ABIGAIL

Magda Szabó

ABIGAIL

Translated from the Hungarian by
Len Rix

MACLEHOSE PRESS
QUERCUS · LONDON

First published in the Hungarian language as *Abigél* by Móra in 1970
First published in Great Britain in 2020 by

MacLehose Press
An imprint of Quercus Publishing Ltd
Carmelite House
50 Victoria Embankment
London EC4Y 0DZ

An Hachette UK company

A CIP catalogue record for this book is available from the British Library.

ISBN (TPB) 978 0 85705 848 5
ISBN (Ebook) 978 0 85705 851 5

10 9 8 7 6 5 4 3 2 1

Designed and typeset in Scala by Libanus Press, Marlborough
Printed and bound in Denmark by Nørhaven

Papers used by Quercus are from well-managed forests and other responsible sources.

Gina is sent to boarding school

The change that came about in her life robbed her of so much it was as if a bomb had destroyed her home.

Her first loss was Marcelle – the Marcelle she had always addressed as "mam'selle", though she had never thought of her as simply the young Frenchwoman who for twelve years had slept in the room next to hers and had brought her up. Marcelle had become much more than a governess or mere employee. Just to be in her presence was usually enough for Gina to forget that Marcelle was not actually a member of the family, someone who could never truly replace the mother she had lost at the tender age of two. Marcelle always knew what Gina was struggling to express, what was really on her mind, the thing she could only stammer about incoherently, and there were moments when Gina felt as close to Marcelle as she did to her father. Whenever the governess was assailed by homesickness, or Gina reacted negatively to something said or done, Marcelle would tell her to be glad that at least she had a father by her side, and one who loved her more than anyone: she, Marcelle, had long ago lost her own parents, and now she had to earn her living from the one thing they had taught her, her mother tongue. She never failed to add that, if that was to be her lot in life, then how lucky she was to have found a home with Gina and her father. Though she had never married, it was as if here at the Vitays she had a family, or at least a daughter, of her own. Marcelle was the sort of person you would always miss when away from home as you would a real parent, and Gina knew that she was so very good to her not because she was paid to be but because she truly loved her.

But Marcelle was no more: she had gone back to France. Gina's father, the General, had said it was impossible for her to stay a moment longer, and he surely knew best. He would not have sent her away if he had not been absolutely obliged to. He knew as well as anyone the nature of the bond he would break in forcing them to part. But there was a war on, he explained: Marcelle's and Gina's countries were on opposing sides, and it was impossible for the young Frenchwoman to continue living with them. When there was peace again she would be able to return and they could carry on with their lives where they had left off. She had left all her belongings behind; they had simply been packed into trunks and moved down to the cellar.

But Auntie Mimó wasn't French, and even if Marcelle really had to go home, why was it necessary to send Gina away to a boarding school? Why couldn't her education be overseen by her aunt? When she asked her father why, if he insisted on her being under constant supervision whatever the cost, his sister couldn't just move in with them, the General shook his head. If she hadn't been so busy clutching at every straw in the hope of being allowed to remain at home, she too would have recognised that Auntie Mimó could never be a successor to Marcelle: she was quite unsuitable. However much Gina loved her aunt, she had made fun of her on many occasions and had often thought that at fourteen she was actually more grown up than her aunt was, even if the latter was a widow and by now over forty. But the moment it became clear to Gina that she would be parted from her too, the thought of losing her as well as Marcelle somehow enhanced her image. She forgot the many times she had giggled at Auntie Mimó's efforts to preserve her long-vanished youth, her desperate need to be the centre of attention when in company and the anxious interest she would take in every new item of fashion or cosmetics in the hope of a miracle. Gina also forgot just how quickly she and Marcelle had realised that those famous afternoon teas, the afternoon teas with ballroom dancing that Auntie Mimó held every Thursday and which no amount of pleading could persuade the General to attend, were arranged not for the reason her aunt gave – to provide an opportunity for her little motherless niece to make herself known, to help her learn how to conduct herself in society, and to practise her dancing. No, Auntie Mimó was simply out to enjoy herself, to show off her new clothes and her ever-changing hairdos, to dance, and, with luck, to find herself a husband. That was why the guests on those occasions were generally old enough to be Gina's father (or even grandfather), with scarcely a young person in sight. Marcelle was no doubt right when she declared that it was not at afternoon teas and dances that a young girl would learn that fundamental something she would later need to know in adult life; and she had surely been proved right that time they found Auntie Mimó in floods of tears because her hairdresser had cut her hair badly. Life undoubtedly calls for dignity and self-discipline, and for a person to be able to react to things in an adult way it was necessary to distinguish between what was merely unpleasant and what was truly bad, especially in wartime, when all over the world people were dying in their tens and hundreds of thousands. A badly cut lock of hair was an utterly trivial matter.

On the other hand, it was at one of Auntie Mimó's famous afternoon teas that Gina had met Feri Kuncz, and had not failed to notice that, almost to the point of rudeness, the Lieutenant had had eyes only for her. She was moreover to receive an unexpected and perhaps somewhat premature gift – the alarming, almost too joyful realisation that she had fallen in love with him, and that she wanted one day to become his wife.

This business of Feri (it was the only thing she never had the courage to tell her father about) was, most unusually, something that Marcelle did not approve of. Her aunt, from the moment she spotted what was developing between Gina and the Lieutenant, had been altogether more understanding. It was she who explained to Gina that there is nothing more innocent and beautiful than the blooming of first love, the memory of which – even if it did not end in marriage – would always burn brighter than any other, and how happy she was to be the guardian of this pure, noble and entirely mutual attraction. Happy she certainly was. But Marcelle did not like Feri, and she liked this association with Feri even less. Not long before the General's announcement that she would have to go back to France she had told Gina that she would have to tell him about it – about everything, the regular

Thursday afternoon meetings and the whispered exchanges. Her father had repeatedly said that Marcelle, rather than his own flighty sister, should be the one to keep an eye on Gina. No-one from the officers' mess should be allowed to come anywhere near her: that was all it would take for one of them to start trying to court her. In the end Marcelle kept her counsel. She was too busy preparing for her departure and the actual moment of separation. As things turned out, she might just as well have told him. Along with the governess and Auntie Mimó, the Lieutenant would also soon disappear from Gina's life. If she were no longer in Budapest, how could she keep up the connection with him?

So now there was no Marcelle, and by tomorrow there would be no Auntie Mimó either, or Feri Kuncz. And with them, plucked away as if by a bird, her life at the Sokoray Atala Academy would have gone too. That fact was no easier to bear. She had been a pupil there ever since she had been old enough to go to school. She knew every brick in the building, every nook and cranny. It was an old and prestigious Budapest school for girls, and the staff were highly qualified and conscientious. Whenever Auntie Mimó invited Gina to one of her tea dances, to celebrate the Feast of St Barbara or St Nicholas, the headmistress always granted her leave, and it seemed no less natural that she should be allowed regular visits to the theatre and the opera. Often (for they had a season ticket) the General would join them at the performance, sitting behind them in the box Gina shared with Marcelle and her aunt. The door would open, a cold draught would caress her back and neck and the crimson-carpeted floor would creak gently as her father took his seat. More often than not his arrival gave her more pleasure than the performance itself. When she turned to greet him, it was into her own face that she smiled: her own grey eyes gazed back at her from beneath eyebrows shaped almost exactly like her own. Even their hair, in its fineness of texture, was alike, though Gina's was brown and his was now greying. Their facial features, their mouths, even the shape of their teeth, were the same: father and daughter. In all the fourteen years of Gina's life, although neither of them had ever expressed it in such elementary terms, they loved each other with a passion and both felt the world complete only when they were together.

And that was why it was so impossible to fathom his sudden decision to send her away to a boarding school in the provinces the moment Marcelle had gone. In the past she had been able to persuade him to do almost anything; now he seemed deaf to all her pleadings. He had decided on her fate without discussing a single detail and had merely informed her what would happen. If he had given any kind of explanation, anything she could understand and accept, it might have been easier for her to bear the thought of being torn from her familiar world. But her father had clearly not been telling the truth when he made his announcement. His reasons – that it was time for her to acquire greater self-discipline than she could learn from a governess within the walls of her own home; that the country air would be so much better for her; that he would henceforth have less time to spend with her and would feel happier if her upbringing were placed in the hands of only the very best teachers – were simply not worth thinking about. The villa on Gellért Hill stood high above the Danube and the city beyond. Where could the air have been healthier than here, in their large garden on the upper slopes? And what greater self-discipline be acquired than what Marcelle had instilled in her? More upstanding governesses? As if he had not personally chosen the best possible school for his daughter. No, for once he was not telling the truth. He simply did not want to have her in the house. And that could only mean that Auntie Mimó was almost right. For months she had been telling Gina that her brother had changed. He had grown more irritable, more reticent, and the amount of time he claimed to be spending on his military duties was quite implausible, in fact beyond belief. No, there must be a woman involved, she had said: one day Gina would see the truth, when he suddenly took the plunge and married. And perhaps the new wife wouldn't want her around. Was it so impossible that her father should love some new woman more than his own child?

Gina was very much her father's daughter. After hours of fruitless pleading she abruptly fell silent. There were no more questions, no more complaints. The General, who knew her every bit as well as if he were her mother, understood what depths of hurt and hopeless misery lay behind her restrained silence. When she gathered her things together the night before she left there was not the slightest hint of tears and no great emotional scene. Even without Marcelle's help the packing did not take long, so few were the possessions she was allowed to have with her in the new school. Her father, it now became clear, had already visited the provincial town in question and had told her that the pupils were issued with their own clothing and equipment. All she would need to take was her underwear and her dressing gown; everything else would be supplied when she arrived. Before she finally shut the lid on her suitcase she ran her eyes slowly around the room, then stuffed her favourite toy, the spotted velvet dog, deep down between the nightdresses. Then she had second thoughts and put it back. It too would have to stay. Her adaptation to this unfamiliar new world would have to be total. The textbooks, the exercise books, everything would be completely new. So far she had been at a state school, now she was being sent to a religious one, where the books, and even the blotting paper, would be different.

That day they went on a round of farewells, first to her aunt and then to the cemetery.

When she learned the reason for their coming Auntie Mimó's fit of hysterics was a model of its kind. She was outraged, of course, by the fact that Gina was to be taken from her side, but also because it was only now that she was being told. The girl was leaving the very next day, and no-one had said a word! Listening to the endless torrent of reproaches Gina felt utterly wretched, though there was nothing that she herself could have done differently. The moment she had learned from her father what was in store for her she had wanted to fly to her aunt for comfort and consolation, perhaps even help. But it had been impossible. She had run to the hallway to telephone her but had not finished dialling the full six numbers when her father was standing behind her and lifting the receiver from her hand. "You must tell absolutely no-one," he said, addressing her not in his usual tones but as to a soldier receiving orders. "I will take you to visit Mimó, but there will be goodbyes to no-one else – not your girlfriends, not your acquaintances, not even the domestic staff. You will never mention the fact that you are leaving Budapest. We'll shake hands on that." Gina gave him her hand, but she could not bear to look him in the face, so upset was she that this too was being denied her, the chance to vent her grievances, the precious moments of parting, the fond words of farewell that she would have exchanged with Feri.

It was the first time Auntie Mimó had ever really fallen out with her brother. When it became clear that he was unwilling even to let her know where he was taking the girl ("You'll be writing to her every five minutes, or sending her parcels, and you'll be calling on her every other week. I'm not telling you, Mimó!"), she rose to her feet, thanked them for their visit and expressed the desire not to see her brother again for a good long while. Then she burst into tears, covered Gina with kisses and rushed out of the room, weeping ever more angrily. They left the house in such haste that Gina did not even have time to whisper a message for her to pass on to Feri. This was especially worrying. On the previous Thursday afternoon she had known nothing of her father's plans and had parted from the Lieutenant with a promise to see him there next week. He would look for her in vain.

From her aunt's her father took her to the cemetery, where they stood in silence before her mother's grave. Gina imagined that this valediction might be rather different from those previous occasions when they had gone there, as they always did before going away for any length of time. Was he perhaps bidding farewell to her dear departed mother, saying a last goodbye to her before embarking on a new life altogether?

That evening was, to all appearances, like every other since Marcelle's departure. They dined, the General sat by the fireplace to read, Gina pulled her stool under the standard lamp and took out her book. She stared at the lines but made nothing of the text; she did not even turn the page, she was merely pretending to be reading. Soon she became aware that there was no susurration of turning pages coming from behind her either; no reading was in progress in the depths of the great armchair. She caught her father's gaze. Talk to me, was the message written on her face. Tell me what you intend to do, and what all this means. Whoever it is you want to bring here, I will love her. Your taste and your choice can never be wrong. How could anyone you love be a stranger to me, or someone I would choose to hate? Tell me what you have in mind. Don't shut me out of your life. Don't force us to live apart just because there is someone else. I won't get in the way or make difficulties. I've always loved you too much for that. It's still not too late. Don't send me away! Make that woman understand that I will be a friend, not an enemy. Speak to me, father!

"You are going into a very different world," he said. "It's strange to think how often you've been to Switzerland and Paris and Italy with Marcelle, and with me to Vienna, and yet you've never lived in the provinces. Please try to bear with it."

She made no reply. What could she possibly have said? The book slid from her lap onto the carpet. Up there on the hill the evenings were cool, even in summer. Now, though it was only the first of September, they already had the heating on. The electric fire with its imitation logs glowed a bright red.

"There is no other way," he continued. "Please understand that, Gina. There really isn't. If Marcelle had been able to stay the situation would have been different. Marcelle was sensible and responsible. But nowadays I am hardly ever at home. Mimó is superficial and frivolous. You cannot depend on her for anything. I have to send you away for a reason I simply don't wish to talk about. I am no happier about it than you are, believe me."

The girl looked at the fire, then held out her hands towards it, to warm her fingers. In her mind she had already decided what that reason was, the one he refused to discuss. But if he wasn't going to mention it, then she too would say nothing. The unexplained *reason* would console her father well enough in her absence, and everything would work out very nicely. If you were sent away to a boarding school in the fifth year of your secondary education you would almost certainly stay there till your leaving exams and come home only for the holidays, so why would you change again after that? "You've never lived in the provinces. Please try to bear with it." What kind of place could he be taking her to, if he had to give her such a warning in advance?

"Tomorrow we have to be up early, so do get to bed," the General said. "I will take you there myself, in the car."

They both stood up. Her father drew her into an embrace and held her face against his. How sad he is too, Gina thought. How much it hurts him that I am leaving. That woman is pitiless. For the first time in his life my father is being weak.

She ran up the stairs to the second floor, where the bedrooms were. In every window the shutters were closed, as required in wartime. With the view of the city and her own garden blocked, her room now felt quite alien, as if it were no longer hers, as if she had not lived and slept there since the day she had been born. Feeling like a guest in her own bedroom she sat down uncertainly on the edge of the bed and stared at the pattern on the quilt: red cups of poppy flowers on grass-green silk, as on a lawn. Feri's words, "Ginny, little Ginny, little fairy girl", flitted to and fro in the silence, like butterflies over the poppy-covered material. The temptation to creep back to the telephone in the hallway and try to call the Lieutenant assailed her once again. Soon it was irresistible. The General was still sitting by the fireplace in the drawing room and the staff were having supper in the basement: no-one would hear her making the call. She got as far as the door, then turned back, feeling utterly helpless. It reduced her to something like despair that she was incapable of breaking her word even when what she had promised had been so incomprehensible, so inhuman and so totally unacceptable. She went back to the bed and tried to imagine where she would lay her head the following night, and what her new bed and surroundings would be like. But it was impossible.

The Bishop Matula Academy

They set off early the next morning, without telling anyone where they were going, or why, or even how long they would be away.

János, the General's batman, who had got the car ready, was clearly under the same impression as both Auntie Róza, the family housekeeper ever since Gina had been born, and Ili the maid: they were presumably going on a last excursion before the start of term. The three of them were still in the hall when the telephone rang. Before anyone could pick it up the General called over his shoulder to say that, whoever it was, they were no longer in Pest. Gina heard Ili telling the person, "I'm very sorry, but they've already left." Auntie Mimó, she reckoned. One last try. Poor thing, after what it must have cost her to get up so early!

She had said her farewells the previous night, both to the staff and to everyone she loved, and she did not look back, either at her old home or at Auntie Róza, who stood loyally waving to them as her father started the car and drove off. What was the point in craning round when everything and everyone was receding into the distance and becoming harder to see? She stared straight ahead, trying to work out where she was being taken. The road she knew best was the one to Lake Balaton. They had often gone that way to the Adriatic coast. But instead of skirting

Buda Hill they turned right and crossed the bridge. So it's somewhere else – not towards the lake, she mused. Ah, but the trains to the west leave from the Eastern Station, so we could still be on our way to that side of the country. What large towns are there on the road to Vienna? Győr? Sopron?

Passing through Kalvin Square she thought of her two best friends, Edith and Alice. They lived close by, Edith beside the Hotel Astoria, Alice a little further on, behind the University Church. It seemed unthinkable to be leaving them like this, without a goodbye or a word of explanation, and then writing to them later to tell them that they would no longer be at the same school. Even at this early hour the traffic was heavy, and while he sat waiting for a light to turn green the General took his hands off the wheel and looked, lingeringly and earnestly, into her face. Right now he must be thinking about Edith and Alice, and how he wouldn't let me say goodbye to them, she thought. And he can see my response: totally impassive. Why should I care where he's taking me?

They were now leaving the outer suburbs. They talked very little. Gina felt that there was nothing to say and her father was concentrating on the road. Out of his uniform he seemed almost a stranger, and somehow older. She noted the names of the villages they passed through. She knew the geography of Hungary well enough to feel sure that they were now travelling eastwards, and when, at 8 a.m., they reached the Tisza, she knew she had been right. They took breakfast in a large town on the banks of the river, where they ate without appetite, making polite conversation. The General said that his legs were stiff from sitting so long, suggested they go for a short walk and took her arm. Gina was rather tall for her age, and when she stood up straight she was barely a head shorter than he was. They wandered about the streets, looking into shop windows. Every now and then he would stop to point out a scarf, a pair of gloves or a handkerchief, and ask her if she needed them, or perhaps would just like to have them, because he really did want to buy her something. Gina surprised herself by the crisp tone with which she declined. It wouldn't be quite that easy to make things right again between them. Once, when she was very little and had been refusing to take some medicine, her father had come and stood beside her bed and suddenly produced a toy from behind Marcelle's back, whereupon, though still pulling faces, she immediately swallowed the liquid just to get her hands on the present. But those things were now in the past, along with measles and other ailments of childhood, that age of total unselfconsciousness. These days she took her medicines without flinching. There was no need for either persuasion or bribery.

In one of the side streets they came across a jewellery shop. There was of course no gold in the window – it had all disappeared at the outbreak of war – but there were some silver chains and medallions glittering on velvet cushions.

"I would like to buy you something all the same," the General said. "And I shall do that here. So no more of this play-acting, please. You've always enjoyed shopping. Shall we go in?"

Inside it was astonishingly bright, especially beside the table where the jeweller was repairing a watch in the blaze of a powerful lamp. He was a polite little man and did his best to find something that would please them. Gina proved a difficult client. The modest selection of goods on display was all very pretty and exquisitely made, but she seemed reluctant to settle on anything. If the aim was simply to dispel her feelings of sadness and disappointment, then she had no desire to be fobbed off with a present, whatever it might be, or however trifling. In the end the General chose for her – a beautiful moon pendant on an obviously valuable chain. Despite herself, the moment it was hung around her neck she fell in love with it. It was such a chaste little moon, with its mouth shut tight, secretive and rather mysterious, not a moon in an operetta. There was nothing showy about it, just an air of calm seriousness. Once it was around her neck there was no giving it back, and she had her present. But she still needed to make her father feel that having been given it changed nothing; that she both accepted it and didn't.

She looked around. There were no neck chains or jewellery in the drawers, only seals, metal ornaments, figurines and ashtrays. All cost considerably more than her weekly pocket money, which was regularly topped up by Auntie Mimó.

"And I would like to buy you something," she said. "As a memento. To remind you of me when I'm not there."

They glanced briefly into one another's eyes, then both suddenly averted their gaze, as if too much had been said in the silence between them. The jeweller watched uncomprehendingly. He could never have known that what Gina's look had declared was: And I shall do as much for you, though there is nothing to celebrate. This ashtray here you would see as the sort of thing you gave someone simply out of politeness. Nobody knows better than I that you don't smoke. But after bringing me all this way and telling me nothing about where you are taking me, or why we are going there, you can't just hand me a present the way you used to.

And this was the answer in his eyes: Well then, give it to me as to a stranger, if that is what you wish. That's what we've taught you to do, Marcelle and I. If you are made a gift by a stranger you should give one in return. One day you will ask my pardon for this. May God grant that we both live to see that day.

They took to the road again. The countryside east of the river was very different. Gina did not know the Great Plain, or indeed any other place like it. Her trips had been only to the great cities of western Europe, or to snow-covered mountains and the sea. Everything she knew about it, and its general character, she had gleaned from the poems of Petőfi, but his lines celebrating the Puszta had never really struck a chord with her. Now, as the car raced steadily eastwards, she could see nothing but the work of autumn going on in the fields, the occasional white homestead in a distant smallholding, a few thinly wooded copses or isolated clumps of beech trees dancing in the breeze, and murky canals filled with water the colour of copper. Then the wind – the distinctive wind of the Great Plain – sprang up. They found themselves enveloped by three of the four elements, water, earth and air, and she experienced something she had never known in her life, something altogether new, to which, as she sat there huddled in the car beside her father, feeling altogether over-whelmed and infinitely sad, she could put no name. Much later, when there were no more secrets to distract her, and her eyes were no longer blinded by misery to such important new experiences, she would look back and remember her first encounter with the Great Plain, in the bleak light of autumn, so different from the deep luxuriant glow of summer.

Árkod, she thought. We're going to Árkod.

She had an excellent memory. Everything she had ever learned about the country's geography had stayed with her almost word for word. "Árkod, the oldest university city in eastern Hungary; population 70,000; 97.5% Protestant; developing industries; its medieval guilds were world-renowned. The university is twinned with similar institutions in Scotland, the Netherlands, Scandinavia and Germany. Also known for its outstanding commercial school, for the Reformed Church Gymnasium for Boys, and for the Bishop Matula Academy for girls, the first institution of pedagogic excellence in Hungary to accept full-time female students."

So here was the answer! She had to stop herself shouting it out. Árkod was not a city she knew, and she had no idea what sort of school the Bishop Matula might be, but even if it were paradise on earth it was a very long way from Budapest: she had never thought she would be quite so far from the capital. Well, if she couldn't go home on Sundays, perhaps her father would be able to visit her. But then, Árkod was almost on the eastern border: it wasn't somewhere you might just nip over to on a whim. This was worse than she had feared in her darkest hours. What was going to happen to her? Why was everything going against her? What had she done so wrong? The whole business was unimaginable.

"Don't say a word," the General said, his eyes fixed firmly on the road. "I beg you, don't make things more difficult than they need be. It's bad enough as it is."

Ever since she had been a child the two of them had been so close that they would often come out with the same remark in the same instant, or one of them would smile at the other and tell them what they were thinking. This time she would say nothing. There was nothing she could hope to achieve by it anyway. She sensed her eyes growing heavy with the strain of holding back tears, and she allowed them to close. She tried to calculate how far it might still be, and what sort of reception she would receive when she arrived, and what the other girls would be like: in short, she was looking for a source of strength in her misery. Then everything became confused and all thought faded away. The next thing she knew was that she had slept, apparently for some time, and that her father had spoken to wake her. The car came to a halt.

She pulled herself up and blinked. The countryside looked just as it had when she had fallen asleep. Trees tossed and swayed in the same watery light. But in the near distance there rose a cluster of tall towers, dozens of them, on a small patch of ground, some standing apart, others in pairs, like twins, and the sky above the city that now appeared beyond them seemed to be impaled on their tops.

"You were up early this morning," the General said. "I'm glad you managed to sleep for an hour or so. I'm sorry I had to wake you, but we'll be there in a few minutes, and I won't be able to say a proper goodbye once we get to the city and the school.

It'll have to be here, with no-one else around, just the two of us."

She gazed at him in silence. Was he going to tell her at last? It was not what she had been expecting.

"Promise me that you will take good care of yourself. As if you were an adult. As if you were not yourself but your mother, the mother who is no longer with us. Do you hear me, Gina?"

She heard, but she did not understand. Why was he suddenly so anxious? Here, alas, there would be little need for her to exercise caution: she would be under constant supervision by the teaching staff.

"Give me a kiss, and, I beg you, when I leave you at the school please don't cry, or at least not in front of me. I would find that very hard to bear."

He should not have said that; it was quite unnecessary. He should have known that she would never make a scene in front of strangers. She needed no instruction on what to feel, and she would certainly never expose what was private between them to the eyes of people they did not know. They kissed, awkwardly and unhappily. It was as if the words that had been left unspoken had changed things irreversibly.

They set off again, and a few minutes later they were in the city. Gina could not decide what she felt about it. She had never before set eyes on such a town. Árkod bore little resemblance either to the capital or to any of the provincial cities she had been to. Later, very much later, she came to see that it was indeed like nowhere else, a unique entity, a world set apart, a world of black and white. He drove on until they reached the school. He seemed to know the way rather well. It took them past a large, four-square-looking church, almost as white as chalk, its dome covered in huge glittering stars. Next to it was the entrance to a side road, named after Bishop Matula, and there, straight down at the end, a vast white edifice stood before them: the school itself.

Another squat, four-square building, Gina thought. Four-square, severe, stark-white. Tiny windows covered with iron bars; iron bars across the entrance. It must be terribly old. It isn't like a school at all. More like a fortress.

Getting inside the fortress was not easy. The barred entrance was shut and they had to ring. They waited for what seemed ages before anyone noticed their arrival. The person who finally opened the grille, a sombre man with a moustache, was as squat and stocky as the building itself. The caretaker in Gina's old school was always smiling, always attentive to the girls, even when he had to tell them off for dropping peanut husks or shrieking in the corridors. This new face now turned towards them and they were questioned in detail about whom they wished to see, and for what exact reason. No glimmer of gaiety or humour ever crossed it – an unmoving face of stone, the face of an idol. On the General's insistence the man finally made a call on the internal telephone, leaving them to stand on the other side of a metal screen that separated the inner vault from the huge courtyard until at last someone, presumably the Director, managed to persuade him that the visitors were telling the truth: there really was a Georgina Vitay on the register, and she should be allowed to enter with her father. The porter opened a hinged section of the grille and held it open for them.

They were taken up a side staircase to the first floor, over stone steps worn down in the middle by the tread of countless feet. Once again Gina had the impression that here too the white was somehow whiter, starker than elsewhere, and that, after lively, elegant, teeming Budapest, everything here was broad, four-square and blank. Apart from one or two plants, and rows of black plaques with biblical quotations in gold lettering, the corridors were bare. The door to the Director's office was surmounted by a huge coat of arms – yet another square, if spared the usual black and white by the need for colour in heraldry: on a gold background two hands came together in prayer around a Bible or book of psalms; around and above them flowed the semi-circular inscription, *Non est currentis*. Gina had studied Latin since the third year and she was rather good at it, but she could make nothing of what she read: the three words taken together seemed to make no sense. *Non* – "not"; *est* – "is". Put together: "is not". *Currentis* was the present participle of the verb *currere*, "to run", in the genitive case. "The person running has nothing" or something like that. But what did he or she not have?

The corridor was empty. No doubt the school term was not due to start until the following day, or perhaps the pupils were not allowed to show themselves outside the classrooms or near the staff room? The General's hand was already on the door handle when he felt Gina's touch. Somewhat vexed, he looked round. Why prolong the moment? Doesn't she realise how hard this is for me too? She's going to plead with me once again to take her home and not send her away. As if that were possible!

"When will you be getting married?" the girl asked.

The look of stupefaction on his face said more than words could ever have. This was Mimó's doing! Mimó with her obsession with love and romance and her stupid fantasies: only Mimó could have dreamed this up. My poor little girl, my poor unhappy little girl! But surely she doesn't really think that that is the reason why I've brought her here?

"Never," he replied. "What sort of idiocy is this? Whatever put that silly idea into your head?"

Her father never lied. The shadowy figure of the unknown woman faded away: clearly her father had no intention of making that change in his life. But why then could she no longer stay with him? Opening the door, he left her no time to ponder these questions. They stepped forward, and were obliged to continue because their presence had been noted from within. In passing over that threshold, Gina was entering her new world, the one that represented her new home, the one that would so totally transform her life: she was like a child being born, or a dying man exhaling his last breath.

The walls of the Director's office seemed even whiter than the white outside, and the man himself blacker than black. There were no pictures, just a few charts and a map of Europe pinned with blue flags representing, as she later discovered, foreign institutions twinned with the school. The full suite of furniture included a fortified cupboard, a second desk of the roll-top variety and, to her surprise, a large tank of fish.

She took it all in as uncertainly as if she had been anaesthetised. She seemed to be in another world, floating on air. It occurred to her that, although her father and the Director were addressing each other in the familiar second person and chatting away like old acquaintances, the man had not even shaken her hand. He had merely glanced at her, nodded, and offered a chair to the General but not to her. Her father handed over some papers and an amount of money. It was obviously a large sum, to cover her enrolment, her expenses and the equipment the new school would provide. He was given a receipt, asked to read through some documents and sign his acceptance of the school rules and conditions. One clause detained him for what seemed ages, but in the end he signed.

"Sister Susanna will be the Prefect assigned to her," Gina heard the Director say, as if she were not standing in the room right beside him. "Letters should be addressed to the relevant Sister, indicating the name of the pupil."

"I would prefer to telephone," said the General, "and not to write. I really don't have the time. How often can I ring her?"

"Every Saturday. The girls are given their post on Saturday afternoon."

That was good news. So they would not be totally out of contact. And if they could talk to each other every week, she would always have something to look forward to.

"Otherwise, everything will be as we agreed last time."

The General nodded briefly, but did not look at Gina. It was as if he was feeling guilty about something. The girl allowed her gaze to stray out of the window. From where she was standing it was clear that the side of the Matula that faced the road was just one part of a vast U-shaped building that stood open to the rear.

The Director picked up the telephone and asked the porter to take Georgina Vitay's luggage up to the dormitory and to send Sister Susanna down to his office. She immediately began to wonder if she really would be able to keep up the disciplined and adult bearing that her father expected of her at the school. She felt even less sure of that now than she had been when she thought that he intended to marry. The Director had made repeated reference to the Sister Prefect, so she knew that a Deaconess was on her way to meet her, and now there she was in the flesh – a grave-looking young woman, someone who smiled at her at last. Gina would have liked to return that beautiful smile, but she found herself incapable of doing so. Her face remained stiff and unmoving. All she wanted was to escape from the room and put an end to the unbearable tension. Her strength was utterly exhausted.

The Director introduced her: "Georgina Vitay." Then, as to a babe in arms, he instructed her: "Georgina Vitay, say 'goodbye' to your father, say 'goodbye' to the Director, and off you go."

"Bye," she muttered, not daring to look at her father.

"That is not how we address a parent," the Director said.

"I wish you good day, Father." She sighed.

The General stood up, put his hand on her shoulder and, with infinite tenderness, began to steer her in silence towards the door. They were just about to leave the room when Susanna stopped her with a touch. With another smile, she lifted the chain from around Gina's neck – the newly purchased silver chain with the solemn, frowning moon.

"The girls are not allowed to wear jewellery or other

adornments," she explained. "Would the General be so kind as to take it with him?"

The little moon tinkled softly as it fell on the table in front of her father. Once again there was no exchange of glances between the two of them; both kept their eyes fixed on the carpet. The silence was like that when a bee wanders in through an open window and drones on and on, without ceasing.

"Thank you," said the Deaconess. Gina stood and waited, not knowing how, in this blunt, four-square world of black and white, she should address the Director. Would "good day" be enough?

"I wish you good day, Director, sir," Susanna sang out to her, as if to a first-year pupil.

"I wish you good day, Director, sir," she whispered, her neck flushing crimson. Never in her life had she felt so hapless, so perplexed, so utterly out of her depth. Marcelle, Auntie Mimó and her old school had between them taught her everything she needed to know for her life in Budapest. Here, she was totally disoriented; she could make sense of nothing.

"Good day to you," the Director said, and promptly turned his back on her.

In her felt-soled slippers, Susanna glided down the corridor in silence. Beside her, Gina's leather-soled shoes made an embarrassing clatter and she desperately wanted to take them off. They came to a low door cut into the wall, one that might have been designed for a child. It led to another wing of the building, no doubt where the dormitories were. They stopped, Gina turned and looked back. If she could stand there for just a minute or two she might see her father once more, and run towards him, press herself against him and feel the familiar warmth of home, the warmth of her old life, now already further off than a dream. But Susanna took her by the hand and gently led her through the tiny opening.

New acquaintances

Never before had she been in such a strange building, with such a tangled branching-out of corridors.

As she discovered later, the renowned Bishop Matula Gymnasium was an old monastery dating from the Middle Ages, which explained the massive outer walls, the vaulted ceilings and the unusual shape of the classrooms. The inner walls had been either cut through or taken down and moved to create suitably large spaces out of the old monks' cells. On the other hand, the furniture and fittings were rather more modern than in Gina's old school, and everything sparkled with cleanliness. Through a door someone had left open she glimpsed the white tiles of an enormous built-in bath. Susanna immediately closed it, as if it were somehow improper for anyone to set eyes on a place where the girls would strip naked, even when there was no-one in there.

They continued on their way, ever further away from the front wing, where her father was no doubt still in conversation with the Director. Here all the windows were shut, and their panes of thick frosted glass obscured the view of the garden. They had reached the part of the building where the boarders lived, and now she had her first sight of the pupils. Girls of different ages were standing at the wall organising their lockers. As Gina and

Susanna came in they all turned, stood to attention and greeted them. They all wore the same long-sleeved uniform with red piping around the shiny black material. It covered the whole body, almost down to the ankle, and the wearers looked so alike that Gina began to wonder if she would ever be able to tell them apart. Their hair was done in exactly the same way, with a parting down the middle and tresses of various lengths woven into plaits and tied by a black ribbon that looked more like a shoelace.

Susanna took her on to the storeroom, where the Sister Housekeeper issued her with her own uniform and equipment. She was sent to an enclosed space where she had to change not only her clothes but also her underwear. Her petticoat, with its bluebirds hovering over a lake of yellow silk, earned a look of such disapproval you would have thought they harboured some virulent tropical disease. The new outfit she was given in exchange for her own – hat, gloves, jacket and the long uniform with its sleeve ends reinforced with protective ruffles – was all, on close inspection, well-tailored from cloth of the finest quality. But Gina was still shocked. It was as if someone, presumably the designer, had done all she could to make sure the pupils of the Bishop Matula Gymnasium should never attract attention, and, if they did, the onlooker would simply stare in horrified wonderment that anyone could have deliberately created a costume like that for an innocent child – a Sunday-best outfit that resembled nothing so much as a naval uniform, sharply cut and sitting high against the throat, where, instead of a collar and tie, it was held tight by a narrow band embroidered with white tulips to add a festive air.

A locker had been cleared for her, and she was now able to examine the things she had been carrying: slippers, a towel, a dressing gown and a bathrobe. The ones she had brought had all been rejected and replaced – even the twelve new handkerchiefs. In her mind's eye she went through the objects she had packed with so much love and care in her trunk: the fluffy sky-blue and pink towels, the scented nightdresses that brought back such vivid memories of the home she had left, of her father, of Auntie Mimó (and Marcelle too, who had made the soft, playful dressing gown for her), and the bathrobe with the fantastical reed beds in which baby hippopotamuses frolicked and open-mouthed crocodiles lay in wait. The Sister Housekeeper told her to take that desperate look off her face: surely she did not have to be told that such trumpery should be of no interest to a good Christian girl. The only thing she and Susanna disagreed on was whether, because of the wartime shortages, Gina might be allowed to keep and use her own toothbrush and soap, but in the end they decided against it. These last had come to Gina through some secret source of Auntie Mimó's: the soap was green and smelled strongly of camellias, and the handle of the toothbrush was a bright cherry red. But even setting aside the question of colour, the housekeeper declared that it clearly failed to meet the regulations and its slanting tufts were a disgrace. In its place Gina was given a white one, on which the woman immediately inscribed her new registration number in permanent ink, and she was handed a large block of the school soap. "It's made here, on the premises," Susanna said. "Everyone uses it, including the Director."

As she pulled on the black ribbed stockings and the tall black boots she thought that that would be all. But she was wrong. What came next was, in its own way, even more horrifying than the new outfit. Susanna teased out her long tresses with the new wooden-handled brush that had replaced her old silver-backed one, then chopped them short to match the other girls' and added a parting down the middle and plaits, tied by the same black shoelace. Gina was now trembling with shock. They have swallowed me whole. I am no longer myself, she thought, and her breathing became a rapid pant. The Prefect, knowing what this meant in a young girl, hurried to finish her task. And now they've taken even my hair. I have nothing left.

"I advise you not to cry," said Susanna. "If you must cry, let it be for something other than your hair. To cry for that would be quite unworthy."

Gina did not cry, if only to make it clear to the two of them that she considered them absolute strangers whom she could never allow to witness her suffering.

"So there we are," said the Deaconess. "This is how we dress here, and how we wear our hair. You will have to get used to it, because it's the regulation. There are good reasons, you may be sure."

"What are those reasons?" Gina asked. It was the first time she had spoken, apart from simple greetings.

"I will tell you when you have learned not to ask for explanations. You will also have to learn that you do not ask questions without prior permission. Goodbye, then," (to the Sister House-keeper). "We are off now."

The new shoes were too large for her feet; they felt heavy and unfamiliar. Tagging along behind Susanna over the stone floor (which had been scrubbed until it shone), she had to take care not to trip and fall. Her personal belongings had been locked away by the housekeeper and she was carrying the new outfit she had been issued with in her plundered suitcase, while Susanna carried the bedlinen. They came to a door above which a plaque read "Day Room A, Years V and VI". Inside, girls were sitting and chatting around a long table. The moment the door opened they all stood up and greeted Susanna.

"This is where you will be when you aren't in the dormitory, the refectory or the classroom. Girls, this is Georgina Vitay. She has just arrived, so do give her your help."

The girls greeted Gina the same way they had addressed Susanna: "Good morning," followed by, "and welcome."

"Good morning to you too," Gina murmured, echoing what the Director had instructed her to say. It must have been the right answer, as this time Susanna did not correct her.

They continued on their way. Susanna took her to the dormitory, laid the linen on the bed nearest to the door and told her it would be hers. She would find a locker in the corridor where she could keep her things. Her name was already on it, and the key was in the lock. When she had finished she should be sure to turn the key and then hang it around her neck. If she lost it she would be punished.

The dormitory was not quite empty. Two girls were there, busy making their beds. They stopped when Susanna came in, stood to attention, as the others had done in the day room, and lowered the sheets they had been unfolding. Susanna introduced Gina and prepared to leave. Gina realised with horror that now it really was about to begin: she would be left alone with these girls she had never met, she would have to talk to them and answer their questions. What sort of person can you be, she wondered about the Deaconess, if you can't see how terrified I am? Say something, if only to show me that you feel sorry for me, or at least that you understand. Show me that, for all your strange customs here, you are still a human being. Say something, so that this won't be so terribly hard!

"May the Lord be with you," Susanna called from the doorway, smiling her beautiful smile, and out she went.

She might have said something more to the point, Gina thought. Something a bit more personal, if only to help me breathe more easily.

Later, many months later, she came to understand that this laconic remark was indeed the simplest and in fact the only possible way the Deaconess, who lived so close to her God, could have said: "I truly pity you, my child. It will be difficult for you here, and in my own way I shall do all I can to help you get used to it. But I don't count for very much in this place. Someone more powerful than I must find a way. But fear not: find it she will."

Gina looked around the dormitory and counted the beds. There was a row of ten against each of the two longer walls. The two girls carried on unfolding their sheets and she started on hers. Feelings of intense gratitude to Marcelle began to well up inside her. Her governess had insisted that besides her lessons she should also learn housekeeping, and she would have been ashamed to show herself less adept than these two. The three girls finished their tasks at almost the same moment and the two parties stood looking at one another for a minute or two. Then the shorter of the pair, whose pitch-black hair had been squeezed into such tight plaits they must have been hard as iron, came towards her. The taller one, the blonde, followed behind. Her eyes were red, as if she had just been crying. They introduced themselves: the shorter, dark-haired one was called Mari Kis, the one with red eyes Torma, Piroska Torma.

Mari Kis asked Gina what school she had come from and was amazed that it was as far away as Budapest. Gina explained that her father was in the army, that he was so often away from home that he didn't have time to look after her; her governess was a Frenchwoman, but she had had to leave the country; and her mother was dead, so she had been sent here as a boarder. It surprised her how very logical it all now seemed, and how natural the other two found it. She would have loved to believe with them that the General's conduct had been quite so straightforward and unambiguous, and that there was no other reason why she had become an inmate of this fortress.

"I don't have a father either," said the red-eyed girl. "Neither father nor mother. I never knew them. I grew up here."

"Ungrateful girl!" said Mari Kis. "You've got no-one? What about the Director? It's no bad thing to be the Director's niece. You should see the trouble he takes over her education! He's already made her cry once today. My own parents are primary school teachers, in a rural village. They sent me here because there's no proper school there, just the elementary one."

40

"Look at her handbag!" the fair-haired girl gasped.

Before starting to make her bed Gina had placed her silver-monogrammed handbag on the chest of drawers beside it. It caused her no surprise that it should be admired – Auntie Mimó had bought it for her in Lajos Kossuth Avenue one Christmas. She ran the tips of her fingers sadly over the soft leather. Its powder-blue elegance was so totally out of keeping with the shapeless school outfit.

"They've forgotten to give you your bag," said Torma. "Have a good last look at your work of art. They'll take it from you, and everything in it, soon enough."

"Here we have school-issue bags," Mari Kis explained. "We carry everything we need in them. Handbags like yours are strictly forbidden. And you'll have to redo your hair. You look awful. There's a mirror in the washroom. Come, I'll show you where it is."

What were they saying? That the handbag too, and everything in it, would be confiscated? They were going to take away the miniature photo album with the pictures of her father and Auntie Mimó and Marcelle, and even the one of Feri – Feri taking a fence on his horse Silkworm? And all her money? The hundred pengő note and the change left over from her purchase of the ashtray? And her powder box, her little calendar, her comb and the key to the house? I'll have to take them out and make sure they don't see them, hide them somewhere. But where? In the bed? Impossible. They'll be sure to look under the mattress. Where could I possibly find a place to hide my last prized possessions? They're all I have now to remind me of my vanished former life.

"So, are you going to do your hair? It's time to go."

She slipped the handbag over her arm and followed Mari Kis out. There was no refuse bin in the dormitory that she could see, but she hoped there might be one in the washroom. If there was, she might be able to hide her things behind or underneath it until she found somewhere more suitable. Mari Kis went with her to the bend in the corridor, held the washroom door open and told her to be quick, because Susanna made a note of how much time each activity took and doing your hair twice before lunch was frowned upon: in fact it was against the rules. The reason they had to wear their hair like that was so that you only needed to comb it once in the morning and again at bedtime.

The washroom was permeated with the damp odour of scoured bathtubs, but through the large, sunlit sash windows of the communal area came a stream of fresh air, rich with the scent of autumn and harvest time. In one corner stood a tall house plant. Some disease had begun to attack its leaves, so it must have been put there to convalesce in the warm stream of moist air. On the sills of the high windows geraniums glowed a cheerful red in the sunlight, in boxes placed behind a protective metal barrier to protect the varnished wood from random splashes when they were being watered. There was a waste bin, under one of the basins, but it was made of some cheap white material and was quite unsuitable as a hiding place. The toilet roll was not tucked away in a holder, as at home, but left exposed. There was no boiler or water heater to be seen – the hot water must have arrived from some central point elsewhere, though no pipes could be seen on the walls. She had no qualms about standing on the toilet seats to feel the tops of the cisterns, but they were covered with sheet iron and screwed firmly down.

She had failed. They were going to take away the last mementos of her former life. She was simply too weary to cry, and she no longer felt the urge to deal with her hair. That was not why she had come into the washroom: she no longer cared what sort of scarecrow they had made of her. She went over to the window and tried to look out, but she failed there too. The narrow opening above the thick pane of frosted glass showed her only the sky, nothing of the garden. She stood on tiptoe and gripped the geranium box, wanting to pull herself high enough to feel the fresh air blowing on her skin and caressing her face – the crisp, free-wandering breeze that would speak to her of the world outside, the one she would be deprived of for God knew how long. Her fingers slid into the gap between the protective shield and the flower box behind it, and almost brought the whole lot down on her head. She leaped backwards, her throat so dry with excitement she began to choke. She had found the answer.

It would be difficult, for most people almost impossible, to take the flower container down from behind the protective barrier. But her fencing and horse riding had given her a great deal of strength in the arm, and it might just be possible for her. Gritting her teeth at the unusual effort, she lifted it down as quietly as she could and placed it on the floor. She took everything out of the handbag, apart from the handkerchiefs. If anyone came in now, all would certainly be lost: it would be such a poor start to her life in the school that she might never be able to redeem herself; but if no-one disturbed her, she might get away with it. Nor could she afford to rush. If she didn't go about it very carefully then it would all be in vain. Delicately, meticulously, one after the other, the photo album, the calendar with its attached pencil, the purse, the key holder, the powder compact and the silver comb were laid carefully side by side behind the protective shield. Once in position they all reached to about the same height. By the time she had replaced the box of geraniums her brow was covered in sweat, but her things were so well hidden you would never believe there was anything there. Her heart was beating so fast it was almost painful.

She took a few steps back towards the door and ran her eyes over the line of flowers, and then again from closer up. There was no sign that anything had changed. She was aware that the geraniums now stood a full centimetre higher above the barrier, but as she was the person responsible for the difference she was sure no-one else would notice it. And she had rescued something from the hands of Susanna and the housekeeper. She stood a moment for her racing heart to slow, but there was no time to dawdle. Mari Kis kept calling out to her that they weren't allowed to spend so much time in the washroom except for a bath and she really must come now or they would be in trouble.

She went out and found her dark-haired companion waiting for her in the corridor. She took one look at Gina and shook her head. She declared that she couldn't see any change – it was just as awful as it had been before Gina went in – and she promised to do it herself the next morning. Gina slung the handbag over her arm, and when they got back to the dormitory she tossed it onto the freshly made bed.

Torma had started to line the drawers of her bedside cabinet with paper and had her back towards Gina when she returned. She called out over her shoulder to ask her if she ever went to the theatre in Budapest, and which actresses she had seen or perhaps even met. This was balm to an aching wound, and her sadness began to melt away. Auntie Mimó's house had been frequented not only by celebrated actresses but by male actors as well. The names she was able to mention made Torma stop and turn her head. She gazed at her with the look her uncle had hoped for in vain during Advent – a look of utter self-abnegating reverence.

At that same moment they realised that Susanna was in the room and was speaking to them. It was impossible to say when she had arrived. They had been talking rather loudly, and the Deaconess' felt-soled shoes completely silenced her footsteps. She was carrying a bag on her arm, a large black school-regulation bag, with a white tulip and two white leaves sewn onto it, dangling from a length of black braid and held shut by two mother-of-pearl buttons.

"I forgot to issue you with your bag," she said. "Your handbag, please, Georgina."

For the first time, the very first time since she had become part of the fortress-world, Gina felt the urge to smile. But she resisted it and handed over the offending object. Susanna immediately opened it and searched inside. Of course she found only the handkerchiefs, the fine, polka-dot handkerchiefs Gina had deliberately left there. The Deaconess told her that if ever she needed money, for a church collection or an act of charity, she

45

should apply to her, as her father had left the permitted boarders' annual allowance with her, and off she went with the pale-blue handbag. Mari Kis picked up the tulip-embroidered replacement and, with a gesture of mock reverence, held it out to Gina.

"This is just the thing for your big-city life," she said. "A supreme work of art, in the very latest fashion; a unique creation."

She hung it over Gina's shoulder and burst into laughter.

The outer windows of the dormitory were made of thick, grainy glass, but those inside were transparent, so that if you held something opaque behind them they made a perfect mirror. Torma hung her dress behind one and, with some effort, piggy-backed Gina over to it so that she could see just how ravishing she looked. Gina noticed that two nails had been driven into the back of the window frame: they had found a way to see themselves at least down to the waist, as opposed to the face alone, as in the much smaller mirrors in the washroom. Seeing the image she presented in her regulation school outfit, Gina stared into the mirror in total disbelief, then – to her own surprise – she too exploded with laughter. A brown-haired scarecrow of a girl with misshapen plaits stared out at her from a hideous black straight-jacket; a bag such as a vagabond might carry was slung over her shoulder, and a key dangled from her neck on a length of string.

"Don't worry," said Mari Kis. "It isn't really so bad here. Actually it's pretty dreadful, but you learn to live with it. We have an awful lot of laughs."

"We'd better do our talking now," said the blonde, "while I'm not being punished. I'm almost always being punished. When I am you can't talk to me at all, only after lights out, and even then it's not a good idea, because Susanna pops up out of nowhere, and she's got ears like a rabbit."

"But why are you always being punished?" Gina asked. Torma had such a kind and gentle face it was hard to imagine that she would ever be insolent or misbehave.

"Actually, it's for love," Mari Kis explained. "Don't be so naive. I told you that the Director is her uncle. He's also the poor girl's guardian, and he's like the good Lord – those whom he loves he punishes. Now we really must go. We aren't allowed to stay in the dormitories after the beds are made. Most of the time we just hang around in the day room, but lessons haven't started yet, so perhaps we can persuade Susanna to let us go out into the garden."

They set off for the day room. Someone had opened windows in the corridor and the sunshine was flooding in. Perhaps, Gina was thinking, perhaps . . . Perhaps there aren't any grown-ups about, only the girls in my year. And perhaps not all the grown-ups are the same. Perhaps I'll even come to like one of them, if one of them is, if only a little, like Marcelle.

As they walked, the two keys, the one for her locker that hung from her neck and the one for her drawer in the study-room table, clinked dully together. The other girls' did likewise. Gina detested the idea of wearing a key around her neck. They were supplied with bags, so why not keep it in there? What else was it for?

"The key doesn't belong with the things in the bag," Mari Kis explained. "The bag is for a handkerchief, a folder for the warnings they give you, the snack they give you at breakfast if we're going on an outing (it comes wrapped in wax paper), a Bible and psalm book for different occasions in the year, and a box for your pens. That's it. The keys stay round your neck. It's compulsory. Instead of jewellery."

"Jewellery." The word reminded her of the sad little moon that Susanna had stripped from her neck. That too was now just a memory, if not a very old one . . . but at that moment something else caught her attention, something her companions had noticed too: through one of the opened windows a tune could be heard, a tune coming from somewhere down in Matula Street, at the front of the building. It was a repeated triple blast on a motor horn, a motor horn on which, in a far-off world, a happier world across the oceans, a world beyond the Seven Seas, a father was sending a message to his daughter. *Gina my child, Gina my child*, the motor horn called out merrily each time he pressed it. *Gina my child*, ran the cheerful refrain, again and again, ever more insistently, until it seemed not in the least happy or merry but appallingly, overwhelmingly sad. Gina turned towards the wall and leaned her forehead against it to stop the others seeing her face. She felt she did not know either the blonde or the brunette well enough to give way to her feelings in front of them without embarrassment. *Gina my child* . . . The sound was already fading . . . now barely there at all . . . and finally no more. The car was now speeding away from Matula Street. Somewhere on its way it would go past the great church, and she would be left behind in the mighty fortress.

"Well," said Mari Kis, turning towards her to look gently into her face. "You mustn't cry. I told you this place is bearable. You'll see. It's going to be a really nice afternoon. If you like, Torma will think up something to make it fun. Torma doesn't care. She's always being punished anyway."

They were being so kind, so very kind, but they could not change the way she felt. The motor horn could no longer be heard, but it carried on and on sounding in her head: *Gina my child* . . .

"Tomorrow is the service for the start of the school year. The whole town will be there, staring at us as we walk down the street. Perhaps one or two boys will manage to slip into the balcony," the dark-haired girl said. "Then the term will begin and we'll all get married. We get married as soon as lessons begin. You will too. If you're really lucky, you'll get Bishop Matula himself."

And despite herself, the thought of that made Gina laugh.

The legend of Abigail

The garden was enormous, and they were given the hoped-for permission to walk in it until lunch. Mari told Gina that they tended the flowers themselves. There was a school gardener, but this was another of the things they had to learn, along with dressmaking and Lord knows what else. According to the Director there was nothing worse than inactivity; the road to Hell was paved with hours of idleness. But there was no need to worry, there was no chance of that in the Matula. When lessons were over and they had finished their homework they would then be tested on what they had learned by the Deaconess. There were no weak pupils in the school. Those who couldn't keep up, or didn't work, were sent away at the end of the year, never to set foot in the building again. The Matula was the strictest school in the whole world. When you had done your homework and repeated aloud what you had learned you were free to go and work some more, either in the garden or in the sewing room, wherever you were sent. You could even take extra lessons in music or a foreign language if your parents were mad enough to ask for them, and they didn't even have to pay. If, after all that, you still had some free time, you could of course read, because the school had a huge library, or you could do embroidery, or whatever else came to hand. You walked for two hours each day, and spent another in the gym: both were compulsory. So there was no need to feel anxious. She would never be bored.

What she was hearing about her new school left Gina with mixed feelings. On the one hand it rather alarmed her. She felt that such a strictly regimented life, with every minute accounted for, must be truly oppressive for anyone whose misfortune brought them there; but she also was aware that these two did not seem too discontented with their lot. On the contrary: though they had never said as much, you could see on their faces that they felt rather proud to be part of this exclusive world, in which everyone was clever and hardworking and would demonstrably have learned so much more by the time they left than people educated elsewhere. What surprised Gina most was being told that there were no day-pupils, only boarders. The fortress was unlike any other school of its kind in the country: it was a proper boarding school, like the ones abroad. Those citizens of Árkod who didn't want to be separated from their children sent them either to the local state school or to one in the nearest town. Between the state school and the Matula there existed, sometimes openly, sometimes covertly, a permanent state of war. The state pupils called the Matula girls the "Holy Tripe Sausages", and the Matula responded with "Cock-a-doodle-doo", because their rivals' school was named after the zoologist Paul Kokas.

Among the Matula traditions was a celebratory feast for the eighth-year leavers at the end of their final term, not of course in one of those dreadful hotels in the town but in the school's Great Hall. It was so grand they even gave you a mug of hot chocolate with your brioche, after which you went over to the state school – the first time you had ever been allowed out without being chaperoned by a deaconess – and bellowed out the dreaded "Cock-a-doodle-doo". At some point in the distant past the wife of the Chief of Police had been a pupil at the Matula, and, strangely enough, ever since then no policeman had ever been seen on the street outside the Paul Kokas on these occasions, and the Matula girls had been free to crow at will; but whenever the visit was returned and the state pupils began their "Holy Tripe Sausages of Matula / No Father Christmas your way. / You're so afraid of damnation / All you can do is pray", there always seemed to be one on duty. The previous year the townees had registered a double setback. They had thrown a huge sausage over the fence, made of stuffed-linen and complete with a halo. Not only did their headmaster receive an indignant letter from the Director, but he was so angry he refused to accept their explanation that they had added the halo purely out of mockery and there had been no sacrilegious intent.

There were many other legends and traditions in the place, like the one about getting married. This one was thanks to a former pupil, Mitsi Horn, who had become engaged in her final year and came back at the start of the September term with an engagement ring on her finger. She was sent immediately to the Director and made to leave it with him until she left. First of all, just imagine: she had had the nerve to bring a profane piece of trumpery like that onto the premises, and second, think of the scandal! She was still a pupil and she had been mixing in the outside world, with grown-ups, which raised the inevitable, and painful, suspicion that whoever had given her the ring, clearly a person of the opposite sex, must have kissed her; I mean, real kisses.

But the matter was not put to rest by her not wearing the ring. The contagion was already inside the building, and all the other girls wanted to become engaged too. Finally, in a flash of inspiration, a former pupil, who had been in the third year at the time and had left the school almost a thousand years ago and then, by one rather amusing means or another, gone on to become a famous actress in the capital, thought of a way for them to do that. Since there were no young men around to serve as fiancés, actual fiancés of flesh and blood, they would be paired off with some object or picture. It became the tradition that every year each girl should be betrothed to an item in the class inventory. These inventories hung by the door in every classroom and listed everything that could be found in the room: pictures, furniture, teaching materials, all recorded against a number. The first girl in alphabetical order was given item number one, the second item two, and so on. It was considered highly amusing to get yourself married in this way, and the teachers were of course totally unaware of what was going on. The Director himself was included in the distribution, but only to the eighth year, or he would have too many wives and he was allowed only one. Best of all was when, for whatever reason, he spoke to this wife of whose existence he was totally unaware. It was a perfect scream, though sadly you couldn't laugh out loud because you would never be able to explain what was so funny. But the most interesting thing of all, they told Gina, was that they all invariably ended up somehow falling in love with the husbands they had married in jest. Sometimes the school inspectors would be taken aback at how much one of them knew about some famous person or other – for example, the girl who had married the bronze statue of Marcus Aurelius and had read everything she could find about him and knew every detail of the life of the man who was now her life-partner. Even Torma who, having the misfortune to have a name beginning with "T", had been married to an etching of the first-ever printing press, had once stunned her uncle in this way. He had found some dust in the classroom and scolded the luckless "girl number eighteen" for not having cleaned it properly during the break."Just look at that dust on this picture of the printing press! But then, what would someone like you know about a fine thing like that?" She started to reel off everything she had read in the library encyclopaedia and other reference books on the subject. He stared at her in disbelief, incapable, for the first time in his life, of coherent speech, while she went on and on in the same endless monotone: "The invention of the movable type printing press took place in the last three decades of the fifteenth century. Opinions differ as to the identity of the inventor, though most commentators agree that it was John Gutenberg of Mainz. Another possibility is that it was a certain Metel, or Mentel, of Schlettstadt. The name of Albert Pfister of Bamberg is also mentioned, although he was merely a pupil of Gutenberg." By the time she had got to Pfister he had turned on his heel and sailed out of the room like a black barge. Several of the girls noted that he was so shocked his forehead was covered in sweat. But Torma was punished all the same, not for the monologue about the printing press but for her failure to clean properly.

Gina listened to their stories and laughed along with them, but at the same time she had the feeling that compared to herself these girls were as immature as primary school children. She thought of her friends in Budapest, of the experiences she had had there, and of Feri, above all of Feri, holding her close against himself while dancing during that last afternoon tea at Auntie Mimó's. He was real, and he was young, not just a picture. If jewellery was forbidden, then obviously an engagement ring would be too. But why resort to this bizarre method of finding yourself someone to daydream about? To take a printing press as husband was all very droll, but real boys were a lot more interesting.

"Real boys?" said Mari Kis, and her eyes grew round with wonder. "Where are there real boys? They exist only in the school holidays, if you can find them. But who would want to start something with a girl from this place, someone you could never write to, and who, even at home, all that way from Árkod, would be afraid of being seen standing in the street talking to a person of the opposite sex? You can only love someone here if you are so committed you don't care what happens to you; either that, or you are just about to take your school leaving exams and know you will soon be free."

Gina was in two minds: should she tell them about Feri? But she said nothing. Not that she did not trust them, but she had known them for such a short time, far too short a time. Mari Kis had already noticed that she was shocked rather than amused by what she had heard.

"It doesn't do to draw attention to yourself here," she said, and Torma nodded in agreement. "My parents pay only a quarter of the fees because they aren't rich. If I made a nuisance of myself I would lose my bursary. Torma has no-one at all, only the Director. If the school hadn't taken us in, who would look after us and give us an education?"

This was the first time Gina had ever thought about what it meant that her father was able to pay her school fees, however considerable they might be, or had reflected on the difference that had made to her daily life. It had never occurred to her that others might have to be on their best behaviour, be submissive at all times and respect the rules, or be denied the chance to finish their time in a school where they were being educated for a min-imal fee or none at all. But even now she was listening with only half an ear to what the other two were saying: she was wondering how she could evade Susanna's vigilance by writing to Auntie Mimó and slipping a covert message for Feri into a text that would certainly be censored. And would Feri send a reply? Would they even post the letter? Torma and Mari Kis were now trying to guess who would be teaching them the various subjects, and the names they reeled off meant nothing to her.

She was walking with her eyes fixed on the ground, trying to think of a way to make contact with the world she had left behind. With her head lowered, she stumbled into something and almost fell, but Mari Kis caught her arm. Raising her eyes, she saw that they had reached the far end of the garden, where a high stone wall marked the school boundary. A curving recess had been cut into its considerable depth, and in it stood a statue, the statue of a young woman. Curly locks spilled out from under her head-band, over a gentle brow, and she held a classical-style stone pitcher.

Torma mounted the two steps at the base of the semi-circular plinth and kissed the stone face on both cheeks. Mari Kis followed her and did the same, and they chorused, "Hello, Abigail."

The statue also had a smile on its face: a rather solemn smile, not unlike the one on the happy faces of the two young girls.

"This is Vitay," said Mari Kis. "Georgina Vitay. She's going to be with us. So now you know who she is, Abigail."

(Oh dear, another of their games, the same childish nonsense.)

"Say hello," Torma insisted. "You must say hello! This is Abigail. The miracle-working Abigail."

That was too much. Gina stepped back. Oddly enough, she now felt more sure of herself than ever before in the fortress: true, it might be a strictly controlled world, a squat, four-square sort of world full of rules to trip you up, but at least there was something rather childlike about it. It was like when they brought out a figure of the Devil to frighten you on Christmas Eve, when you knew all along that it was really your father's batman in fancy dress.

"That's fine," said Mari Kis. "You might want to say hello some other time – just wait till you're in trouble. We don't have guardian angels in this place, or carry amulets, nothing of that sort, and you can't be pestering God over every trifle. But if you really think you can cope on your own, you go ahead."

"Abigail is always there for us," Torma said. Her voice was

perfectly serious. "If you're in trouble, serious trouble, she really will help you. She always does."

(Oh, well, let them enjoy their fairy tales.)

She was now feeling almost liberated, cheerful even. They're just children – this Torma who married a printing press, and Mari Kis, who introduced her to a stone statue. She was thinking of Mozart's "Don Giovanni", the last production she had attended in the Opera House, and once again her heart was torn. The singer who played the part of the Commander was an acquaintance of Auntie Mimó's, and during the interval they had been able to visit him in his dressing room. He had greeted her with "*Kezét csókolom* – I kiss your hand!"

"Here nothing is that simple," said Torma. "You'll see. People have so many dreams that never come to anything. We live in fear because of all the horrible things that can happen. Abigail has been here for hundreds of years. I don't know why she's called Abigail. She's been called that since the Matula was the Matula. Someone must have given her the name at some point."

(Very good: so here we have a statue, a rather fine neoclassical sculpture from the end of the eighteenth century, dressed in the style of Mme Récamier and holding a Greek pitcher – a true daughter of the Empire.)

"It was Mitsi Horn who discovered that she wasn't just a statue, she was also a miracle worker. Mitsi Horn was sobbing and howling because the Director had taken her engagement ring away and her young man had gone off to fight in the First World War. When she was forbidden to wear his ring she went to the statue, weeping and complaining how wretched she was, and when she went back a few days later she saw something sticking up out of the pitcher, and she pulled it out. It was a letter from her fiancé. She almost went mad because just then the bell rang for her maths lesson and there was no time to read it, not until the next break. She wrote back the same day and put the envelope in the pitcher, but it wasn't there long. And for the rest of her time in the school these letters came to her from her boy and she was always able to write back to him."

"How very exciting," said Gina. She knew that her tone would be hurtful. It made clear that she did not believe a word of it and was becoming bored by everything they were telling her – bored by the statue, which wasn't even medieval, and bored with these two girls. Her anxiety returned: how on earth was she going to be able to put up with the childishness of her companions on top of the black-and-white rules of the fortress?

"It was an awfully long time ago," Mari Kis explained. "In 1914. Ever since then Abigail has always been there to help us. But only on one condition: we must never talk about her to strangers. She even wrote as much to Dorka, when she spilled some ink on the school Bible. She told her that she could help us only if we had really serious problems, and ever since then we have kept her secret. I don't know how she does it, but one way or another she always manages to sort things out."

(What an imagination these people have! This Abigail, who always comes to your aid! And all this inside the fortress, where we live like soldiers in a barracks and with nothing but biblical quotations on the walls. They are so superstitious they might just as well worship idols!)

"Of course, she doesn't help people who don't believe in her," Torma said, and she changed the subject. As they walked back to the school Gina did not look back, but the kindly eyes of the Empire girl Abigail followed them, as if to tell them that she would always be there if they were ever in serious trouble, for life in the fortress was hard and one couldn't pester the good Lord about every tiny thing.

The garden was filled with both colour and fragrance, a relief after all the black and white. Somewhere a bell rang, a correct, formal little chime, instructing them to wash their hands, as Mari Kis explained. It was lunchtime. Torma added a word of warning: once she had been shown to her place in the refectory she was not to sit down straight away, and certainly not reach for her spoon. First, someone would read from the Bible, then there would be hymns, followed by prayers; only after that were you allowed to start on your food. It was the same at the end of the meal, and you were not allowed to leave the table until given leave to do so. Conversation was forbidden while eating; the food was good and the servings large, but you should never ask for seconds unless invited to, and you always had to wait in sub-missive silence, because all through the meal a girl on duty read aloud from a book by some ghastly Swiss priest. It was supposed to show you how to live, and how to be a good Christian girl, and you really had to pay attention, because they had been known to question people about it after evening prayers.

"Today we'll be free from lunch until supper, and after tomorrow you'll have a chance to learn about the housekeeping arrangements – actually, that's from the day *after* tomorrow, because tomorrow is the start-of-term service instead, and that's a very special occasion. You'll also meet your teachers and be given your timetable and textbooks, and your first set of instructions. The teachers live in the same building as we do, over in the wing, and you'll be seeing them around rather more often than you want, because although it's supposed to be the Deaconess who supervises our studies, other members of staff are always popping in on the pretext of helping her."

They had now arrived back at the building, at a different door from the one that led up to the dormitory, a low doorway studded around the edges with cast-iron stars. Beyond it the entrance to the refectory stood open to receive them. Gina felt that never in her life had she been in such a spotlessly clean place. Susanna was standing outside the ablutions to make sure that they washed their hands properly and shared out the paper towels fairly between them.

The aquarium, and a betrayal

They were free for the rest of the day, until suppertime.

The Librarian, another deaconess, was already at her post, and other sisters had been busy in the kitchen and the sewing room, but nothing had yet been arranged for the pupils. Nor could it have been. They came from all over the country, as did several members of the teaching staff, and they arrived by train at widely different times, which precluded any organised activity. But by evening everyone was present and at dinner there was not a single empty chair. Gina finally met one of her teachers, after evening prayers – the Chaplain who led services in the school and would be taking her for religious studies.

She had been watching the behaviour of the girls Mari Kis and Torma introduced her to and had been doing her best to copy them. In fact she found it hard to stop herself doing so, which rather distressed her. But when it came to religious worship there was a problem. There had been nothing very intense about her religious life at home. Her father and Auntie Mimó were Catholic, but Gina had been raised in her mother's Protestantism. At the Sokoray Atala the girls had been encouraged to follow their own faith, but there had been no supervision or compulsion and religious studies lessons had all been purely academic. Gina went to church infrequently, though Auntie Mimó had sometimes taken her to Mass, which was rather more interesting because Feri would go with them, and afterwards they went for walks in the centre of town, stopping for a rest in one of the famous patisseries. But she was shocked to find that the hymns, which the other girls knew by heart, were all new to her, ones she had never been taught.

At the end of the service Susanna took her to meet the Chaplain.

She felt rather self-conscious standing before him, not because she felt especially diffident just then but because she knew what he was going to ask her.

"Did they not teach you any hymns in Budapest?" he enquired.

"Not many," she whispered.

"That's a pity," said Susanna. "Here everyone knows the hymns and psalms by heart. But we'll help you catch up. Gardening is too important for your health to miss, but we can excuse you from needlework lessons for a while. When the rest of the class are in the sewing room you must go to the music room, and you'll get to know the tunes as well. Are you learning the piano?"

Of course she was. At the Sokoray Atala they did not teach handicrafts and she did not feel the need to start on needlework now, though it might be rather more pleasant than memorising hymns. Susanna turned away and Gina went back to join the other girls. The little bell rang again. She was getting used to hearing it whenever anything began or ended.

She was afraid that at bedtime there might be another arcane rule preventing her from washing herself the way she was used to at home or from taking a bath every day, although in the end no-one tried to stop her. But you were not allowed to lock yourself in the bathroom; instead you had to hang a placard on the door handle, with a picture on it of a bath and a running shower to say that someone was inside, and not to open the door and disturb them. She was enjoying a nice long drenching when suddenly there was a knock on the door and she heard Susanna telling her that her time was up. Enraged, she dried herself down with the coarse linen towel she had been given and pulled on the shapeless white nightgown. The slippers might have been made for a chimney sweep. Her classmates were already in bed by the time she got back to the dormitory and all the lights were out, except for a tiny one near the door, next to her bed.

The darkness made it impossible to read, or even listen to the radio: in fact there was nothing to do at all. The girls were busy whispering to one another, but they were all some way away from her and she felt very isolated. It would have been so good if someone, even Susanna, had asked: "Are you alright, Gina? How do you like your bed? Sleep well!" But no-one came, and when at long last Torma asked her softly if she was still awake she made no reply, although she was; and she stayed that way until the last of them was deep in slumber. She listened for noises from the corridor outside, or from the unknown city that lay beyond, but there was not a sound. Someone might have been walking in the corridor, but she heard nothing. She never knew at what point she did at last fall asleep: she had forgotten to wind her watch and it had stopped at ten.

When it was time to rise the next morning she struggled to get out of bed. But she did not complain. Instead she forced herself on as she had never done in her life before. The bell rang almost non-stop, always to announce some new task: time to go and wash, time to get dressed, time for prayers, time for breakfast. Soon it would ring again to summon them to the day room, and finally to get themselves in line. That morning they were to wear their dark-blue going-out uniform and the impossible blue hat: it was like something worn by traditional horsemen on the Puszta, with the same wide brim but without the frond of maidenhair fern, emblazoned instead with the coat of arms she had seen outside the Director's office. There was no time or opportunity for her to check in the mirror to see whether this creation suited her, and in truth she had no wish to know what she looked like in such a disguise. Better not to see.

They were now lined up in the corridor. At another command from the bell the column moved off towards the main entrance and out through the iron-barred portal at the front of the building. They were marching three abreast. This suited Gina, as she found herself next to Torma and Mari Kis. It was only when they were out in the street that she realised quite how many they were: the blue uniforms filled the entire length of the pavement. They were lined up in order of height, with the smallest of the first years at the front. Ahead of them were the Chaplain, in all his regalia, the Director and the male and female teachers, while in front of everyone went the school flag, carried by one of the older girls. The form tutors and the class prefects marched alongside their own pupils. Seeing who was next to her class, beside Susanna, she was so surprised she missed a step and had to adjust her pace to catch up. "So?" Torma asked in a loud whisper. "Well, then?" There was no chance to reply because Susanna would have heard, but in fact there was no need. Torma had read her face perfectly well: she was no less thrilled and astonished than they had been when they first set eyes on Péter Kalmár. They had told her the day before that their class tutor was the most handsome man in all the world, and they had not hidden their own feelings about him either. Everyone was in love with him. They all stole the pieces of chalk he left on his chair and collected bits of thread from his clothing. Varga, the girl who had been sent down from their class the previous year and whose place Gina had taken, had cut the letter "K" from the hat of Kőnig, the Latin teacher, and sewn it onto her blouse. It was tucked away under her arm, but of course it was noticed – everything was noticed here – and when she was reprimanded for having the letter "K" sewn onto her dress she replied that she wore it in memory of Johannes Kalvin, whereupon the Director launched into a tirade about how the founder of the Puritan religion would have been appalled to be remembered in such an idiotic way and would she kindly remove it at once. This scene had taken place in the refectory after dinner, and the girls, knowing who the "K" really stood for, were almost choking with suppressed hilarity. Varga kept her eyes fixed all the while on Kalmár, who for his part maintained a small sliver of a smile. He knew exactly what was going on. Only Kőnig seemed not to notice, but that hardly mattered. Even if he had, he never complained about anything.

Gina was not in a particularly good mood; she was still sleepy after spending the night lying awake tossing and turning in her bed; but she felt suddenly cheered by the fact that one of the teachers walking near her had the air of someone from her old world, the world of Auntie Mimó. To think that a mere school-teacher, in a place like this, should be so much a man, a real man! The flag bearer had now turned into the street, with the whole school following, a long dark-blue serpent moving steadily away from the Matula towards the white, four-square church. Gina's eyes never once left Kalmár, and Mari Kis had to pinch her arm whenever she fell out of step. Susanna noticed this too, but she simply wagged her head and said nothing. Her eyes were certainly not on Kalmár. They were on the girls in her class.

The actual service turned her mind in other directions, and she found it rather soothing. The priest talked about how they should all work diligently because there was a war on. The enemies they faced were ignorance and laziness, and as they went about their lessons they should also pray for the soldiers at the front. Gina thought of her father, and of Feri, and her eyes filled with tears. She looked at the branches outside the window, tossing in the breeze, and she thought how strange it was that the priest should say, "We should fight against our sins, our negligence and laziness, just as the soldiers are fighting against the enemy *until the final victory is won.*" How interesting that she should hear this phrase from a priest, this mention of a *final victory.* Her father, who was in the army, had never used the words, and had never promised her, or Auntie Mimó, that "we will win the war". No doubt he considered it so self-evident he didn't think it worth mentioning.

Everyone sang the psalms without even glancing at the words; Gina was the only one who needed them – she and the first years – and she felt ashamed. Worse, she did not even know the tunes, and she stared dumbly at her hymn book: "Hallelujah, hallelujah, our gates stand open to the daughters of the people . . ." She gave up the struggle and studied the faces around her instead. Susanna and Kalmár were sitting next to each other, and the Prefect's fine soprano rose clear of all the others. Kalmár too was singing at the top of his voice, which rather surprised Gina; his eyes were lowered and focused on no-one and nothing in particular. The girls are wasting their time ogling this man, she thought. He couldn't care less if they sewed his monogram onto their dresses or not. Something does seem to interest him, and it isn't the admiration of his pupils.

During the sermon she tried to imagine herself, dressed in her proper clothes and wearing her hair the way she usually did, meeting Péter Kalmár not inside the fortress but in a purely social setting, and she wondered what they would say to one another. At her aunt's afternoon teas she had danced with officers older than he was. What bright blond hair he had, and what a noble profile! It was the face of a soldier – so brave-looking, so decided. Gina had always loved paintings. With Marcelle she had often been into grand salons and museums, both at home and abroad, and they always visited the great collections. Kalmár's face was that of a particularly handsome St George, and seeing the connection made her almost laugh with delight. How lucky it was that our faces didn't betray what we were thinking, and that no-one knew that she, or anyone else in this great squat building, was thinking of him as St George, the greatest knight-errant of all . . . But of course these Calvinists didn't recognise saints.

The dragon slayer had the bluest of eyes, quite unlike any other blue, a pure essence of blue, and his eyelashes were as black as in a painting. And how long they were! It didn't seem right that a man should have such beautiful eyes. At that moment she would have loved to reassure herself in a mirror that her own eyelashes were even longer than his, but of course that was impossible, even if she hadn't been sitting in a church. All she had with her was the bag with the school handkerchiefs in it. Her powder box and its mirror were lying where she had hidden them, under the row of geraniums.

She allowed her gaze to wander along the pews, trying to see where Kőnig was sitting – the man who had failed to complain when a girl stole the monogram from his hat. For Gina, beauty and bravery went hand in hand, as did a lacklustre appearance and a dull mind. She searched along the teachers' pew for the dullest-looking man and told herself that that must be him. As it turned out, she had hit on the right person. The man with grey-ing hair and glasses, sitting directly in front of the sacramental table in a badly cut jacket, was indeed Kőnig. He was tall and broad-shouldered, but held himself badly, almost like a hunch-back.

"Oh Lord our Comforter . . ." Which one is it now? Hymn number 63 . . . She had to scramble back and forth through the book . . . "Send us thy salvation, that we might not stray from the path of righteousness, or lose our courage in the battle to come . . ." The war, yet again! she thought, as everyone stood up for the closing prayer. She recited the Lord's Prayer and received the blessing with her head bowed, not daring to look up. As soon as the Amen was over she raised a foot in preparation to move off, and instantly put it down again, pretending that it had slipped: everyone else had remained standing, with their hands clasped together. Even the first years had known what she hadn't, that at the end of the service it was the practice to say a short private prayer for all mankind.

When they were finally on their way back to the school, Susanna fell in beside Gina. She had noticed, she told her, the degree of devotion with which she had involved herself in the service, how intently she had followed the sermon, and how thoughtfully and sincerely she had prayed. "Thank you," she concluded, with a solemn nod of her head. The girl looked at her for a moment in astonishment, then blushed. She was ashamed at having deceived Susanna, however inadvertently. She had been taught to speak the truth, and she was no coward. She opened her mouth to say that she did not deserve these compliments when Susanna turned away and hurried on ahead. Mari Kis, who had heard everything, hissed at her, "Are you mad? You're not going to tell her you weren't? Susanna would drop dead if you let on that you were really thinking of God knows what."

They were still forbidden to talk, but Susanna and Kalmár were by now a long way ahead and Torma and Mari Kis were busy telling her, sotto voce, what would happen next. When they got back to the school they would go to their various classrooms.

First they would sit in their old places: if they hadn't given her one beforehand Gina could take that of Edit Varga, who had been expelled. Then, after fifteen minutes, their new class teachers would appear, read out the timetable and hand out textbooks and so forth. The purpose of the fifteen minutes' wait was so that the pupils could exercise restraint and observe a fitting silence to show that they were worthy daughters of the Reformed Church and could do this even when there were no teachers around. A funereal hush would fill the entire building. Neither the Director nor the teachers would have the slightest idea that at the end of this fifteen minutes' morally improving "silence" every class from the third year upwards would be holding their own service, in honour of Mitsi Horn, and getting married. The two lower years were so gormless they would sit and wait with their arms folded for their teachers to appear. They were really green.

By the time they reached the school some of her classmates' good humour had begun to rub off on Gina. She did not of course take the game as seriously as they did, having rather different memories and experiences and an altogether different notion of love and marriage, but she did find the general idea rather amusing – of being married to someone or something for a whole year, if only in jest. They had to mount the staircase slowly and calmly, because teachers on duty were standing looking down to observe them. The same had happened at Gina's old school, but somehow it had felt very different there: the teachers would be chatting or even reading, and did not see it as a complete tragedy if the girls were a bit lively or noisy on their return from the service. Here in the Matula no-one was allowed to say a word:

you had to place your steps as carefully as in a solemn dance, and the supervisors kept telling you to tread softly and not march or stamp your feet.

The group now split into their various classes, and for the first time Gina found herself inside a teaching room. Once again she was taken by surprise. It was brightly modern and much better equipped than the Sokoray Atala, which it outclassed in every respect. It was not in the least like a conventional classroom, more like a classical amphitheatre. Between the wall at the back and the teacher's chair there was a semi-circular row of desks every second step up, with a narrow walkway between them and a wider central aisle to allow access. Reproductions and portraits were ranged along the walls, and at the highest point in the room, behind the back rows of desks, there was a projector.

Here, she thought, they don't let you copy other people's work, but at least you can see the blackboard. And, how interesting, it looks as if they use films and slides in the lessons.

Torma let her in between herself and Mari Kis, at the end of the fourth row. No-one had told her what would happen next. As they were taking their seats, an extremely plump girl took down the register hanging beside the door ("Szabó," Mari Kis said, "Anikó Szabó.") and with Murai standing beside her began to read out the list of names. She pronounced them slowly and clearly, stopping after each one and following it with an item from the inventory.

– Ari: *Pasteur.*

– Bánki: *Olympian Zeus.*

– Barta: *Homer.*

– Cziller: *István Bocskai.*

– Dudás: *Emperor Joseph the Second.*

– Gáti: *Rodin.*

– Jackó: *Johann Sebastian Bach.*

– Kis: "The Laocoon Group."

– Kovács: *Mendelev.*

– Lengyel: *Galileo.*

– Murai: *Shakespeare.*

– Nacák: *Goethe.*

– Oláh: *The unknown chronicler of King Béla.*

– Rideg: *Michelangelo's* "David".

– Salm: *Bishop Matula.*

– Szabó: *Friedrich August Quenstedt.*

– Tatár: *The Cloak of Ivan the First.*

– Torma: *The Via Appia.*

– Vajda: *The Graduation Song.*

"All done!"

"Not all done," said Mari Kis crossly. "You haven't finished. What about Vitay?"

"Oh, yes," said Szabó, peering into the register. "Number 20. *The empty aquarium.*"

Oh God, not that! At first she had thought the whole thing quite amusing, far more so than she had expected: Torma, married to the Appian Way, where she had so often strolled with Marcelle and which now came so vividly to mind, the two of them passing through the Porta Sebastiana and moving on towards the distant tomb of Caecilia Metella, and Mari Kis as the wife not of one person – or in this case object – but of three, since the Laocoon group consisted of three statues . . . or indeed four, because there was also the serpent: that was so funny it almost brought tears to your eyes. The girls were almost prostrate with laughter at the husbands they had been given; of course they didn't dare laugh out loud, and having to suppress it made the atmosphere in the room all the more hilarious and effervescent: it was as if they had all suddenly become drunk. Rideg, who happened to be sitting beside her, pointed out that her husband had only a head, because that was all that the picture on the wall showed, which made it even funnier – to have a husband whose body stopped at the neck. But while Szabó had immediately accepted the husband she had been given, Gina's own pleasure in the proceedings had come to a sudden end. It was amusing enough to be married to an empty aquarium, but it also made her angry. She stood up to protest. Could she please have another husband? She certainly didn't need an empty aquarium. She wasn't going to take part in such a stupid game as that.

"You can't do that," whispered Szabó, not crossly but wanting to explain. "It's against the rules either to choose or to change. You're number twenty, and that's what you get. Don't waste your time."

"It's the rule," Mari Kis added, in a whisper.

A rule indeed! Gina shrugged her shoulders and replied that that wasn't a rule, it was a piece of downright stupidity.

"You can't do this!" Szabó whispered again. "It just isn't possible. Everyone gets married. It's the custom here. Do you think I'm happy with this Friedrich August Quenstedt? I don't even know what it is!"

"I'm not going to have an aquarium," said Gina. "I'm not going to join in. Don't any of you understand?"

"Come on," said Mari Kis, wagging her head. "Don't be silly. This is one of our most important traditions. It has been ever since Mitsi Horn got engaged, and it's great fun. If it's an aquarium, so it's an aquarium. Isn't an aquarium human too? I never saw the likes of you."

Her voice was a mere whisper, and her tone was neither hectoring nor sharp, but it put Gina in such a rage she could no longer think clearly. If Mari had never seen the likes of her, well, they hadn't seen anything yet. Gina could be impetuous and short-tempered: Marcelle had often told her off for it. The exchange had driven her to the point where she was speaking without giving any thought to what she was saying.

"I don't want any of this, I'm not going to have any part in it and I'm not interested in your stupid traditions. I've got a real man courting me!"

"A real man?" Torma protested. "How can you possibly have a man courting you when you're shut up in here with the rest of us? Stop moaning! Why can't you see the funny side?"

Gina completely forgot that they were supposed to be sitting in silence. At the top of her voice she shouted that she didn't see anything funny in their stupid games – they were all a bunch of idiots. She wasn't used to people who behaved like that. Her friends in Budapest were the normal ones, and that included her suitors. (She only had one, but it sounded better in the plural.)

There was an instant silence, a silence she should have realised was quite unnatural, even in the Matula. But she was thinking only of herself, of her anger and her feelings, and she failed to notice it. All she wanted to do now was to tear the shoe-lace from her plaits, run out of the room and hammer with her fists on the iron-studded door to be let out.

"Very well," said Szabó. "If that's what you want. It isn't in the rules, but never mind. Vitay won't be taking part with the rest of us. Vitay will have no husband. She'll be an old maid."

Gina felt she would explode. She had thought about her coming marriage a thousand times. She ran her eye over Szabó, from top to toe – the plump belly, the stumpy legs, the whole shapeless body almost bursting out of the ugly uniform.

"You're the one who'll be an old maid," she shouted. She failed to notice that at this point all eyes had turned away from her. The attention of the class was elsewhere. They had seen something she had not.

"Who would want to marry you, you horrible fatty? Who would ever want to kiss you?"

Szabó did not blush; she went deathly pale. Gina immediately realised she should never have let herself say that. Szabó was truly, alarmingly, morbidly overweight, like someone with a longstanding hormone problem. She did not attempt to reply. She would not have been able to even if the offence had not left her speechless, because the whole class had now risen to their feet. Gina, who like Murai and Szabó had been facing away from both them and the door, now turned towards it. There, gazing steadily at her, was Kalmár.

"What manner of speech is this?" he demanded. "Who was shouting in that disgraceful way? Who on earth are you?"

The class were all standing to attention. How wonderful it would have been just then if someone had come to her assistance, had tried to defend her, or at least to offer the man some explanation. But the others just stood there, gazing at Kalmár in silence. Gina had refused to join the fifth year in their game, and now, in her hour of need, they rejected her in turn.

"Who are you?" Kalmár asked again. "I haven't seen you before."

"Georgina Vitay," she muttered.

"Shouting in the fifteen minutes' silence, and such language?"

"She's a new girl," Torma said softly. Gina's heart filled with gratitude. It was Torma who had spoken – Torma who was married to the Via Appia.

"You've given a fine first impression of yourself, I must say. And Szabó and Murai, why were you standing next to my chair, and what were you doing with the class inventory?"

Szabó and Murai were nowhere to be seen. They had melted away like snowflakes in the warmth of the room, absorbed back into the protective body of the class. Only Gina was left standing alone. No-one came to her aid. Kalmár took his seat at the teacher's desk and, without the slightest anger in his voice, as if there were no point in paying too much attention to this unpleasant episode at the start of the new term, said, almost laconically: "The girl who was shouting will leave the room."

He did not have to say it twice. Gina fled. She was shaking, as if in a fever. She now hated everything to do with her new school with a violence she would not have thought herself capable of. As soon as she was outside she burst into tears, leaned against the row of lockers that ran along the wall and wept so furiously it made her face ugly. Having nothing to dry them with she dabbed at her tears with the back of her hand: her bag was still on the bench inside the room.

For the second time she was being spoken to before she realised. It was only when a hand was placed on her shoulder that she noticed that someone was standing there. She looked up and found Kőnig.

"What's the matter, my girl?" he asked. "What has happened to you?"

How could she explain, to this person who had stood by and said nothing when the monogram was stolen from his hat? She offered no reply; she pulled herself away from him and began to weep even more furiously, as if she would never stop.

"What's going on here?" another voice demanded.

A stockily built man in black, with a stern, expressionless face: the Director himself. An altogether worthier opponent.

"Why is Georgina Vitay standing in the corridor?" Gedeon Torma wanted to know.

"I think she's unwell," Kőnig said quickly. "The poor girl is not at all well."

No! Not him! She didn't need *him* to defend her. Gina drew herself up and said that she had been sent out of the room.

"Sent out of the room? In your first lesson? And for what reason, may I ask?"

She hesitated for just an instant, then almost shouted at him: because she had refused to be married to an aquarium!

She knew that as long as she lived she would never forget the look on the man's face.

"It's a game they play," Kőnig explained, though no-one had asked him. "They are very young, these girls. Girls of this age often play at getting married."

"Very interesting," said the Director, "but I don't see the connection. How did you come to be playing this game during the fifteen minutes' silence? And what's all this about an aquarium? Don't look at me like that. Answer me!"

"Everyone gets married during the period of silence," Gina whispered.

Kőnig's eyes flickered behind his enormous glasses, and only then did it dawn on Gina that this was the one thing she should never have said. She had betrayed the great secret of the school, the legacy of Mitsi Horn that had been kept from the teachers since 1914. But her regret lasted only a moment. What did it matter to her? People who tried to force her to marry an aquarium were beneath her consideration.

"Even more interesting," said the Director, nodding his head. He opened the door to his office. "You must tell me the whole story. So the fifth year have all been married, in the first half-hour of lessons after returning from the service? Come this way, Vitay."

He pushed the door wider and went in. Gina followed him. Kőnig tried to slip in with them, but the Director told him he wished to interview Vitay on his own, and, very politely, shut the door behind him.

Cast out

The moment she finished detailing her grievances Gina's anger began to melt away. She was left instead with a feeling of despair: what had happened in the last half hour had been the result of something utterly trivial – a simple, good-hearted bit of fun – and she had responded with blind anger. Poor Szabó, trapped in her fat, ungainly little body! How could she have had the heart to insult her? And those other poor girls! They had accepted her without question and invited her to share in the one thing that lightened their lives inside these oppressive walls – their games, their jokes, their harmless petty pranks. What stupid pride had made her say that she would never accept the aquarium and that she refused to take part? She made up her mind that as soon as her present difficulties were behind her she would stop being so proud, and would ask pardon of Szabó and the other girls in all sincerity.

The Director remained silent for a moment, then he informed her that her behaviour had been so utterly disgraceful she properly deserved to be expelled from the school, but instead she would be forbidden to set foot outside the premises for a fortnight. She would be allowed to go into the garden but not to visit the town. As for the fifth year, he had still to decide how to punish them. What he had just been told was so scandalous, so abominable, so outrageous, so base, so wicked, so unworthy – that a group of girls in an institution renowned for raising its girls in a true Christian manner . . . ! He might be forced to involve the entire teaching staff, and perhaps the school governors as well. But for the moment he would be sending Gina back to her class while he continued his investigations.

Kőnig was still hovering in the corridor, but the Director failed to notice him. Gina felt almost sick with remorse. If only she had not implicated the whole fifth year! If only she could have held her tongue! But it was too late now. As so often before, she had acted without thinking. When she and the Director re-entered the classroom she was met on all sides by a stony stare. Having so recently been sent out, she did not dare return to her seat but hovered near the door, like a bearer of bad news. Kalmár immediately stepped over to greet the Director, shook his hand and made a bow. He scarcely glanced at Gina. That really hurt.

"I hear that we are all about to be married," said the Director, "to various objects. Show me the class inventory, so that I can see who or what has had the good fortune to marry the pupils of year five."

The inventory was still on the desk where Szabó had left it. Kalmár picked it up, looking bewildered. When the Director repeated to him what Gina had said he lowered his eyes, as if reluctant to look at his charges. The man in black ran his eye down to the end of the page, and Gina discovered for herself what Torma had said it was like when he started to shout. He bawled out his rage and indignation in a voice that seemed barely human: pagan gods and pious bishops, long-dead German scholars and famous poets married off to girls whose education had been entrusted to his care! The fifth year kept their eyes fixed on the floor. Gina learned later that this was what you did when you were being reprimanded, to show your sense of guilt and remorse. Then one of the heads looked up, emerging as from the depths of a pool. It was the slim, intelligent face of Mari Kis. And Mari Kis did not just raise her head, she indicated that she wished to speak. This was an act of such daring that the Director stopped in mid-flight. Mari stood up and apologised on behalf of the class, to both the senior management and the form teacher, but what Georgina Vitay had told him was based on a complete misunderstanding. They had never had the slightest intention of playing such a game with the great men, or any of the objects, listed in the class inventory. It was just that Georgina Vitay was so homesick they had wanted to distract her with a bit of silly nonsense. The sole purpose was to amuse the poor heartbroken girl from Budapest and make her laugh. She was so very unhappy they wanted to make her laugh with a bit of silly nonsense, but she hoped in good taste. She now realised, of course, that how-ever well they might have meant it they should not have led her so astray, because what they did was an offence against the ethos of the school, and she humbly begged pardon of the Director and all the senior teachers, and of Georgina Vitay herself. She had meant no harm, and she regretted from the bottom of her heart the way it had turned out. She had let Murai and Anikó Szabó in on the joke and asked them to help, but the rest of the class had known nothing about it. It was nothing to do with a tradition, and how could it have been? Unfortunately Vitay had misunderstood this well-intentioned joke, and instead of being amused she had got very angry, and that was why she, Mari Kis, once again wished to apologise.

The face of the man in black seemed to soften. The idea of a childish prank was easier to accept than the story the new girl had told him – that such a godless custom had survived in his institution since the days of the First World War. He told Mari Kis that for her part in this tasteless jest – one that might have damaged the reputation of the school – she too would be gated for a fortnight, and since Murai and Szabó had been so eager to help her perpetrate this brainless scheme, perhaps they could show the same loyalty in sharing her punishment. Furthermore, it might be a good idea for Mari Kis to consider her general behaviour. There were plenty of candidates to take her free place. One more of these clever schemes and she could say goodbye to her bursary. The class watched in grim silence as his black shape disappeared through the door.

Kalmár gestured to Gina to return to her seat. Her heart was beating wildly as she took her place between Torma and Mari Kis. She wanted to say something to them immediately, but there was no chance. Kalmár had begun to hand out textbooks, exercise books and writing materials, and while they were being given them and were busy arranging them on the desks no talking was allowed. Her moment came only after the lesson, when they arrived back at the day room. First, she whispered to Mari Kis not to be angry with her. Mari replied that she wasn't angry, and said no more. She then asked Murai and Szabó to forgive her, and they too assured her that they bore her no grudge. She was filled with gratitude: what thoroughly decent girls these were!

It took her a while to work out what this "not bearing a grudge" really meant: "I don't know who you are. You are not one of us, you simply don't count. For us you no longer exist. You are nobody."

At home, she had been at the centre of her father's life, and to a certain extent of Auntie Mimó's; in her old class she had been, if not the very best student, highly praised and respected, someone who both counted and was liked. Now, in this squat ugly world of the fortress, she found herself alone. There was no-one now to put her right or come to her aid, and she belonged to no-one. From that point on the behaviour of the class towards her would have revealed nothing to an outsider. At lunch they would politely pass the salt or the basket of bread when they noticed her indicating by her glance that she wanted them, but the moment there was no-one else around it was as if a glass jar had been set down over her, one that seemed to cut her off even from the air. For a while she continued to make efforts in the hope that they might soften towards her; then she fell completely silent. She kept her nose in her books, telling herself that they would eventually come to see reason – the situation was so absurd it simply couldn't continue for very long; she had been in this position before, sometimes with more than one person; it went on for a bit, but it had never lasted. They would sulk for a while and do their best to avoid her, then there would be an explosion of laughter and all would be well again.

But as the hours dragged by she began to panic. This was

something she had not reckoned with: the terrifying self-discipline of the Matula. These girls were not like any other. They had been brought up in their own special world and trained to keep their silence. She remembered what Mari Kis had said: "The Matula is one of the best schools in the whole country," and the idea that she would have to live among these people, in such inconceivable isolation, brought tears of helpless despair to her eyes.

At five in the afternoon they lined up for the usual walk. Susanna now knew of the ban the four of them were under and stood shaking her head gravely throughout the long talk she had with Mari Kis. Mari listened with head bowed and trembling lips, but made no attempt to defend herself. Then the rest of the class set off, once again in their appalling hats and with the tulip-embroidered bags on their shoulders, like an elongated swarm of identical blue insects. Mari Kis, Szabó, Murai and Gina stayed behind, in the garden. The other three were chatting and laughing, and at first Gina traipsed along behind. Finally she tried to join them. They made no attempt to send her away: they simply ended their conversation, drew a circle on the wide path and began a game Gina did not know, though she picked it up quickly enough. They did not invite her to join in. She stood and watched for a while, but they remained completely absorbed in their game, and soon she wandered off on her own into the garden.

Apart from the sister on duty sitting by her window and casting an occasional supervisory glance in their direction, the fortress seemed almost unbelievably dead. Gina wandered about, pausing every now and then to touch a flower and trying to persuade herself that what was happening was not so very painful. Every so often she peered through one of the open windows on the ground floor corridor, which the day before (day? ten years? a hundred?) Torma had told her were always shut because behind them lay the section where the unmarried male teachers and the Director lived, unlike the female teachers, who lodged alongside the deaconesses next to the dormitories. She squeezed her head through the bars and peered around, but saw no-one. What might the teachers be doing at this time of day? Those who weren't on duty had obviously gone into town, where everything was: cinemas, theatres, people they knew. They were under no obligation to spend all their time in the fortress. As she turned away from the grille she found herself facing Abigail. Everything that welled up inside her at that moment predisposed her against the smiling statue. She could hardly bear the sight of the miracle-working maiden with the pitcher in her hands. The tradition of Mitsi Horn! Would that this Mitsi Horn had never existed!

She heard sounds of movement outside the school gate. Those lucky enough to go into town were obviously back, and she went to meet them. Mari Kis and Szabó had snubbed her, and so had Murai, but perhaps the others' anger might have run its course? Perhaps one of them would take pity on her, would see her standing there hoping to be spoken to at last and forgiven? But even Torma's glance passed over her. Susanna was the only one: she adjusted the bow at the end of Gina's plaits and asked her how she had spent the afternoon. "Very well," she replied, with bitterness surging through every drop of blood in her veins.

During supper she tried hard to follow the reading. It was written in old-fashioned language and concerned the spiritual growth of a noble-minded orphan who had lived in Geneva in 1827. But she found it impossible. Instead she gazed in silence at the faces of her classmates and reflected that if she had accepted the husband she had been offered she would at least have an aquarium to think about and would not now be feeling so unimaginably alone.

After they had gone to bed Gina listened carefully to try and hear what the others were whispering in the darkness. They were talking about the Director, and Kalmár – whether he would be getting married soon – and how they had discovered some new information about the Prefect: Susanna looked so very young on the outside, but she was already over thirty. There was talk of the new textbooks, and of an outing that had been held every autumn to date but might not happen this year. While they were walking back Susanna had rather surprisingly said that they shouldn't hope too much because, with the war going on and all the bombing, the Bishop hadn't yet decided to approve it; but how wonderful it would be if they did manage to visit the vineyard, because things were so much more relaxed there. They chatted about everything except the class inventory and of course Gina. Gina had never lived. She did not exist. They had never set eyes on such a person. It proved a difficult night. It weighed on her as heavily as the punishment itself.

The next morning was no easier. The first lesson was taken by the class tutor, and officially a history lesson, but several other matters arose. Mari Kis asked if she could sit nearer the front:

she thought her eyesight must be deteriorating; then Torma stood up and asked if she too could move – she seemed to have developed long-sightedness over the holidays and she thought she would be able to see the blackboard better from the back. Kalmár made an entry for Susanna in the day's notes suggesting that the two girls be sent for an eye test, and sat them for the time being in new places, one nearer the front and one further back. He doesn't seem to realise, thought Gina, red-faced with humiliation, that they just don't want to sit next to me. Why can't he see that?

The second period, with Miss Gigus, was less eventful. It passed more easily for Gina because the teacher spent most of the time talking to her, trying to establish how well she knew German. That presented no problem: Marcelle was from Alsace and spoke German as fluently as she did French. The rest of the class turned a deaf ear to their conversation, but Gina made a special effort to speak not just accurately but choosing her words with great care. She impressed no-one: her classmates stared at the blackboard without interest. Miss Gigus congratulated Gina and called on Szabó to follow. Gina quickly saw that she was making a real mess of it, pronouncing words with a thick Hungarian accent and constantly placing the wrong inflection on her nouns. At the Sokoray Atala Gina had always been happy to help the weaker girls practise their languages, and she wondered if she should offer to do the same for Szabó. But she dared not suggest it: she had had all the rebuffs she could cope with. She would raise the subject later, when the others had cooled down.

Of that happening there was no sign at present. The fifth

year, she suddenly realised, were now playing a game that did not originate with Mitsi Horn. They were amusing themselves by seeing how long they could carry on treating one of their number as an outcast without anyone noticing. This was hardest to keep up during gymnastics, when some of the exercises had to be done in pairs. Gina's partner Bánki started to limp, pretending to the gymnastics teacher that she had hurt her foot, to avoid having to work with her; and when that excuse no longer worked, she simply let go of Gina's hand and allowed her to fall off her back. Had Gina not been so agile she might have been seriously hurt, so severe would the impact have been when she landed.

The days passed, and her efforts were getting nowhere. By now she had got to know all her teachers, and, contrary to expectation, she found she liked them all: all, that is, apart from Kőnig. She was working very hard, harder than she ever had before, hoping to hear some kind words, if only from the staff. She had never in her life enjoyed a teacher's praise as much as she did that term. Quite why she had taken against Kőnig she could no longer say: she must have been influenced by having heard, and by continuing to hear, what Torma and Mari Kis said about him. The Matula was used to the iron fist, but Kőnig was gentle. He marked generously. If someone burst into tears during the lesson after giving a poor answer he would always be happy to postpone the questioning until the following day. The girls were forever complaining about being kept on a tight leash, but as soon as someone applied a lighter touch and allowed them a looser rein they showed how deeply the system was ingrained in them by despising his kindness as weakness. They even played practical jokes on him. One day they hid his glasses and then pretended to be searching frantically for them. While he stood at the desk complimenting them on how kind and attentive and considerate they were, they were passing the huge spectacles from one to another beneath the benches and almost exploding with mirth. But the glasses never reached Gina. They're afraid I'd give them back to him, she thought bitterly.

The school year had begun on a Monday and nothing had changed for her by the Saturday, when the post was given out. The days leading up to it had passed a little more easily, because she knew that on that afternoon she would hear her father's voice: as soon as Budapest made contact she would have a chance to pour out her grievances. Her father would then give her some wise counsel and tell her what to do to put things right with the class: he always managed to find a solution – it was inconceivable that he would not be able to do so now. He would obviously be deeply upset when he learned that she felt so very alone in the school, but she could hardly conceal the fact from him because who knew how long it might go on for? And that would be something she simply could not bear.

On the Saturday, when the others were back from their afternoon walk, they all gathered in the day room. Susanna handed out sheets of writing paper to everyone except Gina. She was sent to the music room to learn the psalms, so that she need not be idle while she waited for her father to telephone.

When, as an adult, she thought back to the hymns and psalms of her youth, she never remembered them in isolation; particular sounds and scents drifted around them, and with them too the smell of the home-made soap that filled the corridors of the Matula, the soundless opening and closing of doors, the timid, hesitant movement of her fingers on the piano keyboard, and even her face as it had looked at the time. But just then she was busy pretending to study the texts she had been set to memorise. Her mind was elsewhere; it was as if her body and her whole being had been reduced to an ear listening out for the stabbing ring of the inter-city telephone. She had to wait a long time. The bell had already begun to summon the staff to lay the tables for supper by the time Susanna came in and told her to be quick because her father was on the line. She banged down the keyboard cover and ran. Her heart leaped when she realised that the Deaconess was taking her towards the teaching rooms and the school office. Her father had obviously rung the Director's number, so the conversation would at least take place away from the other girls. As they reached the door to the office the Prefect called her back. She stopped, barely able to conceal her reluctance to obey. Could they not leave her in peace even at a moment like that? After a full week in this appalling Matula, a week in which she had spoken to no-one in a normal way, she had to be given a lecture while her father waited at the other end of the line.

"Georgina," said the Deaconess, "your fellow pupils must have told you that we do not forward letters that mention complaints."

Gina stared at her dumbly, not grasping what she was getting at. She had spoken so little to Mari Kis and Torma that she had been told nothing about this.

"Our parents are far away, and they have quite enough problems of their own. If we trouble them with our day-to-day disappointments we shall only make them worried and anxious. Things always happen in a school that might upset a pupil for an hour or two, but experience shows that by the time the letter reaches home the particular difficulty has usually passed and the family have been needlessly upset. Do you understand what I am saying?"

No, no, no!

"You are allowed to discuss only positive things," the Prefect continued. "Only things that will reassure them. Anything bad, anything seriously bad, we will tell them about ourselves, officially, once a term. There are always difficulties at the start of the year in a new school, but apart from those you clearly have no cause for complaint. And even if you did have, you are not allowed to mention it on the telephone, just as the others in your class may not mention them in their letters. Your father the General is battling with the problems of the whole country and he should hear only cheerful, positive things from you."

Gina felt that what was happening to her was beyond anything she could have imagined, beyond anything that she could possibly bear. Sometimes a nightmare can be so cruel, so murderous, so horrifying and hope-destroying that it leaves you whimpering and moaning for someone to come and wake you. Susanna pushed the door open and Gina followed her in helplessly. She was not surprised to find that the room was not empty. There next to the telephone hovered the black presence of Gideon Torma. The moment he saw her he said into the receiver: "I'm passing her on to you now."

To take the telephone she had had to go right up to him, and there she stood, between the Director and Susanna, both of them watching the expression on her face. Her fingers felt so cold she could barely hold the instrument. Her father's voice came to her from across a vast distance, as if it were addressing her from the end of the world.

"Hello," it said. "How are you, my darling?"

"Very well," she replied.

"So it's not so terrible then?"

"No."

"What are the other girls like? Have you made any friends yet?"

She stood staring into the telephone, without answering.

"Hello," said the faraway voice. "Are you there? I can scarcely hear you. I asked you what the other girls are like."

"Very nice," she replied. She was almost choking.

"Mr Torma tells me you are in good health, and that they are very pleased with your work. He read out your marks to me, and they were all outstanding."

"I'm working very hard," she replied.

"Hello, Szeged," a woman's voice butted in. "Are you still on the line?"

"One more minute," the General said. "Look after yourself, my little one. I have asked Auntie Róza to bake you some pastries. You'll get them next week. Won't that be nice?"

"Father!" She was now shouting. At the sound the Director's head went up, as if she had banged a fist on the table. "Father, I beg you, please come and see me! Come!"

"As soon as I can," she heard the faraway voice say. "At the moment it's impossible. But I shall ring you every week. Good-bye, my little one."

The line buzzed loudly, then subsided into a steady crackle. A voice asked, "Have you finished?" and the connection was cut off. Finished indeed, thought Gina, and she stared dumbly at the receiver, as if it were something she had never seen in her life before. She doesn't know just how much is finished. Now they've taken even this away from me. They haven't given me any writing paper, and even if they had I wouldn't be allowed to tell the truth, and there's no point in telephoning because I'm like a prisoner standing between two guards. My classmates have rejected me. I'm not allowed to complain. What will become of me now?

She flinched: someone seemed to have said something. How long had the Director been speaking to her?

". . . so once again we have the extraordinary situation in which it fails to occur to a girl to thank the Director and the Prefect for sparing her anxious father any further worry by not mentioning that she has already had to be punished for highly inappropriate behaviour, and yet . . ."

"Thank you," Gina whispered. "Thank you very much."

"Georgina Vitay may leave the room," the Director said.

Gina took her leave and followed Susanna into the corridor. When they reached the pupils' quarters the Prefect stopped her outside the day room. She could hear music coming from inside, Mozart's "Eine Kleine Nachtmuzik" – the first secular music she had heard since she had been locked up in the fortress. Apparently once the letter-writing session was over a concert was held in the sitting room. The Prefect peered inside to make sure that everything was in order. The fifth year were sitting around the gramophone and Salm was choosing the records. Seeing the new arrivals, they all stood up. Susanna nodded for them to carry on and closed the door again. Her grave, intelligent face looked into Gina's for what seemed ages, then she asked: "Is something the matter, Georgina?"

She shook her head. Nothing.

"You don't seem very happy. Has someone upset you?"

"No."

"Can I do anything to help?"

No, *she* couldn't help her. There was one thing that would have helped – to leave her alone with the telephone. But she hadn't done it.

"I realise," Susanna went on, "that your mood has been influenced by this unhappy start to the year, when you had to be punished so very early on and barred from going into town. But you can learn from Mari Kis, and Szabó and Murai. They have submitted to their punishment with fortitude. They don't walk around with long faces. This will all be over soon enough, and the shame of not being allowed out will become easier to bear."

She doesn't imagine, she cannot possibly imagine, thought Gina, that that is the reason why I am so unhappy! Here now was her chance to take revenge on them all – all those who had been looking straight through her for a week: surely not even Susanna could be capable of pardoning these good Christians for their implacable refusal to forgive her?

But then again, here was a tiny ray of hope, one that helped her breathe more easily. This time she would not stubbornly persist in her anger as she had before. This time she would be no traitor. She knew that if she told Susanna the truth she would certainly believe her, and she would see to it that justice was done. Once she knew that Mari Kis had lied about the Mitsi Horn tradition and that the class really had been married to the likes of the Founder-Bishop and the graduation song, she would probably inflict a punishment on them as hard as Gina herself had suffered. But if Gina said nothing, would the others appreciate that when she told them?

"May the Lord be with you," Susanna said in parting. Gina went into the day room. The music had come to a stop and Salm was searching for the next record. She sat down beside Cziller, who immediately stood up and moved her chair away. The sense of injustice that rose up in her forced her to break her silence.

"You can stay where you are!" she said. "This time I am not guilty. They asked me what was wrong, but I didn't tell them. I didn't tell them about the way you are behaving towards me, even though both my father and Susanna tried to make me."

Once again silence – that terrible silence that the fifth year knew how to produce when they wanted. She thought they were not going to reply. Then Mari Kis spoke up.

"You couldn't have told your father because a Matula pupil is never allowed to complain – as they must have told you. Even the first years know that. As for Susanna, you might think it a great thing to have said nothing, but we don't. You're just weak, Vitay. You said nothing because you knew that if you betrayed us a second time we'd make it so hard for you you'd end up running away."

Salm put some Beethoven on, the Fifth Symphony. Mari Kis placed her elbows on the table, her plaits fell forward and she gave herself up to the music: it was as if she had immersed herself in an infinite river of serenity. She did not look at Gina again. No-one did. Gina remained where she was, her heart beating wildly. Mari Kis, my bitterest enemy, you may not have meant to, but you have given me just what I need. You have shown me the answer I couldn't find myself. If I can't ask my father for help, and you are going to reject me forever, then I can't stay here. At home I could explain everything. My father would understand and forgive me. And if I can't stay with him, he'll find me another school for clever children. Thank you for showing me what I must do. I shall run away.

Gina prepares to escape

So she was going to run away: but how?

Only the intention was clear. She had never been allowed out of the fortress on her own, and now not even as part of a group. She did not know the city, having moved there only recently, and she was banned from even setting foot outside the gate. As soon as she got up the next morning she raced through her chores to allow herself more free time. She walked round the courtyard examining the gates, the perimeter wall and the windows, looking for a way out. As soon as she was in the street she would ask the first person she met to tell her the way to the station.

She would also have to get her own clothes back. In those happy days when the others were still talking to her she had realised what a significant presence the Matula was in the city, and she knew that any adult seeing her wandering about unaccompanied in her school uniform would know that the girls were not allowed out on their own: anyone might accost her and take her back. The housekeeper would never voluntarily hand over any of her belongings – she could be very sure of that; she would have to make the attempt dressed as she was. She would leave the hat behind, and take off her school stockings – those ugly black ribbed stockings that stood for everything Matula –

and the uniform. That would leave the shapeless everyday school smock, but perhaps no-one would notice it.

So far she had seen the road only as far as the white church. The main thing was to find a way out. Over the wall would be impossible. She was now familiar with the extent and layout of the main building and knew that there was a gate cut into the perimeter nearby, but it was made of cast iron. Naturally, it was locked, and apparently it had no key. Every window opening onto the street was barred. The only way to get out would be if some-one, perhaps the porter, opened the main gate for her.

But of course, the porter!

She remembered the surly, thick-set man who had met them on their arrival. She ran across the garden, between the two wings of the U-shaped building, to the vaulted portal where his office was. If she could strike up a friendship with this man and get him so used to seeing her about that he no longer thought any-thing of it, she might be able to steal the key and nip out through the gate. Never mind if it was raining or whatever else the weather might be doing: coat or no coat, she absolutely had to escape.

She stood at the door of the lodge and peered in through the glass. The man had his back to her and was reading a newspaper. On the wall facing him was a board hung with keys, and halfway down there was a large, old-fashioned one, clearly the one for the main gate. In her old school she had been on very good terms with the porter. From his office he sold all sorts of goods – sweets, pretzels, exercise books and pencils. Why not try to make friends with this one? She might just manage it. Well, she would do her best.

The porter put down his paper, as if he sensed that he was being watched. He turned round, spotted her immediately, and came out of the office to ask what she wanted. She had no idea what to reply. She simply smiled at him, unable to think of a sensible answer. She could hardly come straight out with the announcement that she found the dear old boy so very congenial she would like to have a chat with him. It was a bit too soon for that! In fact, impossible.

"You must go back to the school," he told her, not angrily or sternly, but in a matter-of-fact tone that invited no contradiction. "You are not allowed near the office. Haven't you read the house rules?"

She hadn't read them, though there were copies posted up everywhere, in the corridors as well as the dormitories. The sight of their contents, the long lists of what was allowed and what was not, filled her with such repugnance that she had always just glanced at them and turned her head away. She went back to the main building and began to read the framed typescript.

Rising: weekdays, Sundays and public holidays, 6.30 a.m. Breakfast: 7.30 a.m. It was the daily timetable, which she already knew. *Boarders are not allowed to borrow money from one another. Money must not be carried on one's person.* That wasn't what the old chap had been referring to. *It is forbidden to fraternise with the auxiliary staff . . .*

So that was it. The reason was pretty obvious. If you hung around with the non-teaching staff you might make friends with one of the cleaners, or the porter, or the gardener, who might then offer to smuggle letters in and out for you, or turn a blind eye when you slipped out through the gate. It was no good: if she couldn't rely on the porter she would have to think of something else. And she would have to bide her time. From now on she would be so conscientious, so hard-working, so meek and mild, so cheerful even, that people would think she had come to terms with the place, perhaps even come to like it. And as soon as a chance came up, on one of the outings, she would disappear.

For that to happen, she would first have to familiarise herself with the list of excursions. She would also need to know which routes led out of town, and what shops and public buildings there were for her to hide in before her final escape. All this would take patience.

At their next meeting in the staff common room the class teachers agreed that all was going well in the fifth year. The new girl from Budapest was exceptionally hard-working and the others seemed to be doing their best to keep up with her: no doubt they wanted to show her that no newcomer was going to outshine anyone who had been at the school from the start, and they were certainly matching her diligence. Miss Gigus, who had also taught this group the year before, both German and French, praised Kalmár for the way he was guiding them through the difficult stage of puberty. Last year it had been hard work keeping them in check; this term they were behaving well, and were most conscientious. The Vitay girl spoke French and German as if they were her mother tongue, and, as Sister Susanna would testify, the others spent every afternoon coaching one another so that they could keep up with her, and they were all making remarkable progress. Kalmár met this with a modest smile. He had no doubt that the change was entirely due to the fact that he was the form tutor. They were simply trying to please him, to impress him with their impeccable behaviour, and of course Vitay herself would want him to forget the painful circumstances of their first meeting. He would never be able to imagine that there was a covert war going on against the girl. They were all so much in love with him they just didn't have the time for one.

For the four girls who had been gated, the second week of their exclusion from outings was coming to an end. The practice was that after the last lesson on a Saturday the subject teachers and prefects would attend a brief meeting presided over by the Director to share their experiences of the class. On this second occasion everyone spoke so highly of them that, after a short pause, the Director announced that, if the standard of work continued at the present level, then they might perhaps be put forward for the annual invitation to a certain event in October. The teachers exchanged smiles, Kalmár gazed round complacently, Miss Gigus expressed her strong approval, the Chaplain said he could see nothing against it, and even Gertrúd Truth, the physical education teacher for whom nothing was ever good enough and who always demanded more than was humanly reasonable, nodded and made no objection. "They must not be told beforehand," the Director concluded. Everyone agreed. It had happened more than once that the implied compliment had gone to the girls' heads.

It was Kőnig who had argued most strongly that the decision should be kept a secret. But the moment the meeting was over he raced over to the refectory, where the pupils were sitting waiting for the teachers to arrive so that they could start eating. Only the deaconesses ate with them. The teachers' table stood on a raised platform, which greatly annoyed the girls. It meant that it would be noticed from above if anyone had spilled her soup on her napkin, or let a morsel slip from her spoon, which did nothing for the appetite. He went straight to the fifth year and told them what had been decided. Their faces lit up. Gina did not know what the invitation involved, and it would have been pointless asking the others – she would just have to wait and see what would happen. Someone sitting near her mentioned Mitsi Horn, and that only increased her bitterness. She had never met this person, but she loathed the very sound of her name.

She also had her opinion of Kőnig. He had begun his little speech by saying that really he should not be telling them what he was about to: he just wanted to put them on their guard and warn them against denying themselves the anticipated pleasure by some stupid prank. To think that a grown-up should be so incapable of managing his tongue! Especially when what he was saying was in their interest rather than his own!

It was a grey, joyless Saturday. Her father telephoned again in the afternoon, this time not from Budapest but from Sümeg. The conversation went exactly as it had the week before, but this time both Susanna and the Director thought that she had been much more natural and less depressed.

The next morning at breakfast the Prefect seemed unusually preoccupied. Since it was a Saturday the meal was at eight. She had a prolonged conversation with Sister Erzsébet and then disappeared. She returned with a radiant face and went straight to

Gina. It was now clear where she had gone, and for what purpose. She had been to see the Director.

The two-week gating was due to end on Monday evening, but it would mean that the offenders would miss a second church service. Since its purpose was obviously to fortify their minds and souls, she had asked if she could take them to it, and the Director had decided that yes, considering their exemplary behaviour over the last fortnight, they could go, and they could also join the afternoon walk into town.

The four girls were delighted, but none of them as much as Susanna. They donned their going-out uniform and set off. Once again Gina found herself walking between Mari Kis and Torma. They pointedly whispered to each other over her head, but it no longer upset or even interested her. She was studying the road to the church with fresh eyes, looking out for any possibilities it might offer for escape, and this continued once they were inside the building itself. But she quickly realised it was probably the least suitable place of all. Every class was assigned to its own pew, and members of the clergy stood at all the exits. If she feigned illness it would achieve nothing. Susanna would simply leave the church and take her back to the school.

When the service was over they had some free time. After lunch came the handing-out of the post. The parcel that her father had promised the previous Saturday had also arrived. Going up to receive the large cardboard box Gina could almost see Auntie Róza carefully placing the delicacies in rows, her hands caked with icing sugar, flour and jam. Her father must have had more time than usual to spare, because he had written:

For my daughter Gina, in the care of Sister Susanna. And perhaps he also thought it unsoldierly to use his rank when naming the source: she read *Sender: János Tóth* (the name of his batman). *Place of sending: Monor.* He certainly seemed to be doing a lot of travelling.

It was now time for her to hand them around, though you were not required to share anything sent from home. She began by offering the pastries to Susanna; she took a small sugar-coated star and placed it beside her place setting, but did not eat it.

"Bring some side plates," she instructed the girl on duty. "You are all allowed to have some of Georgina's pastries."

The girl on duty was Bánki. She fetched a large round platter and twenty side plates from the kitchen. Susanna went over to the window and stood looking out into the garden, where Miss Gigus was walking arm in arm with Eszter Sáfár, the Head of the Lower School. Instead of her black gown Miss Gigus was wearing a brightly coloured dress and blue shoes with enormously high heels, and Susanna was completely unaware of what was happening behind her back. Though she knew exactly what would happen, Gina started to offer the platter round, beginning with Ari, who was sitting across the table from her. Without even a "thank you", Ari turned her head away. Salm, sitting beside her, hissed: "Don't waste your time, there's no point. You can stuff the whole lot yourself."

She stood with the plate in her hand, helpless and mortified. If Susanna discovered that the offerings had been refused it would be seen as another betrayal. But the Prefect was still staring out into the garden, at the extraordinary dress, and had noticed nothing.

Eventually she came back. She looked at the untouched platter in surprise.

"Did you not offer them to the others?" she asked.

"She did," the fifth year replied with one voice.

"Has everyone had some?"

"Everyone," she was assured.

"And there's all this left? You have been very restrained. I shall hand the rest out myself." She took the dish, counted out the pastries and put two on every plate. Gina was given three. The dish was now empty.

"Now say 'thank you'," Susanna said.

"Thank you, Vitay," the class chorused.

"May it do you good," Gina muttered.

Susanna went back to the window. Mari Kis slipped her two pastries into her pocket, and the others all did the same. The honey cake that Gina had put into her mouth from a sense of duty turned bitter and she struggled to swallow it. When the time came to leave the refectory she concealed the other two in the palm of her hand, then threw them down the toilet.

The funeral for the remainder of the General's offering took place the next day, in the garden. With much digging and raking, the class prepared a space in the vegetable patch. Szabó built a low mound of dry leaves and twigs; Mari Kis gathered a second pile from around the plot, took them to Szabó, and dropped the two pastries from her pocket on the pyre. "Are you ready?" Szabó asked triumphantly. "Ready," replied Mari Kis. Gina watched as each girl in the class came up one by one and added her own, every single one of the pastries that they dreamed of and longed for. There were so many that Szabó had to build another mound. More twigs were raked up, and more dried leaves. Bánki lit the pyre, and Szabó, like a tubby little priestess conducting some ancient rite, kept the flame going by prodding it with a stick. They all knew that Gina was watching, and they kept glancing to see the expression on her face. But she stood where she was at the other end of the garden and did not so much as tremble.

Only when the lights were out did she give way to tears – tears for the cremated pastries, the poor innocent pastries. She wept and wept, all the while hating herself for not being stronger and for not having removed herself sooner from that hateful scene. But she was unable to stop either the sobbing or the desperate, choking flood of tears, or wondering as she wept what sort of girls these could possibly be that not one of them came over to speak to her.

She came to with a start. The light had gone on and someone was leaning over her. Through eyes strained with weeping she beheld Susanna, a Susanna without her bonnet and with her shock of blonde hair, which seemed to have been hastily brushed, coiling down to her shoulders. She was wearing a dressing gown, a rather comely grey. She looked so beautiful, and her appearance was so unexpected, that Gina stopped crying.

"Is it you crying?" Susanna asked, and sat down on the side of the bed. "You were sobbing so loud it could be heard in the corridor: everything is so quiet out there. It's very late, past midnight. What has happened, Georgina?"

She could not, did not want to, reply. She simply opened her hand and took Susanna's arm. It was against the rules to touch a member of staff, she now remembered. She was aware that the Deaconess had flinched, and realised that she too was thinking of it, but the hand stayed where it was, and Susanna remained at her side.

"Don't cry," said the Prefect. "You mustn't cry: you have no reason to. Everything is going nicely for you here, your father rang on Saturday and all is well at home. I know this is about the parcel. It brought back memories of your family and made you homesick. It's why I don't like people sending these parcels from home. So you really mustn't cry."

She spoke very softly, almost inaudibly. Gina held her arm even more tightly and this time Susanna felt obliged to withdraw it.

"Shush, Georgina. You'll wake the others."

She stood up and looked around. The fifth year appeared to be fast asleep in their beds, but the Prefect's long experience allowed her to read those blank faces as clearly as if their open eyes had declared: "We know she's been crying, and we don't give a damn."

"A member of the fifth year in so much distress and no-one takes the blindest bit of notice? That doesn't show much generosity of soul." Her gentle tones took on the hardness of steel blades clashing in an icy wind. "Such a cold-hearted class hardly deserves to take part in the invitation from Mitsi Horn. I know that you know what I am referring to. Mr Kőnig has told us that he spoke to you about it."

For a while no-one stirred, and the pretence continued. Then one by one they began to yawn and rub their eyes. Eventually Bánki said: "No, really? If I had known poor Vitay couldn't sleep and was feeling sad . . ." and they all gathered round her bed, as many as could fit themselves into the space, and Gina burst into tears again, all the more grievously because Susanna could not see that their concern was only a game, an act they were putting on.

"You must show her some sympathy," said Susanna. "If I find her still crying after half an hour I shall hold you all responsible. Everything here is new to her. She isn't used to this kind of life. Her father is a long way away, and the parcel made her homesick. Tell her about our dear Mitsi Horn's invitation."

And she left. The girls nearest to her, Mari Kis, Torma and Murai, Szabó and Bánki, went and sat on Torma's bed and looked at her.

"Go away," Gina said. "I don't need anyone, least of all the likes of you."

"Are you sure you don't need us?" asked Mari Kis. "But we're supposed to be entertaining you, so that you won't feel sad in the night. Like a king with insomnia."

"And we have to tell you all about the wonders of Mitsi Horn's invitation," Szabó added angrily. "Well, you can find out for yourself."

"We have to tell her," said Torma, nodding her head. "Susanna will be asking about that when she checks up on us."

"That's true," said Mari Kis. "So listen to this, you pathetic weakling. Every month Mitsi Horn invites girls to afternoon tea at her house, a whole class at a time. It's incredible what she serves up. What you get to eat is unbelievable. It's a real banquet, with games and sometimes even dancing, and it's all so wonderful you want to faint. She has this amazing house near the station and the front door key is just as fantastic: there's a laughing man's head on the end of it. She gives a tea party every fourth week from October onwards, and the best class is always invited. We've never been there. This will be the first time in our lives. So you'd better make sure that we don't miss out because of you, or you'll see what we do to you."

Gina stared at them for a moment, then abruptly turned away and buried her head under the quilt. Her heart was beating so hard she thought it must be making the bedcover shake. When Susanna looked in again the whole class was still up and whispering to her, expressing concern and chatting, while Gina slept like a newborn baby. Her cheeks were dry and her face fresh. She's calmed down, thought Susanna, and nodded. Then she did something she never would by day: she gently stroked the girl's brow. She could not know that behind that forehead lay the liberating, sleep-inducing, all-comforting idea of using Mitsi Horn's tea party in the last week of October to make her escape. If an entire class were being entertained in the house, and the house were right beside the railway station, you could nip out the way you went in; or if not there, then through a ground-floor window, or one in the cellar. In a private house probably neither would be covered with iron bars.

At Mitsi Horn's; the escape

Now that she finally had a plan, a real prospect of escaping, the behaviour of the other girls bothered her less and less. As for the teachers, she came to see that there were some she would be sorry to leave behind. Kalmár, for one: he taught history in a way that made the eyes of his students light up with excitement. Whenever he spoke of the love of one's country Gina felt more than ready to take up arms herself and, mere slip of a girl as she was, rush off to join the soldiers at the front. Kalmár had become a significant person in her life, and if the figure of Feri still shone in her recollections of the happier world she had lost, he was far away. Kalmár was there to hand, right before her eyes.

Kőnig's lessons she detested, yet he was a wonderful teacher, not just highly cultured but also very well-spoken. She was sometimes astonished by how very fine, and how lucid, his explanations were, but her conscience would not allow her to acknowledge what she was hearing. And if she could not approve of Kőnig, she could hardly approve of some of his material. The classical virtues he described in his Latin lessons, so admirable and convincing when Kalmár talked about them, seemed in his mouth dull and boring. Kalmár's character was the one she associated with the Roman virtues of manly fortitude, and equally with the

111

love poetry of Catullus, while Kőnig was everything that a virile Roman was not, and as for love, he would certainly not still have been a bachelor at fifty-two if he had what it took to stir a woman's passion. He invariably responded to the literature with a far deeper sensibility than his pupils did, and that too seemed to her unmanly, as did his feeling for poetry and his ravings about "ideal beauty". What irritated her most was that things happened in his lessons that never did with the other teachers. Kalmár had no qualms about sending a fifth-year girl to stand in the corner, but when Kőnig tried to do the same it always descended into farce: the offenders would smirk and pull faces or take a book and read it when his back was turned, and after a while Kőnig would start to show signs of embarrassment, of worrying that he might have been too strict. He would then announce that the punishment was now sufficient, and effectively apologise to the girl concerned.

Gertrúd Truth she did like, but the woman was such a tartar in the gym that Gina sometimes feared the rope-climbing sessions would strip the skin off her hands, and if a girl said she was feeling giddy during an exercise she was simply ignored. Gina also liked Kerekes, though his maths lessons could be terrifying. He had a habit of suddenly asking you about something from last year's work, or even from the year before, and always when you least expected it, so you had to visit the lower form's day rooms to ask the Prefect there how to calculate percentages or compound interest, or whatever it was you had forgotten. If you didn't get it right, Kerekes would blow his top. Éles, the science teacher, was like his name, sharp or caustic. But Gina liked him too. His white coat made her think of her family doctor, and the smell of acid chemicals that pervaded his lessons, indeed his whole universe, brought back the fierce perfumes worn by Auntie Mimó. She also enjoyed the practical tasks they undertook under his supervision, looking after the frequently restocked terrarium that stood beside the huge fish tank, both of which he had entrusted to her care, or picking fruit and doing other little jobs in the garden. She was less fond of Hajdú, the music teacher, though she still preferred him to Kőnig. He was moody, he could be woundingly sarcastic, and he really seemed to think that his was the most important subject in the whole world. She often had her work cut out to keep up with the giddy pace he set, and it was becoming more and more clear to her that in Budapest it was not only the religious songs and chants she had not been taught as well as the Matula girls had: her knowledge of Kodály and Bartók also fell short. They not only knew the former's songs by heart, they had also been put through a thoroughgoing history of music, including church music, and had no difficulty recognising the extracts Hajdú played for them on the huge school gramophone. What saved Gina was that, although she had still not yet learned a large number of the psalms, she was fairly well up on the classical side, thanks to the many concerts she had been to with Auntie Mimó and Marcelle.

She used Miss Gigus' lessons as a time to relax after the exertions of the morning. She no longer needed to learn new grammar or vocabulary, and her written tasks and translations were dashed off within minutes. Susanna had asked her to help the weaker ones in the day room. She had of course agreed, in the certain knowledge that no-one would ask her, and none of them did. When they were given one of the harder exercises they simply surrounded themselves with a wall of textbooks, exercise books and dictionaries, and did the best they could. On one occasion the Director called in to observe the class during one of Kőnig's lessons. Gina failed to answer one of his questions, so he turned to Torma, who was so intimidated by the piercing black gaze of her uncle that she instantly forgot the most elementary rules of grammar, whereupon he made a personal entry in the day's notes that she had been "slacking". The moment he left Kőnig asked her the very same questions. This time she returned perfect answers, and Kőnig went straight to the Director's comment and added: "Much improved now. Excellent." Torma should have shown her appreciation of what he had done but instead she turned to look at Gina. Gina, to her own surprise, had been nodding her approval as, his face beaming with pleasure, Kőnig made the redeeming entry. Now she simply felt ashamed. Any of the others could also have noticed that she shared their view of the teacher's behaviour, and at that particular moment she did not wish to seem to be making common cause with them.

In the interests of the Mitsi Horn invitation they were making a show of being very concerned about her. The moment Susanna appeared, or a teacher came in during one of the two breaks, one of them would go up to Gina and anxiously enquire if she was taking proper care of herself: would she like something to read, or did she need any help? In the day room or the refectory, when they were given permission to talk quietly among themselves, the two girls sitting nearest to her, Mari Kis and Torma, would put on a smile and whisper the list of Latin prepositions that take the accusative case. From a distance it gave the impression that they were genuinely talking to her. At first Gina would smile back, though it felt as if her muscles were being stretched from ear to ear, and she quickly tired of it. But Mitsi Horn's party was drawing closer by the day, and she thought she could bear anything until then.

As he had promised, the General called her every week, and they exchanged the usual banalities permitted under the watchful eyes of her teachers. Gina would be told that everyone at home was well, including Auntie Mimó and her friends. She did not repeat her desperate plea for a visit, but she did wonder that her father, who knew her so very well, should be so unable to sense that she was in difficulties from the way she limited her conversation to strictly impersonal things and expressed herself in a manner so very different from the one she had used in Budapest. It was hardly the way a normal girl might speak of her life at boarding school. To her relief, no more parcels arrived. One ritual burning of the pastries had been quite enough.

Mitsi Horn's tea party was designated for the last Sunday in October. At the end of lessons on the Saturday the entire school assembled in the Hall of Honour and the Director read out the aggregated marks of each form for the month: the results for the fifths were the best they had been since the start of the school year, and for that reason he felt able to overlook the regrettable failure of self-discipline they had shown on the first day back. As a reward for their proper remorse, for their exemplary behaviour and their unstinting work, they would be allowed to take part in the tea party that an esteemed former pupil held every year from October to June for the best-performing class of the month. Departure was at 3.30 p.m., return at 7.20 p.m., and they would be accompanied by the class prefect and form tutor.

That Saturday in October was almost as bright as a summer's day, with the autumn flowers in the garden in their full splendour. As soon as lunch was over the girls set about their preparation work for the following Monday. Gina took great care over hers, and even memorised the Latin, though she knew there was now little point. She was about halfway through when she was called to the telephone. This time the conversation was much shorter than before. Her father clearly had nothing of special interest to report, and she mouthed only the platitudes approved by her guards. Besides, by the afternoon of the day after next she would be back home.

When she was ready she went down to the garden to say a proper goodbye. Susanna was nowhere to be seen, and there was no sign of anyone moving behind the iron grille of the teacher's wing: it was a free afternoon for everyone, a sacrosanct and blessed time. She went over to the statue, sat down on a bench in front of it and looked around the garden. There was a book in her lap, but she made no attempt to read it. It was there only in case a teacher spotted her, decided she must be lonely and sent her to join the rest of the class. The book was Daudet's *La Petite Chose*, in the original language. She knew it almost by heart. If anyone questioned her about it she would have been able to respond in fluent French. She was looking out over the top of the page when she heard footsteps on the gravel behind her. She turned her head to see who it was and found Aradi, a girl in the eighth year, the tall head girl who had carried the banner in the procession. She was walking very slowly, and her face showed grief and despair.

Gina moved over to make space for her, relieved to know that even an eighth year such as she could have problems. Aradi had always spoken to her whenever they met, so there was no fear of being subjected to a list of prepositions. Thanks to their Matula command of silence the fifths had managed to keep their secret intact: all knowledge of the traitor's punishment had been kept from the other classes to stop one of them blurting out Gina's story to a teacher.

Aradi sat down beside her, rather reluctantly, and returned her greeting; then, to her surprise, she asked Gina to run back to the eighth-year day room to see if the rest of her class had finished their homework. It was so obviously a pretext to get rid of her that Gina was troubled. Perhaps the older girl had caught wind of the fact that she had been ostracised and no-one was talking to her? She stood up, feeling rather offended, but then the urgency of Aradi's request made her think that something else might be going on. She dashed off as requested, then stopped behind a large stone urn, which hid her completely. It was most unlikely that even a senior girl could have an assignation in this place, so what else might be her secret?

When she saw the slip of card Aradi pulled from her pocket, Gina underwent a sudden loss of the respect due to the head girl and standard bearer. Had she no proper sense of shame? She had actually come to petition Abigail about some nonsense or other! Preferring not to witness the actual moment when the note went into the pitcher, Gina carried on to the day room to look for the eighth year, who, as Aradi knew full well, had of course long finished their homework and were now being worked hard in the gym by Gertrúd Truth. When she returned to the garden the head girl met her with the happy air of someone who has successfully fulfilled an intention. Gina told her what the class prefect had said, that the others were now having their free exercise session with Miss Truth: they had been entered for a competition involving the Cock-a-doodle-doos and given permission to do extra training. She suggested that her companion should get there quickly before her absence was noticed. Aradi raced off in the direction of the gym, and Gina found herself alone in the garden again.

What was the secret that so troubled this superstitious older girl? She went over to the pitcher, slipped her hand in and found the note. It read:

Dear Abigail,

I know that we should turn to you only when we are in serious difficulties, but that is my situation now, believe me. I forgot to remove the photo of Jani, the one taken before he left for the front, in my maths exercise book. It's the one where we are standing arm in arm. What will happen to me when they find it? How will I be allowed to take my school leaving exams? I'm on a scholarship, we can't afford the school fees, and it looks like the end of me. Please help me, Abigail!

And this was the girl who had carried the school flag! How could she not feel ashamed of herself? Much as she felt like crumpling it up, Gina put it back where she had found it. So now Abigail would step down from her pedestal, nip over to the staff room, open the cupboard where the exercise books were kept, take out the photograph from Aradi's homework book and return it to its owner; then she would titivate her hair, and, since she was now out and about, would stroll out through the gate and off to the cinema. Gina was so aggrieved that for the entire time it took her to collect her afternoon snack and eat the croissant and the apple she had been given she found herself thinking of the senior girl as a mere baby.

After the walk Sister Erzsébet came on duty. It was Susanna's afternoon off, and the fifth year had gathered in the day room: Gina learned later that it was a Matula tradition that before Mitsi Horn's monthly tea party the invited class would devote their Saturday afternoon rest period to revising their knowledge of the Bible, as a way of showing gratitude and self-abnegation. They were testing each other on the text and Bánki was asking the questions. Gina had long admired the assurance with which Bánki identified quotations, knew in which gospel a passage was found, who had written it and who the speaker was. But she also knew that no-one would ask her anything. They had never done so before, so why would they now? Moreover, Sister Erzsébet would be so delighted by their pious afternoon activity that this would be just the moment for her to do what she had to. Susanna would be back by the evening, and she was much more alert: she took regular walks up and down the corridor and even went into the washroom.

After one particularly difficult question had been posed, Gina got up behind Sister Erzsébet's back and crept out of the room and down the corridor. Much as she wanted to run she took care not to hurry. She slipped into the washroom and, as quickly as she could, with beating heart and in frantic haste to get the job done, lifted the boxes of geraniums down from behind their protective metal shield and recovered the objects she had hidden. They were all a bit damp, no doubt from the flower-watering, but there was no serious damage. She returned the boxes one by one, and then, back in the dormitory, slipped her possessions under her mattress – everything except the hundred pengő note. But she was not going to leave without a word of farewell. She tore a sheet of paper out of her diary and, in her very best hand, wrote: *I despise the lot of you. Carry on with your stupid little games in this prison. I'm leaving. Vitay.* It would be found when the bed was stripped.

She tucked the hundred pengő note into her shoe: it would go into her stockings when she went to bed. Her father would write to the governors to say that he was sending her to another school and to ask Susanna to return the personal items she had been keeping under her mattress, along with her other possessions that the Sister Housekeeper had taken.

She managed to slip back into the day room without her absence being noted: Sister Erzsébet still had her back to the door and did not turn round.

That evening they were shown a geography film, one that succeeded in holding even her attention. For the first time ever in the school, she felt calm and serene. Kalmár had to explain some of the details as there was no soundtrack, because the projector lacked the necessary equipment. Following that, she was the first into bed, but she soon rolled onto her side. She needed time to think, and to review the steps she would have to take. She knew the others were talking about her – she could hear her name being whispered from time to time – but she no longer had any interest in what they might be saying. Aradi's was another name that regularly surfaced, like the flash of a fish above the general susurration, but she was no longer interested in her either: Aradi had fallen too low in her estimation.

Having been the first into bed she was the first up the next morning. After washing and dressing she went and stood in the corridor where they lined up. The hundred pengő note had been taken out of her shoe when she undressed for bed and was now inside her stocking. During the service in the chapel she was surprised to find herself murmuring a rather different prayer from the one led by the Chaplain. It asked for only one thing, success in the enterprise that lay ahead. After prayers the fifth year did not go back to the dormitory wing with the other classes: they had been granted an unscheduled walk to make up for the one they would lose to the afternoon tea party. Gina's face was now so radiant with harmony and good humour that Susanna noticed, and remarked how glad she was to see this, though it was of course understandable and no doubt a lot to do with the forthcoming tea. You can forget about that, thought Gina. These Mitsi Horn traditions are a lot of nonsense. But for once I don't hold them against her. She doesn't know it, but she's going to help me get out of here.

That afternoon Kalmár led the procession, with Susanna

bringing up the rear. In her black formal dress and the little white cap perched on her luxuriant hair, she too had a kind of festive beauty. Although she had a great deal else on her mind just then, Gina could not help thinking for the first time how very well suited the two of them were. Salm had arranged the bunch of flowers they were to present to Mitsi Horn and had given it to Kalmár to admire, but he handed it straight to Gina: Vitay had never set eyes on this remarkable lady and she should have the pleasure of giving it to her at their first meeting. In later life Gina often recalled the look of pure venom on Salm's face – that the bouquet she had put together with so much love and care should be presented to their benefactor by the ostracised Vitay!

As they were leaving the skies had darkened and the rain set in, so they had brought their raincoats. That doubly pleased Gina. On this day of days a leaden sky would be the perfect ally, and she would certainly need a coat for her planned overnight journey: she had no wish to spend the entire trip back to Budapest in a black cardigan, with her teeth chattering with cold – it was all the warm clothing they were allowed to wear on the afternoon walk, even in November.

They had taken a route that Gina had never seen before. With every minute that passed, every step that brought them closer to Mitsi Horn's house and the station, she grew more excited and nervous. They turned down a side street and began to cross a square, in the middle of which stood a statue. It was the mutilated torso of a woman. She had no arms, or legs, and her expression was one of absolute grief. So, thought Gina, even in Árkod there is a monument to The Sorrows of Hungary. Kalmár called out to her to take some of the roses from Mitsi Horn's bouquet, run over to the statue and lay them at the base.

Normally she would have welcomed this order, if only as a brief distraction, but not now. She was too preoccupied with her problems for that, though she was more than happy to do something to please Kalmár. She stepped out of the line, went across and examined the monument, looking for somewhere to put the roses where they would best be seen. Her glance fell on a small white placard, presumably bearing the name of the sculptor. How odd, she thought. It would normally be carved into the stone. She leaned down to place the roses next to the statue, and as she did so her eyes fell level with the notice. In fact it was not a notice at all. It was a sheet of paper that had been attached to the monument, inscribed, rather like the plates one saw at the front of books, in a florid, elegant hand:

STOP THIS POINTLESS SHEDDING OF HUNGARIAN BLOOD! WE HAVE LOST THE WAR. SAVE THE LIVES OF YOUR CHILDREN FOR A BETTER FUTURE.

Scarcely able to believe her eyes, she stood stock-still. Kalmár called out to ask her what she was waiting for, and she turned round with such a look of astonishment on her face that the teacher left the class and went over to join her. He leaned down to study the inscription, called Susanna over and sent Gina back to the line. His face was as scarlet as if someone had struck him a blow.

This was a special moment for Gina. She alone knew what was happening and no-one else in the class did. None of them were allowed to leave the group to go and see what was so very interesting about the statue. She smiled into the faces of Mari Kis and Torma, but said nothing. The procession remained at a standstill but none of them asked her what was happening and she felt a chill air closing around her: it was like coming into a room left unheated for the whole winter. Never mind, she thought. Two hours at the most, and I shall never see you again.

In his lessons on national defence Kalmár had explained that in times of war hostile elements would always seek to undermine public morale, but Gina had never been able to imagine how that might apply in reality. Now she could see for herself. It wasn't exactly a propaganda leaflet as he had described them in the lessons but what he had termed an act of provocation. What would the General have to say about that when she told him?

Susanna was standing with her back to the class and it was impossible to see her reaction to what Kalmár was telling her. They spoke very quietly for a while, then Susanna went back to the group and announced that the form tutor had some special business to attend to and would join them later; they would carry on slowly, and he would catch up with them outside Mitsi Horn's house. They set off at the funereal pace she dictated. Szabó turned her head to look, but the Prefect called out, "Face forward, everyone!"

He must be peeling it off, or tearing it down, Gina thought. Then he'll go and find a policeman and show him what we found. He'll have to, because it's what he told us to do in class. He looks a real St George standing there, the Knight of The

Sorrows of Hungary. The rain started to fall again, very gently, and the few passers-by that she had noticed in the distance retreated into their homes and disappeared. That's good, Gina thought. The fewer people there are on the streets, the better for me.

Mitsi Horn's house was proving to be further away than she had thought, or perhaps it only seemed that way because they were walking at such an unimaginably slow pace. Kalmár soon caught up with them and resumed his place at the front as if nothing had happened. No-one pointed out to Gina which house was Mitsi Horn's, but she spotted it at once. Only one former pupil, with her extraordinary notions, could be the owner of the tall, narrow, angular, eccentric, fairy-tale building with windows in an attic that leaned out over the street as if to peer down on what was going on below. The other windows were tall and set deep into the walls. There was no porch as such; a short run of covered steps led up to a cheerful red-brown door with a large brass ball for a knocker. No garden was to be seen – it must have been round the back of the house; but she then spotted something that gave her more pleasure than any garden might have: a cellar with windows, all of them unbarred and almost on a level with the pavement. And the station was close by – she could smell the smoke from the engines. She wouldn't even have to ask her way, she would need only to follow her nose. What extraordinary luck that Mitsi Horn should live just there, right beside the tracks! Well, that was how they were all referring to her, but it was absurd to think that the name she had heard so often could refer to this actual person. She must be nearly a thousand years old! If she had been in her final year and become engaged in 1914, at the start of the First World War, she must now be forty-seven or forty-eight – an old lady!

Susanna rang the bell. The door opened immediately: their hostess must have been looking out for them through the window. The diminutive, smiling person who stood there was not in the least like the Mitsi Horn Gina had imagined. In her elegant afternoon gown she looked slim and graceful; not a grey hair was to be seen among her carefully brushed locks, and she had large, beautiful eyes of emerald green. Kalmár kissed her hand, and Gina became so busy wondering what it would be like if one of her former teachers did that to her after she had left, having attacked her year after year with, "Go and get some chalk," or "Where is the register?" or "Why has the blackboard wiper not been washed properly?" that she instantly forgot what she was supposed to do. It was also dawning on her that this Mitsi Horn might be a rather more agreeable person than she had allowed. To have so many of them to afternoon tea was no small thing, let alone to do the same month after month . . . And what was more, you really could not describe her as unattractive: extraordinary as the fact was, she was much, much prettier than Auntie Mimó.

The fifth year were being unbelievably restrained and well-behaved. They deposited their raincoats in the entrance hall in total silence and queued up outside the drawing room without the slightest show of haste, as Susanna noted with an approving nod of the head. Then it was Gina's turn to go in. The moment she set eyes on the décor she knew at once what it was that, even more than her personal problems, had so oppressed her inside the walls of the fortress. The beauty and the harmony to which she had been accustomed at home were totally lacking in that austere and charmless place, where everything was functional and utilitarian. Mitsi Horn's salon, on the other hand, was just like theirs at home and Auntie Mimó's.

Kalmár introduced her. She handed over the flowers, and Mitsi Horn asked her if she was new to the school. She said she was, and stood expecting a comment along the lines of, "How lucky you are to be there. If you need to go to a boarding school then the Matula is the only one. It's the centre of the world, and it stands in for both your father and your mother." But Mitsi Horn said nothing. Instead she put her hand gently on Gina's arm, as if to convey, "My poor girl, how very hard it must be for you," and Gina felt the woman's strange charm acting on her, as it did on everyone in her presence. But she had no wish to like her, and she struggled against the warm response that rose up inside her.

Merriment and laughter began to fill the room. Six tables had been laid with the most exquisite silver and porcelain dishes, and Mitsi Horn said they should start at once to allow more time for games. Susanna told them where to sit (in the same order as in the refectory) and Gina found herself once again with Torma on her right, Mari Kis on her left and Ari facing her. They were well placed, next to the main table, which their hostess shared with Kalmár and Susanna. They collected their tea from a silver samovar that hummed and bubbled non-stop; it was poured into their cups by the hostess herself – real, fragrant tea, not the noxious brew served up at the Matula. Gina sipped hers in near-ecstasy and, knowing that she would have nothing more to eat before she reached Budapest, consumed an unseemly number of the sandwiches that were piled high on every table, at the same time reflecting that some other people might also not have much to eat that night, especially the two in charge, Kalmár and Susanna, who would be out searching for her once her absence had been noticed.

From what Mari Kis was saying Gina gathered that the silver-framed photograph on the shelf above the fireplace was of Mitsi Horn's son, who had fallen in battle the year before at the Don; and, Mari went on, it was really interesting why she had never remarried after the First World War, when her husband died from some disease contracted at the front: it was because she didn't want her son to be brought up by a stepfather. But she was still so attractive she could easily marry again if she wanted, now that he was no longer alive.

Gina listened with only half an ear, trying to decide on the precise moment to ask Susanna where the toilets were. She would pretend to have a stomach ache so that she could go out and explore the house, and when she had found a suitable window to escape through she would climb out from the basement into the street. She would leave the drawing room three times, each time for a little longer than before, and the fourth time she would not come back. For the moment she was trapped where she was: she would have to bide her time.

Ari, Torma and Mari Kis were now working through the list of suitors Mitsi Horn had rejected, so she turned her attention to the conversation taking place at the main table. It was so close she could hear everything that was said.

"Another one?" Mitsi Horn was asking. "Where was it this time?"

"On the monument to The Sorrows of Hungary," Kalmár replied.

"It's incredible that they still can't find the person who is doing this," said Mitsi Horn.

"They will," said Susanna.

"The other day, in church, I found a typewritten leaflet lying on the pew. I picked it up, thinking it must be an invitation to tea with some women's group, or some matter of church business, but it was a summary of a propaganda broadcast by Radio Moscow. I thought I was going to faint. There were piles of them on every pew."

"Let's hope they catch him soon," said Kalmár. "The scoundrel deserves to be hanged. I spoke to a policeman and there's now someone watching the statue in case he comes back. Our boys are pouring out their blood at the front and here he is, undermining morale and upsetting their mothers."

Mitsi Horn finished stirring her tea and then, as the others had already done, looked up at the mantelpiece. The photograph in the silver frame showed a young man in an open-necked shirt standing beside a horse, holding it by the reins and smiling out at them. The resemblance to his mother was striking. Gina could easily imagine what Abigail's friend the eighteen-year-old Mitsi Horn must have looked like in the days when she could still laugh so loudly it could be heard, they said, at the porter's lodge.

"I should like to be there when they string him up," Kalmár added.

"Mr Kalmár!" said Susanna. It was the tone of voice she used when upbraiding a pupil in the strongest possible terms, or standing on her dignity. Kalmár dropped his gaze, then raised it again and stared at her defiantly. This is not someone to be easily intimidated, thought Gina. He is a man, and he knows about these things. He teaches us about them in his lessons. He isn't going to be lectured on them. And he certainly knows how to deal with our enemies.

Mitsi Horn smiled a quick smile to change the subject and pressed the bell beside her. It was answered by an old lady bringing in a large platter of pastries. She was acting as a domestic servant, but Gina found her as formidable as a princess, even as she kicked herself for her stupidity in not realising that a woman as well-to-do as Mitsi Horn would hardly be living alone in such a large house: of course there would be other people too. Never mind, she would still find somewhere in the basement to make her escape from, somewhere no-one usually went.

The old lady was now going from table to table setting down cakes and pastries on everyone's plate. Mitsi Horn issued instructions from where she was sitting, and announced that she had prepared a tombola. When they had had enough tea and eaten their fill they should clear the tables and take the used crockery to the sideboard. The class monitor would then deal out the marked sheets in the box to the right of the fireplace; she would draw the numbers herself, so that their teacher and Sister Susanna could also take part. There were several prizes waiting, plenty for everyone; the winning numbers were in the hatbox on the piano stool.

The girls cleared their tables at lightning speed and in total silence, and each was given a tombola card. Enjoy your bit of fun, Gina thought to herself. You might even win yourselves a few pen nibs or sheets of Bristol paper covered in biblical quotations printed in gold. I shall be playing for higher stakes, and for a rather more exciting prize.

Soon Susanna was looking at her with an air of concern. She stood up, went over and leaned over to speak into Gina's ear. "Is it your stomach? Oh dear. Would you like me to come with you?"

"No," was the reply. It was rather embarrassing, as Mitsi Horn and Kalmár had stopped their conversation and were listening.

"Truly, it isn't that bad."

"There are bathrooms upstairs and downstairs," Susanna went on. "But you mustn't use Auntie Mitsi's, so go down to the basement."

She could rest assured about that! As she went out she heard Susanna telling Mari Kis to play two hands, one for herself and one for Gina until she came back. A wonderful idea, and all the better as Mari Kis would refuse to call out any lucky number she had, to stop her winning anything. But Mitsi Horn objected. She asked for Gina's sheet and announced that she would play in her place. Mari should not have the double burden of having to worry about her classmate's hand as well as her own. Whereupon Gina left the room.

She looked around. As everywhere else, including the school, the windows were covered in the regulation blackout paper. But the hallway was well lit and there were lights at the side of the stairs, going both up and down, and she could see her way easily.

She went quickly down to the basement. There was no sign of the old lady, but she could hear her moving around somewhere, perhaps cooking – there was a faint whiff of vanilla in the air. Gina peered into two rooms, then found what she was after in the third. Here too the blackout material blocked all light from outside. She felt around for the switch and turned it on. It was the washroom used by the domestic staff and the bath was set against the wall backing onto the street. If she stood on the rim she would be able to open the little window just above it, pull herself up onto the sill, and be out in less than a minute.

She flushed the toilet to give the impression that she had used it and left immediately. Once she was back through the hallway she would have only to reach up and take her coat: no difficulty there. She wasn't going to risk taking her hat as well. It was just too conspicuous, too unmistakably Matula.

Back in the drawing room she found that Mitsi Horn had won two wafer biscuits for her. She was pleased by that, and popped them immediately into her school bag: they would be good for the journey. Someone said, "Hark at the thunder!" and the old lady, who had just come in with yet more pastries, confirmed that it was pouring down out there like the start of another Great Flood.

Twenty minutes later Gina made her second request. This time Susanna felt her brow to see if she had a fever and Mitsi Horn asked if she could give her something for it. Kalmár looked away: these female things embarrassed him as a man. Susanna told her not to eat anything more and took away her plate. Mari Kis and the others looked at her with malicious glee on their faces. They were all clearly delighted that she should have been taken ill just when such a magnificent supper was before them. As Gina went out Mitsi Horn took over her tombola sheet once again, but this time she won nothing.

The third time she went out Gina did not ask permission. As she got to her feet she heard the Prefect saying that perhaps it would be better if she took the poor sick child back to the school, and Mr Kalmár could bring the others later. Mitsi Horn said no, she couldn't possibly let them go in this rain. They should at least stay a bit longer: the girl would be just as sick at the school as she was there. Now Gina knew that she really had to make her move: if the ever-conscientious Susanna was to follow her to the washroom or drag her off back to the Matula she would utterly ruin the plan.

So this was the moment. The final one. The real goodbye. She gazed round at the others for the last time. How strange it was that this should be the last image of them that she would take with her, so untypical of life in the Matula – the girls sitting on silk-upholstered chairs and tucking into wonderful cakes and pastries, surrounded by nothing black-and-white or squat and four-square, with the fire blazing in the hearth and the glitter of silver everywhere. Susanna was looking more than usually beautiful at that moment, and Kalmár, after calling for the unknown dissident's head, more manly than ever. Farewell, Mari Kis, pitiless and loathsome as you are, and goodbye to you too, Torma, and all you others! At that moment Feri seemed once again real and Budapest closer than ever. She even thought of the aquarium, but it no longer made her angry.

The old lady passed close to her in the hallway, this time carrying a large porcelain dish piled high with baked apples. Gina waited until she had disappeared into the drawing room, then took her coat from the rack and raced down to the wash-room. This time she did not turn the light on: that would have been a serious mistake. The only safe thing now was to feel her way with her fingers: this is the bath, this is where to stand on it, that's where the window must be . . . just hold on here . . . and success! It took some effort to get the window open, and pulling herself up onto the sill had been even harder, but thanks to Gertrúd Truth her limbs were in good condition and she managed. She pushed her head out and looked around. There was no-one in the street, only the endless, pouring rain. Once outside, she pushed the window back into its frame as best she could, and ran off down the unfamiliar, dimly lit road in which she had smelled smoke when they first arrived.

She was free! She wanted to shout for joy, but she restrained herself. Emerging from the side street she found herself, from what she could see in the dull haze of the wartime lighting, in a large square. She knew she must be very close to the station: she could dimly make out the words "Railway Restaurant" in the gloom, and a low, wide building with a portico over the entrance, which stood open. Every minute was now vital, but she needed to walk slowly to avoid drawing attention to herself. Why would a solitary girl be running at breathless speed towards the station, with neither an umbrella nor a hat, in the driving rain? Only when she was almost there did she quicken her pace. She had realised that if someone did accost her she could say she was afraid of missing a train that was about to leave. She entered the main hallway. A light was on in the ticket office, but, worryingly, there were no passengers about. Oh my God, she thought, why aren't there more people here? Perhaps there are no trains due for some time?

She pulled out her hundred-pengő note and placed it on the counter.

"I would like to go to Budapest," she told the sleepy official. "When is the next train?"

"In another hour and a half," the man yawned. "If it isn't delayed."

"Nothing before then?"

"How could there be? You're lucky there's one at all. Don't you know that since the start of the war there's been only one train a day?"

She hadn't known. They had always travelled around by car. Stunned, she gazed into his indifferent face. In much less than an hour and a half they would have found her and taken her back. The man rubbed his eyes; obviously all he cared about was his lack of sleep. As if mimicking his yawn, a loud hissing noise came from outside. She looked out through the door that opened onto the track. Alongside platform one a train was pumping out steam.

"Where's that one going to?" she asked. She was so excited she could barely speak.

"To Dömölk. It's leaving in two minutes. It goes in the opposite direction."

"Never mind. A ticket, please. To Dömölk. Quickly!"

She got her ticket, but not before he had tapped his brow, first on one side and then the other, wondered how it was that some people were able to travel wherever the fancy took them – if not Budapest then why not Dömölk? – and said how nice it was to be young. But why was she in such a panic? She had almost torn from his hand the ten-pengő notes given in change. If she was in such a hurry, why hand over a hundred note? And then fly off like that to the platform? Oh, to hell with her.

Just let me get out of here, she was thinking as she ran. Anywhere will do. I'll be safe in Dömölk, or at least until the next Budapest train gets there. I can telephone home in the morning. There are army units everywhere. I'll introduce myself to the senior officer and ask if I can wait with them until my father comes. But I must get away from Árkod. As long as I'm still here they can catch me and lock me up again.

The stone paving in the hallway was covered in water, shed no doubt by passengers arriving on earlier trains. In her hurry she slipped and almost fell to her knees – but the exit was straight ahead, and there was the train. Just a couple of seconds now, or less, and she would be there, on board.

As she went out onto the platform she bumped into someone coming at full tilt into the foyer. If he hadn't caught her she would most certainly have fallen. She wanted to apologise, but the words stuck in her throat. The stranger got there first.

"Please excuse me," said Kőnig. "I do beg your pardon. Have I hurt you? I am so sorry. But where on earth are you going, and in such a hurry?"

His eyes blinked at her. He seemed completely unperturbed.

His hat and coat were dripping with rain. She could not even cry. She stood and watched as the train on platform one set off for Dömölk.

Disaster. The General

Gina's father had never liked hunting. He took no pleasure in it at all. But Feri did, and Gina had on many occasions listened in raptures when, at one of Auntie Mimó's afternoon teas, the conversation turned to his exploits in the field. Now, to her surprise, she found herself thinking of them again. She had remembered something very strange that Feri had once told her. It was really absurd, the Lieutenant had said, but it often happened on a hunt that the quarry would fall to a Sunday sportsman who barely knew how to handle a rifle. As they danced together she agreed with him, adding that the poor deer or stag would care very little about who it was that had taken its life. But now, at this most dreadful and distressing moment, with the train for Dömölk pulling out of the station, she thought she had been wrong. Perhaps it did make a difference: it was far less shameful to be taken down by some world-famous hunter than by some insignificant nobody. She herself would much rather have been caught by Hajdú, or Gertrúd Truth – there was no hope of outrunning her, everyone knew she could still see off champion athletes – or any one of Kalmár, Éles, anyone who actually counted. But Kőnig? Why did it have to be Kőnig?

She trembled in the grip of his enormous hands. They held

her drenched shoulders with a firmness that astonished her. The man had unexpected strength, and now he was intent on steering her back inside. She did not resist: there would have been no point. Once there, he took her left hand in his and, holding it as if it were that of a tiny child learning to walk and needing help, began to talk to her in a low, gentle voice: what a surprise it was to see her there, and how lucky that they had bumped into one another. The poor girl had lost her way, had she not? She had obviously become separated from her group – the fifth year were being entertained at Mitsi Horn's. It must have been because of the blackout; you could hardly see where to put your feet. But what a happy coincidence that he should have been at the station at just that moment to enquire about the current travel situation and to check if it was still possible and safe to organise a full-day autumn outing! And he would now see her on her way so that she wouldn't get lost again.

She gazed into his innocent face. Everyone knew about Kőnig's credulity. It was legendary. Perhaps she could find a way to take advantage of it, if not just then, then sometime in the future. She would have to keep very, very quiet on the way back, to avoid betraying her true intentions, and think carefully about what to tell Susanna, who was certainly no Kőnig.

They had crossed the foyer and were already outside in the rain when the door of the ticket office opened and the sleepy official emerged. He stared at them in surprise, and smiled a sour little smile, as if even to move his lips was an effort.

"So you didn't take the train to Dömölk? How was that? When I sold you your ticket it was still at the platform."

Gina thought that her heart would stop. Without intending to, the wretched man had betrayed her.

Kőnig studied the official and his uniform with a look that combined surprise and genial curiosity. It was as if he had never seen a railway employee before.

"I think there has been some mistake," he said amiably. "You have confused little Vitay with someone else. Little Vitay is not going anywhere."

"Not going anywhere? I sold her the ticket myself. She was in such a hurry I thought she was possessed. The money is right there in her hand, see – the money I gave her in change; and so is her ticket. Do you think I'm stupid?"

It was all over. All over for good. In her panic she had completely forgotten to hide the change in her pocket, and there it was indeed, in her right hand, next to the ticket.

"Not at all," said Kőnig. He took Gina's hand, snaffled up the ten-pengő notes and the ticket in his ice-cold fingers and stuffed them into his pocket. "It must have been some other girl, a girl who looked like her. Where would this one be wanting to travel to? The poor thing had lost her way. She isn't from these parts; she doesn't know the town. Luckily, we happened to bump into each other."

The clerk stared at them, first at one and then the other, turned on his heel, went back into his office and slammed the door. The hand that was holding hers was now pulling her forward with an irresistible might. She allowed him to lead her away, keeping her face completely blank. She had certainly been wrong about Kőnig. He wasn't as dim as she had thought. He had taken the money and the ticket so that he would not have to reveal her crime at the Matula: he would play it as if nothing had happened. He didn't have the courage, and he didn't like her enough, to help her escape, but he was too sentimental to give her away: let's just carry on the way things are; little Vitay never intended to abscond or break any rules; little Vitay is such a nice girl, she shouldn't have to be put through a tribunal, good Lord no! And certainly not asked to leave . . .

Asked to leave? Expelled?

She was dumbstruck. How could she have been so dull, so incredibly stupid, not to have thought of that before? If you did something really terrible you were hauled before a disciplinary council, your parents were summoned, and if you couldn't give a satisfactory account of your behaviour they kicked you out. If the offence was serious enough you could be denied a place at every other school in the country, but if it was less dreadful the punishment was just that you had to go to a different one. As she was General Vitay's daughter they would probably not go so far as to destroy her chances of an education completely; he would simply be asked to send her somewhere else. It was another example of Columbus' egg: nothing would have been lost, and everything could start again from scratch.

They were now out in the square. Kőnig was still holding inexorably on to her hand, almost running, and she was doing her best to keep up with him. By now she was near-ecstatic. Her legs were splattered up to the knees in mud from wading through slush, but she did not mind in the least. She was revelling in it: she was now a scruffy, neglected-looking waif, a true runaway.

The square was as empty as it had been before, but as they neared the street that led down to Mitsi Horn's she spotted Susanna standing at the corner in the dull haze of the wartime lighting. She had no coat on, there was no umbrella in her hand, and her face and clothes were every bit as drenched as their own.

"Gina," she said – it was the first time she had used the intimate form of her name – "where on earth have you been? I thought you must have been taken ill in one of the bathrooms. I looked for you everywhere. When I realised you weren't in the house I came out without telling anyone. I didn't stop to bring an umbrella or anything, but never mind, here you are at last. Where have you been?"

"I ran away," said Gina. Her voice was not as calm as she would have liked it to be. It was not that she was afraid, but she was now very tense, and she wanted this farce to end as quickly as possible. "Mr Kőnig stopped me on the platform. I was trying to go home."

"Well, you know," Kőnig began, "this girl is not at all well. As soon as we get back we must have her seen by a doctor. Trying to run away? The poor little thing was wandering about in the general direction of the station, but how could she possibly have known where to go? I hate to think where she might have ended up if she hadn't chanced to bump into me."

Susanna's mouth moved as if she were about to speak, but she stayed silent. She took Gina's other hand, as if she were afraid she might free herself from Kőnig's grip and disappear a second time.

"My ticket is inside Mr Kőnig's pocket, and so is the money

I was given in change for my hundred-pengő note. Have a look in his coat. That's where it is. He took it from me."

Kőnig and Susanna spoke at almost the same time. Kőnig said: "The poor little thing must be feverish. So now I've stolen something from her! It's ridiculous." Susanna's voice was icy with suppressed anger. "How dare you say such a thing about your teacher?"

Gina looked at each of them in turn, feeling utterly helpless.

"Yes, I suppose she must be ill," the Prefect agreed, as if thinking aloud. "She left the party several times, and I couldn't find her after that. But what is this all about?"

"As I said, it's the fever talking," Kőnig said mournfully. "She's such a good-hearted girl she obviously didn't want to upset Auntie Mitsi by admitting that she was ill, so she set off back to the school. Unfortunately she went in the wrong direction. How could she have known the way back?"

"If only she hadn't been so stubborn, so irresponsible, so headstrong," Susanna went on – as if Gina were not right beside her and able to hear every word she said. "Properly speaking, I ought to punish her. She knows perfectly well that she had no right to go out on her own. But she showed real unselfishness in not wanting to spoil other people's pleasure. Perhaps I can find a way to overlook her conduct."

Gina felt that in all her life she had never hated anyone as much as these two, the soft-hearted Kőnig who was telling all these lies and the saintly, simple-minded Susanna, who were taking her back, one of them holding her left hand and the other the right. This time it was Kőnig who rang the bell and the old lady who opened the door. As soon as she saw them, each dripping even more profusely than the last, she clapped her hands and wailed so loudly that Mitsi Horn left her guests and appeared in the hall. She took in the situation at a glance, calmed the domestic down with a few quiet words and sent her back to the kitchen. Kőnig apologised profusely for having turned up uninvited, but he had chanced to bump into little Vitay. She was not at all well, the poor thing. She was trying to make her way back to the school and had got lost in the rain. He had brought her here again with the help of Sister Susanna.

Gina, her mouth clamped shut and her face devoid of expression, stared back at Mitsi Horn. She did not try to explain a second time that there was not a word of truth in the whole story and that she had simply been caught. She felt that Mitsi Horn would play it the same way as Kőnig and pretend to believe her innocent; she might even offer her some sort of reward for having been such a model of selfless consideration. There was no point in fighting against all these adults: she would speak to Susanna once they were back at the school. Even if Kőnig had hidden the train ticket to Dömölk and the money, she still had one piece of evidence that she had tried to escape. How lucky it was that, thanks to the hated Mari Kis, she hadn't left without writing a farewell letter!

The game of tombola came to an end. It would have had to anyway; the time permitted for the outing was almost over. As the fifth year lined up, Kalmár gently reprimanded Gina: she had not behaved very responsibly. She had broken the rules. There was no shame in having a stomach ache; in fact everyone would have sympathised with her. It was extremely foolish to venture out into a city she did not know, but they would soon have her well again in the infirmary. Throughout all this Gina had to be very careful not to weaken or to betray her sense of despair, as the whole class was watching. She now rather hoped that they would think she really had acted unselfishly: they must not have the pleasure of mocking her because she had tried to run away and Kőnig had stopped her.

The umbrellas were produced. Susanna told Torma and Mari Kis to take her by an arm to warm her up, while Gina held one over their three heads. The old lady appeared once again and shared out the remaining pastries, which went into their bags. Kalmár led the chorus of farewells, and the door closed behind them. From somewhere far away came the call of an engine blowing steam. That was all. That, and the endless rain.

Susanna had ordered them not to talk, but of course they whispered. Szabó, walking immediately behind Gina, kept saying how never in all her life had she enjoyed herself as much as she had that day, and how nice it was to be so cosy and warm after all that tea, and not to have to mind the damp. This was directed at Gina, of course: Szabó could not feel her arms shivering the way Mari Kis and Torma could, but she was perfectly aware that Gina must have been feeling utterly miserable in her sodden clothes. Her behaviour was of no concern to Gina. She had more important things to think about than the petty pinpricks of her classmates.

Their route took them back the way they had come. A policeman was now on duty beside the monument to The Sorrows of

Hungary. As they passed by he flashed a blue light over them, recognised Kalmár and saluted him. The roses were still there at the feet of mutilated Hungaria, but the placard was nowhere to be seen. At this point the girls were saying that Kalmár must surely have spoken to the Director about the autumn outing by now, and how nice it would be to know what the Prefect thought about it, but, as always, you couldn't tell a thing from her face. When out of school they always walked in step, it was quite difficult in the deeper puddles, and every so often Mari Kis would deliberately get her timing wrong, do a little sashay, and splash a bit of mud onto Gina's shoes.

When they got back they were sent to the day room. After one of Mitsi Horn's teas the invitees did not usually go to supper – they would hardly have been able to eat anything. They were given permission instead to amuse themselves or to read, as they chose. Susanna called Gina aside. She told Mari Kis to go and fetch Vitay's night things and toiletries from her bed and bring them to the sick bay. Torma was despatched to find the doctor.

At this point Kőnig disappeared, presumably to go and change his clothes or run a hot footbath. Kalmár also abandoned the class, though he was the least sodden of them all. In the sick bay the nurse stared in horror at Gina and Susanna, clearly unable to decide which of them should go in the bed. The Prefect was every bit as soaked as the girl from Budapest and in just as much need of warmth and rest.

Gina undressed. She had only just lain down when the doctor appeared. Susanna explained that she had put the girl to bed because she was having severe stomach pains. The doctor prodded her all over, examined her tongue and peered down her throat. Gina made no attempt to stop her. What would be the point of telling them all that there had been no stomach pains and that her repeated trips to the toilet had been for an altogether different reason? She would do that when she was alone with Susanna. All the same it was rather amusing that the doctor made her stick out her tongue three times, was puzzled every time because it wasn't furred up, and placed her on a strict diet for twenty-four hours. And why all the fuss about the fact that she had got a bit wet? It was laughable. Was she now supposed to take her temperature five times a day? What would be the point? If she had a fever, wouldn't they just bring her a cup of tea and an anti-inflammatory pill? But why would she have one anyway? She was given permission to read until nine if she wished. She said she didn't want to read. She needed to talk to Sister Susanna.

"Later," the doctor said. "But first the Sister should go to her room and change her clothes – everything, from top to toe, if she doesn't want to get seriously ill herself."

Susanna promised to be back soon, and Gina was left alone. The Nursing Sister had thoughtfully placed a book next to the bed, another soul-uplifting work by the tedious Swiss priest who so delighted them over supper, but she snuggled down and closed her eyes. Now that she could finally give way to it she felt more tired than she had in her whole life. She lay and waited for the Prefect to come back, thinking about and trying to decide what to tell her. Susanna was as stern as the Good Book itself. Once the evidence was in her hand, and she finally realised what Gina had intended, would she, if indeed she *had* ever liked her

(Gina had never been able to work out if Susanna genuinely liked someone or if she was just following her Christian duty), would she set aside whatever pity or sympathy she had for her and immediately inform the Director that, as surely as she was now lying in that bed, Georgina Vitay had tried to run away? Susanna wasn't Kőnig. Susanna was hard. So perhaps everything would be resolved within the next few days. They could no longer persist in their game of not letting her talk openly to her father. Once he knew what her life in the class was like, after she had spoken candidly to him (it would only take fifteen minutes), he would surely take her away, even if the school allowed her to stay on out of charity. He would never leave his daughter to be tormented the way she was.

She had to wait a long time for Susanna to return.

She had indeed changed her clothes and was once again wearing her usual grey outfit, including the dull, rather shabby shoes she wore every day, but now, instead of the usual bonnet, she had a towel wrapped round her head, like a turban. Even in her current state of mind Gina could only stare in wonder at this strange beturbaned Susanna . . . But of course, her hair had been dripping wet, it was long, and she had not had time to dry it.

"So, how are you feeling?" the Prefect enquired. She pulled up a chair next to the bed and sat down. "You know, our dear Mitsi Horn has been incredibly kind. She was here not five minutes ago, so late at night, to find out how you are. You aren't shivering with cold, Georgina? You don't have a stomach ache? You don't feel as if you are going to be sick?"

On the contrary; she was starving. But that wasn't important now. What was important was that they should understand each other. And that Mitsi Horn would just leave her alone.

"So, what have you to tell me, then?" Susanna asked. "You can't have anything to eat. That's out of the question. It isn't real hunger. You wouldn't be able to eat on such an upset stomach."

"I don't have a stomach ache," Gina said. "I never did. I just wanted to go to the bathroom in Auntie Mitsi's house to find a window I could climb out of, go to the station and get back home at last."

Susanna reached across from her chair and felt Gina's forehead.

"I don't have a fever! I had almost got away when Mr König caught me. You must know what sort of person he is. He can't bear to see anyone in trouble. He hid my ticket in his pocket, and my money, and he lied to you that I had lost my way."

"What's this you're saying?" Susanna asked. "You still dare tell me that your teacher is a liar? What exactly is going on here? You aren't still trying to say that you told me the truth – that a Matula girl could ever be so underhand as to climb out of a bathroom window like a thief and have to be brought back from the station? If that were the case, you would not be allowed to stay here another week. You would be out of the school immediately."

"Would you please go to the dormitory and look under my mattress," Gina replied. "There you will find the farewell letter I wrote. I didn't want to go without saying anything. That should make you believe me. It's under the mattress, with my other things – my powder box and my photograph album and my diary. Please just read what I wrote to my classmates, and then telephone my father to come and take me away."

The look on Susanna's face reflected her inner struggle: should she go, or should she not? Should she give sufficient credence to this impossible story to run down to the fifth-year dormitory to see if there was any truth in what the child was saying? Her face became so sad that, even in that unreal moment of drama and tension, Gina thought she must be genuinely distressed. Was she really so upset to discover that Gina was such a wicked person, someone who fully deserved the punishment she had mentioned? If so, then Susanna must love her indeed.

The Deaconess left the room. Now she's at the end of the corridor, Gina reckoned. Now she's turning into the main one . . . now she's almost at the dormitory . . . and now she must be there. What will the others say when she rummages through my bed and finds the letter? I don't care what they say. The important thing is that they know I tried to run away. Let's just hope I can get out of here, in a few days at the most.

She found herself trembling all over and covered herself with the quilt. But this time it wasn't her nerves. She must have caught a cold after all.

Susanna was back very quickly, and she was not alone. The Nursing Sister came in behind her. This surprised Gina. She had thought the two of them would be talking in private and that no third person was needed. Moreover, Susanna was empty-handed. Where had she put the letter. In her pocket?

"This child is not well," she told the nurse. "She is delirious. She keeps accusing herself of the most extraordinary things.

Can we give her an aspirin and half a sedative to help her sleep through to the morning?"

The nurse held out the medicine and Gina pushed it away. Susanna took hold of her hand and gripped it firmly.

"Calm yourself down, Georgina. What sort of behaviour is this? Drink your medicine, please! Of course there was nothing in your bed. Not a letter, or anything else. And how could there have been? Or perhaps you have already forgotten what you were rambling about just now?"

Gina tore her hand out of Susanna's. She jumped out of the bed and started to scream, and the two women had a struggle to subdue her. She kept shouting that the letter had been stolen either by Mari Kis, when she brought her night things to the infirmary, or that she, Susanna, had taken it, because she was in league with Mr Kőnig, and she had deprived her of her last chance to escape; she hated them all so much she could kill them.

"Oh, my word," the Nursing Sister groaned. "Now she's been robbed – by Mari Kis, who's been with us since she was ten, and by Sister Susanna too. Dear, oh dear! The poor little thing, what a state she's in! Kill us all! What a thing to say! Now take this medicine, my child. You are very ill."

She held both of Gina's arms. Gina relaxed and opened her mouth. If there was no letter and her hidden treasures had vanished, then she no longer had any proof. She was simply a thoughtful, unselfish person, a sick little girl shouting out in delirium with no hope of ever escaping. Wiser just to take the sleeping pill and let the world disappear from sight. She gulped the sedative down, lay back, closed her eyes and said not a word more, not even to answer questions. She was aware of a thermometer being slipped under her arm and taken out again, and she heard the nurse telling Susanna, "Not good: it's very high." The door opened, closed, opened, and closed a second time, but she kept her eyes shut. She had no idea who was now standing beside the bed, but at one point she had the impression that Susanna was leaning over her and her face was very close . . . Then the anger and disappointment she felt towards the Deaconess started to give way under the effect of the sleeping pill. She tried to huddle into the corner of the bed, but as she did so the drug completed its work, and she fell asleep.

The next morning she woke feeling thick-headed with an unpleasant taste in her mouth. The Nursing Sister read the thermometer and again shook her head. There was now a raging fever. Susanna did not come to see her, but the doctor called in, examined her again, and told her she had a serious inflammation of the throat, but luckily not of the tonsils. She would not be having any visitors. She had a bad cold and was coughing and sneezing.

It was true: she could barely swallow and was having to blow her nose continually. She felt very unwell, she had no desire to eat anything or to read, and all the time the fever was on her she had difficulty gathering her thoughts. She simply lay there in a leaden drowsiness, without hope, like a captive who has just discovered that he has dug his tunnel in vain: a large rock bars his route and there is no way for him out of his prison.

In the afternoon Susanna looked in on her. She brought flowers, she said, from the other girls. I can imagine, Gina thought to herself, with what pleasure and affection they gathered them, and what good wishes they sent. The doctor visited her on three consecutive days, but from then on she saw no-one apart from her, the Nursing Sister and Susanna. By the fifth day the temperature was still there but she was able to get up; by the sixth it had gone. Susanna told her she would be going back to the dormitory that same evening: the doctor had given permission. Gina listened to these words as if they were not addressed to her and referred to someone else. Susanna took a long look at her face – it was now much thinner – and told the nurse she would advise the kitchen staff that for the next few days Vitay was to be placed on a special regime.

The final afternoon was spent entirely alone. She was still in the infirmary, away from the other girls, but she was now much better and the time dragged on, devoid of interest and totally boring. She was waiting for someone to come and take her to the Director's office: it was a Saturday, when her father usually telephoned. She was also wondering when and how Susanna would punish her, or whether she might decide that everything she had said and done had been due to the illness and punishment was no longer appropriate. She made no attempt to think about what her situation in the class would be now. If Mari Kis, going to collect her nightgown, had poked around under her mattress and stolen the letter and the other things she had hidden, what might she have done with her booty? She pondered all this while standing at the sick bay window. She found to her amazement that the weather, which had been so gloomy on the day of Mitsi Horn's tea party, was again bright and sunny, lending an unusually rich redness to the leaves that still hung in such numbers on the trees. In past years they had seemed to shed them almost all at once, towards the end of October, as if in obedience to some unspoken word of command.

It was now five o'clock. She was surprised that no-one had come to call her to the Director's office: her father must have had difficulty getting a connection. She started to pack her dressing gown and other belongings into the laundry bag and put on her school uniform. She was just doing up the ribbon on her blouse when she heard someone coming down the corridor. It was a strong, firm step, not the usual sort one heard in the building. There was a knock at the door. How odd. No-one knocked on the door of a room used by the girls. Perhaps someone was bringing a workman – a plumber perhaps: that morning the nurse had said there was a tap leaking. She called out, "Come in," and turned to face the now wide-open door. Susanna came in first, and next the General. As on the day when he had first brought her, he was in mufti. Gina threw herself into his arms and burst into tears.

At the Hajda patisserie

None of the adults present tried to quieten her. When she had calmed down a little she wiped her eyes and noticed that her coat was draped over Susanna's arm. The Deaconess had gone to collect it, along with her hat and school bag. She glanced at her father, and then again at Susanna, as if scarcely able to believe her eyes.

"As you can see, instead of telephoning the General has come to see you," the Prefect said. "I am so pleased for you. The stomach bug or whatever it was that laid you low has affected you far more than we imagined. It has made you depressed and highly strung."

"May we go?" the General asked. "I have very little time. I have to be back in Pest by the end of the day."

"But of course. Put your coat on, Georgina. The Director has given you leave. This is your pass. You must be back by six, no later."

You can wait for me as long as you like, Gina said to herself. Her hands were trembling so violently that the Prefect had to help her button up the collar of her coat. By six I shall have been in my father's car for hours, and we'll be well on the way to Budapest. You'll never see me again. If I am being allowed out it's obvious that you haven't told anyone what I said to you. You really do think that it was the fever speaking. You chose to believe König and not me. Now I shall tell my father everything. I know what he's like: it will be goodbye to the Matula for me. He would never leave his daughter in a class where they've been tormenting her since the start of the year.

Her father seemed very subdued, as indeed he was, but when he saw his daughter standing there in her school uniform, with the school bag hanging from her shoulder, his lips twitched and he struggled to suppress a smile. Wait till you hear the rest of it, she thought. This is just the outside, and it's already enough to drive any sane person up the wall. Now I'm going to tell you the rest of it. In this place you aren't even allowed to complain to your parents. They censor every letter we write home.

Susanna bade them goodbye at the door to the outer court-yard, waited for the two of them to go a few steps down the gravel pathway, then called Gina back. She returned reluctantly. She was desperate to find herself on the other side of that huge studded door.

"I just want to remind you that your father is burdened by the problems of the country, and that the life of an adult is a difficult one. Don't make it any more difficult for him, Georgina. If there is anything about the school that you don't like, don't complain. Allow him to go home feeling happy and reassured. I didn't trouble him with any of that nonsense you were shouting about when you were ill. The Director himself has done nothing but sing your praises, and he made no mention of the unfortunate exhibition you made of yourself at the start of term. Let this be a brief moment of happiness for your father. Do you under-stand me?"

Oh, Susanna, strict, severe Susanna! Gina gazed at her as if she, Gina, were the older of the two and not the other way around. What are you thinking? That after I've been hammering on this door all these weeks and it suddenly opens, I won't run straight out into the fresh air and freedom? That humility, or self-sacrifice, or any other of the virtues you beat into your charges with your rod of iron, will make me ultra-diplomatic and lie to my father? But she made no reply, either yes or no; she just nodded her head, a gesture that belonged less to the Matula than to the polite world of Auntie Mimó's circle. Susanna turned away, closed the door behind her, and Gina hurried back to the General's side.

The air outside was mild, almost unnaturally springlike, and twilight was beginning. To Gina's surprise work was going on in the courtyard. As a mark of honour for the Director the fifth year had volunteered for outside duty, even though it was a Saturday and a holiday. The school had had a delivery of coal that morn-ing; the ground-level windows of the cellar stood open and the girls were shovelling it inside, under the watchful eye of Sister Erzsébet. Everyone saw the two of them making their way out. Seeing Sister Erzsébet, Gina automatically stood to attention and gave the due greeting for the occasion, "I wish you good day, Sister Erzsébet. I wish you good day, girls," and the General bowed. Sister Erzsébet, deciding that Gina had behaved well and shown the politeness of a good Matula girl, ordered the class to stop what they were doing, stand to attention and return the greeting. Choking with rage and resentment, they stood holding their hated shovels and chorused the appropriate formula back to Gina and the gentleman with her, who was so very like her in appearance that he could only be her father, and who would now take her out for a nice long walk and then stuff her full of wonderful things to eat, even though she had been suffering from some ghastly stomach ache ever since last Sunday at Mitsi Horn's and they would still have to give up their precious free time to tell her what she had missed. The porter studied the exit pass at great length, scrutinised Gina from top to toe, and eventually opened the gate. At last they were out in the street, just the two of them, beyond the watching eyes. She was free!

She had spent so much time thinking about what she would say to her father when they met that as soon as they had taken their seats in the Hajda patisserie the torrent of words burst from her. The General listened with an impassive face, the face of a man only too used to hearing unpleasant news, and he studied her in silence as she held forth, ignoring the delicacies piled high on the plate before her. The things he was hearing he would normally have expected to have been accompanied by floods of tears, but Gina was not crying, or indeed complaining. She was simply reporting the facts. She laid out the reasons why she could no longer remain where she was, and why he had to remove her from the Matula forthwith: her communications were strictly censored, she wasn't allowed even to mention her problems, either in writing or on the telephone, her class had cut her dead and she had not a single friend. She couldn't live like that, it was impossible.

My God, what a tale! The weird traditions of the Matula; the brutal revenge of classmates she had betrayed in a fit of anger; Gina the despised, Gina the traitor, Gina the girl who was too proud to be married to an aquarium! The General pushed his plate of pastries away: he could no longer bear to look at it. Before leaving home he had gone to the Ministry of Defence and seen reports of the actual state of the war, details he had never previously been shown. It was all death and destruction, battles lost, armies in retreat, and the panic-stricken actions of a deranged national leadership – all that, and now the medieval freakery of the Matula, the petty cruelties of a pack of young puppies who could think of nothing more than that, in a moment of fury, Georgina Vitay had blurted out something she should not have. No, my girl, no, he said to himself. In this I cannot help you, however hard it may be for you. I simply cannot take you away.

Of course, when he was first thinking of sending her to Árkod he could have had no idea that once there she would be so alone, would have not a single friend, and that even her attempts to complain would be silenced. It was something he could never have guessed but that was how it had turned out. One way or another she would have to sort things out with her classmates, and sooner or later she would find a way.

He realised she was expecting an answer, and that far from merely hoping she was confidently expecting it to be a favourable one. To avoid her gaze and not to have to see the light in her face die with disappointment, he pulled her towards him, took her by the shoulders and told her never again to ask him what she had: he would not be taking her home. For the time being it was completely impossible.

Gina tore herself away from him as if he had not spoken but had struck her. Her eyes were filled not with the sadness he had expected but with steely defiance and rebellion.

"Then I shall run away again," she said. "And I shall do so again and again until they expel me. Would you prefer it that way?"

Run away? Again? She had already done that?

His face was as white as a sheet. And now he knew, because she spelled it out for him. He was filled with a sense of horror such as he had never felt in his whole life. The fits of sulking, the business of the aquarium, the bizarre traditions, the censorship, had all seemed a kind of game, a matter of childish pranks, childish loneliness, childish punishments for childish crimes, but what he was hearing now – his daughter climbing out of a bathroom window, fleeing across a completely strange city towards the station – was altogether different. Now it was a question of real danger, mortal danger, and not just for her but for himself and for so many others.

He would have to tell her the truth, to put his terrifying secret in the hands of this young girl, the secret he had kept from her for so long, the one that for love of her he had hoped never to have to spell out. He had to tell her, because if he did not she would run away again, and if she did manage to make her way to Budapest, it would take just one person to discover where she had been living and then it would be impossible to send her back. But there was no other school in the country where he could feel sure that no-one would be able to get at her, or from where she could not make contact with anyone outside.

Gina leaned back, took her father's hand and smiled for the first time. She had delivered her most powerful threat and she felt sure it would have its effect. It had been a struggle, but she knew she would win. They could now go back to the Matula, collect her clothes from the Sister Housekeeper and, if she really had to, say goodbye to everyone. Everyone except Kőnig. Kőnig she would never forgive.

The General stood up. There seemed no reason for him to do this, and then crane his head around like that, but there he was, on his feet and with his eyes searching every corner of the room. He was obviously looking to see if there was anyone close by, either to the right or to the left. There was not. The two love-birds who were the only other people anywhere near them were clearly no more desirous than he was of having their whispered conversation overheard: there were booths on either side of the central aisle and they were sitting in the furthest one away. There was also a large group celebrating a family anniversary, but there were too many of them to fit into a single booth and they had pulled tables up to the window and were chattering away. Mr Hajda noticed that the gentleman who had brought the little Matula girl was gazing around and immediately took umbrage. The man was unmistakably the girl's father (what else could he be? He looked so very like her); he seemed to have found something unsatisfactory with the table he had been given and was looking for somewhere more appealing – or cleaner? As if there were anywhere in the town more pleasant or more spotlessly clean than his! This gentleman – obviously not a local – was clearly ignorant of the fact that his was the best patisserie in Árkod, that it experienced none of the usual difficulties sourcing its ingredients, that it offered the very finest confections, and, whether he knew it or not, was frequented by military officers, was in fact the only such place in the city they were allowed to patronise. There might not be any of them there at the moment, but they would certainly come later that afternoon. This critical inspection was positively insulting. To spare himself the sight he withdrew into his kitchen. As he opened the door the shop filled with the delicate aromas of his trade. The scent of sugary cakes and cream buns, Gina's entire childhood paradise of happiness and laughter, became forever fused with the moment when her father sat down beside her and told her, very quietly: "My girl, you cannot leave the school, now or at any time, for as long as the war goes on."

He spoke softly, and his tone was neutral, matter-of-fact, the way it was when he talked to her about her late mother. Now she was really frightened. Her father loved her more than anyone, and if he was not going to take her home, knowing as he did how very unhappy she was in her imposed silence and rejection, and after hearing that she had already tried to run away and was prepared to do so again, then he must be about to tell her something she could never have imagined. It was like pronouncing a life sentence on a completely innocent person. There was no point in saying anything. She knew his decision was final, and that no floods of tears would ever change it.

"People's lives depend on what I am about to tell you. I never wanted you to know this, not because I didn't trust you but because I didn't want to frighten you, or heap worries on your head that you might be too young to bear. But I can't leave you here again without an explanation. If I did that you might try to run away again, or begin to lose your trust in me and in the love that binds us together. So I shall tell you, but there will be a price. From this moment onwards, Gina, your childhood is over. You are now an adult, and you will never again live as other children do. I am going to place my life, and yours, and that of many other people, in your hands. What can you swear on that you will never betray us?"

Again she leaned back in her chair, but she continued to return his gaze. Now they were both deathly pale, and the General felt his daughter's fingers grow cold in his hand. Susanna's reproachful voice was echoing in her ear: "You must never swear an oath: thou shalt not take the name of the Lord thy God in vain." But the Matula and all its precepts seemed light years away.

What will she say? he wondered. She is barely fifteen years old. What will her response be? Will she even answer me?

"On your life," she said. "I love you more than anyone in the world, and I have no mother – you have been all the mother I have. I swear on your life."

So she had understood. The colour returned to his face. He was over the first hurdle.

"Gina, we have lost the war. In truth it was lost from the start. Its aims were always bad, and so has been the way it has been conducted. We have lost so many lives now that God knows when the country will recover, and we are not yet at the end of it.

There is nothing left but to try and save as many people – the people in our towns and cities and the soldiers on the front – as can be saved, before the Germans invade and occupy the country. Those of us who know this also know what must be done. We are trying to put an end to the war. If we succeed, countless people will live. Budapest and the other cities, and what is left of the army will be spared. If we don't succeed, then the loss of human life and the general destruction will continue, and I will be caught up in it, and so will my colleagues."

She could no longer see his face directly. He had turned to look at the window, at Mr Hajda's large glass bay window with its pretty lace curtains that brought memories of peacetime and happiness and families sitting eating ice cream. But he knew she was watching him, and looking at him in a way that she had never done before.

"There is an active resistance in the country, involving both soldiers and civilians. I am one of the officers who organised the military side. If we fail, or if I personally make a mistake, I will be arrested and they will come for you. I am like any other man who fears for his child, and if, in order to blackmail me, they arrest you and torture you in my presence, I might not be strong enough to stay silent: all I will care about is that they let you go. I cannot take the risk of your becoming an instrument in the hands of our enemies. We cannot let ourselves get into the position where they try to make me forfeit my honour by means of you, or, if I do stay silent, they kill you. You would have become the sacrifice I would have to make to stay true to my oath."

She opened her mouth as if about to reply, then said nothing.

She continued to grip her father's hand, but it was now the grip of a comrade in arms, brave and comforting. It was what he had hoped for, and it gave him strength.

"Mimó is incapable of seriousness. There are always people in her house, and if anyone came after me that is where they would find you. They would use trickery. They might lure you out into one of the streets on the basis of some lie or false information, a bogus telephone call, or they could ambush you anywhere in the city. I spent months looking for a place that would be as impenetrable as a prison before I found the Matula. The reason why I don't write to you there, and why you don't write to me from there, is that no-one at home must ever know that you are in Árkod. Every Saturday I telephone you from a different town. I go to the post office in mufti to ask for the number, and when I am put through I never give my name. All I say is that I want to speak to Gina. Here, you are never allowed out of the school without an escort and no-one can get inside. As long as the war carries on, and until I can at last take you home, this is the only place in the country where you will be safe. The other day you tried to run away. If you had succeeded, and if, once you were back home, you had complained to anyone about the way things were in the Matula, I would never have been able to bring you back here because the secret would be out. If the worst then happened, and I came under suspicion, perhaps a couple of months later you would be taken hostage and the only way I could save your life would be to forfeit my honour. Is that what you want?"

She shook her head. Every contour of her face had come from

her father, but now she had taken on the look of her mother, and the General met the steady gaze of his long-dead wife. So, it's happened at last, he mused, as he studied her. It's finally happened, just as I thought it would. Your childhood is over. You have grown up, my darling.

"Apart from myself there is one other person I can entrust you to. I have already asked him to watch over you. He is the leader of the civilian opposition in the city."

It came to her in a flash:

"Another one? Where was it this time?"

"On the monument to The Sorrows of Hungary."

STOP THIS POINTLESS SHEDDING OF HUNGARIAN BLOOD! WE HAVE LOST THE WAR. SAVE THE LIVES OF YOUR CHILDREN FOR A BETTER FUTURE.

"If that person contacts you, then you can go with him. And go you must, because if he sends you anywhere outside the Matula it means that they are on your trail and he has found somewhere to hide you."

"How will I know who he is?" she whispered.

"You have known him for some time without realising who he is. When you discover who it is you will be very surprised. Now, do you still want me to take you home?"

"No," she replied.

"If by any chance I am unable to telephone you, don't try to write or contact me. Just wait. If I can, I shall call you every week, or come and see you. If I do neither, there will be a reason why I am keeping away, why I can't come. At all events, stay calm. Will you promise?"

"I promise."

"And now we must part. I know you have been given a bit more time but I must get back to Budapest. If I never see you again . . . –" his voice did not waver; it was as if he had mulled over what he was about to say many times – ". . . then you will at least know that I loved you, and you will know that I died because I wanted to free my country from a war in which there are no heroes, only victims. Kiss me, and then we must go."

Her kiss was cold, her normally glistening lips dry and lifeless. The General tapped his fork on a glass, Mr Hajda appeared and cast a reproving eye over the untouched plates. The General's gaze followed the line of his glance.

"How many girls are there in your class?" he asked.

"Twenty, including me."

"Twenty, plus the prefect with the fair hair. Shall we treat them?"

"They won't accept them, father. I tried once before."

"You must try again. There is no anger that lasts forever."

Mr Hajda's face brightened. He was asked to pack up the pastries left on the plate, along with another thirty. They filled two large boxes; Gina had difficulty carrying them.

Once outside, they barely spoke. She did not look at him. She kept her eyes fixed on the road ahead, while he kept his on the street, in the squat black-and-white city to which he had entrusted his greatest treasure. An austere city, a stern one, worthy of his trust.

"I won't go in with you," he said, when they reached the gate. "You go on by yourself. It will be easier for us both."

"Yes, father."

"Have you forgotten anything?"

"Nothing."

"So now you know everything. Can you be true to your word, even when you feel you can bear it no longer?"

"I shall be true," Gina replied.

This time they did not kiss. Gina did not cry, nor did she smile. "You have given me your word," the General said again, and the girl nodded once more. He rang the bell and the great studded door opened before them. Gina immediately went in, and the porter – as if he knew what they had been through at parting – left it open until her youthful form reached the end of the corridor and finally disappeared. The General watched her as she went, a large parcel in either hand; she never once looked back, perhaps to ease the pain of parting. As she walked towards the dormitory block her back seemed to stoop a little, as if she carried the weight of the world's burdens on her shoulders.

The statue speaks

She was now in a hurry, on her way not to the sick bay but to the dormitory, and trying hard to think of somewhere to hide the boxes of pastries before another ritual humiliation could take place. But she was stopped by Susanna, coming the other way down the corridor. She expressed surprise that Gina should have claimed so little of her permitted time and asked her if she had come back early because she was feeling ill again. Gina reassured her: she and her father had discussed everything that mattered and he had to get back to Budapest; she was now on her way to the kitchen with these boxes of pastries. The sight of them filled Susanna with delight: the class had finished their voluntary labours and were sitting in the bath washing off the coal dust before getting ready for their tea, and a bit of extra cheer would be most welcome after all that shovelling. Except that they won't eat them, Gina thought. They'll throw them away again. But she no longer cared.

This was the new Gina, the one who had come into being such a short time earlier that day in the Hajda patisserie. She no longer saw life in terms of petty wrongs and insults, and certainly not by the number of pastries that might or might not be eaten. She was trying to take on board everything she had learned from her father – not something to be done all at once – and she was relieved when Susanna reminded her that she had an hour of her free time left and if she liked she could go to the music room after tea; she should take her book of psalms and her Bible, read the Holy Scriptures, memorise some hymns, and play the piano if the urge took her.

She hung her coat up in the deserted corridor. Going into the washroom she could tell where the others were by the voices coming from behind the closed bathroom doors. Those who had finished must have gone to the day room – she could hear someone singing. She was not feeling especially happy just then, but she could not help smiling. Much to the delight of the deaconesses the class had taken to singing canticles in their so-called "quiet time". Following a rota, one of them would bellow out a psalm so that the others could carry on talking without fear of rebuke ("filling your precious moments of contemplation with idle chatter!"). Their little games and cunning schemes, their anger and their acts of spitefulness seemed miles away from her now, she in whom the General had placed his trust, who was the bearer of secrets in whose recesses lurked the shadow of death. At this point she would much rather have been left on her own. If one could put a name to what she now felt towards her classmates whispering their silly school jokes and nursing their petty grievances under cover of the sacred music, it would have been envy rather than anger. Happy those whose greatest concern was what practical joke they might play on Kőnig the next day, what was the worst sort of punishment they could expect if they were caught, and what a fine blow they could strike at her now by treating Mr Hajda's pastries like so much rubbish. "We have lost the war, our soldiers are dying pointlessly, every one of them who falls is a victim, nothing more than a victim, and the reasons for the war are all bad. The war is illegitimate. That's not what Mr Kalmár teaches us, and it's not what he thinks, but then everyone I've met here thinks as he does – apart from someone I don't know, or rather do apparently know but haven't yet identified, the leader of the civil resistance."

By the time she had washed, tidied herself up and collected her hymn book and Bible the rest of the class were ready too, and they all trotted down for their tea. Erzsébet, who had supervised the coal-shovelling, had already shared out the pastries, along with the usual apples and croissants. "Those who do good work deserve a special surprise," she told the class. They seemed paralysed with joy for a few seconds, then promptly devoured them. Gina heard Nacák say that the school must be suffering from senile dementia, or the Last Judgement must be at hand, because that was what she had read in the Book of Revelations. A few weeks earlier the seventh year had been given a similar voluntary task on a day when the school was due to send a parcel of food to the front, and the Director had suggested that, to honour their splendid efforts, their weekly apples and cakes should be included in it.

"These are from a patisserie," Jackó whispered. "Perhaps Erzsébet has fallen in love. It's such a new experience for her she's lost her wits and this is the result." Gina prayed that the others would believe this, and she was on the point of thinking she might escape a second humiliation when Erzsébet, with her inborn love of the truth, spoiled everything and told the class the full story. They stood to attention, as required, while the class monitor expressed their gratitude to the Director and Governors for acknowledging their voluntary work through the gift of pastries, though of course they were always happy to labour without reward because God loved the work of busy hands. At this point Erzsébet shook her head and told them that the pastries were a present from Georgina Vitay's father, and he was the one to be thanked. There was a moment's silence, and all faces turned towards Gina. The monitor stood up again and, with a diplomatic froideur that would have withered an elder statesman, delivered the approved formula: "We thank Georgina Vitay's father for his kindness from the bottom of our hearts."

"You may now leave the refectory," Erzsébet concluded, "and go to the sewing room and mend your clothes until supper – except for Georgina Vitay, who has forty-five minutes of free time left."

The class filed out. Gina went to the music room, sat down facing the door and waited. She was so sure that something was about to happen it was as if she had been forewarned. She wanted only to get it over and done with, not just because it might be extremely unpleasant but because she had no time now for these games. She needed to think, and to incorporate what she had been told into her thinking.

The fact was that there could be no escaping her situation. Whatever the attitude of the other girls to her, and whatever the consequences, she would have to remain where she was. So far she had thought of the fortress simply as a prison; now she knew it as much more than that. It was a place of refuge. A bleak one, no doubt, but one she would have to put up with. She would have to make her peace with the rest of the class and persuade Mari Kis, as quickly as she could, to give her back the things she had found in her bed, beginning with, and above all, the letter. The great solution that had so far presented itself to her, to get herself expelled if she couldn't run away, was now out of the question. But if her letter, that dreadful farewell note that Mari Kis now had in her possession, should ever, either from anger or revenge, be put in the hands of a teacher or Susanna, she would not escape expulsion. How, without betraying what her father had confided in her, could she persuade Mari Kis, first, not to make a terrifying use of what she had found and destroy her, and second, to forgive her? If Gina tried to speak to her she would simply turn her back and refuse to answer her. The idea was out of the question. And then, why had Mari waited so long? It was almost a week since the tea at Mitsi Horn's, following which she would have found the letter. She could have given it to the Prefect at any time during the last five or six days. She would have to have a word with her in private, keeping calm and rational. But when? Mari Kis would never give her the chance. It was unthinkable.

But the chance soon presented itself. The attack she had been so long expecting was under way, and Mari Kis was the standard bearer for the class. She marched into the room, closed the door behind her and went straight to the piano, where Gina's psalm book lay open on the music stand. Her bag was slung over her shoulder. She unhitched it, opened it and hurled the contents onto the piano. Ten- and twenty-fillér coins came tumbling out in a shower.

"Nineteen times two pastries, thirty-eight pastries," she announced. "One pastry, thirty fillér – at least that was the price when we were last in a patisserie. If the price has gone up since then, let me know and we'll make up the difference."

"Give it back to me," said Gina. She did not look at the money. "I beg you, in the name of all you love and hold dear, give it back. If you want, I'll clean your shoes for a whole year, I'll do anything, whatever you ask, anything. I'll wear a sign on my back saying what an idiot I am, and what a traitor. I promise I'll even wear it in the garden. In the name of mercy, Mari, give it back to me!"

Mari Kis stared at her. A completely different Vitay returned her gaze, one she had never seen before: either she had gone mad or she was drunk.

"It's our money for Sunday's church collection, you scum. Because of you the entire class will now have to put nickel-plated buttons in the collection box, and where can we possibly find enough between now and tomorrow? If Susanna notices that we aren't putting real coins in we'll be done for. Perhaps you should just give us away first, before she catches us – just go and tell her to watch us on the day, and watch us closely. We have nothing left now, after what I have just given you. From now until Christmas the only cash Susanna will let us have out of our pocket money will be for the church and charity."

"Just give me the letter and you can do what you like with me," Gina said. "Anything, do you understand? If that means hitting me, then go ahead. I won't hit back. Or if you prefer, I could fall from the top of the wall bars in the gym and make it look like an accident; if you're lucky, I might even break a leg. You don't know what I'm talking about? My letter, the one you found under my bed! You can keep everything else – my comb, my powder box, my diary, the purse, the photo album, even the bunch of keys, though I've no idea what you would do with the keys to someone else's house. Do you hear me? Just tell me what I have to do! You wouldn't even have to talk to me. I no longer want you to take me back. All I want is the letter."

"I found something under your mattress?" Mari Kis retorted. She was now furious. "I never met anyone quite as shameless as you! You made us eat your filthy pastries, we ate them in good faith because we had no idea you were trying to foist them on us again, and when we try to pay you for them – because we want nothing from you, we would rather starve – you are as brazen as ever. So I've stolen something from you? If I had found anything of yours in your bed, when I went and fetched your nightdress, do you really think I would have picked it up and stolen it? You have the gall to tell me there was something in your bed when there was absolutely nothing? Just you wait, Vitay! If you think that these slanders will get you out of trouble, then you really don't know the fifth year!"

And she flounced out of the door in such a passion that she forgot that she was supposed to walk on tiptoe and behave decorously, not least because she was not officially allowed to visit Vitay, who was still in her allotted free time and supposed to be reading the Bible and strengthening her soul with religious music. Instead she slammed the door behind her with such force that the painting of Geneva Cathedral over the mantelpiece jumped in its frame and almost hurled itself to the floor. Gina stood staring after her. She did not doubt for a second that Mari Kis had been telling the truth, that she truly had not taken anything from the bed, only the nightdress. So then, her things must be with Susanna. She must have found them when Gina sent her to the dormitory to look for evidence. She could now breathe easily again, because if the Prefect had kept silent about them all this time then she obviously intended to protect her: she must have destroyed the letter and hidden the other things to stop their being used against her. Dear, lovely, noble Susanna! Her heart spilled over with gratitude: with the Prefect's help she had been spared. The class still hated her, and when they knew what she had accused Mari Kis of they would hate her even more, but never mind. She could put up with that.

She gathered up the coins and stuffed them into her pockets until they were so full they bulged visibly. When she left the music room she would shield them with her Bible, and tomorrow she would take them to church in her shoulder bag, push her way to the front of the queue, and as soon as someone was watching she would explain that she had been asked by the rest of the form to put all their money into the collection in one go. Then perhaps they wouldn't try their stupid stunt with the buttons. The trick would be discovered soon enough anyway, as soon as the box was opened and word got back to the Matula, so what would have been the point?

The old Gina would have been only too pleased if they had

got themselves into trouble; she would have paraded her own sixty fillér before one of the teachers as proof that she had had nothing to do with the buttons and been more than happy to leave the others to incriminate themselves. But not now. It would be yet another problem that she had brought upon them, and it would enrage the innocent Mari Kis even more.

She raised the lid of the piano and started to pick her way through a particularly difficult psalm. *In the greatness of Thy wrath, do not chastise me.* (There was something they didn't show in that news film we saw: all that blood was shed to no purpose.) *Do not chastise me, oh Lord* . . . (Auntie Mimó knows nothing about these things. In his lessons on national defence Mr Kalmár says that this person who is trying to undermine public morale . . .) *as You look upon me and grieve in Your heart* . . . (. . . is a traitor. The person he thinks of as a traitor is actually a hero. And I have been entrusted to his care. He must be the one who left the leaflets on Mitsi Horn's pew, and who wrote those words on the monument to The Sorrows of Hungary. Kalmár is quite wrong. They have all been misled . . .) . . . *do not chastise me, oh Lord* . . . (I can't let them track me down here. I must make myself as indistinguishable from the others as a drop of water in a stream . . .) *In Thy great wrath* . . . (so that my father can go about his work without worrying about me. I cannot take the slightest risk that they might use me to blackmail him.) . . . *In Thy great wrath, do not chastise me, oh Lord* . . . (We must try to save the lives of our soldiers. The war was started for all the wrong reasons. My father's associates are trying to save the country.) . . . *as You look upon me and grieve in Your heart.* (I shall be strong. I shall be wise. I shall be patient. If only my father's enterprise can succeed! And may we all get out of this alive.) *Do not chastise me, oh Lord.*

"You aren't singing?" It was Susanna.

She was standing behind her. Gina had not noticed her come in. The gratitude she felt rose up in her and she had to stop herself from rushing towards the dear, kind person who had saved her without even knowing what she was saving her from. But she stayed where she was. She knew that any such behaviour would bring instant correction – girls were not allowed to touch, let alone kiss, a member of staff. And she realised that if Susanna was indeed protecting her she would want her to keep very quiet about it.

"Your time is up," the Prefect said. "Your class have finished their sewing, so you can go and join in their games in the day room."

Gina left the room walking very circumspectly, holding her Bible out in front of her and taking care not to jingle the coins in her pockets. Susanna did not follow her, so she went down to the end of the corridor and poured the money into her bag. Then she slipped into the day room, fully aware that the Saturday relaxation period before supper would not bring her very much pleasure. The fifth year knew some rather spiteful little games and this session would give free reign to their mood: the teacher in charge that evening was Kőnig, who never seemed to notice anything.

The game consisted of one person leaving the room while the others decided who she was supposed to be. She would then be called back in, and her task was to find out who they had decided that person was by putting questions to people she called out by name. Oláh drew the first lot. She slipped out quickly while Kőnig dozed. It was impossible to guess what he was thinking about, but they could be sure that he wouldn't hear a word, and even if he did hear he would have no idea what was going on.

Mari Kis nominated Gina with a toss of her chin. That's right, Gina thought. Go ahead with your little prank, you lucky people. Pretend that Oláh is now Vitay, and use your questions and answers to show what a nasty, loathsome person I am. Enjoy your little frolic if it makes you happy. Our soldiers are dying at the front and no-one in the country knows the truth. And neither do any of you.

Oláh was called back in and put her first question to Torma.

"Human or thing?"

"Human," said Torma with a smile.

Oláh turned towards Ari. "Real or fictional?"

"Real," Ari confirmed.

"Am I a boy or a girl? Salm."

"A girl. *Feminini generis.*"

"Do I know this person? Lengyel."

"Only too well."

"Am I a Matula girl?"

"That's what you think you are."

"Do people like me? Vajda."

"About as much as a goat likes having his throat cut."

"Good God, why? Mari Kis."

"Because you're scum."

Oláh's eyes lit up. She's got it, thought Gina. Who else could it be but me? Who else here is liked about as much as a goat likes having his throat cut, who isn't a real member of the school or a true member of this form, and who is considered scum?

"Good God! What have I done?" was the next question. Oláh's eyes shone with suppressed mirth as she gazed round her classmates. Equally amused, they returned her gaze but said nothing.

"So what can I possibly have done? Vitay."

"You stupidly betrayed a secret," Gina replied quietly. Everyone's eyes were now trained on her. Her face showed no emotion. Vitay was neither complaining nor angry, or even embarrassed. She had denied nothing, nor had she pretended not to understand the thrust of the question. As strange as the feeling was, they could not shake off the impression that she was playing with them, but playing the way an adult does when joining in with the children. But that made no sense. If she wasn't hurt, or fuming with rage, then what was the point of it all? Oláh was thoroughly confused. She had expected an entirely different answer, something altogether more tearful and angry, that would have set her up for the final thrust. But what could she ask her now? She thought the game would have been more fun than this.

"I know who I am," she said sulkily. "Who's going next?"

By the rules of the game it should have been the person whose reply had produced the answer. But Vitay? Could they let her join in? How would that work? They couldn't have the same person again, and there was no-one else who would make it worth the while. The class stood silent. Not even Mari Kis could think of a solution.

Kőnig looked up. Strange as it might seem, it was as if the

sudden absence of noise had a greater effect on him than its opposite.

"Who was this person," he asked, "that you identified so quickly?"

"Augustus Caesar," Szabó replied sulkily. "But we aren't playing anymore. May we talk instead?"

"But of course," said Kőnig. And he sank back into his ruminations.

Gina went over to the window and stood with her elbows resting on the sill. She couldn't see out because the view of the garden was blocked by the blackout lining, but at least she was away from the others and did not have to hear Mari Kis telling everyone about her latest crime, and how it surpassed all the others. She tried to imagine what it would be like if every window in the country could be left open and every street flooded with light, and there was no war and none of this dying, no burdensome secrets, no danger or destruction. She thought about her father, and the car, now approaching Budapest, its horn sounding from time to time, and remembered that moment when it sang out to her *Gina my child,* and she thought of Feri, who almost certainly must know everything her father knew, being so clever and wise, and so unlike anyone else she knew; he was part of Auntie Mimó's circle, he always spoke of her father with great affection and he had so often asked if he could visit her at their home, even though, as she also remembered, every time she raised the subject the General had replied that no officers would ever be allowed there and Lieutenant Kuncz was no exception. Perhaps he especially wanted to keep Feri away from the house to avoid putting him in danger? But surely a lieutenant would attract less suspicion than a general?

The bell rang for supper. Kőnig – it singled him out for special derision – was chronically afraid of catching a cold: even if he was going by way of the internal corridors rather than through the open courtyard he would always tie a scarf round his throat and take his overcoat, which he kept hanging on the window latch instead of on the rack. As the class were about to leave he lifted it down and discovered to his amazement that there was not a single button on it. Oh my God, tomorrow's church collection! Gina thought. They've stolen his buttons. They must have started collecting already. And though her mind was filled with other, more serious matters, she almost laughed at the faces he was pulling, and at Mari Kis dancing around him with a face of sympathy and concern and asking had he been on the tram that day, because, you know, people often lost their buttons in the crush, and, what a shame, they were such lovely pale-grey buttons too, every one as bright as a coin, and how hard it was going to be to find new ones to replace them. Kőnig moaned and groaned, and then, as always, resigned himself to what had happened and led the class off to supper.

Gina ate only half of hers, pleading her illness. Yes, she was on a special regime but no, she didn't want any of the stewed fruit, she really couldn't eat a thing. Susanna asked her who she wanted to give it to. Gina stared helplessly in front of her, knowing that none of the girls would accept it. But then that notorious gourmand Kőnig called out from the staff table and put in his bid for the unwanted delicacy. The other teachers lowered their eyes, as did Gedeon Torma, fighting down the urge to bark a reprimand at the glutton. Gina flew to Kőnig's side with the dish and set it down before him, desperately wanting to see it disappear and not to have to look at it again: now at least she wouldn't have to explain why the class had refused it. Miss Gigus and Eszter Sáfár muttered something to one another, Kalmár shook his head, and Murai whispered, "This Kőnig is capable of anything." They were even angrier with him than usual because if he hadn't been such a barrel of lard Vitay would have had to pass the wretched bowl of stewed cherries round the table.

Things were calmer during evening prayers. The Chaplain was talking about the honour of being a Christian woman. His theme was that, "As the scented rose adorns the rose bush, so do the virtues of long-suffering, patience, gentleness and neighbourly love adorn a Christian maiden."

All my life I have been a wild thing, Gina reflected. I am impatient and impulsive, and I have never learned to love people who annoy me or try to hurt me. Now I shall try to learn these virtues, and I shall do so for the sake of my father: for him I shall seek to be gentle and patient.

She looked around, though to do so was considered inappropriate and was in fact forbidden, and caught the eye of Piroska Torma. Torma gazed steadily at her for a moment, then turned her eyes away. It was only later that Gina learned that she was thinking the same about herself, how she lacked these adorning virtues, as did almost everyone else in the class, and how could they hope to be welcomed at the Lord's table at Christmas if they had not themselves forgiven Vitay?

The class did not go for their usual bath before bedtime, having already done so after shovelling the coal. Instead Susanna allowed them an extra hour of reading or quiet conversation, as they preferred, in the dormitory. Being back again was a change for Gina, and, after the loneliness and silence of the sick bay, a welcome one. But no-one spoke to her, not even to say hurtful things. She was not mentioned once: it was as if she had never existed. She made no attempt to read; she just snuggled down in the bed in which she had not slept for a week and thought about her father, and their last conversation, and what she had been taught about the war by Kalmár and at her old school, and what people had said about it at Auntie Mimó's.

Salm stood guard at the door while the girls giggled away. Tubby little Szabó was doing an elaborate oriental dance in her nightdress; the others had gathered round her and were doubled up with laughter. Gina wanted to fall asleep quickly, but it was impossible. Too much had happened during the day, she had far too much to think about, and somehow the bed felt different; it felt more like the one in the sick bay, even though she had made it herself the previous Sunday morning. Of course! Susanna had been poking around under the mattress; she must have put it back differently . . .

It was now very late. Only the nightlight was on, and the class, worn out by their games and their laughter, were deep in slumber. She decided to get up and deal with the problem: she really needed to sleep. From now on she would have to be strong and fit, and she had promised to take better care of herself. She slipped out from under the quilt, pushed back the sheet and gently lifted the mattress to make it level and put it back the way it had been. She slid her fingers underneath it, and drew them back as quickly as if they had been cut by a knife. For a few minutes she squatted beside the bed, her heart beating wildly; then she recovered herself, pulled out everything her hands had felt and spread it out on the bedcover: her powder puff, her comb, her pocket diary, her purse, the photograph album, the key to the house – everything that had been there before, and then . . . the letter, the farewell note, the one she had so earnestly begged Mari Kis to give her back. There it lay, the very page she had torn out, unharmed and intact. But the words she had written seemed to have grown in number.

I despise the lot of you. Carry on with your stupid little games in this prison. I'm leaving.

I KNEW WHEN YOU TRIED TO RUN AWAY THAT YOU WOULD NOT DO SO WITHOUT LEAVING A NOTE. AS SOON AS YOU LEFT FOR MITSI HORN'S I GATHERED UP YOUR BELONGINGS, INCLUDING THIS UNFORTU-NATE NOTE. TEAR IT UP AND MAKE PEACE WITH YOUR CLASS – THEY ARE A FINE BUNCH OF GIRLS. IF YOU ARE IN DIFFICULTIES, WHY NOT TURN TO ME? YOUR SECRET IS NOT THE ONLY ONE I KEEP.

ABIGAIL

Air-raid practice

All this time she had been crouching down beside the bed. Now she fell to her knees and laid her head on the bedcover next to the letter and the precious mementos of home. Her eyelids began to droop, as if weighed down by the immensity of what had occurred, as if the reality of what she had seen was too blinding to contemplate. Abigail, you worker of miracles, you who always come to our aid, who resolve all our little difficulties, why did I not fathom your secret when I was first told about you? What, in my contempt for the credulity of the others, when I still thought of them as childish and stupid, made me think that you too were just another example of Matula imbecility? Why was I so slow to understand that in this forest of rules and instructions and prohibitions there might be someone, not a mere stone statue but a real person hiding behind it, ready to help anyone with a genuine need? My classmates are totally unforgiving, and any kindness shown here by the staff, when it is ever shown, is remote and impersonal, simply the way of the school. This place gives me security, but there is no warmth. I ran away because I was desperate for human contact. I did not know then that I am not alone, that there was someone here who cared about me, was here to help me, who had been watching over me without my ever suspecting it or asking for it, and doing so even when I refused to believe that such a thing was possible.

Who are you, Abigail? You live with us here in the Matula, you move among us, shout or smile at us, are so familiar to us that you can walk in and out of the dormitories without attracting attention, or rummage in our pockets and leaf through our exercise books. You always know what we are whispering about, you see everything, and yet no-one ever even notices you. There is someone inside these fortress walls who lives a secret life, who keeps their face hidden, someone who shouts at us and scolds us, treats us either with obsequious politeness or presents him- or herself as harsh and overbearing, so that they can maintain that disguise and move around freely; someone who understands that we are all far from our parents and relations at home, and also knows how much the school demands from us, that it is often more than we can bear, and that it puts us in situations in which any one of us might come to grief. Who are you, Abigail, you whose true face no-one has ever seen, whom we know only by the actions that you've been carrying out inside these walls for thirty years? You must be either the same person who heard the young Mitsi Horn weeping or you are constantly being replaced by a new Abigail, like the Cumaean sibyl. She changed too. A fresh young priestess would always take over, don the dread robes of the underworld, and continue the tradition. Are you old, or young? A woman, or a man? What does your real face look like? When I stand before you in your everyday form, do I like you or am I afraid of you? How could you know me so well that you knew I wanted to run away, and that once I had decided to do so I would never go without leaving a note? If you hadn't discovered that, or worked it out for yourself, how could you have been so sure that I would do what I did? You couldn't possibly have overheard what I told Susanna in the sick bay. If only I could see you, and take you by the hand! As it is, I can't even thank you for what you have done. Who are you, Abigail?

She opened her eyes again. The sheet of white paper lay there before her eyes, but its physical form told her nothing. Any member of the school, any of the teachers, the deaconesses, or indeed the pupils, could have shaped those capital letters; the school had its own distinctive way of writing them, one that imitated the slender elegance and open clarity of print. So that was no help. If she wanted to track down Abigail's secret she would have to follow a different trail. The person she was trying to identify must be truly remarkable if they did not share the general Matula view of what was unacceptable or indeed criminal. They would have to be immensely brave to take on the enormous risk that one day they might be exposed. Any one of their colleagues with different ideas about how to educate children might easily realise who they were and unmask them. But which member of staff was clever and resourceful enough to come unfailingly to the aid of those needing help, in so many different situations?

And thus she knelt before the familiar objects, racking her brain and making no progress. Abigail would not be Abigail if she or he were the sort of person who might easily give themselves away through their actions. It must be someone very un-Abigail-like, someone, say, like Gedeon Torma, with his dreadful bellowings and unbelievable demands for conformity, or Susanna, with her puritanical streak that could verge on the terrifying, or even Kalmár, who was so aloof and so distant, and so strict. It could be any member of the teaching staff who was adept and quick-witted enough, able to react at lightning speed, and a good enough actor never to have given herself or himself away in all these years, moving quietly among the girls at every level in the school, and standing with arms opened wide behind any one of them who might slip on the narrow path that wound through the thousand-and-one prohibitions and injunctions of the Matula, ready to catch her as she fell and hold her until she could stand firmly again on her own two feet.

Midnight.

Yes, Abigail, I am coming. I know that you want me to sleep.

She stood up and put on her dressing gown. She gathered up her newly recovered possessions and the letter, and tiptoed out to the washroom. The first thing she did was to destroy the piece of paper, tearing it into pieces small enough to make it impossible for anyone to reassemble it; then she took her belongings out of her handbag and laid them where she had on the first occasion, under the box of geraniums. On the way back she met no-one, and none of the girls so much as stirred in their slumbers. She put her bed in order and lay down. Now at last she could sleep. For the first time since she had fallen out with the class she felt that someone, some unknown person inside those massive walls, was thinking about her, and had smiled, she fancied, at the look on her face when she discovered her precious belongings.

The next morning the groans of the others told her that the

wake-up bell had rung half an hour earlier than usual. No-one knew what was happening until Susanna ordered them to line up and at last they were told. The service would not be taken by the Chaplain. It was to be a visiting priest from the city, one of the leading lights of Árkod theology and a well-known preacher. Especially good behaviour would be expected from every one of them, and the purpose of the early waking was to give the prefects time to make sure that their charges would rise to the occasion, would behave as they should in church, and would set forth to hear the word of the Lord immaculate in both person and dress, and with their hair done with a respectful and modest grace, in honour of the distinguished speaker.

Susanna's notion of "modest grace" was never likely to accord with the desperate attempts the class made, at least on Sundays, when their afternoon outing put them in full view of the citizens of Árkod. They did their best to make something aesthetically pleasing of their locks while ostensibly conforming to the boot-lace-and-plaits-style favoured by the regulations, and naturally the Prefect made almost every one of them comb and tie their efforts afresh. Salm whispered that they looked as if they had dead mice strung up behind their ears and the shoelaces were tokens of mourning. Normally the prospect of having to venture outside the gate with their appearance rendered even more hideous than usual would have produced an outcry, but this was not now their main concern. What exercised them just then was the importance of the event and how that might affect the collection. If the sermon was to be given by such an eminent speaker, then, as had happened on previous occasions, it would not be the usual members of the parish council (all of them more or less senile and purblind) who would be standing there to receive their offerings but their teachers, and God help them if the box allocated to the fifth year fell to Gedeon Torma, or Éles of the piercing eyes that could see through brick walls! Mari Kis began to be seriously afraid; she whispered something to Murai and dashed out of the dormitory. Gina guessed where she had gone, and for what purpose.

They were now about to set off, and Mari still had not returned to her place in the line. Though she had no reason to wish her well or to be concerned on her behalf, Gina wondered what would happen if Susanna gave the order to go and she was still missing. But she appeared at the very last moment, took her usual place on Gina's left, and whispered to Torma that "it hadn't worked". She had raced round all the other classes to ask if by chance any of their parents had given them some money on the recent visit that they hadn't declared, and if so, could they borrow it? But no-one anywhere had a brass farthing more than what had been doled out for the collection. Gina longed to say to her, "Don't you worry, the full amount, every single fillér you so insultingly threw at me yesterday, is here in my bag. Everything will be fine. When the time comes I won't let the teachers catch you putting those buttons in the collection box, the ones you stole from Kőnig and God knows who else." But she said nothing, not because she wanted to prolong the girl's anxiety but because she simply did not dare to speak to her. Ever since she had been accused of theft Mari Kis had been more implacably angry than ever.

Later, as an adult, Gina often thought of that particular Sunday service, during which she had heard not a single word of what was said and knew that none of the rest of her class had either. They had just sat there, every one of them, stealing occasional glances at their watches to avoid being caught by Susanna and wondering anxiously which of their teachers would be standing beside the box on the left-hand side of the church, near the door through which they would have to file out. The visiting speaker had no doubt composed a particularly fine sermon for the edification of their souls, but even the Lord's Prayer passed them by, and not one of them could have said which hymn had been sung to the mighty rumblings of the organ as they moved towards the exit, though it was one they had practised so many times down the years that they had begun to intone it as soon as the instrument started up. Normally too, they would have had to be reminded how unseemly it was to be in such haste to get out onto the street, but this time Susanna had to urge them in a loud whisper to move along more quickly. And there, at the door on the left-hand side, beside the collection box, stood a personage even more terrifying than Gedeon Torma: the Chaplain himself. Gina heard Mari Kis draw her breath in the moment she saw him. He stood there patiently, viewing them with the solemn air of benign and complacent pride that he reserved for girls who were always so immaculately turned out, who were meek and silent and so very well brought up – such fertile soil for the good seed he had sown. Torma uttered a faint squawk, which only Gina walking beside her heard, under a particularly loud blast of the organ. "Sweet Jesus," she whispered. "What's going to happen when he sees the buttons?"

As usual they were now in single file: it was impossible to proceed otherwise down the narrow concrete strip between the pews. Alphabetically, Ari was supposed to lead them to the collection box, but as she stepped, ashen-faced, towards the Chaplain, Gina broke from the line and, acting as if under instruction, hurried forward and pushed in ahead of her. Susanna was supervising the procession from the rear and had no chance to send her back or ask what she was up to, and Gina arrived at the collection box unhindered. She opened her bag, reached inside and began to spill the coins out very slowly, while the fifth year stood waiting behind her like a row of geese, unable to move forward until she had finished. Everyone saw what she was doing, the Chaplain best of all. He nodded to show that he had taken note, and when Gina had finally crammed everything into the large wooden box he stepped back to allow the others to pass. They went out as fast as they could, in total silence, and began to line up again in the street. Gina said nothing, and no-one asked her any questions. Susanna came up to her and told her that if ever again she wanted to speed up the departure by collecting the money in advance and handing it in for the others in this way, she should ask permission. She might have found a clever solution to the problem of how quickest to leave the church, but she should never again attempt any such thing without speaking to the Prefect first.

Mari Kis maintained her silence, as did Torma, and, most unusually, none of the fifth year said a word until they had hung up their coats and bags and were back in the dormitory. Then of course they all began to talk at once. Gina went out into the corridor, not wanting to hear what they had to say. Eventually she began to worry that one of the deaconesses would find her loitering there (they were supposed to stay inside the day room until supper) and she decided to go back in. During her absence a decision had been made: unanimous rejection. She was not surprised, nor was she especially pained by it. Listening to Mari Kis she reflected that she hadn't done what she had to win their approval but because she couldn't bear the thought of seeing them get themselves into trouble for the second time, over those stupid buttons.

"If you expect us to be swooning with gratitude, then you are very mistaken," Mari Kis told her. "We aren't swooning with anything. We don't want or expect anything from you, and you needn't fancy yourself as the person who came to our rescue."

Gina looked at her, said nothing, but did not lower her gaze.

"Nacák's aunt is coming next week, and she's asked her for the money. She'll give it to her in private and we'll be returning your crummy fillér. Try to get it into your head, Vitay, that you aren't going to ingratiate yourself with us either with your pastries or your self-sacrificial deeds, so there's no point in trying."

"That's fine," Gina said. "That isn't why I did it. You can give me back the money if you like, and I'll put it into the Christmas collection box for the soldiers. I don't want any handouts from you. I don't want or expect anything from you. But setting that aside, I am truly sorry for what I said yesterday, that you had taken my letter. That was another stupid thing I did."

Mari Kis turned her back on Gina, as if to say that she didn't need anything from her either, and certainly not her apologies. But once again she noticed Torma looking at her pensively, and Salm too, no less steadily or thoughtfully . . . as was Csató, and even Murai. But nothing further was said, and soon the class were chattering away again. Gina picked up a book and sat reading it until supper. Susanna came hurrying down the corridor, looked into the day room and told her that she could have the rest of the day to relax, but it would be back to work for her on Monday because she had missed a full week's lessons.

Supper was a rather more sombre occasion than usual, and it ended on an unexpected note.

Gedeon Torma, who led the after-supper prayers, made an announcement to the whole school: Georgina Vitay, knowing that the Sunday service called for an especially high standard of conduct from the pupils, and wanting to speed up the process of leaving the building, had taken the trouble to gather the collection money from all the girls in her class beforehand, and, acting on their behalf and wanting to express the depth of their sisterly solidarity, had put the thirty fillér each of them had raised into the box. That allowed the fifth year to be the first out of the church, and in a much more orderly way than on previous occasions. Although she acted without first securing permission, the governors considered that she had found a practical and elegant solution to the problem, and they urged all the other classes to choose a different member of the form every week to do the same for them, following Vitay's fine example.

"Sisterly solidarity . . ." But Torma had turned her eyes away. Once again, as so many times before, Gina had a sense of being trapped in the chilly, suffocating air inside a bell-jar. And this time it really did hurt, because she could do nothing about it. How could she have known that the action she had taken to help them would end up this way? Susanna beamed at her, and Erzsébet too. Susanna seemed delighted beyond words that for once Gina's name was being linked to something other than acts of dire delinquency.

She spent the afternoon before the usual walk sitting in the day room. Without telling her, the fifth year had asked for and been given permission to put on their gym clothes and were enjoying ball games in the sports hall. When Susanna next saw her, as they were lining up to go out, she asked her with an air of concern if she had a sore hand, and had that stopped her joining in with the others? And she gently reproached her: the next time she fell in the corridor and hurt her wrist she should tell either her or the doctor, one never knew whether it was something simple or a bad sprain. Could she move it more easily now? She should be sensible and take better care of herself. (Oh, these girls: what liars they were!)

Gina was no longer interested in where the walk took them. Now that she no longer planned to run away there was no point in getting to know the city better. The previous day had vanished into the remote past: it was as if she had not seen her father for years. The Hajda patisserie – they were now passing in front of it – was the site of a long-vanished paradise, the last place where she had been happy and buoyed up by hope, where she had still believed that she might one day escape from this place where there was such unrelenting hostility towards her, and where, even when she tried to do something good, it turned out badly and every step she took left her in an even deeper mess. If all she could do was wait to be released, then it was going to be difficult to go on living there. But wait she would. She had given her word.

The latter part of the afternoon passed as usual. The lucky ones who had friends sat in the day room while one of their number belted out psalms so that the others could chatter to their hearts' content. Gina decided to go into the garden: she wanted to visit the statue of Abigail. She picked some bright yellow Michaelmas daisies, thinking she might put them in the basket to tell her that she had received her gifts and they were her way of thanking her for what she had done. But she never got there. She was still some way short of the statue when Kalmár found her and asked her, rather brusquely, what she was doing in the garden at that time. She had not been given permission to be there on her own, so would she please go inside? As she made her way back, with the now pointless flowers in her hand, the bizarre thought struck her that perhaps Kalmár was the person she was looking for. She had always seen him as a kind of St George, a knight in shining armour. If it was true, as she now thought, that there was an ongoing succession of Abigails, with a stream of new people taking on the role, why should it not be Kalmár, who was so brave, so quick, so competent, and so young? She was still toying with this idea when she reached the foyer. She was trying to think where outside the staff living quarters he was free to pass without attracting attention, and the answer was: everywhere. The school was as open to him as it was to any of the boarders.

Supper was a quiet affair, extremely dull, and the story of the pious Swiss maiden seemed to her more tedious and oppressive than ever. After evening prayers she made no attempt to join in the activities of the rest of the class. She was the first to have her bath and get into bed: all she wanted to do was to lie down and surrender to oblivion. Perhaps a nice long dream would refresh her. She had fallen asleep late the previous night, and the morning had brought her nothing but stress. Soon she was deep in slumber, and shortly afterwards so too were the rest of the class. Silence and peace reigned throughout the Matula.

At one in the morning the sirens went off.

They knew at once what it meant. Kalmár was the school's air-raid warden and he had taught even the littlest ones what to do in the situation. They had practised enough over the past month to know that they should all have their air-raid packs at the ready and form a line, and the older girls all knew exactly which part of the site to run to and present themselves for duty. They also knew that the Civil Defence people would regularly sound these alarms during the night, both for practice and to prevent panic in the event of a real attack.

The girls were familiar with that wail, but what was so frightening now was that the whole school had been roused from sleep, and they milled about in the dormitory in a state of confusion and dismay. They would have been even more restless had Susanna not appeared and helped dress those whose hands were trembling too violently to do it for themselves, and as a result of her efforts they were all lined up in the corridor well within the allotted time and ready to leave for the cellars. The two senior years had been assigned to first aid, stretcher duty and fire watch, and the sixths were to run messages, but the fifths had no responsibilities and had only to make their way down to the refuge area inside the cellars. There they found the blue lamps already lit and the entire teaching staff present. Some of the smallest girls were crying and whimpering, but fear could also be seen in the faces of the older ones. To them it did not feel like a rehearsal, a mere exercise: what they registered was the terrifying strangeness of it all – having to leave their beds and run down to the cellars, to this special underground place, because one day real bombs would come raining down on them. Susanna took up a position next to the entrance so that when the imaginary blast occurred she could take the force of it herself and spare the pupils; the fifth year sat on benches brought down from the gymnasium, with their backs to the wall. Mari Kis reached out her hand, and Murai took it; Murai held out hers, and Szabó took it; Szabó offered her other hand to Bánki, and so on down the line, until nineteen girls sat with tightly interlocked fingers, as if trying to measure their collective strength by the warmth of their neighbours' hands. There was just one gap in the chain, between Mari Kis and Torma, where Gina was sitting. Neither of her neighbours reached out to her, and she looked to neither right nor left.

There was the sound of running in the corridor outside and Aradi in year eight came dashing in to announce that incendiary flares had been spotted from the watch tower and the fire brigade were on their way. At one point Kalmár strode in, with his gas mask-helmet on his shoulder: he made a splendid sight, looking more St George-like than ever. Next, though of course there was nothing to be seen, they heard the boom of a distant explosion, and Susanna explained that the townspeople had earlier prepared a special building for the demolition squad and the rescue services to practise on.

It was all a simulation, but no-one experienced it as such. Gina was thinking, Please God, don't let us all die! Once again there was the sound of running in the corridor, followed by slower and heavier steps. Susanna, peering out calmly, reported that the eighth years were carrying the supposedly wounded to the doctor on stretchers. And Gina was now thinking, I really should have thanked them for inviting me to join in their game. It was only a bit of fun, something that had nothing to do with the war and the bombing, and all this danger and death. And I should have thanked them for inviting me to marry the aquarium, but I was stupid – stupid and proud. And Mari Kis was thinking, What would happen if a real bomb fell tomorrow? My father is at the front, and my brother, and we were too mean-spirited to accept Vitay's pastries. And Torma was thinking, I have no parents. I don't even know what it's like to have parents. My uncle bullies me all the time, but if the Matula really was hit and he was killed, I would have no-one, and if the building burned down, I wouldn't even have a home.

Susanna clapped her hand to her head. Vitay had leaped to her feet and turned to face the rest of the class. "Please forgive me, I beg of you," she pleaded. "You would if you knew how very ashamed I am. And may I please have the aquarium as my husband?"

The Prefect could only watch as the girl from Budapest burst into tears; and she could only sit and listen as Mari Kis began to sob, and then Torma, and Szabó, who was now weeping as if she were about to drown in tears.

"And you must forgive us too, Gina," Mari Kis sobbed, "for what we did with the pastries and the buttons." Again the Prefect could only look on as she fell on Vitay's neck and began to kiss her again and again. There came a shout from outside, Kalmár's voice, telling the seventh year to get a move on because they still had to put the fire out in the east wing. Susanna had to clamp her lips to avoid rebuking the class, who had now, contrary to all instructions, stood up, and were crowding around Vitay, taking turns to kiss her, and then, with her head pressed against plump little Szabó's shoulder and her eyes closed, Vitay went not to her own place in the row but to one further along, and sat there holding tight onto Mari Kis' dress until the sirens sounded the all clear.

An outing in the country

Years later, when everything that had happened in the fortress was long in the past, and her memories of the war, and those historic times, and of everyone she had feared and loved and despised had become mere shadowy presences among her recollections, the period that followed the night of the air-raid practice seemed to her the most wonderful of her whole life. She continued to miss her father desperately and the anxiety she felt about him never diminished, but she thought less and less about Budapest, about her old circle, the Sokoray Atala and the faces of her friends there; and one day she caught herself thinking that if she could only see her father more often, and have regular contact with Feri and Auntie Mimó, she would be happy to remain in Árkod for as long as was needed. The black-and-white building no longer frightened her, and she slept in peace beneath its vaulted arches.

She was among sisters, nineteen of them. After that stormy start to the year, and those painful early confrontations, she now lived among them in an intimacy and harmony such as she had never known before. One of the reasons for this was that every class in the school was a real community: you either joined in with everyone else or were totally outside. The other reason lay in the nature of life in the Matula. Once she had shed her isolation and was always among friends and comrades, Gina began to realise how exhilarating it was to live in a forbidden forest. Like hungry little foxes, they were always on the qui vive, looking to squeeze out every bit of fun they could in the thicket of rules and regulations and constant supervision. It was a never-ending quest, in which twenty pairs of shoulders and twenty young minds forever looking for love and laughter supported and sustained one another. Gina had also learned how much more special something was if you had had to struggle to achieve it, and how much stronger you were if you faced life as a group, like mountaineers whose very lives depended on an invisible rope linking them together, sharing the same passions, the same hopes, the same waiting and worrying, and were ready to act as one to help any of your number who needed it.

After the air-raid practice something had changed too in her attitude to the adults. Without particularly analysing it, she had come to see that they were not so much enemies as opponents, the way the class itself was divided into two teams to compete against each other in the gym. This permanent fixture against the adults could even be a source of amusement: you had to dodge them or sidestep them, outwit them, and finally take the ball from their hands with a piece of nimble footwork.

If she could only have spoken more often to her father she might more easily have endured not seeing him, but although he kept up his regular weekly call he never repeated his visit. Once she had won back the confidence of the class she started to worry that someone would ask her why she and he communicated in the unusual way they did, rather than by writing. But the girls' attitude was not what she had anticipated. That was because the censorship that was supposed to spare their parents undue anxiety made it impossible to write a proper letter home. The girls were very happy to receive them, but writing the same deadly boring platitudes over and over again was not to their taste, and they felt they would gladly give up writing if they could at least hear the voices of their mothers and fathers once a week.

By now they knew everything about Gina – Marcelle, the world of the Sokoray Atala, the weekly afternoon teas, Auntie Mimó, and of course Feri. Just as she had taken the aquarium to heart, so they had adopted Feri, and every one of them doted on him as if he were not her suitor but their own. They often talked about him after the lights had been turned out. Gina had described what his eyes were like, his hair and his uniform; she had told them that no-one had such wonderfully scented locks, and how he kissed her hand and tried to get her father to invite him to their home, because if they couldn't talk to each other every day then their lives were nothing. Anna Bánki urged Gina to marry him as soon as she could, if possible before her school leaving exams: plenty of people as young as she was were married in wartime. It could be done by the Chaplain, here in the school. Every bit of her dress would be covered in shiny spangles – it would make the Director explode! There was a cherished tradition that members of the school should marry in the chapel rather than in town. Mitsi Horn had in her day, to that certain young man. She loved the school, Bánki reassured Gina, and often came there to walk about the garden for no particular reason, just to see it. The porter adored her, as everyone did, including Gedeon Torma, and she was allowed to come and go whenever she pleased. Surely Gina must have seen her?

Gina had not seen her, nor was she very interested. The memory of Mitsi Horn still rankled. However kind she had been towards her, and however true it was that everything that had happened at that time had turned out for the best, the name of Mitsi Horn was linked in her mind with the memory of that failure: she really had no wish to see her strolling about the building or in the garden.

But playing with the idea of marriage was a source of pleasure, as was tending to the aquarium. She took such good care of it that Éles was often moved to praise her. As a relationship it was so much more real than what she currently had with Feri. She was not allowed to write to him; if she should ever manage to get hold of an envelope and wanted to smuggle a letter out of the school, her father had made her promise not to; and even if he hadn't, she had no idea how she would send it. Whenever they came anywhere near a postbox Susanna marched them past at near-running pace, and gave it such a wide berth that they would have needed arms four metres long to be able to reach it. But for all that, Feri was alive among them, in the same way that Murai had her philosopher, and Salm her Samuka. This "Samuka" was really called Pál, but by another Matula tradition every theologian was given that nickname.

Moreover, as she now discovered, they too, every one of them except Torma, had someone to dream about other than their husbands from the class inventory – some living person in the outside world, a real boy, a young man of flesh and blood, whom they could talk about and compare with the object of other people's desires, someone they could hope to meet again in the school holidays and perhaps even exchange a few words with, away from the prying eyes and ears of the Matula. And there was another thing they had in common: they were all just a little bit in love with Péter Kalmár.

This last feeling was genuinely disinterested, not only because they knew that it was hopeless but because they were so attached to the idea of Kalmár that they argued all the time who he himself might be in love with, and how they could help him find happiness with her. They were sure that his chosen one, if she existed, would have to be kept as much a secret as their own husbands from the class inventory. Kalmár would be watched just as closely by the Director as they were by Susanna; if he really were courting a woman it would have to be with the specific intention of marrying them, and not in the long term either, because that would be considered most unsuitable: the teachers in the Matula were either not involved in relationships or they married immediately and moved out of the staff residence to live in the town. The class might not be able to follow his movements beyond the school gate, but they were confident that he was seeing no-one outside, because if he were he would be wearing a ring. To track down whoever it was who filled his private thoughts they would have to look elsewhere, somewhere closer to home: perhaps even in the school itself.

That they had been right in this became clear on the country outing.

When she had bumped into Kőnig on that stormy evening of her attempted escape, Gina had not paid much attention in the pelting rain to what he had said about an outing. It was only later that she learned from the others that this was an event that happened twice a year, in the spring and autumn. The trip took them a short way out of town, to where the school owned a piece of land consisting of a vineyard and an orchard. In the past they had always gone in October to pick the grapes, but since the start of the year there had been doubt whether the Bishop would authorise it. In the end, he did give his permission, though it came a full month later than usual, and Kőnig was sent to see if there was somewhere they could shelter in the event of another air-raid warning and to check that there would be a suitable train connection. He found that neither the wine-pressing room nor the hut could be considered, as both were too small, but there was a little wood nearby to which they could withdraw if the need arose. It was not improbable at that time, November 1943, that any vineyard or orchard around Árkod might be attacked.

Kalmár made the welcome announcement in person, with a warning that they should make very sure that none of them did anything that would result in their having to be left behind. The class breathed a sigh of happiness, but the only time they dared let off steam was an hour later in the gym, when Gertrúd Truth emerged from her office and tossed the big ball over to them. She told them afterwards that she had enjoyed listening to the lively enthusiasm they had been showing, but in fact they had ignored the ball completely. They had been rolling about on the mats clinging to one another, and thinking of anything but gymnastics. A country outing that broke up the weekly routine of the Matula – now *that* held possibilities.

During the next seven days their behaviour was exemplary. By the Saturday assessment not one of them had incurred a single punishment. Sunday passed as usual. Because every form of physical labour was forbidden on the Lord's day, even on outings, the trip was set for the following Monday, a normal working day that Gedeon Torma had declared a school holiday. Apart from the porter everyone was going: the kitchen staff, the cleaners, the doctor (no-one was currently ill) and the entire teaching body. As the procession reached the front gate Gina was struck by the thought that not since she arrived had the fortress been so dead and deserted: there was now only the porter in his office and Abigail down at the end of the garden.

Abigail had not shown her hand for some time, or if she had come to anyone's aid Gina had not heard of it. But she thought about her constantly, and kept trying to imagine the face, the real face, of the person behind the statue. She began by thinking that if she could keep a steady watch on it, by night as well as by day, she would be able to spot which of the grown-ups was taking the messages left in the stone pitcher, but she soon realised that would be impossible. It would be unwise to be seen lingering there for too long. The site was in full view of the staff residence, and anyone standing in front of the Empire-style recess in the wall for hours on end would inevitably attract attention sooner or later, and besides, there would be little point in watching it by day. The person behind the mask surely went there at night, when all doors and windows had been shut and the pupils were safely in their dormitories. The moment they had got back to the school after the party at Mitsi Horn's, that old gossip Kőnig would surely have prattled away to one and all about how he had found little Vitay at the station, soaked to the skin. That would have been how Abigail knew about it, and immediately realised what she had been up to. The contact they had had, the fact that Abigail had written to her, was the one thing she had not told the other girls about, even when they had become indispensable to her. The reason, oddly enough, was not that she wanted to hide the fact that she had run away because she was so angry with them but that she could not bear to admit that it had been Kőnig who had not so much found her as caught her, that in his soft-hearted benevolence he had told lies on her behalf, and had physically dragged her back. To have been rescued by him, to have been his victim, as she felt it, was so humiliating that she had not yet got over it.

The procession was now on its way to the station. Everyone was dressed for work and the girls had scarves on their heads. The early November morning was crisp, and the outlook was promising, but they had come prepared for both rain and seriously cold weather. Instead of their usual school bags they had brought rucksacks to carry their lunch boxes, a raincoat, an extra coat and gloves for picking fruit.

They were now passing down the street where Mitsi Horn lived. As they neared the monument to The Sorrows of Hungary Gina involuntarily glanced to her left, but this time there was no placard. Mitsi Horn's windows were open, but they did not see her, only the old lady, who was shaking out a duster and who called out a greeting. At the station they had to mark time briefly. It was still rather early and there was little daylight in the large waiting room, where some passengers whose train was due were dozing on the benches. Now that they were sitting side by side, rather than walking in line, Gina could study the adults more easily. Kőnig was wearing a battered old loden coat, knee breeches, a scarf and a very strange-looking hat. Kalmár did not have a hat. He looked cool, dapper and elegant in his freshly ironed, russet-coloured sporting gear, a joy to behold in the morning light.

Kőnig went from one class to another, as if he had not yet decided which one to join, but no-one invited him to stay. He asked the fifth year if they were glad to be on the outing. Their reply was so frostily polite that he quickly moved on and started to stroll about the room. Finding it rather dark, he looked around for the light switch and turned it on to help everyone see. He wandered up and down, yawned, gazed around, then suddenly stood rooted to the floor and shouted, "For heaven's sake!"

All eyes followed his gaze. Gina clapped her hand over her mouth, as if to stop herself completing the response that was rising inside her. One of the walls was covered entirely with posters about the war. The nearest to them showed a map of Hungary, Hungary as dismembered at the Treaty of Trianon, surrounded by all the lands she had lost. Above it, in huge black letters were the words:

NO, NO, NEVER!

The slogan had been extended with yet more letters in black, heavily daubed to make them stand out even more dramatically.

Around the map of Hungary as she now was, these words followed the original three:

DO NOT SEND YOUR SONS TO HITLER'S BUTCHERY!

The Director threw a murderous glance in Kőnig's direction, and Gina heard him asking in a loud hiss why he had drawn attention to it. If he ever saw something like that he should keep it to himself and inform the station authorities later, not point it out to the pupils. The sleepy travellers were all now staring up at the wall; some of them had got up and moved nearer the offending poster. The Director ordered the school to turn their faces away, with the result that even the youngest and most naive of the first-formers now knew exactly what was there. At this point Kőnig disappeared. There came the sound of boots marching their way, but their train was drawing into the station, it was time to board, and they never saw the soldiers standing on one of the benches, trying to tear down the poster. It was later found to have been attached not with nails but with an unusually powerful glue.

The dissident of Árkod. The man into whose care she had been entrusted!

She felt her heart beating so violently that she imagined its trembling must be visible under her coat. This was the second time she had seen his handiwork. Oh, how brave he must be, how incredibly daring! He must have slipped out during the night, climbed up onto the same bench and painted his message at lightning speed before he could be spotted. If only she could have seen him and found out who he was! But his face was as great a mystery as Abigail's.

It was of course forbidden to discuss what they had seen, though some of the teachers felt free to comment. As soon as they were on the train the girls' faces all turned towards Kalmár, as the person who always spoke most eloquently and in the manliest terms about the war. But at that moment he was not much interested in the poster and he ignored the questioning eyes. His own were fixed on someone else – Susanna, who had just sat down beside him. He had whipped out his handkerchief, rubbed the bench vigorously (it was not quite as spotless as it might have been) and given her a look that made the fifth year draw in their breath. It was no longer a matter of supposition, of mere conjecture: this was certainty. He was in love with the Prefect; she was his chosen one – the severe saint who every morning hid her golden locks beneath her grey bonnet (pointlessly, of course: by midday they would have slipped out to shed their golden glow on her kindly forehead again). Their suspicions were confirmed: his hopes were in vain. And then, to make the journey even more memorable, something of even greater significance occurred, something that made Gina disloyally turn her thoughts away from the dissident of Árkod. Kőnig had not found a seat for himself or a hanger for his rucksack, and was still hovering between the different classes, and he too – she saw this quite distinctly – had noticed what Kalmár had done and his face had immediately darkened. Kalmár and Susanna had their heads bent over the fifth year's work schedule. He was making the decisions and she was writing them down on sheets of paper. They were so close together they must have been able to feel each other's breath. Kőnig immediately turned away, found somewhere to sit at last, and began to root around in his rucksack.

This was beautiful beyond beauty and exciting beyond excitement. Kőnig, the clown, had he not pursed his lips at the sight of Kalmár and Susanna leaning their heads together? Was this not hopeless love? Was this not pure jealousy? "Are we allowed to sing?" Nacák asked ecstatically, and Kalmár sent Bánki to the Director to ask permission. She came back with a favourable answer, and Mari Kis asked Susanna for her favourite song. The Prefect hesitated for a moment, as if she were unsure whether it was entirely proper for her to have such a thing, then said that she liked songs about flowers. The class immediately started on "Lily-of-the-valley", and she sat listening with her eyes closed. Hajdú came in from another compartment and almost managed a smile at the sounds of love and youth and joy welling up from the fresh young throats, so much lovelier and more meaningful than even under his baton.

Suddenly Kalmár rose to his feet and moved away, as if it were now all too much for him. Kőnig emptied his rucksack, took out his lunch pack and gazed at it thoughtfully. The Director, who had also come to hear the singing, noticed what Kőnig was up to and shook his head in disapproval. Everyone knew why: yet again he had been obliged to point out to the teacher that his behaviour was out of order; it had been made quite clear from the start no-one was to eat anything before lunch. "Sausage heals a broken heart!" Torma whispered, and the class began to laugh until they were almost choking, each girl egging the next on to further hilarity, and Susanna's eyes snapped open.

The Director, sensing that his niece's remark was somehow the source of this unseemly delight, told her to go and sit in the corner until the next stop. Then his dark presence vanished through the door.

The train trudged slowly along: it was wonderful – everything about the journey was wonderful. The sun eventually broke through the clouds and shed a golden light on the autumn landscape. They got off at the second station, and a short walk took them to the estate. It had been left to the Matula by a former pupil; some of its produce supplied the school kitchen and the rest was sold to provide free education for those in need. Gina knew that they had not come to enjoy themselves, or at least not only for that: for the first part of the day they would be doing serious work. Gedeon Torma's educational principles were well known to her. There was no point in training the mind if the body was left idle. It was his practice to drive them to exhaustion every now and then, physically as well as mentally, to teach them to respect all forms of manual labour.

On their arrival the older girls, who had taken part in grape-picking and other autumn-harvesting activities in previous years, knew what they had to do; it was only the juniors who had to be instructed. There was no running about or standing around fretting, no voices raised in anger or rebuke. Attached to a map of the estate was a work schedule assigning tasks to each year group, and every class tutor and prefect had one.

The farmhouse was occupied by the estate manager and his family; it had been passed on to him by the previous owner, a former pupil of the school. They hung up their coats and bags in the designated places and got themselves ready for work. Gertrúd Truth issued them with bags, boxes, baskets and step-ladders from the storeroom, supplied the group leaders with large wicker containers and explained the overall plan. Apart from the two lower years, the teams were to change tasks every hour. For one of those hours they would pick apples or bring potatoes and vegetables up from the cellars and underground storerooms; in the next they would fill their bags and baskets with them (they would be waiting in clearly marked piles), and haul them off to the wagons. The younger girls would act as runners for the management team directing operations from the pressing room. Like a priest conducting an arcane rite, the Direc-tor insisted on opening the first of the cellars himself, then spent fifteen minutes working with Aradi as her partner, carrying vegetables, before lending a hand with the potato-picking, and finally showing the others how to grade the harvest into three separate piles. The best were to go to the front, the next best were for the school kitchen, and the smallest for the orphanage.

The estate was not so large that it could not be taken in at a glance, but it was inconveniently laid out in two sections, divided by a raised railway line. This was no more than a secondary line, carrying very light traffic, but it proved difficult to cross when lugging large, two-handed baskets or sacks, as the fifth and sixth years would have to, having already carried their hoard of late-maturing apples and hazelnuts from the distant weighing station. The little ones were not allowed to cross at all, even to take messages: those would be taken on by either a prefect or a teacher. The fifth year quickly busied themselves among the apple trees and, although getting the ladders there and manoeuvring them into position had brought them out in a sweat, were relishing the exercise, and the girls at the top kept glancing down to see if Kalmár was looking at them. Gina was not involved in the picking; her job was to sort. She loved breathing in the fresh scent of the apples, and she enjoyed the serious business of deciding which should go into which pile. The teachers took turns to stand on the embankment, keeping an eye on the rail track and sending back anyone who got too close when one of the local trains appeared.

In truth these were very few. At one point a goods train came trundling past, and then a second, transporting troops. When that happened, all work came to a halt. Seeing the class, the soldiers stopped singing and turned their faces to take in the sight of schoolchildren labouring in the countryside – young men on their way to the battlefront, gazing in silence at the girls and the apple trees.

It was one of those experiences whose deeper significance struck Gina only much later. All those soldiers suddenly falling silent, their eyes fixed on her and her companions . . . it took time for her to understand just what it had meant for them, the young men on their way to the frontier and beyond. They had been thinking of their own children, their families, the little patches of earth that were their own gardens, and the grand order of nature to which mankind had been subject since the dawn of time. It was what they too would have been doing had the train not been taking them off to kill or be killed.

At that moment Hajdú was on duty beside the track. He went

to the edge of the rampart, raised an imaginary baton, and the fifth year and the sixth, from slightly further away, launched into "The soldiers are going away / To defend our beautiful land," and waved at the young men, who waved back and resumed their own song. Gina did not join in. She stood gazing in silence at the slowly disappearing train. She was thinking of her father, and of the placard she had seen on the monument to The Sorrows of Hungary.

She remained there until Susanna called out to ask what she was waiting for. Has she any idea, this Susanna, Gina wondered, that the person who risks his life day after day in Árkod to try and save his people is telling the truth, and that he wants to spare the lives of those men too, the ones on that train, going off to the war . . . or that there might be a father somewhere who has had to send his daughter away so that he can work in the same cause without having to worry about her? Susanna called to her again, to ask if she had heard: her time for sorting the apples had finished. She should go and help with the baskets. They were ready to be taken away.

Towards the end of the next hour, while they were hauling apples that they had collected, something happened that none of those involved – Susanna, Kalmár, Kőnig, the Director, indeed anyone who witnessed it – would ever forget. By now the fifth year were almost completely exhausted. They were in the process of lugging the huge wicker baskets loaded with their carefully sorted pickings over the rails to take them to the pressing house. Kőnig was on track-watching duty at the time, and Susanna and Kalmár were working with them. Kőnig was dancing from toe to toe and holding on to his hat with both hands in the strong wind that had sprung up. Gina knew rather than saw that he was there because she was looking at Susanna and Kalmár when they glanced towards him. Kalmár had said something that had clearly displeased her. She had stopped in her tracks, dumped her basket on the ground, and called to Cziller to come and help her class teacher. She went over to the choicest pile of apples, asked Oláh to bring her one of the sacks and called across to Kalmár to carry on the work with Cziller: she had just remembered that they were supposed to have set a sack aside for the Bishop. She obviously doesn't want to hear any more of whatever it was he was saying to her, Gina sensed. What could that have been about?

Kalmár's face darkened with suspicion. The delighted Cziller took her place beside him, and Susanna began filling the barrel at speed. Susanna was always beautiful, but never so much as at that moment, a timeless figure bent over a task of autumn and completely at one with the landscape. The sack was soon brimming over, and the blood-red apples seemed almost to smile as Mari Kis and Torma eased her two arms into the straps that would hold it on her back.

Kalmár and Cziller had been at the pressing house for some time before she finally set off with her load. She was carrying the huge bag by herself, with Gina and Bánki following a few steps behind under their own enormous burdens. Arriving at the embankment she quickened her pace and reached a point close to where Kőnig was standing. He turned a sleepy glance towards her and – in the same instant as the fifth year – watched her long dress catch on a piece of metal sticking up between the rails, causing her to miss her step and tugging her backwards, and her load with her. His shoulders flinched, and his hands moved as if to catch and hold her until she regained her balance, but he just looked on helplessly as she stumbled and fell onto the rails, and then, with the class watching in horror, slid down the other side of the embankment and out of sight from where they were among the apple trees.

Gina later thought how very Matula it was of herself not to have screamed. In fact none of the girls had. There was so much to take in during those few seconds – Susanna disappearing before her eyes, the fifth year throwing down their baskets and running towards the embankment, Kőnig's face, first bright red and then deathly pale, and that strange gesture when he had almost leaped after her, thought better of it and held himself back, before clambering up from between the rails and rushing to the side of the embankment and standing there staring down at the Deaconess with that look of anxious enquiry . . . and a voice calling out from the other side of the track, a single word that in its intensity of feeling dispensed with the formal "Sister". Kalmár was now back, he had been standing there for some time with Cziller, and had yelled, "Susanna!" while Kőnig remained rooted to the spot, staring down in horror at what the fifth year could not see from the other side of the embankment. Just then a train appeared. Had the class not instantly begun to scream at him he might have stayed where he was until it hit him. At the last moment he came to his senses, turned round, uttered a cry of terror and scrambled shamefacedly down the side of the embankment. By now the fifth year had been joined by Miss Gigus, newly arrived from her place beyond the apple trees, where she had been putting the last of the hazelnuts into boxes with a group of year six girls. In true Matula style, her voice conveying neither alarm nor any other emotion – things they had been told time and time again to avoid, and in which both Kalmár, with his unseemly display of feeling, and Kőnig, in his cowardice, had fallen short – she ordered the girls back to work. Vitay was told to wait until the train had passed and then bring back a report on the Prefect's condition. It obviously wasn't too serious, she added. If it had been, the doctor and two of the teaching staff would by now have been at her side with the first-aid box, and besides, Sister Susanna would have been the first to be upset if she knew she had created a fuss. The train chugged by belching smoke, with the driver leaning out of the cabin window and shaking his fist at Kőnig for dancing about on the line. As soon as the track was clear Gina ran up the embankment and stood waiting for Kőnig to give approval for her to cross. From up there she could see the whole of the estate.

On the other side, the bright red apples destined for the Bishop lay scattered on the ground. Susanna had been disentangled from the sack she had been carrying and was now sitting with her back resting on Kalmár's knees. The doctor was holding her wrist. Kőnig was standing a short way away, next to the stretcher, looking at them. There were no other teachers present, only the Director. Behind Gina the work had resumed, and the seventh and eight years were once again weighing their potatoes in silence, as if nothing had happened. Below her the doctor was now dipping a wad of cotton wool into a solution and holding it up under Susanna's nose. The Prefect's forehead was bleeding slightly, and her eyes were closed. As in everything she did, her self-discipline was absolute. She did not so much as sigh or ask a single question.

"Susanna," said Kalmár. "Are you feeling any pain? Are you able to stand?"

The words could not have been simpler, more professional, but the tone . . .

She became aware of where she was, that it was very uncomfortable, and sat up. She ignored Kalmár's question, pretending she had not even heard it, tested an arm briefly, then leaned forward and tried to stand, with the doctor's help. She took a few steps and pronounced herself fit and well, ready to carry on with her work. She seemed to feel something on her forehead, wiped it, and stared at her crimson fingers in surprise.

"I'll deal with that right away," the doctor said. "You've grazed it on a stone. Luckily, there's no harm done, but you must take a short rest. You should be working in your usual clothes, not that long dress. Mr Kőnig, you are the only one here whose hands are clean: could you give me a hand while I see to the sister?"

Clearly embarrassed, Kőnig mumbled something about not being able to stand the sight of blood. Kalmár snatched up the first-aid box and his voice took on a murderous edge. The astonished girls standing on the embankment then overheard speech that no Matula person should ever utter: "If you weren't so damn useless you would have caught her. Get the hell out of here!"

"Vitay, you go and help her instead," the Director said. Gina shrank back reluctantly, but even from where she was she could see that Susanna was blushing a bright red. Kőnig, feeling older and more crushed than ever, turned and went back up the embankment to resume his watch. Gina noticed the Director whispering furiously in Kalmár's ear, while the nurse led Susanna out of earshot. In short, she had witnessed yet another of those miraculous little scenarios at which the Matula was so adept: nothing had happened at all, or, if anything had, it was of no importance, there had been no unseemly language or ugly behaviour, nothing had been said that was unworthy of the school, and no hard words had passed between members of the teaching staff. Gina went back to her class and told them that Susanna was fine and carried on with her work. Shortly afterwards Kőnig disappeared, the Director took his place on the embankment, Kalmár went off, stiff-faced, with restless emotion showing in every movement of his body, and Cziller, who had been working happily alongside him all this time, had difficulty keeping up with him.

They did not see Susanna again until dinner, when the work was over. She had a sticking plaster on her forehead but was moving as gracefully as ever, as if there had never been any accident. Kőnig was keeping his distance from her, sitting on his own, but this time the Director did not invite him to come and join him. Gina felt that the man hardly deserved to be treated like a pariah. Was he really such an object of loathing? Of course not. Better just to ignore him.

Kalmár too was sitting well away from Susanna; he had found a place among the girls. Gina knew the Matula well enough by now to realise that after making Susanna sit against his knees and bawling at his colleague he was now watching his every step and every movement.

After supper and a short rest it was time for games, including netball. Susanna elected to join in. She wasn't able to run, she said, her foot was a little sore, but she took part nonetheless, laughed a great deal, and took it in good part when it was their turn to shout at her. Kőnig did not fall in with any of the classes, and for a while he disappeared altogether. They did not see him again until they were on their way back and had boarded the train, but he was still avoiding the fifth year. The girls were all now singing the same song. They were tired but they were happy, their nostrils filled with the scent of apples and the autumn land-scape. Suddenly Susanna stood up, as if there was something she needed to go and reassure herself about. Mari Kis and Gina followed her discreetly to see where she was going, and if she had gone to look for Kalmár. He was with the Director, who had ordered him to spend the homeward journey in his company, and the two men were sitting together in a coupé, where the older man was now explaining – in exactly the tone he used with his niece, according to Szabó – what was considered right and proper, in good taste and generally polite.

But it was Kőnig that Susanna had gone to look for.

Gina had missed him because he had been still on the plat-form when Susanna went to look for him. The two of them were now hidden from her by a panel that protruded from the wash-room, but their voices could be clearly heard: the song had finished and Hajdú's messenger had not yet arrived to tell them what he wanted them to sing next.

"Mr Kőnig," Susanna said. "Won't you join us? There is an empty seat for you."

"Thank you, no," he replied. "The air is fresher here."

"Did you have your supper?"

"But of course. I like eating."

"I would be very happy if you came and sat with us."

"May God reward you," he responded. "Your goodness surpasses even the standards of the Matula."

She said not a word more. She turned and went back to the compartment, arriving just a few steps behind Gina and Mari. The amazing thing was that Kőnig should have been so arrogant, though that might have been because he was reflecting on and grieving over the consequences of his (in)glorious discharge of his duties. But if he had ever nursed any such hopes he had now blown his chances with the Prefect forever, even were there no such rival as Kalmár. When Susanna was safely back in her seat the two girls, rather daringly, asked her if they could go and wash their hands, and went back to the Director's coach. Through a narrow slit they could just about see the speakers. Gedeon Torma was explaining something of grave significance, with a face of funereal gloom. St George was sitting there like a block of wood, almost soldier-like, wearing the ecstatic look of a martyr in extremis, while Torma turned the screw. "What a fine match these two would be!" Mari Kis whispered to Gina. "Aren't the deaconesses lucky to be allowed to marry!"

Caricatures

So now the central problem was the question of Kalmár and Susanna.

The fifth year had decided that they certainly should be married, but they could think of no way to help them attain that goal in the shortest possible time. In fact they soon realised that there was very little they could do. There was no point in dreaming about it. They would somehow have to find a way of making it possible for the two of them to spend time together away from other people. They took their meals in the same room, and every Saturday Susanna joined Kalmár for the weekly class assessment, but generally their lives were lived within such narrow constraints that if they hoped to avoid the most painful consequences there was absolutely no hope of their ever being able to spend time together. Susanna seldom left the school, and when she did, to go to her professional association in town, the Bishop's office or the dentist, she always left a telephone number with the duty sister, so that even the day staff knew where to contact her in an emergency. The idea that she would ever venture outside other than on business or to carry out some charitable task was unthinkable.

The same could not be said of Kalmár. First of all, he lived on the other side of the grille-gated corridor, in the staff residence from which there was another exit onto the street, and when not on duty he could come and go as he pleased. And their daily timetables were very different. There was simply no chance of their ever meeting without other people being present unless they themselves planned it, which, knowing Susanna, was not likely to happen. None of the girls doubted that she had been far from indifferent to the way he had looked at her on the train, or imagined that he could be any less attractive to her than he was to them. They spent many hours considering the possibilities.

It was therefore both hilarious and confusing that night, when the Prefect came unexpectedly into their room to stop them gossiping after the lights had been turned out: at just that moment their "gossip" had been every bit as altruistic as she expected from them at all times in other areas of life. How could she possibly have guessed that it was her own wedding that they were busy organising, and debating how she should do her hair for the great occasion, and what indeed could be done with such long tresses. Torma knew the most about these in-house Matula weddings. She had been barely seven when she first visited her uncle and met some retired former employees who had been there at the start of the century and had actually attended Mitsi Horn's wedding, the first ever in the school, in which, she claimed, Kőnig had acted as a witness. No-one was ready to believe that, but Torma swore "honest to God", which brought a temporary chill to the proceedings (to swear an oath in regard to such matters was considered a terrible sin). She also insisted that the previous porter, who had retired two years earlier, had always said of Kőnig that not even Jesus could understand how he turned out such a coward, because he had not been like that in his younger days. Again they refused to believe her, or rather, they decided that if he had said that then he must have been pulling her leg. That Mitsi Horn – Mitsi Horn of all people! – would have allowed the young Kőnig to be a witness at her wedding was completely improbable. Murai told Gina that when her time came to be joined with Feri, if the wedding was to be in the Matula, then perhaps she too should have him as a witness. He would stand at the holy table, a lunch box in one hand and his hat with the ear flaps in the other and listen dewy-eyed as Gina vowed her undying loyalty to Feri. After all, if Mitsi Horn had done as much, she had a duty to keep up the tradition. The idea was so hilarious they nearly fell out of bed laughing, and Gina was reduced to whimpering that she had a pain in her stomach from trying to hold her laughter in. She thanked them profusely for their advice, but as a variation on the idea of Kőnig as a witness she would like to propose a new tradition for the Matula: after all, where was it written that only Mitsi Horn and her successors could start one? The class listened in great excitement as she told them that at her old school girls who hadn't fully prepared their lessons would avoid the usual questioning if they kicked the statue of Sokoray Atala, the man who had given his name to the school; whereupon Salm, whom the class inventory had given in marriage to the school's founder, János Matula, protested vehemently, worked herself into a frenzy and swore that anyone who tried to kick *her* husband would find themselves in real trouble. That made them laugh again until their jaws ached. Murai then asked Gina if she would be so kind, in consideration of the exceptionally strong feelings of Mrs János Matula, née Gisella Salm, as to suggest some other custom from the Sokoray Atala Gymnasium. Nothing sprang immediately to Gina's mind, but the next day, during Kőnig's first lesson, an idea popped up in her head while they were doing a written test, and her face lit up so much that he asked her what had so galvanised her, and was it possible that writing a Hungarian essay could have such power to raise her spirits?

Kőnig had changed since the country outing. He smiled less often, and rarely engaged in conversation with the pupils. It was as if he felt so ashamed of himself for his woeful behaviour that he no longer wanted to be in company. Gina did not answer him – something you could get away with only with Kőnig – and as she bent over her exercise book again she nudged Mari Kis' elbow. (Mari, like Torma, had returned to her seat as soon as Gina made her peace with the class and their view of the blackboard had been somehow restored.) Mari knew instantly that Gina had had the idea she had been searching for, and that in the break, when they circled round the corridor in pairs pretending to be repeating their lesson aloud, as they were supposed to, she could tell them what it involved.

There was still some time to go before the bell. Gina had made very little headway with her composition and she would have to make a special effort if she wanted to excel herself. They were always given two hours for writing, the first of which was spent preparing a draft; that day's topic, "A Letter to the Front", was written up on the board. Like everyone else, she wrote urging the heroes to stand their ground. She promised them that those at home would in their own way also be working for victory, and added that if that victory came at the cost of their lives they should not feel that their sacrifice would be in vain. The war was in a sacred cause, and those left behind would preserve their memory faithfully. But as she warmed to her task and became absorbed in the essay – it was one that every schoolchild in the country was asked to write in November 1943 – she found her buoyant mood fading. Looking along the rows of heads bent over exercise books she thought of how, back in the dormitory, the girls talked about absolutely everything but the war. There was scarcely one of them who did not have someone at the front; the thought of it was always there, just below the surface of their consciousness; and yet all they ever whispered about was love, their teachers, and what had happened in lessons that day. She was the only person in the class who worried about why it had all started and how it might end. Some of the pupils were actually in mourning; they were allowed to ignore the usual rules and wear whatever they chose under their school uniforms to mark their grief. The father of one of the first years had fallen in the summer, and the same had happened to a girl in the seventh year. The orphans whimpered and shed tears whenever they thought about it, but their loss never led them to ask whether things could have been any different.

The clarity that Gina owed her father in this matter was a real burden. In his lessons on national defence Kalmár painted a horrifying picture of anyone who opposed or even questioned the war and thereby undermined national solidarity. His voice took on a special edge whenever he held forth about why the struggle was necessary, repeating over and over that whatever sacrifice might be called for, in the end good would come of it. It would restore order to our neighbours in Europe and secure the return of our lost lawful territories. Had she not had that fateful conversation with her father in the Hajda patisserie Gina might never have thought otherwise: it was also what she had heard time and time again in Budapest, at the Sokoray Atala and at Auntie Mimó's.

It would have been so good if there had been someone in the Matula who knew what the truth was, the way her father did – someone who could keep her abreast of what was really happening, so that she would know at every stage how long the war was likely to last and when life might return to its usual course. But in the Matula, to all appearances at least, there was no-one who did not enthusiastically support it, and Kalmár was such a persuasive speaker that at times she had to shake herself and remember the things her father had told her.

And that was difficult, because Kalmár's expositions were always so much more comforting than the grimly objective picture painted by the General. She had even managed to persuade herself that his zeal was genuine, that he really did believe what he taught them. There were moments when she pitied her class tutor for being so grievously mistaken and predicted that when he did wake up to the truth he would realise that he had been an advocate of pointless bloodshed. The poor man, how astonished he would be to find he had been wrong all along. Perhaps by then, she hoped, he might already be married to Susanna, and she would help him regain his self-respect.

At break she told Bánki and Salm about the Sokoray Atala tradition she wanted to introduce. In her old school, she said, there had been a senior girl who liked to write two versions of her Hungarian essays, the first as the school expected it to be and the second for private consumption. She was a clever, rather daring sort of girl, who had had a very unusual upbringing. Even while she was still a pupil her parents took her everywhere, including going out dancing in the evening and to nightclubs. Of course, none of the teachers knew about that, and as for what else she might have got up to, best not think about it. She was not only a bit of a madcap, she was also the best in her class at essay writing. She absolutely hated having to write on the topics she had been set, so, to relieve her boredom, and because she enjoyed a bit of mockery, she would produce two versions. In the lesson she would write what was required, and when she got home she did the whole thing again, both for her own amusement and to entertain the class. The home versions were of course secret. They would be passed round from hand to hand, and the girls almost died laughing when they read them.

For example, if they were asked to write on "An Evening at Home", she would conjure up a picture of sitting with her family after supper. Her mother and father would both be there and she would be playing the piano and singing traditional songs for her dear old grandmother dozing next to the stove, until the old lady took herself off to an early bed, devoutly told the beads on her Rosary, and went on to dream of the smiling faces of those she loved.

The private version went as follows: it was really her grand-mother who liked the nightclubs; she was much younger at heart than the girl's own mother, quite astonishingly so; she smoked like a chimney day and night, she made the best cocktails of anyone in the family, she hated schools and was forever telling her to clear out of that stupid academy because what was the point of staying for your leaving exams – those endless lessons must be so boring, so why not just have a good time? Whenever she gave a party the grandmother would dance with the boys until even the ablest and fittest of them would throw in the towel. Her father was never around, and no-one could ever find out where he went. His wife would be at the dressmaker's or the women's club, or if she wasn't at the hairdresser's she would be sitting in the cinema. The girl could not recall a single occasion when they had all dined together. By sheer good fortune they all loved going to shows and dances, and that was how they met and how she and her parents and grandmother were able to get together on a regular basis.

Salm and Bánki instantly saw the possibilities this presented, and when at the end of the second hour Kőnig announced the topic for their homework preparation, "Portrait – a Character Study in Words", Bánki squealed with delight, then excused her-self for having a hiccup. It could be a portrait of anyone, Kőnig went on, anyone they knew personally. By the afternoon, when the time came to prepare for the next day's lessons, the whole class knew what the game involved. Susanna, sitting in for the teacher, was astonished at the zeal they brought to the task: natu-rally she had not the least idea that they were writing a double essay, the second one hidden from her sight under the blotting paper and destined for one another's amusement back in the dormitory, a very different audience.

In their class exercise books almost everyone wrote about their father or mother. Gina had found it harder to choose, and considered three people. Of her mother she had no first-hand memories, only what she had heard from other people. As for her father, from what she now knew about his secret activities it was unthinkable that she should present him as an enthusiastic soldier. His real character was a secret she could never reveal, and she did not want merely to describe his appearance, so she decided to write about Marcelle. She described what the young Frenchwoman looked like, outlined her character, explained their close relationship, and ended by saying how much she missed her, and how much she hoped that when the war was over she would be able to return to her former position in the house on Gellért Hill.

During the lesson Mari Kis had sent a note round under the table asking everyone to say who they would be writing about in secret. When the list reached Gina, she noticed that while most of them had opted for Kalmár, Torma had chosen the Director, two others Mitsi Horn, and four Susanna. Only Szabó had chosen to write about Gertrúd Truth and their difficult relationship in gym lessons: because she was unable to climb ropes, the teacher was constantly making remarks about her fat legs and how she would be good for nothing but the harem, spending the whole day sitting around on cushions eating sugary sweets and waiting for the sultan. Perhaps next time they'll choose more wisely, Gina reflected. How could you make fun of Kalmár and Susanna when we are all so fond of them? And the Director is such a fearsome figure he is hardly a suitable subject. Why didn't they think of the one person who really would be right for this sort of exercise, Kőnig himself?

They were working in the large study room they shared with the year six girls. Susanna was the only one who noticed the Bishop's entry. With him were the Director, the Chaplain and five of the teachers. The long table at which the fifth year were sitting was nearest the door. The Bishop nodded genially at the sixth year, spotted an empty seat beside Dudás (Gáti was absent just then), and lowered himself onto it. It was almost directly opposite Gina. The teachers remained standing beside the table. At a sign from the Prefect half the class stood up to offer their seats to them and to Gedeon Torma. The fifth year stood gaping at the Bishop as if they had been turned to stone, though his manner was so affable and self-effacing you would never have known that he was an even more important person in the school than the Director himself.

"Close your exercise books," Susanna ordered. "Vitay, Kis and Torma, go and bring some chairs from the day room."

Their heads spinning, they went out and picked up two chairs each. No more were needed because the Bishop was already seated, and the only other teachers present were Miss Gigus, Hajdú, Kalmár, Kőnig and Mrs Sáfár, who taught the second year.

"We're done for," said Torma. "If they open my exercise book and the blotter comes up with it, it's the end of me. They'll throw me out."

"They'll throw all of us out," Mari Kis said darkly. "If they see what I wrote about our beloved Deaconess I'll be on my way this evening. I said that she wasn't a member of the Reformed Church but a closet Buddhist, and not a real deaconess but a film actress come here to prepare for her latest role."

"They can't throw us all out," Gina said. Her hands were icy and stiff with tension: once again she had put the class in jeopardy. "They would never do that."

"You don't think so?" said Torma. "You halfwit. This is the Matula, not the Sokoray Atala, where you can go to nightclubs and your granny makes cocktails. Haven't you learned anything yet about the sort of place this is? If my uncle caught himself doing anything wrong he would throw himself out."

On their way back to the study room they heard laughter. Torma's eyes filled with tears and she began to rattle through the Lord's Prayer, and the proud and fearless Mari Kis kept muttering, "Jesus, sweet Jesus." Gina was the first to pull herself together. She was thinking that if they were laughing then perhaps it wouldn't be quite so bad. She was about to go in when her fingers went numb and the chairs fell from her hands with a clatter in the doorway. The Bishop was reading aloud. It was clear from his tone that he found the text amusing, but he was by far the most restrained person in the room. Study room A resounded to howls of delight. The sixth year were shrieking with mirth, the teachers were all smiling, and Kalmár was actually laughing. The only person who was not was Susanna. Her face was solemn, in fact almost grave, and she was staring fixedly into her lap. Kőnig was blowing his nose and his face was hidden behind his handkerchief. Gina froze. It was her essay that the Bishop was reading – not the one copied out in her fairest hand into the exercise book but the secret one. He was only halfway through.

". . . he follows the latest fashions with a keen eye, as can be seen in his extraordinary hat with the ear flaps and the ties he purchases with such unerring taste. The dazzling sharpness of his wit is admired by all, but even that is surpassed by the spirit of heroism, the manly fortitude and the almost legendary courage he shows. His ability to cope with the sight of blood makes one wonder why he does not retrain as a surgeon. The moment he qualifies he should waste no time in claiming the hand of his beloved. She will surely respond with an immediate yes, for who would not happily entrust her life to such a man? – although not perhaps at apple-harvesting time with a goods train approaching."

"This is grotesque," said Mrs Sáfár, who had been looking after the second year during the outing and had witnessed none of the events that it referred to. "Utterly grotesque."

"Isn't there something rather sarcastic about this, something rather contemptuous?" the Chaplain asked anxiously.

"There certainly is," said the Bishop. "It has obviously been conceived as a satire. Who wrote it? And what kind of exercise is this? Surely not something for a Hungarian essay?"

The writer's eyes were fixed on the floor. She sensed that everyone was looking at her – Kalmár and Susanna, Kőnig himself, the Director, her own class and the sixth year. Dear God, she kept thinking. Give me somewhere to hide. Don't let them send me away. If I can't stay here, what will become of my father?

The Director leaned angrily over the table and seized Torma's exercise book – and the page under the blotter with it. She was almost sick. Everyone saw the blood drain from her face.

"A black man in black clothes with a black name, black in his rages and black in his dreams," the Director read out. "What is this nonsense? What can Mr Kőnig tell us about this?"

My God, thought Gina. If he recognises himself! What have I got Torma into now?

"I am aware of all this," Kőnig said, through a blocked nose. "These references to black are an echo of Babits. They were asked to come prepared to write a character portrait. Either a straightforward one or a caricature."

"Aha," said the Bishop, and he put Gina's essay down. "But aren't they a bit young for that sort of thing? In my opinion the writing of these caricatures as a stylistic exercise is something for the seventh or eighth years. I have nothing against lightening the task of essay writing with something more amusing – the girls have quite enough cares and sorrows already – but we should make sure that the satire does not become hurtful or demeaning. Who was the model for . . . ?" He glanced down at the name on the exercise book and read out the name: ". . . for Georgina Vitay?"

"Who was the model for Georgina Vitay?" the Director repeated, like a dark echo, after a moment's deliberation and with a quizzical expression on his face. Torma breathed a deep sigh of relief. Every teacher, the two deaconesses and every girl in both classes knew that the crisis had passed. Gedeon Torma had thought the matter through and decided to catch the slender rope that Kőnig had thrown him. If he was to avert a scandal he would have to become an accomplice in the man's readiness to forgive. The alternative was to denounce the two fifth-year pupils, and the gravity of their offence against the respect they owed the school would call for the ultimate sanction. In addition, the Bishop would be left with the impression that such abominations were possible in the Matula. And if in his fear of the Bishop the Director went along with the ruse and accepted Kőnig's explanation, then Vitay and Torma would be spared for the time being, and what followed would be a purely internal matter. It would be kept within the school walls and run its course without his superior hearing anything more about it.

What could she say, about who her model had been? She could think of no-one. Her horrified glance went from one watching face to another. Kalmár's eye twinkled with merriment: she had never seen him show such pleasure before. Susanna was sitting at the head of the table, utterly mortified. Only her headscarf could be seen, nothing of her face. She was really taken in, Gina reflected. She never noticed that we were writing two essays. She couldn't see what was under the blotting paper.

The silence was heavy and oppressive: unbearable in fact. Eventually someone spoke and answered for her. Again it was Kőnig. She could hear the smile in his voice as he told them that it was an imaginary figure, most probably someone she had read about, not a living person. The girl had been told she could base her portrait on someone she had come across in a book. The Director swallowed audibly, as if he were nursing tonsillitis, but he said nothing, and the Bishop let the matter of the caricatures drop. He rose and went over to the sixth years' table. Nacák later told them that she had overheard him discussing the apples that Vitay had mentioned: were they a biblical reference, or something from pagan folklore, or perhaps Greek mythology? Not at all: in the Matula the only logical answer was that they were an echo of some passage in the Old Testament.

Nothing more could happen before prayers. The Bishop stayed on to make himself available to the teaching staff. During the meal the fifth year, who normally devoured their food like wolves, took tiny mouthfuls and nibbled at them nervously. The pockets of their uniforms were filled with the shredded remains of their compositions à la Vitay. The evening prayer was led by the Bishop. The strongest voice when the hymns were sung was Kőnig's.

When the visit was over, and he was taking his leave of the assembled school community in the foyer, Susanna kept the fifth year back. She waited until the other classes had filed out and the rest of the staff with them, then planted herself before them, completely silent, and with a sad and sombre expression on her face. They stood to attention, their hearts beating, waiting to see what would happen and feeling distinctly uncomfortable. It would have been easier to bear if she had raged at them, but she just stood there, saying nothing. They remained like that until the Director returned from escorting the Bishop to the gate. He did not come into the foyer, he merely addressed them from the entrance. Georgina Vitay was not to go to bed until she had copied out the line from the First Psalm: *Blessed is the man who walketh not in the council of the ungodly, nor standeth in the way of sinners, nor sitteth in the seat of the scornful,* five hundred times, in red ink, in a fresh exercise book. Torma was to stay with her and illustrate each line with an initial letter executed in black: that might serve to free her from her urge to write the word. Susanna dismissed the class with a nod of the head, and then, still maintaining her silence, took a bottle of red ink and two exercise books from the wall cupboard, directed the two offenders to a desk with another silent gesture, sat down near them, opened her Bible and immersed herself in it.

It was almost daybreak by the time they finished. Torma had had to wait for short periods while Gina worked her way to the bottom of each page and she had managed to catch a few short bouts of sleep. Gina was still wide awake. She felt tense and restless. She felt no self-pity, though she had long wearied of the business of writing and her wrist ached. Her feelings were divided. She had been punished before in Budapest when she had misbehaved, and she knew that the class would not hold it against her for having made them endure those torrid several minutes because of what she had put them up to; nor was she concerned about the effect it might have on her relationship with Kőnig. He was stupid, but he was certainly no fool. Like the Director, he must have known perfectly well what lay behind that reference to a surgeon. No, what really worried her was Susanna, and what her attitude might be. Susanna had not uttered a single word to them throughout the entire episode. She had scarcely raised her eyes from the Holy Scriptures, had responded with a simple nod when the time came to collect the two exercise books, and merely glanced after them to make sure they were on their way back to the dormitory. What upset Gina most was that not once had she reproached them, and she had given them no opportunity to apologise. In truth, what they had done had not been so very dreadful. She and Torma had been chastised for their disrespectful compositions and had submitted to their punishment, and even if everyone – apart from the Bishop and the Chaplain – knew what the truth was, they could not now be punished for their real crime because Kőnig had said he had given them permission to write in that vein. If he had been willing to smooth the matter over, why was Susanna so unforgiving?

The moment they had turned the corridor and were out of her sight, Gina put the question to Torma. Torma simply groaned something unintelligible: she was beyond sensible conversation. Gina expected to fall asleep as soon as she got into bed, but for some reason she could not stop thinking about it until at long last she dozed off, and for the rest of what remained of the night she kept waking, trembling from head to foot, from a fitful, formless dream that gave her no rest at all.

A visit to Kőnig, and another message from Abigail

The next day she struggled to get out of bed, and if Bánki had not helped her do her hair, button up her blouse and lace her shoes she would have been late for morning prayers. Torma could barely stand. She stared so fixedly ahead from her aching eyes that seeing her the Chaplain grew thoughtful: this was a thoroughly decent girl who took every reproach to heart, and Vitay, how strained her face was looking! But what could one say? Christmas was approaching, and it was a good time for serious soul-searching.

Neither of the girls had any idea what was said during that morning service. Torma sang along with the others because she had grown up in the Matula and there was not a single hymn she could not intone in her sleep, but Gina did not even open her mouth. Her eyelids were raw and she kept them firmly closed. Susanna stood near them, immersed in her prayers, with eyes and ears for no-one. As always, all the teaching staff were present, including the Director. Kőnig showed not the slightest sign of being offended by the unmistakable portrait Georgina Vitay had painted of him: he belted out the hymns and psalms at the top of his voice, which could be clearly distinguished among those of the other teachers.

The first lesson of the day was taken by Kalmár. He had barely begun testing them on their preparation when Susanna appeared. She was such a rare visitor to the class that normally her arrival would have received a delighted welcome, but on this occasion the class were still suffering from a bad conscience and the faces that turned to meet her were distinctly troubled. Kalmár was no less surprised than they were. He almost leaped from the dais to greet her, his eyes shining with pleasure: he was sure that everyone must have realised she had come to listen in on his lesson, and the one he would deliver now would be one to make the very walls glow with emotion. Everything that he felt towards her, everything he had been either unable to express or unwilling to put into words, would be subtly woven into it.

But Susanna had not come to observe. She directed not a single smile towards the class, refused a chair and remained standing by the door, from where she said what she had come to say. She apologised for interrupting the lesson, but the matter could not wait until the afternoon. There was a matter still to be resolved following the Bishop's visit. She had spent a long time during the night considering what to do about it, and had decided to ask Mr Kalmár, as the class tutor, to help her get to the bottom of the regrettable events of the day before. If Mr König had not, in his extreme kindness, sought to protect the girls responsible – girls who obviously held him in such high esteem – and if the matter had not been decided in the presence of the Bishop, she wondered how differently it might have ended. She intended to find out what lay behind what happened, if only to help the class regain their self-respect. And perhaps they might also learn to respect the concepts of neighbourly love, not to mention compassion and the spirit of forgiveness, and draw the right conclusions from this episode about what was proper and acceptable; in short, what sort of behaviour was expected in the school.

The air turned frosty. Susanna remained with her back to the green door like a stern angel guarding the gates of paradise: it was as if she had suddenly realised, as had Gina and everyone else in the room, that the atmosphere had cooled not only because of the effect her words had had on the girls, who were now tearful as well as anxious, but because of Kalmár's reaction. There was a tension, a charge of undeclared feeling in the air, something that had strayed in from the adult world beyond the school walls, and even the pupils were aware of it. They all, including the guilty ones, now knew that Susanna's wrath was driven by something else, by a parallel emotion that was so hard for them to imagine that they had never before noticed it. They had finally understood that Kalmár loved Susanna but that Susanna did not love Kalmár. And what was so bizarre and incomprehensible about it was that Susanna must therefore love Kőnig – he of the flap-eared hat, the impossible Kőnig, and that she who was too proud ever to respond to an attack on her own authority was capable of acting to defend his. They felt that no man could endure a greater sense of disappointment than Kalmár must be feeling at that moment, and that somehow Susanna had offended them too, for how was it humanly possible to be attracted to someone like Kőnig?

If he had failed to conceal his emotions earlier, Kalmár had been trained by the Matula well enough to make sure that no-one saw how rejected he felt now. The only change in his expression was that the joy vanished from it and he became once again schoolmasterly and impersonal. He invited the Deaconess to take a seat at the desk, where she would have a better view of the class, stood beside her like a presiding judge, and did his best to give both her and the girls the impression that he too had been giving thought to the matter that weighed on her heart.

He too, he declared, intended to look into the unfortunate events of the day before. He wished to draw their attention to Mr Kőnig's extreme magnanimity, and to reproach those who had so abused the gentle and selfless heart of a good man. He also needed to explain to them that if someone did alter the facts in some way, if the intention was merciful and done to spare one's fellow man, it might be wrong but it was not strictly speaking a sin, and should not be seen as such; in fact it was a worthy and noble thing to have done.

Susanna lowered her head and they saw her face turn scarlet. Like the girls, she realised that Kalmár had just declared, in everyone's hearing, that his colleague was a liar. Kalmár went on to say that he would hold a formal inquiry into the matter, so could he and the Prefect now be told exactly what that satirical portrait was about?

His words were so direct, so unimpeachable, so perfectly in keeping with the school's pedagogical ethos that they could have been printed on a board alongside quotations from the Bible and posted up as a guide for aspiring teachers. At the same time every one of them had a covert meaning, and no-one in the room failed to understand what it was: What you are really after, Susanna, is revenge for this person, the school clown. What sort of woman are you if you can turn down what I offer you and make a stand on behalf of a creature who is so unworthy of you?

Gina lowered her gaze. What could she possibly do? It was thanks to her that the class were in this mess: she couldn't allow them to bear the consequences, it was unthinkable. But perhaps there was a way out? If the Director had said nothing when the Bishop was present, then the matter was hardly likely to come before him a second time, and if she were to be punished again it would probably not go so far as to involve expulsion. Susanna was simply warning them to leave Kőnig alone. Gina was not afraid of Kalmár. It was most unlikely that he would take revenge on her on behalf of his colleague. She asked permission to speak, stood up and repeated what she had previously told the class. She explained to Kalmár and Susanna that the idea of writing a double essay came from the Sokoray Atala and that she was the one who had suggested it. Susanna listened without once taking her eyes off her. Kalmár played with his piece of chalk, steadily breaking the full length of the innocent stick down into stubs far too short to use. When she stopped speaking he asked the rest of the class how many of them had also written a double essay, and they all stood up. Susanna watched in silence as he demanded that they hand them over, only to be told that they had all been destroyed. The class were mightily relieved that they had not failed to do that. It would have been all they needed – Kalmár seeing what they had written about him, and Susanna having access to the literary effusions they had produced on the subject of her love life.

Kalmár said that although Vitay and Torma had already undergone a night's punishment it would not be right to leave the matter there. For the next two weeks the entire class, including Vitay and Torma, would be banned from borrowing fiction from the library and would be excluded from the showing of any films. On the latter occasions the Sister would set them more useful and improving tasks. As for the instigator, Georgina Vitay, she should present herself after lunch at the staff residence and ask for Mr Kőnig, tell him the full truth, that she had monstrously ridiculed him, and very humbly beg his pardon. This would be done in the presence of the Prefect. And to make the punishment complete, he would personally accompany the Sister and Vitay as the class representative.

What a brilliant plan! It exceeded their wildest dreams. Once again the girls felt that Kalmár had been the perfect choice as an object of yearning. The idea that Kőnig would have to sit and listen while it was made absolutely clear to him, in case he had ever doubted it, that he had been ridiculed to his face, and that all this would happen that very evening, in his own lodgings and in front of Susanna, made their own punishment seem trivial. Twenty faces turned to the Prefect to hear what she would say. She must by now have realised what she had brought down on Kőnig's head: if she had said nothing the scandal would have been forgotten in a day and rarely mentioned again; no-one would have been insulted and nothing serious would have happened. It had merely been necessary to punish the fifth year for writing some ill-conceived caricatures, and they would know better next time. Now both she and Kőnig would get what they deserved, and all this in the presence of Kalmár.

Kalmár asked her if she was satisfied with the punishment he had imposed. She turned to look him full in the face, said nothing, and did not thank him. She simply nodded her head and left the room. No-one, probably not even Kalmár, could ever explain what happened next. When, two days later, they began to prepare for his next lesson, they found he had filled their exercise books with incoherent notes. It was as if he had scribbled without knowing what he was saying, and even the dates were wrong. Not one of the kings he listed had even been on the throne at the time he suggested, as could be plainly seen on his wall chart.

By lunch, thanks to the breaktime rumour machine, there was not one girl in the upper forms who did not know about the Sokoray Atala tradition and the way Georgina Vitay had introduced it into the Matula. Kerekes had sent the older Aradi girl, the tall standard-bearer, to the second-year classroom to fetch a protractor and she had been almost sick with excitement when she saw what was on the blackboard. They were writing an essay on the first topic on the list: "The Pleasures of Fido: a story based on the passage we read." She was barely able to stammer out that she had come for the protractor. Fido was the nickname she had given her fiancé, a Dr János Jablon, because of the doggy look in his eyes whenever he showed affection. She decided that as soon as she had a spare moment she too would write about the pleasures of Fido, whom she was to marry in the summer as soon as he was given leave to return from the front.

The collective punishment did not much bother the fifth year, and Gina prepared for her visit to the staff residence as if it were merely a social occasion. When her lessons were over she changed into her dark-blue uniform. On her way to supper Miss Gigus asked her why she had put it on. She replied, loudly enough for everyone around to hear, that she was going to the staff quarters to apologise to Mr Kőnig for insulting him in a satirical essay she had written and she thought the uniform would be a sign of respect. Miss Gigus turned round abruptly and raced off to the teachers' table as if fired from a gun: now the class knew that everyone in the building would be aware of what had really happened the day before and what would follow that afternoon. Within minutes the entire staff, with the exception of the Director, before whom they always exercised discretion, and of course Kőnig himself, would know too. The whole school would watch in fascination as the funeral procession of Vitay, Kalmár and Susanna set out, supposedly to complete the poor girl's punishment but in fact to insult him as he had never been insulted in his whole life, and to destroy any last vestige of hope he might still be nursing in his more optimistic moments that the scurrilous essay had not been directed at him. But for the moment he was in excellent humour, asking for a third helping of the vegetables. Miss Gigus did not dare look at him.

The excitement during the meal was so palpable that the Director had to speak sharply to the girls, something he had never had to do before. It was the turn of the seventh year to provide the reader, and fate had decreed that Déak would be the one to continue the soul-uplifting tale from Switzerland. It had reached the point where the virtuous maiden had resolved, from a mixture of humility, duty, affection and gratitude to her adoptive mother, to offer her hand not to the upstanding Theophilus but to her godson, a gibbering, pockmarked, hunchbacked youth, and to submit to a life of loving self-sacrifice in which she would fill his gloomy, bumbling days with joy and sunshine. The girls were shaking with suppressed laughter. Every one of them knew by what magisterial coup Kalmár had seen off Kőnig's claim on Susanna, and they felt that if she were capable of falling in love with someone simply out of pity then it was only right that she be shown the error of her ways.

The atmosphere was so electric that the Director asked each of the teachers in turn what was agitating the pupils. The only one who offered a coherent reply was Kőnig, who told him in all innocence that even in a tranquil institution like the Matula people could be affected by the war, or perhaps it was the change in the weather, because young girls were very highly strung.

In the few seconds she spent standing outside Susanna's door waiting for Kalmár to join them, Gina felt a strange sensation rising in her, as if she were slightly drunk, but when she finally set off for the staff residence, with the two adults on either side, the exhilaration melted away. She felt no pity for Kőnig. In fact she found the whole business rather distasteful. She and he were mere bit-part players in a drama acted out between Kalmár and Susanna; it was a matter between the two of them and there was nothing she could contribute. Susanna was downcast and deathly pale, Kalmár simultaneously offended and triumphant. As they passed the window with the view of the niche in the wall Gina wondered whether, if Kőnig had known earlier in the day what was in store for him and had written one of those messages to Abigail to tell her that he was facing a crisis, she would have come to his aid? Did she help everyone out, or was it just the pupils?

Kalmár unlocked the grille at the entrance to the corridor, and for the first time ever Gina found herself inside the staff residence. The idea of having to repeat the story of the Sokoray Atala in the presence of the man she had humiliated did not now seem quite so amusing, though she was sure he would not rage at her but simply behave as if nothing important had happened. Kalmár knocked on the door, waited for his colleague to answer, and stepped back to let Susanna enter first.

By the time Gina was inside, Kőnig was already on his feet. He must have been marking work: there was a pen in his hand and a pile of exercise books on his desk. Now her heart really began to thump, and she felt desperate to get back to the other girls. His room was beautiful, fitted out with exquisite taste – even in this most difficult moment she could see that – and it took her by surprise. The larger items of furniture must have been his own: the school would never have provided him with all those antiques. The two pictures on the walls were the work of well-known painters, in fact masterpieces. She had been to museums and galleries with Marcelle often enough to know that.

"Aha," he said, and stood there smiling. "This is a surprise! Welcome, all of you. Do please have a seat."

Despite the invitation there was nowhere for Gina to sit. There were only three chairs in the room. She could not directly see the look on Susanna's face, but she sensed what it must be from the way she was holding herself: "This is going to be very unpleasant, so be on your guard." Kőnig's smile, which she could see very clearly since Kalmár had placed her directly opposite him, vanished, then immediately returned, broad, radiant and unshakeably serene.

"Mr Kőnig," Kalmár began, in the tone he reserved in his history lessons for announcing national disasters, "we have come to you on behalf of year five, the Sister as their class prefect, myself as class tutor, and Vitay as the guilty person concerned."

"Guilty?" Kőnig looked puzzled. "Of what is she guilty?"

There was no reply. Kalmár embarked on his important revelation, but before he got to the point Kőnig burst out laughing.

"You aren't still bothered about that essay she wrote? The poor girl has already had her punishment. She had to spend the whole night copying out a psalm, as I heard. I gave the class an unsuitable subject and the blame is entirely mine: write a satire, anything goes, and that includes insults. They are young and inexperienced. Vitay simply described me as she sees me."

This was even more painful than she had feared. She stared at the carpet and could hardly breathe.

"Of course, even if that is how she sees me, she should not have said so. But she is still very young. She'll learn better in due course. Is that not so, Vitay?"

Gina did not reply. What could she possibly say?

"Mr Kőnig is not in the least like that," Susanna said in a hoarse whisper, though her voice was usually strong and clear.

"Your teacher has a noble heart, magnanimous and forgiving. Thank him, Georgina, and beg his pardon."

"Thank you," Gina responded, almost inaudibly. "I beg your pardon."

"Now look, this really isn't important. It's not a tragedy and it wasn't one yesterday. It's just that these are difficult times and I didn't want to worry the Bishop or the Director. So let's just forget about it. Do you like dried plums?"

The question took them so much by surprise that they just stared at him. He dipped his hand into an elegant wooden box in which dark plums were lined up like soldiers on parade.

"Mitsi Horn brought these this morning. They are from her own garden. Do try one, Sister."

Susanna could only shake her head, and Kalmár also declined. Gina stood rooted to the spot. More than ever she wanted to be somewhere, anywhere, else. Once again she had the feeling of being caught up in a play, a play in which she had a totally insignificant role and whose plot was impossible to follow: just as the tragedy reached its climax one of the actors smiled and asked the others if they would like a dried plum. Seeing that no-one was ready for a little light refreshment, Kőnig ate one himself, a gesture that made it perfectly clear that he had no idea how he could be of further use to his visitors, that he had drawn a line under the matter of Vitay's essay and it was no longer of interest to him. It was obvious that the visit had been futile. His insatiable appetite and total indifference struck them as downright insulting; Kalmár had been denied the pleasure of embarrassing him, because he had not been embarrassed; Susanna was left feeling that there was nothing she could do or say. The man had not been in the least disturbed in the way she had expected; he seemed interested only in his stomach, and perhaps in Mitsi Horn. It isn't worth even trying to make fun of him, Gina thought. He's so utterly insensitive he doesn't even notice.

They took their leave. Kalmár went back to his room and Susanna to the chapel, where Gina felt sure she would give way to tears, something she would never normally do. Once again Kőnig had failed to grasp what he had done. Perhaps he had not consciously intended to reject this second approach by her because he had simply not seen it for what it was, but he could scarcely have made it more obvious that he was perfectly happy on his own.

She made her way back to the day room. There she was besieged by questions not only from her own class but from messengers from the two senior years wondering how the story had ended. Her description of the elephantine placidity Kőnig had shown was received with bitter disappointment. They had expected something quite different, either far more serious or simply farcical. She had to tell the story at least ten times, and was still being interrogated when they went out into the garden. They had "chosen" to go there for a short break instead of their usual afternoon walk, after the Director had sent his assistant Suba to tell them that he had decided the garden would provide them with all the fresh air and exercise they needed, but if anyone missed the shop windows and the passers-by and would rather go into town, they should think of the Bishop's visit of the day before, and the satirical essays. They wandered around the wintry enclosure no longer feeling quite so happy. The statue of Abigail gazed on in silence.

It was later that same evening that she spoke again. Gina found another note in one of the exercise books in which she wrote her homework. The message was rather chilling.

THERE MUST BE NO MORE OF THESE SCANDALS. THE REST OF THE STAFF ARE NOT KŐNIG, NEITHER IS THE DIRECTOR. THIS IS AN ORDER. ABIGAIL.

The attack on the aquarium;
the General's farewell

The message reawakened Gina's curiosity and fired her determination to find out who was so attentively following her fate from afar – this unknown person who knew so precisely what was happening inside the school walls and continued to help her. Over the next several days she spent every spare moment wandering around near the statue. She slipped out into the garden at the most unlikely moments, even when she had not had permission, receiving several reprimands in the process. But she saw nothing. She met not a single soul, came across not a trace of the real Abigail. Mari Kis asked her why she was always sneaking out there. She said she was dying of curiosity to know who was hiding behind the statue. "Don't be so stupid," Mari told her. Gina was surprised by the anger in her voice. "Nearly everyone has tried, but no-one has ever succeeded. Even Aradi, and she's really clever. Abigail taught her a firm lesson. She realised that Aradi was trying to find out who she was, so she wrote and told her not to poke her nose in or she would come to the same end as Psyche in the myth – you remember: she dropped burning oil from her lamp on the sleeping Cupid and he woke and left her forever. If you carried on prowling around the statue and did find out who she was, the same would happen.

So for heaven's sake, stop! What would we do without Abigail?"

By now Gina was becoming increasingly impatient to see her father again.

In their last telephone conversation he had told her that they would meet again soon. On the Wednesday of the following week he appeared without warning.

A great number of things happened on that late November morning, but it was only much later that she saw the connection between them. Every episode or image associated with that Wednesday fused in her mind – the gaping mouths of the dead fish, the filing cabinet standing open, the glazier's assistant with his huge moustache, and the General. She tried time and time again to separate the images from the events and to focus on her father alone, but she never succeeded. His figure always returned, but next to his grave and solemn face, in a strange twinning of opposites, would be that of Mráz, his sharp features bedecked with his huge moustache, and the lifeless fish scattered like precious stones across the parquet floor and the carpet in front of the open drawers.

The series of events started early, shortly after morning prayers, when most of the pupils were already in their classrooms and the teachers still in the staff room. The Director had begun the day with his colleagues, as he did every morning, having accompanied them as they filed out of the chapel, glancing back all the while to see if they were behaving as they should. He took out his bunch of keys and unlocked the door to his office. The fifth year were still on their way up to their classroom, and had just reached the top of the stairs when an uncanny howling, unlike anything any of them had ever heard, arose from behind the office door. The teachers, the ancillary staff and the deaconesses all rushed to the scene, fearing the worst – it was the sort of terrified screaming you might hear in Africa when a huge roar brings the shocking revelation that there are lions nearby and you had better run. The only member of the ancillary staff on that floor was Suba; he had dashed into the office, which was right next to the fifth years' classroom where they were now lining up to go in, and had run out into the corridor again, bellowing for the cleaners to come. If he had kept his wits about him and not lost his head in the extremity of his panic he might have realised that there was little point: the cleaning was done only when lessons had finished; the staff room and the Director's office were seen to after evening prayers, when no teacher was likely to be around and the Director had withdrawn to his apartment and had his telephone line transferred across. (By nine in the evening every room in the building would be ready for the next day's work and awaiting the onward march of learning in a state of absolute spotlessness.) He should have realised that screaming would be pointless: none of the cleaning ladies would be anywhere near, as they were all either helping out in the kitchen or dealing with the dormitories and other places used by the girls. But he certainly had his reasons, and the class quickly discovered what they were. The aquarium had been smashed and all the fish were dead.

The Director's collection of fish had been the subject of ongoing debate. According to Mari Kis he was a widower only in appearance: he now had a second wife; it was either one of the fish or, at the very least, a water-sprite, and he kept her in his aquarium. She was a fish only by day; at night she changed into a woman. No-one had ever actually seen the Director gazing tenderly at anyone or anything other than his fishy darlings. If Suba hadn't been drunk (but then, how could he have been, and on what, inside the walls of the Matula?) then something must have happened to justify those incoherent bellowings. From the sound of them every one of those miraculous creatures in Gedeon Torma's aquarium, the ones with the lacy tails, the brilliant blue damselfish and other exotic species, must have been lying on the floor stone dead, the parquet flooring ruined and the carpet a battlefield.

The whole thing was utterly incomprehensible. When the cleaners finished their rounds at nine the Director had personally locked all the doors, just as he did every night, and had seen for himself that everything was in order inside his office. So who on earth could this madman be, to break into the Matula after dark and vandalise an aquarium? How could he have opened the door? And with what? No-one apart from Gedeon Torma had a key to the office. There was of course a duplicate, kept by the porter, who lent it to the cleaner on duty for the short time that her work took her. On the previous evening, at 8.45 p.m. precisely, the widow Botár had hung it back on the board before his very eyes, and it had remained there for the rest of the night alongside all the other keys.

Kalmár, who was in charge of the first-floor corridor on that particular day, did his best to calm the assistant down. "Pull yourself together!" he snapped. "You're setting a bad example to the children." The Director came flying out of the office and told him to take the debris and the unfortunate victims away. Kőnig was still standing at the door of the fifth years' classroom, where, having set them a particularly difficult Latin exercise to prepare for his lesson, he had been waiting for them to arrive. Suba finally realised that there was no point in screaming and that the cleaners were not going to abandon their work in the kitchen. Kalmár promised that he would get him some help with the office, and looked at the class. They gazed back with eyes full of hope and anticipation. They had of course done the preparation, but it would be far more interesting not to have to do the lesson and nose around the Director's office instead: what an enticing prospect, and what opportunities that would give – so much to see and take in, to hear and touch and handle. Looking for a girl to volunteer for this exciting task, his eye fell on Oláh, then moved on, and she clamped her mouth tight in annoyance. She should have known. It was disgraceful the way he had favoured Vitay ever since she had demolished Kőnig in that essay.

Gina's position in the class had changed since the Bishop's visit. She no longer enjoyed the same degree of sympathy from Susanna, but Kalmár had made her his pet. It was not that he ever allowed her to get away with a bad answer; rather, it was as if they were party to the same secret. He treated her less like a pupil and more the way a young man might an adolescent girl who had a private understanding with him. It was that they both despised Kőnig.

Having recruited Gina, he told Suba that the fifth-year girl would sort out the office for him and sent him away. He should telephone the glazier and get him to ask his assistant Mr Mráz, the moustachioed handyman who maintained the school windows, to come and see what could be done with the smashed aquarium. And he should ask Mr Éles, as the natural history teacher, to send a new one and some ornamental fish for the Director.

Kőnig stood at the classroom door listening with obvious admiration to the way his colleague was dealing with the matter – so speedily, so imaginatively and with such decisive energy. Ever since the visit he had paid him with Gina and Susanna, Kalmár had treated Kőnig with an unvarying courtesy edged with a hint of contempt. He now asked him if he would mind letting Vitay miss his lesson. The question was politely put, but was in fact insulting, as he had already claimed her. Kőnig nodded as if to say, "But of course," and the other girls marched inside behind him with daggers in their eyes. He gave Cziller the exercise books to hand out. Murai's last thought before she gave herself up to the fascinating task of translating Ovid from Hungarian into impeccable Latin (it was his poignant farewell to his family and to Rome as he left for exile) was that, as Susanna had so obviously rejected Kalmár, then perhaps if Vitay made a bit more effort she might take her place. Kalmár was young, Vitay was attractive, and her Feri was far, far away.

Gina was shrewd enough not to find the broom, the bucket and the sponge too quickly. She knew exactly where to look for them (there were cleaner's storerooms along every corridor) but she started by visiting each in turn, as a way of spinning out the time: if anyone caught her out, she would explain that she was looking for a better mop and a drier broom. She was in no hurry to get back to the Latin lesson when there were all these wonderful possibilities to look forward to.

She went into the office and found herself alone for a few minutes. Suba was obviously still in the staff room trying to get through to the glazier.

A truly woeful sight confronted her. She had never taken a great deal of interest in aquariums, but the gleaming little corpses spread across the sodden carpet and the parquet flooring, all with their mouths gasping for air, for a last taste of life itself, could not fail to move her. The aquarium had a stand of its own: it was impossible to imagine who might have hauled it down, and why. Eventually Suba returned. Gina slowly and casually mopped the water up and then, taking great care not to put her hand on them, brushed the shattered fragments of glass into a pan and tried to sweep up the spilled sand and ballast. She was reluctant to touch the fish, not because they repelled her but because of the thought of their having slowly suffocated overnight. Suba made no attempt to help. He just walked about talking to himself and muttering that the glazier's assistant was on his way and the Director had told him to keep his eyes open. When he was last there at nine he had found everything in order, and if the aquarium had collapsed it didn't have legs of its own to jump about so someone must have pushed it off its stand, and that could only have been a burglar. Who else would have broken into the office?

As she fiddled about with the carpet Gina kept looking around. Nothing appeared to have changed. Suba knelt down, picked the fish up by their tails and tossed them in the bucket. He told Gina to get a move on, then telephoned the Director to announce that he had found nothing amiss and they had finished cleaning up, but he should come and see for himself. There was no clue as to who might have broken in; it was even possible that no-one had. The door had been locked, there were bars on the window, the cupboard, the table and the desk drawers were all intact, and no-one would have forced their way in just to knock an aquarium onto the floor. Perhaps a very gentle earthquake might have caused it? But none of them had felt anything.

The Director arrived at almost the same time as the glazier's assistant. He walked around the room checking everything, and was just emptying the steel safe (there was a great deal of money in it) when Mráz appeared. Gina continued to dab the carpet, very gently, though by then it was almost completely dry, taking note of all that was happening: crouching there was so much more interesting than Ovid's lachrymose wailings. "Nothing seems to be missing," Gedeon Torma declared as Mráz made his entry, like an actor appearing on stage for the closing lines, his moustache twitching with a small smile as he bade the Director good day. He squatted down beside the aquarium and prodded the metal where one of the panes had shattered into pieces, while the Director sorted through the contents of his desk, murmuring as he did that no-one had been into any of the drawers, rested a hand on the top of the filing cabinet, went through the personal records and archived letters, and pronounced everything in order. The workman turned the aquarium round and smiled once again, as if something the Director had said had secretly amused him.

He had one piece of good news. Purely by chance there were some panes of glass in the workshop that would do to repair it, this famous aquarium that the Director had treasured all these years, and he went off with it under his arm. From outside the room came the sound of the bell. Gina realised with delight that she had managed to miss the entire Latin lesson, though sadly there was no way she could prolong the idleness any further. She picked up the bucket and cleaning implements and followed the workman out. Kőnig had just emerged from the classroom, carrying a pile of Latin translations on his arm, and he accosted her. "Georgina Vitay, have you finished in there?" Since he could see with his own eyes that she had, there seemed little sense to his question, but then what else did one expect from Kőnig? Standing to attention as required, she clasped the mop to her chest like a soldier on parade and confirmed that she had. In the same instant she noticed that Mráz had also stopped and turned round, still clutching his burden, and was studying her closely. Their eyes met, and she had a sudden longing to see herself in a mirror, to discover what sort of face she presented: this Mráz was no beauty, but he was after all a man, and the look he was giving her left her feeling strangely disturbed. Then he disappeared, leaving her alone with Kőnig. The moment he saw what was in her bucket, the ornamental fish mixed in with the water and dirt from the mopping-up, he began to tremble. "The poor things," he exclaimed, and whatever pity she herself might have had for the little lace-tails vanished at the sight of his grief. My God, she thought, I hope he isn't going to weep into the bucket! All that *emotion* for a few fish!

She returned the implements to the closet and made her way back to the classroom, where Mari Kis told her that the divine Ovid had been hellishly difficult. Stupidly, she failed to ask her which passage had been set. Following the afternoon snack, when the others were free to do whatever they chose, she discovered she would have to do it herself. Susanna summoned her to her room, planted her exercise book in front of her and told her that she understood that she had had to miss a lesson. It really worried her when a pupil missed an exercise, so would she have the goodness to make it up? There was the passage; she had asked Mr Kőnig for it to pass on to her. Gina thought she would explode. Susanna sat with her throughout, and though she was busily mending her underwear there was not the slightest hope of Gina nipping out on some pretext to get her Latin book and look over the full extract. She made a very poor job of the translation, the worst she had done in all her time in the school. She was so angry at having to do it at all that she had found it impossible to concentrate.

The General arrived while they were having their supper. He stood glancing up and down the vast refectory while the older Aradi read out further episodes in the life of the pious Swiss maiden. It took him some time to pick out the face he had travelled so far to see, hidden as it was among the many heads peering up from their plates. The Director ordered a setting to be laid for him, and Gina was so excited she could barely eat another mouthful. Her father had never appeared at such a late hour before. She longed to run across to greet him, but Matula self-restraint required that she wait until the meal was over, and even then it was only after Susanna had given permission that she was able to go to him. It would have been impossible for her to leave the school at that late hour, but in any case the General did not ask for it. He said he had very little time to spend in Árkod, and if he could simply exchange a few words with his daughter while they waited for prayers it would be enough. Susanna sent them off to the study room, which was always free at that hour.

Her father had brought her a box of pastries and a beautifully wrapped parcel from Auntie Mimó. Gina promptly hid it in her blouse. Her aunt had sent her a bottle of perfume, a stick of rouge, an eyebrow pencil and a marcasite brooch shaped like a squirrel. She told her father that she was now much happier in the Matula, and gave him a shortened account of the strange circumstances in which she had broken the ice and been reconciled with her classmates. She had been speaking for some minutes when she became aware that, although her father was still listening to her with a smile on his face, and had been telling her what her family and their acquaintances in Budapest had been doing, passing on messages from them and explaining that Ili the housemaid would be leaving them in the spring because she was going to celebrate her engagement at Christmas, there was something different about him. Nothing had changed in his tone of voice or his demeanour, but the two of them had always been so close, there had always been such a deep bond of sympathy between them, such an instant mutual understanding, that she knew something was troubling him. She stopped in the middle of a sentence, as if some voice she alone could hear had shouted: "Don't tell him about what happened in your last session in the gym, it really doesn't matter that you were the only one who could do those floor exercises and that Gertrúd Truth was so pleased with you – it's of no importance now." She sat looking at her father and waited. He gazed back at her, surprised by the sudden silence, then urged her to tell him more about the school and the other girls. He doesn't know where to start, she said to herself. What is this news he is waiting to tell me? It frightens me.

The conversation became very hesitant. If the bell had not called her to prayers she might have become horribly garrulous and superficial, the way close friends will sometimes chat idly about this and that when there is something needing to be said between them, something so important that they spin out the conversation until the right moment comes. The bell brought a brief respite. Then Susanna appeared, and although she said nothing her manner made it clear that she had come to fetch the girl and it was time for the guest to be on his way. Her manner softened only when the General declared that he had no wish to overstay his time, but he wondered if he might join his daughter in the service, then leave for Budapest immediately afterwards. Susanna arranged for him to sit not with the teaching staff but with Gina, and when she noticed that he was still holding Gina's hand after the prayers had started she simply closed her eyes.

The reading was from Paul's epistle to the Romans. The Chaplain explained that the school motto was taken from chapter 9, verse 16, where it states that mercy is not "of him that wills or of him that runs" but belongs to God, because human wishes and intentions amount to little: whatever happens is the result of His will. Gina was so conscious of her father's presence that she listened with only half an ear. It was only much later, when Mráz, the Director's ornamental fish, her father's presence and that reading from the apostle had become no more than memories, that she was able to see the connection between them. It was always a source of happiness to her that the person she had loved more than anyone in her life – more, after she had been married and had her own home, than even her husband and her children – had had a goal and had fought for it, never bothering to ask whether or not it was his own will that he was following or whether the purpose behind it accorded with God's. He knew what he wanted, and he strove for it until the hour of his death.

She was allowed to accompany him to the gate. Passing through the garden they sensed the coming of snow: none had yet fallen, but they could smell it in the air. They stopped just inside the vaulted porch, too far from the porter's office for anyone to hear what they said. And at last he revealed what he had been waiting to reveal all evening. It was what Gina had so accurately foreseen.

"You must say goodbye to me, Gina. Kiss me, but do not cry. Our enterprise is entering a critical phase. It will be a long time before I can come and see you again, weeks or possibly even months, and for a while I won't be able to telephone you either. You must not be afraid or sad. Just wait patiently until I contact you again."

He looked down at the well-scrubbed flagstones under the vaulted ceiling. The weekly telephone calls had provided the momentum that had carried her from one Saturday to the next, even if the inescapable presence of Susanna and the Director had reduced them to banality. Only now did she realise how much they represented continuity. Could she stay on in the Matula without hearing his voice? Perhaps for months? But the holidays were starting in December!

"I shall be here again at Christmas. If there is any chance at all I shall be with you on Christmas Eve. If I don't come, it will be because it is simply impossible. But I will come at some point after that, sometime after the school holidays. If not, someone else will give you news of me. That is as true as the fact that we love each other. Do you understand what I am saying? Promise me that you will never do anything foolish, and that you will wait patiently."

Since the first of September that year Gina had been a daughter of the Matula, trained by Susanna. To prevent him seeing how sad she was now, she buried her head in her father's shoulder and clung to him. But she did not have to try too hard. He grasped her chin and raised her face to look into it one last time, and she saw the same profound sorrow written on his. He kissed her, then pushed her away tenderly, and gestured silently that she should not accompany him to the gate. Her eyes followed him for a few moments, and she saw his face once again when he turned round, his eyes glittering in the blue light of the porch. She was sure she could make out his form even after he had disappeared into the street. She had no idea that she would never see him again.

The St Nicholas' Day service

On November 29 they decided that, as they were never going to be allowed to cook dumplings or make lead castings to discover the names of their future husbands, they could at least try making paper stars. Of the St Andrew's Eve divinatory practices the lead-casting was the only one Gina was familiar with. She had never heard of the one involving meatballs wrapped round a piece of paper (the first to rise to the surface in boiling water would have the name inside it) or of the paper star method: you had to fill five of the six points with the names of all the possible contenders and leave the last one blank, trusting fate to send you someone you had not yet met. Gina worried about the idea of using the names of real people in her own, but Oláh reassured her: the others would also have at least one suitable name besides Kalmár's and they would fill in the rest with the boys' names they liked most. You had to put your star underneath your pillow, tear off one of the points during the night, and then look (but only in the morning) to see who the oracle of St Andrew had given you.

They waited for that moment with mounting impatience. To make sure the magic worked they kept the names they had chosen strictly to themselves. However, when Susanna came to put the lights out she ordered them to lift their pillows so that she could see what was underneath them. They obeyed with downcast looks. She went from one bed to the next gathering up the stars, tore them into shreds one after another, without bothering to read what was on them, and dropped the pieces into her huge pockets. She uttered not a word of reproach, but it was perfectly clear from the look on her face what she thought of all such superstitions. When she finally left them, lying in the dark and feeling thoroughly dejected, they tried to think how she could have known about them. They worked it out soon enough. They had been inadvertently betrayed by Dudás, the good honest Dudás, who hated doing anything badly and loved everything to do with drawing – paints, pencils and the like. She had decided that if they were going to make a star then it should be a really good one, and they should ask for some of the proper drawing paper from the store cupboard. No-one reproached her for her blunder: first of all, it no longer mattered, and second, no-one would ever have imagined that Susanna knew about the St Andrew's oracle and the folk superstition attached to it, or that it would be enough for her just to see Dudás handing out drawing paper to the class – clearly not for writing out endless long division sums or irregular verbs in French – to realise that they would be making name stars back in the dormitory.

Luckily something happened the next day that made them forget their disappointment. Szabó, who tended the plants in the staff common room, returned from her "weed nursing" (as she called it) with some sensational news: the following Friday, the name day of the Regent, was to be a national holiday and a school holiday as well. Gedeon Torma, simultaneously boiling over with rage and puffed up with pride at the promised moment of glory, had told the Chaplain that because the festival was common to both Church and state the school would have the honour of celebrating the day by welcoming the city dignitaries at their usual service. The fifth year were beside themselves with delight. Everyone knew that the requirement to give them a holiday on December 6 drove the Director to distraction: Admiral Horthy could call himself what he liked, Caiaphas or Jebuzeus, but not Nicholas. It gave those reprobate Matula girls the idea that the school celebrated the day and enjoyed all that wonderful food as part of a purely pagan festival that had no place inside the school walls.

"It's going to be fantastic!" Szabó said, between her gasps for breath. "The Mayor will be joining us, and so, believe it or not, will the Lord Lieutenant. He's officially a Catholic, but they ignore that on national holidays, and they'll all be there – the city aldermen and representatives of the local garrison. The Director may be heartbroken because he hates the name Nicholas, but he's also horribly proud. He told the teachers who were there to start preparing their classes immediately and to remind them what sort of behaviour would be expected on the day, because the whole of Árkod would be there to dignify the proceedings." She added that the Chaplain was so beside himself he was like a young girl going to her first ball, and the other teachers were also glowing with pride. The fifth year duly spread the word, and the whole school began thinking about and looking forward to the great event.

Their normal church services were rather dull affairs: those civic leaders who did occasionally worship there rarely came to the school-specific services. This event promised to be something special, a welcome touch of colour in the general greyness. They were so beside themselves that evening that Susanna had her work cut out to keep them quiet. What excited them was not so much the prospect of a celebratory supper (many of the pupils were the daughters of farmers who paid the fees in produce and the food in the Matula was always good) as the prospect of seeing people from the town.

The next day the north wind sprang up.

Gina had thought that she could never again be surprised by anything the weather might do. She knew what it was like to be out at sea, she had even been on a ship during a storm, she had paced the shores of the Atlantic in driving rain, experienced the furnace that was Sicily and stood on the edge of a glacier; but in Árkod she was to encounter something quite new: the wind of the Great Plain. In later years, whenever she dreamed of the fortress and the city the wind would always be present, moving restlessly among human figures obscurely glimpsed in the haze.

The noise it made was tremendous. Coming from the north, it brought a chill that cut to the bone. The radiators lining the corridors pumped out their heat in vain; it poured round the edges of closed windows and the girls shivered in its breath; they heard it night and day, howling without a moment's pause. It went on for nearly a week. At supper on the Thursday before the service the church bell ringer appeared, asked the Director for permission to speak and delivered a message from the Chaplain. The next day they were to dress up warmly. An hour earlier, as the church was being cleaned, the wind had smashed one of the windows. Mr Mráz had been sent for, but his men were unable to do anything before the morning, and by then the temperature in the church would have plummeted. The wind was quite exceptional. Even snow would have been better.

And he added a personal detail, to add spice to the news. The gales had been so fierce that they had gathered dust from the Great Plain and the surrounding farmland and blown it into the city. It was still swirling about in the streets, and it was unclear whether the cantor would be in a fit state to play the organ: he could barely see out of one of his eyes. It was blood-red and inflamed by the dust, and he was wheezing with catarrh from whatever it was that had been blown in his face.

There was little interest in the state of the cantor's eye. The girls had other concerns now. And there was something else that they were starting to talk about in hushed tones in their rest period, something none of the teachers ever mentioned. The gale had liberated something more elemental, a sense of foreboding that they were too young to put into words. The older Aradi sat staring straight ahead, ignoring the open book on her lap. She was thinking of what it must be like at the front, where her Fido would be tending to the wounds of some poor soldier, and she was wondering if the same icy wind was raging over there.

They could still hear it when they went to bed. It sent them to sleep earlier than usual, and the next morning they did not, for once, have to be constantly chivvied to get up. Szabó's eaves-dropped news had worked its effect. Their faces were lit up by the prospect of their encounter with the outside world, the world they only ever became part of during their afternoon walks, and the hope of seeing something really interesting. It was to be a day like no other in the school year.

In the Sokoray Atala, and generally in Budapest, the last Sunday in November and the arrival of December had never been thought of or talked about as particularly special, either at home or at Auntie Mimó's. But here in the Matula the mood seemed to change from one day to the next, as you might re-set a heating system. Like Christmas itself, St Nicholas seemed to be taking forever to come. It was inconceivable to Gina that her father would not find a way to be with her, even if the great project he and his colleagues were engaged in was moving into a critical phase. She was sure he would think of something that would take him to a neutral venue, perhaps on a visit to friends, or he might even stay in the school itself. People from outside had been known to take advantage of its hospitality.

As she was doing her hair before setting off for the service Gina thought about something else that Szabó had heard: people from the garrison would be present. She often thought of the soldiers stationed in Árkod: their uniforms always brought her father and Feri to mind, and with them the incredibly brave, faceless person based there who was working in the same cause as the General. She never doubted for a moment that even if he were the leader of the civil defence he must be a soldier.

That day the blue crocodile glided down the streets with a disciplined elegance it had never managed before. There was one particularly exciting moment on the way, when they caught sight of the Cock-a-doodle-doos in the distance, going to their own service, held not of course in the great white church but in a smaller one built of red brick and altogether less distinguished. They spotted the Matula in their turn, and the teachers of both schools were given strong cause for satisfaction: the moment they caught sight of each other, both the state-educated girls on their way to the red-brick building and their counterparts from the Academy marching to the white one struck out for the honour of their schools, and the standard of their performance reached a level such as no orders or instructions could ever have achieved. Both Aradi and the distant leader of the Cock-a-doodle-doos strove to carry their banners with a self-confident swagger that cried out to be filmed.

A large crowd had gathered outside the church. Gina had never before seen so many people in Árkod, or such a large congregation, and she noted with delight that it did indeed include members of the garrison. Although it was forbidden to stare at them, she took regular glances both at the officers and the women with them, reflecting in wonderment how long it had been since she had seen anyone who was so well dressed. The Matula staff wore a regulation gown during lessons, and when they did appear in their own clothes, for example at mealtimes, they all, with the notable exception of Miss Gigus, opted for decidedly old-fashioned styles, as if to convey that what was important lay within and no manner of garment or display of ephemeral glamour could make up for that. Gina studied these meticulously turned-out city women, with their beautifully coiffed hair just visible under their hats, and marvelled too at the men: they were all so like the ones she had been used to seeing in her former life. It was the first time she had been to one of these special services and now she was experiencing for herself the truly high regard in which the school was held. As representatives of the ancient foundation it was they who led the procession in: it was only when they had passed through the main entrance, with the school standard and the Director at their head, and had been followed in by the civic leaders, that the townsfolk and people who had no connection with the Matula were allowed in.

It was bitterly cold inside, colder even than she had expected, but who cared when they were part of such a magnificent gathering? In Árkod the custom was that the men and women sat in separate pews; only the form tutors broke the rule and remained with their charges. Gina knew she was supposed to be bent in prayer, but she gazed instead around the congregation, watching the officers and the townsfolk dividing off from their wives and taking their seats behind the church officials, and the ladies making their way to look for seats on the female pews. From where she was sitting she had a very clear view, one that included everyone both from the school and from outside. The Chaplain was in a separate pew with his face, as usual, buried in his hands in fervent prayer. Beside him was the assistant chaplain, a man they all knew well by sight. He was the older brother of Salm's Samuka, and the girls often thought that the Director should invite him to lead the evening prayers – though in that case they might pay less than full attention to the Word of God. Gedeon Torma knew exactly why the Chaplain and he had agreed that only he should be in charge of religious instruction, the Sunday sermon and the twice-daily prayers, and why, if he were ever unable to do so through illness, or was away on leave in the summer, his stand-in would have to be some doddering old worthy from the local seminary. Samuka's brother was leaning forward in a mirror image of the priest, and his head too was buried in his hands, on the same level within a hair's breadth.

The cantor started to play. The organ boomed out, but unfortunately not very accurately, and the melody kept breaking down. Word had of course spread the day before that he was having trouble with his eyes, and although years of practice should have guided his fingers the irritation in one of them made it hard for him to concentrate on the music. But it was clear enough that the tune was "Beloved Advent, we greet you", the seasonal hymn that announced the start of the festive season. Gina knew it well but had forgotten its number. She glanced at the board listing the day's hymns.

There were three of them scattered round the church, one facing the pulpit, another over the entrance and one just above the gallery opposite. It had not been the practice in Budapest, as it was here, to display the various texts and psalms to be used during the service, and all three boards carried the full list. They had been concealed behind folding doors while the congregation continued to pour in; it was only when everyone was seated that the three designated church officials would leave their seats beside the organ and make their way, solemnly and with folded hands, towards the wooden steps leading up to them, and fling the covers open with a grand flourish to reveal the chosen hymns. Then, as they processed back to their seats, the congregation would have a chance to thumb through their hymn books and find the songs they were unfamiliar with. The cantor sounded the introduction, everyone rose to their feet and began to sing. Well, Gina thought, I'm certainly glad to welcome you, Advent. I have waited for you long enough. And perhaps I shall even see my father at Christmas.

The organ grew louder and the officials set off on their journey. D, G, F, E, F, E, D, A, H, G, F, G, E, D, A . . . They arrived at their respective galleries and flung the wooden covers open. All eyes, including Gina's, were raised to see which hymn number would be first – surely one of those near the beginning, somewhere between twenty and thirty? She would probably know only the first stanza by heart and would have to look up the rest.

A wave of shame passed through her when she realised how far out she had been. She had reckoned she knew her way around the canticles well enough by now – there were a great many of them and they had certainly given her enough trouble. But once again she had got it wrong. Had Hajdú known he would have sent her straight to the corner. To have confused a hymn with a psalm! It was ridiculous. But the error was logical enough, since the canticles associated with a special ceremony were usually the latter. Right, so it must be Psalm 72. But the tune was exactly the same as for "Welcome, beloved Advent". She leafed frantically through her hymn book, as everyone else was now doing apart from the two priests, who remained slumped forward in their pews and continued to pray regardless of the confusion around them. Psalm 72 was not one she had ever learned, but luckily she knew the tune: it was the same as "On top of Mount

Sion". The cantor must have gone completely mad! Why was he still playing "Welcome, beloved Advent?" Thank heavens they hadn't started singing that out of sheer habit! Hymn books were now open in all the pews. No-one knew this psalm, and they all stared at the text, trying to make sense of it. Everyone was caught in the same dilemma.

And that was why the scandal that ensued would be talked over in such horrified tones and picked over for weeks and months to come, in religious and lay circles alike. The organist continued to boom out the opening hymn, as he had been for the last several minutes, but the entire school and everyone else was now taking instruction from the boards and had started out on a very different tune from that of "On top of Mount Sion". The Matula girls had had a long training in sacred music, and even after the congregation had fallen silent in stupefaction they continued to belt out the first, with all the attention to timing and volume that Hajdú would have wished.

Endow the King with your justice, oh Lord, and his Son with your righteousness, that he may direct his great army with wisdom and rule justly over your suffering people.

At first few people seemed to realise what was happening, but both the Chaplain and the elder Samuka reacted as if they had been rapped across the knuckles and pulled their heads out of their hands at almost the same moment. Lengyel, who had a sore throat and had not been singing but simply miming, reckoned that it would take stronger language than any normal person might use to describe the facial expressions of those around her. As far as Gina was concerned, the words of the

Protestant psalms had always seemed peculiar, and she had been taught at the Matula not to bother her head too much about what the references to Sion or Israel, or the harps in the willow trees by the waters of Babylon, might actually mean. But however bemused they might have been by the fact that the cantor was playing something quite different from what had appeared on the boards, and by the resulting cacophony that was now rising to the heavens, the girls simply ignored what was happening around them and kept their eyes fixed on their hymn books. The psalm was completely new to them, it was one they had never learned, and they trembled at the idea that Hajdú might notice that they had gone astray. Their *fortissimo* and their purity of diction had reached an exemplary perfection when the church officials suddenly put down their hymn books and the Director leaped to his feet, followed by the Mayor, the Commander of the garrison and the County Sheriff. The elder Samuka dashed over to the priests' pew and began an urgent parley with the red-faced elders, while the teachers and deaconesses tried desperately to silence their charges – in vain: it was they after all who had beaten the iron discipline into the girls that forbade the raising of eyes during the recital of a psalm. Their young voices were now sounding forth the second stanza of this appalling text, loud and clear: "May Peace return to the mountains, / Justice be restored on the downs, / the villages spared all this conflict / and the Tyrant overthrown."

The three last phrases could barely be heard. The girls had finally realised that something very odd was happening and that they should stop singing. The pews around them where the adults were sitting had already grasped the enormity of the outrage; the organ fell silent, as did the whole school. Those of the guests who had not leaped from their seats and made for the exits with fury and indignation on their faces were now sitting bolt upright in their pews. Gina, being familiar with the various military ranks, had decided which of the uniformed men present was the Chief of Police, and she was fairly sure that the two rather elegant gentlemen who had been the first to march angrily out had been the Mayor and the Lord Lieutenant. The Police Chief had despatched a lower-ranking officer after them but remained where he was, repeatedly glancing up at the hymn board and noting down the numbers of the psalms and canticles in his notebook. The Chaplain had now taken up position in the pulpit, though his ascent had not been made with his usual processional dignity, or the famous serenity he usually exuded in his glittering silk robes: he had raced up the steps in leaps and bounds as if fired from a gun. Dispensing with the customary "Peace and Mercy be upon you", he gabbled out words to the effect that someone had altered the list of canticles, and would the congregation kindly engage in a few moments of silent prayer while the wardens put them right. He had checked them himself the evening before and again in the morning, and on both occasions, he reassured them, they had shown the correct information.

The silence that reigned was as profound as for the Lord's Prayer, and the whole building hummed with tension. While she waited to see what would come up on the boards next, Gina surreptitiously opened her hymn book at the list of contents page. She was interested to know what the ones displayed had been about and she marked them off with her thumbnail: Psalm 52, hymn number 239, stanzas 1–3, and the Anthem. She knew there would be no chance to look them up straight away, but later that afternoon, when they at last had some free time, all the girls would open the psalm and discover its horrifying content: "Why, oh Tyrant, do you glory in evil? Why in your hour of fortune are you puffed up with pride? The Lord will cast you down forever." And as for canticle 239, it had obviously been given its prominent position because it was the one traditionally reserved not for a patriotic ceremony, and certainly never for a day of festivity such as the name day of the Regent, but for occasions of national mourning.

In a very short time the boards had been restored by the shaking hands of the church officials. It seemed that they should have begun with hymn 28, welcoming the beginning of Advent, and moved on to the main canticle, "Eternal God, Father of your people, You who watch over us" – the one used on occasions of national rejoicing. But by then the girls could have been singing whatever they liked. One by one the city fathers had marched out, and the military officers with them. The first to leave, it later transpired, had gone straight to the presbytery to await the arrival of the luckless Chaplain. He, meanwhile, in a voice quite unlike his usual one, and in jumbled phrases that did more to confuse whoever might still be listening to him, tried to thread together the themes of his Advent sermon, rejoicing in the fact that our destiny lay in the hands of such a wise leader, whom may God preserve. The teachers were trying to behave as if nothing had happened, though it was obvious that Kalmár was very angry and Susanna rather frightened. Kőnig was for once not booming away at the top of his voice – perhaps because he had caught a bad cold and had a vicious cough. The Director's face was covered in red blotches. The older girls were struggling to work out what was going on: the country no longer had a king, the national leader was the Regent, and it was his wisdom that had been challenged by whoever had interfered with the boards . . . and it was also to him – on his name day! – that the pleas for a return to the rule of law and the blessings of peace had been addressed. If one understood the real message of the altered boards it was that this was a day not of rejoicing but of national mourning. How utterly disgraceful!

For her part, Gina finally began to make sense of what had taken place: Kalmár's indignation overruled his training not to mention lay matters during a church service and he whispered in Susanna's ear, "It's that scoundrel once again; he can't even respect a church service."

So it was you again? Gina whispered. Her heart was beating wildly. Another message, and in a place like this! You risked your life on such dangerous terrain? If only I could see your face, you wonderful person! If only you would speak to me, and tell me how the work is going, and what my father is doing, and when he will come!

When this most distressing of services finally ended the congregation sang the national anthem two full bars ahead of the organist, such was their hurry to get out. The Chaplain came down from the pulpit, clinging to the handrail as if he were terrified of falling, and disappeared from the building without delivering the usual prayer of dismissal from the Bishop's throne. Instead of enjoying the usual after-church stroll the girls were taken straight back to the school, with their teachers almost running beside them down the street. You would have thought that they were returning not from a church service but from some appalling spectacle.

Gina was aware of Mari Kis chuckling beside her, and of Szabó and some other girls behind her whispering about what sort of person it must be who would play such tricks on both the church leaders and the civic ones as well. But she remained silent, and kept her eyes fixed straight ahead, not even glancing up as they passed Mr Hajda's window, now ablaze with little St Nicholases and devils made of something that looked like chocolate. The yearning to gaze into the eyes of this unimaginably brave person who had so sensationally cocked a snook at his pursuers made her blush, and a warm glow surged through her body despite the intense cold she had endured in the church. Only he could have smashed that window the night before!

The window, smashed during the night but repaired only in the morning . . .

She realised she had inadvertently stumbled on what the people pursuing him had only just grasped: in their quest to discover who had entered the church through the broken ground-floor window the previous night they had looked everywhere in the presbytery and the church itself, poked around in every cupboard and every nook and cranny and questioned one and all, so now they knew it must have been someone who was familiar with the ways and practices of the church, who knew that the service would start with the opening procession to the hymn boards, and who could be sure that once the display had been set up correctly no-one would check it the next morning. Never had she been as desperate to see anyone's face as she was now, and to gaze into it, blank and veiled in mystery as it was, the face of that unknown person out there, whether smiling or deadly serious. And never in her life had she felt so much respect for anyone other than her father. The walk back to the school was pure agony, not least because she had to listen to König blowing his nose again and again, pulling an endless stream of handkerchiefs out of his pocket and telling everyone he really could not conceive what sort of person would take pleasure in playing such a trick, and that he would not mince his words with Mráz and his glaziers for not having repaired the broken window immediately the night before. It couldn't have been because of anything to do with the defence measures. Did you actually need light to repair a window by? Surely a skilled craftsman could fit a new pane in total darkness with his eyes shut, even if it wasn't possible to take the whole frame out?

Documents

Years later, when Gina thought back to the events of that fateful December and those first few months of the new year, up to that moment at the end of March 1944 when she finally left the fortress, she often asked herself if things would have turned out differently if she had been stronger, if she had dealt better with that period of isolation, or shown greater self-discipline, and she had repeated bouts of tearful self-recrimination. Abigail had told her many times by then that what happened to her father was in no way due to her, and had nothing to do with Bánki's act of loyal friendship, her own failure in that Bible knowledge test, the stormy atmosphere of that Christmas, or even the events of that memorable March evening. The words whispered on that chilly violet-scented evening were not the ones that betrayed her father: that had been done long before, by the person from the counter-espionage unit who, as they later discovered, had been following the movements of the General and his family for over a year. Once they had tracked her down it would have made no difference where anyone phoned the General in his villa from: his enemies had long known exactly what he was up to. It was irrelevant, even, that thanks to Bánki's letter they had known since Christmas that she was hiding in Árkod. The purpose of the hunt she was subjected to in the following days had not been to kill her. What was she but a terrified rabbit fleeing through the forest of the wider war? The real prey, her father and his associates, had been prisoners in Germany ever since the country was occupied on March 19. She would have been of use to them only if they had needed her to compel him to reveal the names of those of his colleagues they had failed to trace, his co-workers in a project that was doomed from the start. By then she had been assured that, whatever else happened to him, he had died with his lips sealed. Abigail had told her that he would have done that even if the alternative had been to sacrifice his daughter, but he had been spared that fate by the actions of the dissident of Árkod. He had been able to depart this life in the knowledge that his beloved child was safe.

But those revelations lay in the distant future. What the immediate future held for Gina was the winter of 1944, the bleak winter of the Great Plain with its fearsome storms and mountains of snow. Meanwhile Christmas was approaching, and it would be even harder to bear if she could not hear from her father.

In the dormitory and the day room the subject of every sotto voce conversation was which train would be taking them home, and when. Their time in the sewing room and for handicrafts was spent making gifts for their families; Susanna had allowed some of them to dip into their pocket money to buy what they lacked the resources to make for themselves. Although her father had told her that they might not be able to meet at Christmas, Gina still clung to the idea that he would come. She was increasingly conscious of the fact that if the fortress offered her the best possible protection then it might shelter him too – Gedeon Torma would surely let him sleep in that very pleasant room used by visiting priests and the inspector of schools. She too was busy making a surprise present for Christmas, something that would be the work of her own hands.

Among the more popular choices at the time were embroidered book-covers and cushions decorated with motifs from folklore. She chose neither but settled instead on a bookmark to be used in a Bible. She was a little unsure of how much actual service it would be to the General – she had rarely seen him with one in his hands – but she thought he might be glad of it as coming from her and keep it for use in some other book. She had difficulty finding a suitable quotation to embroider on it, so she asked Susanna for advice. With the air of cool reserve she had maintained towards Gina ever since the Bishop's visit, the Deaconess reminded her that at the end of term there would be a competition to see who knew their Bible best. If Gina revised for it she might find something she thought particularly appropriate for her father.

Gina had been aware of the existence of this annual competition, but it had never struck her as something that might interest her personally. Compared to the other girls her knowledge of the Bible was extremely poor. She could recall a great many phrases and quotations, but had no idea where they were from, and she confused things that Jesus had said with the words of Paul the Apostle and the four evangelists. But from then on she devoted every spare moment to reading the scriptures, and one evening, in the Book of Psalms, something came up that would do for the bookmark. She had gone to ask Susanna for some fabric and some beads and the Prefect had written on the bunting "Psalm 140, verse 7", and then, without consulting the text, immediately quoted it: "Oh God the Lord, the strength of my salvation, Thou hast covered my head in the day of battle."

December came. On some days the time passed quickly, on others at a snail's pace. When she thought of how long it had been since she had last seen her father it felt more like months than weeks, but when she thought of how much she still had to do the days seemed to last just seconds: the sun had barely risen and it was already evening. The girls were now so caught up with working on their presents that they asked Susanna if they could give up their afternoon walk. She looked at them as if they had addressed her in a foreign tongue and ordered them to fetch their hats and coats. Nor were they given permission to stay up later than the rules allowed, or do their homework in the afternoon rest period; nothing in their routine was to change, and no-one took the slightest interest in how they were supposed to prepare for the competition while carrying on with everything else that they had to deal with. The one minor easement was that in their half-hour reading sessions they could choose to study the scriptures rather than works of literature. If the Director had ever happened to look into the day room and seen the full twenty heads bent over their Bibles, he would have nodded with satisfaction. That was exactly what he imagined a well-brought-up and respectable Matula girl would want to spend her free time doing. By great good luck they were also able to use Kőnig's lessons. For the entire week since the scandalous service in the white church he had lain in his bed with some sort of fever, the result of a cold.

Talk about that notorious event was still very much alive in the school because the investigators had now paid a visit to the Director. That piece of information proved far too interesting for Suba to keep to himself. He had also told his favourite, the older Aradi, that the matter had been smoothed over and the cantor cleared of suspicion. Everyone had agreed that even in the house of God there could be no hiding place for the mysterious spy, or whatever he was: they would be on his trail night and day. Kőnig's lessons were supervised by either Susanna or Elisabeth, neither of whom taught Latin or Hungarian, and they both allowed the class to read the Bible instead.

Bánki knew the scriptures better than any of them and everyone wanted her to test them. At first she obliged one and all; then one evening she became suddenly withdrawn. She seemed anxious and touchy, and she turned everyone away. Her attitude was all the stranger because her mother had come to see her that day, and after such visits you were expected to be especially nice to everyone in your moment of happiness. But not Bánki. She was almost rude to one girl who approached her, book in hand; she shouted at her to leave her alone and dashed out of the room. Gina was in the washroom when this happened, trying to clean ink stains from her fingers, and she looked up in amazement as Bánki burst through the door with the face of someone who could no longer endure her sense of bitterness and burst into tears. Gina put down her nailbrush and tried to get her to say what had happened, but Bánki was too upset to answer; her sobs became even louder, and she ran out again into the corridor, clearly unable to bear being questioned. She eventually managed to calm down and went back to the day room. Cziller asked her what her mother had brought her. "Nothing," she replied sadly. Cziller shrugged dismissively. There was no mother on earth who would come to the Matula and not bring something for her daughter from the magical world outside. Bánki must be out of her wits to do something like that – hiding the sweets or whatever she had been given. Shame on her!

Oláh was the next best on the subject of the Bible and stepped in for her. Gina went over and stood beside Bánki. Some of the other girls were now trying to comfort her: her behaviour was impossible to fathom. She just sat in their midst opening and closing her Bible and glancing at her watch, as if waiting for bedtime. Something's happened to her, Gina thought. To her or her family. Something that Cziller would never be able to imagine. She was crying her heart out in the washroom. Something really bad has happened at home and that's why her mother forgot to bring her anything.

Gina had always been attracted to Bánki, and in the past few weeks they had become particularly close. She was one of the more serious members of the class. She was more grown up than the others, she took things more to heart and often wore a pensive look on her face. Gina had the feeling that even if she didn't have the sort of material problems that many of the others did, or was an orphan like Torma, she must be harbouring some sort of burden, one she could never talk about, just as she herself had to keep silent about the things her father had confided in her. That night in the dormitory, when everything had gone quiet, she lay awake for ages listening to hear if Bánki were crying. But there was nothing: perhaps she had got over whatever it was that had upset her.

Gina was almost asleep when she became aware of something moving on Bánki's bed. She wasn't crying; she was getting up. By the glow of the nightlight Gina watched her take her dressing gown from the hook, step into her slippers and make her way quietly out. Gina put on her own and followed her.

She was in the washroom – where else could she have been? – crouching beside the laundry basket. When Gina came in she raised her head. She wasn't crying: it might have been easier for her if she had been. Her face was the face of an adult in absolute despair.

"Are you in pain?" Gina asked.

She shook her head.

"Is something wrong?"

She nodded.

"Did your mother really not bring you anything?"

Unexpectedly, Bánki smiled, as if to say, My God, she's still thinking about sweets!

"Can I help you in any way?"

Again Bánki shook her head.

"Can you tell me what it's about?"

"I can't," she replied quietly.

"You can't, or you aren't allowed to?"

"Not allowed to."

"Is it very bad?"

She nodded her head to indicate that it was.

"Could anyone help?"

Bánki answered that with a wave of the hand: no-one.

"Not even Abigail?"

She had put the question so naturally she was struck by the realisation that for her too Abigail had become such an obvious source of help in times of need, and one that everyone could rely on.

Bánki considered. Her eyes reflected a great many things, but among them now was a glimmer of hope. Then she shook her head again. The only way to contact Abigail was to write to her and she didn't dare put her troubles on paper. Not knowing what to say, Gina stroked her shoulder, and Bánki suddenly buried her face in Gina's neck. She did not cry. Instead she put her cheek against Gina's and whispered, "Thank you. God bless you!" as if she were about to part with her forever.

Gina was on the verge of asking if perhaps her mother had come to tell her that she was going to remove her from the school before Christmas when the door opened. Standing there was Susanna.

For two girls to go into the washroom together at night was absolutely forbidden. Bánki tore herself away in terror. Gina felt a moment's bitterness. All she had wanted to do was to comfort the poor girl and now she was in trouble again. Susanna was very gentle, terrifyingly so.

"Go back to your beds," she said quietly. "Anna, stop mooning around here, put everything out of your mind and get some rest. You will need to be fresh in the morning. I was watching you this evening. I know you have had some bad news. When we give way to despondency and doubt we lose our faith. I would have thought you might have made better use of the Bible you know so well."

Bánki lowered her head. Susanna's reproach seemed to have given her some comfort.

"The Book of Daniel is a good one to start on," she continued. "Go back to the dormitory and hold your head up high. Vitay, you too. Off to bed. I can't see why you should be here. Do you also have some particular cause for grief?"

How Gina would have loved to shout in her face, "I certainly have!" What could the Prefect be thinking? That her little world corresponded to the real one, the world beyond the school: that nothing existed apart from the Matula? Did she have a cause for grieving? She certainly did. And so did Bánki. How nice it would be if one could put everything right by opening the Book of Daniel. The mocking nickname the Cock-a-doodle-doos had for them leaped into her mind. For the first time she found herself thinking of Susanna as a "holy tripe sausage".

The Deaconess escorted them back to the dormitory. She told them that she was on night duty and would be patrolling the corridors at regular intervals. If they took the risk of leaving their beds again to go and gossip in the washroom she would put the two of them in detention and they could ponder their spiritual shortcomings at leisure. Neither of them dared open their mouth. Even when they were back in their beds they said nothing. Bánki tossed and turned constantly. Listening to her restless movements Gina felt profoundly sorry for her. When Torma was in any kind of pain she would moan and whimper, and Cziller emitted little groans, but all Bánki did was to shift around in her bed in silence, like a thoroughly miserable adult not wanting to burden the children with her pain.

Abigail, you who work miracles!

Bánki had said she did not dare put her troubles in writing, but Abigail knew everything, so perhaps she already knew what Bánki's mother had told her and realised that she needed help because she was so unhappy. They were not allowed to keep things like exercise books and writing materials in the dormitory, so she lay in the dark and tried to plan what she would say to Abigail in the morning.

Dear Abigail,

Something very bad has happened in Bánki's family, but I don't know what it is. She is too frightened to write it down or even talk about it. If you know what has happened and can do something to put it right, please help her. But quickly, because she is very upset.

Vitay

The next morning before prayers she opened the Book of Daniel. It did little to help her. It was about a king called Joachim and some young men with unpronounceable names and it made no sense at all. While they were on their way to the day room to collect their books she pretended she had some homework to finish and scribbled down her message to Abigail. When they reached the corridor that led to the classrooms she nipped out into the garden, leaving her coat behind in case anyone should suspect she was going out and praying as she ran that no-one would see her drop the note into the stone pitcher. In that respect she failed, but luckily it was only Kőnig who had seen her. He opened the door from the teacher's quarters just as she was scurrying back. She stopped, came to attention before him and greeted him, with rather bad grace. He stood there looking at her, and at the snow on her shoes.

"Good Lord," he said, in a voice even thicker with a cold than before. "What are you doing in the garden at a time like this? The others have already lined up. And if it comes to that, why aren't you wearing a coat?"

Kőnig was so insignificant she felt she could lie to him without guilt. She said she had just wanted to pop out and see what the weather had decided to do.

"At this early hour?" he asked in astonishment. "But you won't be going outside before your afternoon walk. Wouldn't it have been simpler just to look out the window?"

Luckily, that was all. He let her wipe her shoes on the doormat outside the teachers' door, and the meeting turned out to have another benefit. When Susanna and her classmates saw her come in with him they assumed that he must have kept her back to tell her something: they had neither noticed what happened nor heard what was said. Gina did not explain, least of all to Bánki.

Bánki seemed calmer now, but she was far more withdrawn than she had been before. Gina observed her closely. She now thought of her as someone like herself, who had problems that went far beyond any that the others had, and she was struck by the natural way they accepted the change in her. They showed not the slightest interest in what had upset her and no-one stopped to think why her mother had not brought her anything special to eat, or, if she had, why she had suddenly become so selfish and greedy and gobbled it up by herself. But if Bánki no longer cried, she began to behave very strangely, and she kept disappearing whenever she could. During break Gina noticed her whispering something to Krieger in year eight and she saw the look that crossed the older girl's face; after the next lesson she spoke to Zelemér in year six, and her face also darkened; and then after lunch she sought out Kun in the third year, though no self-respecting fifth-year girl would normally talk to such babies. During supper and prayers the four of them were together again, and Gina noticed that they all had something in common. In some strange way Bánki, Krieger, Zelemér and Kun had begun to resemble one another: their faces had all taken on the same sombre look of maturity.

The Christmas holidays began on December 22, with lessons ending on the twentieth. In all her time at the school Gina had never received so many bad reports as she did on that last Saturday, when, by some unwritten tradition, the question and answer sessions became particularly searching. The holidays might soon be upon them, but they were expected to show that even at a time like that the only thing on their minds was work. But she could not stop thinking that the holidays began at midday. Her father would be aware that teaching had stopped in all the state schools, and if he had managed to find a way to come it would have to be that afternoon, or the following day at the latest. The girls put a lot of effort into the last lesson, which was in the gym. It was as if they were deliberately taking the opportunity to jump about and exercise to get rid of the tension and excitement that had been building up in them. At the end of the session Gertrúd Truth reminded them not to forget to hand their kit in to the laundry.

For games they wore tops and trousers, gym shoes and special stockings. At the Matula the display of bare feet was considered indecent even when exercising – something Gina's own children could never quite believe when she reminisced about her days in the school. The kit was kept in a row of individual lockers, and everyone had their own numbered shelf and hanger for their uniforms when they changed for gym. It was washed once a fortnight; it went in numbered bags that they took from trays hanging from the shelf for shoes. Gina was in the middle of changing and had started to rummage through her bag when she realised there was something in it. Her hand froze. She felt around inside. Something had been put there. A sheet of paper? No, several sheets. She tried to think who would have given her a present in such a secretive way. A game of hiding things in other people's possessions had been going on for some time now. Oláh had even found a tiny mouse in one of her shoes and had let out such a scream that she was put in detention, along with the mouse-donor, Gáti. Gina decided that if it turned out to be a practical joke it would be better not to say anything while they were still in the changing room but to wait: you couldn't have a proper laugh in there. She would empty the bag when they were back in the dormitory and could have a good look then at what she had been given – probably some satirical lines of verse or a cartoon of one of the teaching staff. She would have to take care not to attract Gertrúd Truth's attention. As they lined up she studied the faces of her classmates to see if any of them seemed to be harbouring a private joke, but they all wore the same expression of deadly seriousness. During this penitential week you could be told off if your face failed to suggest that all the extra prayer sessions and much needed calls for inner reflection had had their effect and you had put all worldly vanities aside.

The class were trying hard not to show how keyed up they were, but they were very tense. This was the moment when the year's work came to a head. The Bible knowledge competition was due that afternoon; the following day they would take Holy Communion, and as soon as the service ended those whose parents had arrived to collect them would be free to leave and enjoy the holidays until January 7.

Gina took care to arrive last at the laundry bin. She waited until she was completely alone before emptying the bag to see what was on the sheets of paper. She peered inside, then turned them over and over again in a state of total amazement. She could not believe what she was seeing. In her hand was a series of documents. They consisted of the baptismal certificates and parental details of Bánki, Krieger, Zelemér and Kun, all of them carrying tiny scars and splatters of ink. With them was a note. Its elongated capital letters were now familiar to her. They were identical to the ones that had so sternly ordered her to keep out of trouble and not provoke her teachers. But this time the message was rather different.

THAT NIGHT WHEN THE DIRECTOR'S AQUARIUM WAS KNOCKED OVER SOMEONE WENT THROUGH THE

FILING CABINET AND REMOVED THESE DOCUMENTS. THEY REFER TO PEOPLE WHO BECAUSE OF THEIR FAMILY ORIGINS HAVE BEEN SUBJECT TO RESTRICTIONS OR PUT IN DANGER BY AN IMMORAL STATE DECREE. IF ANYONE DISCOVERS THAT THE SCHOOL RECORDS ARE NOW INCOMPLETE AND THE PUPILS CONCERNED ARE REQUIRED TO PROVIDE THEM A SECOND TIME, THESE ARE THE ONES THEY SHOULD PRODUCE. YOU MUST GIVE THEM TO THE GIRLS WHO ARE MENTIONED, AND TELL BÁNKI AND THE OTHERS THAT AT THE END OF THE HOLIDAYS THEY ABSOLUTELY MUST RETURN TO THE SCHOOL. IT IS THE ONLY PLACE WHERE THEY WILL BE SAFE, MUCH SAFER THAN AT HOME WITH THEIR PARENTS. TELL THEM THAT THE PEOPLE WHO PROVIDED THESE DOCUMENTS WILL LOOK AFTER THEIR PARENTS AS WELL. AND TAKE NOTE: IF YOU ARE NOT EXTREMELY CAREFUL YOU WILL PUT BÁNKI, KRIEGER, KUN AND ZELEMÉR IN DANGER, AND IT WILL NO LONGER BE CERTAIN THAT I CAN CONTINUE TO HELP YOU EITHER.

ABIGAIL

She stood there paralysed. She was not thinking of her own problems and sorrows now, or about the sort of Christmas she would be having in the Matula: the concerns that had struck her with such sudden force were ones that had always lurked in the depths of her consciousness, only she had never given them much thought because they had not touched her personally. Of course the religion your parents belonged to was now a matter of terrifying importance. It even made a difference whether they had or had not themselves been baptised when they baptised you. And if they had not been Christian for more than a certain length of time, or either of them had not been christened at all, did that not also put you at a disadvantage, or even in danger? From what Abigail had written that certainly seemed to be the case. She looked through the documents again. Everyone named, including the parents and grandparents, was listed as belonging to the Reformed Protestant Church.

She ran into the dormitory to look for Bánki, then realised that she would be in the kitchen, helping the baker make bread. Only after lunch would they be able to talk in private. She slipped Abigail's message into her notebook, the one she had to have about her at all times during the school day for recording things she needed to do, her homework, and any other instructions she might be given. These notebooks were kept in the day room from the end of lessons until breakfast the following morning, but the documents she did not dare leave anywhere out of her sight. Susanna or one of the domestics might get it into their heads to look in the cupboards and find them, and to hide them in the geranium boxes was out of the question: there they could be found at any time during the day by someone going into the washroom. Instead, she pushed them into her blouse and buttoned it up again. It gave her a very odd-looking bust, but the school uniform was so copious and shapeless that probably no-one would notice.

She had no idea what they were singing about or praying for before the meal, and by then she had had more than her fill of the religious life. Ever since the penitential week had started they had all had to be extremely circumspect and attentive to the state of their souls. Her own mind was not in the least taken up with heaven-directed thoughts. She was tense and impatient and just wanted everyone to eat up and leave. That day Bánki stayed late in the kitchen to help with the washing-up, and by the time she got back the class had already changed for their walk. Gina asked Mari Kis and Torma to keep the others away from the two of them as she wanted to speak to Bánki on her own. The girls' attitude to Bánki had softened again: having initially had difficulty believing she had not been given the usual parcel they had realised that her mother must have come to tell her something serious had happened in the family, something that was too painful for her to talk about. Mari Kis was very good at dealing with this sort of request. She took Torma's hand and they stood shoulder to shoulder to create a living screen, at a point where they could turn away anyone who came too near and at the same time block the view of Gina's locker, which was now standing open. Gina called Bánki over and leaned halfway into the locker to unbutton her blouse and fish out the notebook. There was no chance to say anything – Mari and Torma were standing too close. She took her hand and guided it to where the documents were, so that she could see what was there and read Abigail's message.

Among the many other images of her time in the Matula that Gina took with her into adult life was the face of Bánki at that precise moment, with her skin slowly turning red. She often thought back, too, to the many other extraordinary moments and events of that winter, the spring of 1944 and her days in the fortress; and she thought especially of Abigail, the person who had directly involved her in those grown-up matters, fateful as they were, and of her father, who had given her a wider perspective on life and made her understand things that, as a fifteen-year-old girl who was not in danger herself, she had never thought about or would have been able to grasp without his help.

Bánki was incapable of speech. She simply nodded to show she had understood what she had been given, then leaned forward and rested her head against the shelf. Her whole body was trembling violently. Gina waited for her to calm down and for her hands to stop shaking, and to give her time to fold the papers up and stuff them into her blouse as she herself had done. At that moment Susanna appeared, and Mari Kis and Torma instantly let go of each other's hands. Susanna asked them when they thought they might get round to putting their coats on: they must surely have realised that they would be going out earlier than usual because the competition started soon afterwards. And she stayed with the class until they set off.

Even when walking three abreast they were expected to keep in step. Bánki was just behind Gina, with Szabó to her right and Murai on her left, and for the entire outing Gina heard Szabó grumbling that Bánki was weaving about all the time and getting out of step, "and I'm going to be blamed because of her!" Today I did something good, Gina herself was thinking. It wasn't really me, it was Abigail, but in part it was due to me. When I wrote to her I had no idea that she had already been in the office and looked to see who might be needing help. Perhaps when we get back from the walk my father will be here as my reward, or at the very least he'll speak to me on the telephone.

But there was no message waiting for her, he had not telephoned, and he was not in the building. No sooner were they back than they were told to put on their formal going-out uniforms. Susanna was furious with Bánki, the ever meek and gentle Bánki, because she had been wandering all over the place, hanging around the third-year dormitory, holding a sotto voce conversation with Zelemér and another with Krieger next to her locker. When she threatened her with punishment Bánki looked at her with the serene calmness of someone who has just been paid a compliment. Third-year dormitory, Éva Kun, Gina said to herself. She isn't yet thirteen, and she will have to learn to keep her mouth shut, and shut tight, about the fact she has been in real danger and has only just been saved from whatever it was. But what about all those people whose papers are not in order, the ones Abigail is unable to help? And what exactly is that danger? She could not begin to imagine.

She would of course learn later what she could not have known then, when the threat had merely advanced its shadow, that in just a few more months all hell would be unleashed against those affected by the Jewish Laws, and it would become clear that Abigail had indeed saved Krieger, Zelemér, Kun and Bánki, and their parents with them.

If Gina had not performed so appallingly in the Bible-knowledge competition perhaps Bánki might not have felt so sorry for her for having to spend her Christmas holidays in the fortress, and might not have been so keen to make her the gift that she thought the best present Gina could possibly have at the

305

time. But the truth was that Gina could never have hoped to compete with girls who had been brought up in a religious institution from the start; nor could she ever have imagined she would do so badly. There were fifty questions. The Director read out fifty short passages from the Bible and they had just thirty seconds to write down who had said them and in which book they appeared. They were not simple questions – they included quotations from the Book of Revelations and Jeremiah – and there was also a brief interruption when Suba appeared at the door. He stood there with his mouth open until an irritated Gedeon Torma waved at him to tell him not to disturb them, but he ventured in regardless and whispered something in the Director's ear. The Director nodded and told him, yes, he had gathered that, but there wasn't time for it right then, and would he please allow the competition to continue?

Bánki identified every one of the fifty quotations, and she got nearly every detail right; Oláh knew forty-eight, and there were some other outstanding results. Aradi got forty-seven and a girl in year six got forty-five. The two youngest classes did not take part, but, as the final list showed, even the third years did better than Gina, who came last with a score of twenty-six. When the results were announced Susanna looked at her reproachfully. Gina was all the more upset when she realised that she had actually known another ten but had been too scared to write them down in case they were wrong. Never in her life had she come bottom in a school exam. Of course no-one tied her to the stake. Susanna said nothing, but the odious Kőnig came over to her and blathered on about what everyone knew, that she had been brought up in a school of a different denomination and she shouldn't take it to heart: next time she was sure to be among the top few. She found his commiserations so offensive she could have hit him. So she had come last. There was no need for anyone to pity her.

Kalmár did not attempt to console her. He told her to take it in good part and go and congratulate Bánki, who had just received her prize, a fine special edition of a work by Ferdinand Ziegler in the original German describing the joys of the religious life. He told her that at least she wouldn't mind lending it to others because it was the sort of book one could always do without for a while. For the first time in ages Gina almost smiled: it was good of Kalmár to express so delicately the ghastly nature of the prizes given out in the school, and to hint that the competition was not worth grieving over.

Then it was Gina's turn to go up to Bánki. The moment she saw her Bánki dropped the book noisily onto the table and smothered her in kisses. Susanna promptly removed her arm from Gina's neck, but said nothing. She did not approve of these unwarranted outbursts.

"Next year we shall do better, I think, Vitay," the Director said. He had come over and was standing by her side, and she lowered her gaze to avoid looking at him. "You are a bad loser," Marcelle had once told her while they were playing a game in company. "Good manners require that you do not spoil the winner's pleasure by putting on a long face. You really must learn how to lose gracefully." That was something she had yet to do. Now it was the Director gently admonishing her. She had to stand there and hear him through, and she did not enjoy it. The only thing that made it bearable was the knowledge that he knew nothing about something that she and Bánki and Kun and Zelemér and Krieger did, that certain papers had vanished from his office that night when the aquarium was smashed. One day, when he went through the files and realised that the documents of four of his pupils were missing and needed to be replaced, would he notice that the ones that came back were not the same as those that had gone missing? But her chain of thought was interrupted. The Director was speaking to her again. Suba had brought a message, she heard him say: while they were doing the competition there had been a telephone call for her, but she had not been available to take it. Her father had rung to wish her a happy Christmas and to tell her she would be getting some money to buy herself a present. He had left it with the Prefect on his last visit. Unfortunately it would not be possible to have her at home because the boiler had exploded.

There were several fireplaces in the villa, and tile-backed stoves in even the smallest rooms, but she understood what he was telling her. It made her realise that she had not taken him seriously enough when he had said that they might not be spending the holiday together. The disaster of the competition and the thought of spending a bleak Christmas in the deserted Matula, away from both her father and the rest of the class, became too much to bear and she burst into tears. The Director informed her that such displays of hysteria were unworthy of a good Protestant girl, especially during the week of penitence, and sent her out of the room. He told her to come back in five minutes and show the Prefect that she had washed her face and calmed herself down. She was back before the five minutes had elapsed. She was perfectly composed and was determined not to show her grief and disappointment to anyone. When there was no-one else about, she would pour out her heart to Torma. They would be the only girls staying on in the school.

As soon as the event finished there was a prolonged whispering among the other girls, then Mari Kis came over to Gina and stood before her. She told her that as she couldn't go home because the boiler had exploded she could spend the holiday with any one of them. They had all invited her. There was no-one whose parents would not be delighted to have her with them. They would have taken Torma too, but her uncle would not allow it. She was his only living relative, poor thing, and Christmas was the one time when he chose to indulge his idea of family life, which was why she always started the new year in a state of collapse. But Gina had only to choose who she wanted to go with. They would ask for Susanna's permission, and the next day after communion they would leave together on the train.

She looked at each of their faces in turn. They were all smiles, all genuine affection. Murai's invitation was so enthusiastic she sank her nails into Gina's arm to enforce her claim. Gina would have loved above all to go with Bánki, but she knew it was out of the question. She had given her word that she would never leave the fortress except with her father or with the person her father would send. She told them she could not go with any of them and the atmosphere instantly changed. Of course she could not explain other than to say that it was what her father wanted. It pained her very much to see how the mood had cooled. They were clearly thinking that the General must be a very proud man and probably didn't think any of them good enough company for his daughter.

But they soon softened towards her again, and their joy returned as they started to plan their own holidays and think about the presents they might be getting. Only Bánki and Torma had stayed by her side, Bánki because there was now this new bond between them, and poor Torma, who had nothing to offer Gina beyond her status as an orphan, which she felt even more painfully during the holidays. Gina did her best not to show her feelings of bitterness. In this of course she failed, and whenever the others caught sight of her they bit their tongues. There was no point in making her feel even worse; they themselves had only one more night in the building and the next day the train would take them home.

During the communion service the next morning the girls' minds were focused rather less on the sacred vows the Chaplain was making on their behalf than on what might be happening outside. They were burning with impatience to know if there was anyone waiting for them in the drawing room. For her part, Gina believed in, affirmed and, like everyone else, promised everything that service required, but she felt very little beyond a profound sense of sadness and disarray.

By lunchtime more than half the school had gone, including most of the fifth year. When Susanna was looking the other way they hugged Gina and Torma and kissed them, promised they would write and gave them their own addresses in case Susanna took pity on them and allowed them, against the rules, to write to anyone other than members of their own family. Bánki was among those who left before lunch. When she reached the gate she turned and ran back to Gina to say she would think of her all the time, even on Christmas Eve, and that she was going to send her something that was sure to make her very happy. Gina listened in silence, forced herself to smile and kept waving until the last of them was out of sight. The other half of the school had also gone by suppertime, leaving her and Torma to wander the echoing corridors like shades of the dead.

Christmas

It was a very strange time.

Her experience was by no means one of unrelieved gloom. There were some exciting moments and even some happy ones, so different was life in the fortress out of term. Most of the domestic staff had been allowed home for the holidays, as had several of the teachers and almost all the deaconesses. The teaching rooms and the corridors leading to the dormitories had all been closed off – with only two pupils staying on it would have made little sense to heat the two vast wings of the building – and Gina and Torma were relocated to a twin-bedded room in the infirmary. This made for a degree of revelry. For one thing, it was further away from Susanna, so they could risk staying up late, reading in bed and even nosing around outside the teachers' living quarters, and when the Prefect did make an occasional appearance it was now much harder for her to catch them out, as the sick bay was at the bottom of its own short corridor, behind an outer door whose unmistakable squeak heralded her approach from afar.

Along with Susanna, Sister Erzsébet was also spending the holiday in the school, as were the Director, Miss Gigus, Kalmár and Kőnig. The cook was on leave and if anyone were taken ill the community health service would send someone to stand in for the doctor, who was away. Susanna had asked the two girls if they would be willing to provide some much-needed help with chores: they had no schoolwork during the break, the days were long, and there were several things they could usefully do. Of course they said yes. It would still leave them with plenty of free time.

Sister Erzsébet did the cooking. She loved doing it and she had excellent taste. The girls worked with her, laid and cleared the tables and did the washing-up. This was on even-numbered days; on the days in between they helped with the cleaning. That was rather more exciting because they had to deal not only with their own room but with those of the staff. The brief did not extend to the deaconesses' rooms simply because by the time they had risen and gone down to breakfast Susanna had long seen to both her own and to Erzsébet's, and their round was confined to those occupied by the Director and the three teachers. One of the three cleaning ladies had stayed on; she saw to the sweeping and airing, but she left the dusting to them. Would there ever be a better pretext for finding out what they had in there?

Miss Gigus had some wonderful old porcelain artefacts and a leather-covered box filled with all sorts of brooches, bracelets and earrings; they could not imagine where she could have bought them or when she would ever wear them. In Kalmár's room they found some interesting photograph albums with pictures that immediately reminded Gina of the summers she had spent abroad with Marcelle, and Torma listened in raptures as she explained what they showed. "This is Kalmár in London, leaning against one of the lions in Trafalgar Square with his eyes half-closed against the sun; this is the Sorbonne in Paris (it's the university); and that paved road . . ." But Torma swore she knew it; it was the ruins of the old cavalry barracks; she had seen it on one of their walks, on the other side of the station. "Don't be daft, it's Pompeii. Isn't that Vesuvius in the background, just above your so-called barracks, issuing smoke?" Sometimes there were women standing next to Kalmár, rather attractive women. The girls stared at them in disgust, and Torma dropped a spot of Indian ink on the face of the prettiest and turned her into the ugliest.

Kőnig had a huge library. He clearly read a lot, in several different languages. Kalmár's collection, by contrast, consisted mostly of reference works on Hungarian history. The Director's sitting room continued his theme of black, with a series of carved ebony animal heads that stared out at them from among black apple and pear trees in the corners of a bookcase. And there could be no doubt about how he spent his time in the holidays: dusting in his room they found the Hungarian homework books of all eighth years in the school stacked on his desk. Torma confirmed Gina's suspicions with a nod: it was his practice, his holiday pastime, to go through them and point out in green ink any errors that the marker had failed to underline, and to pen comments at the end of the relevant exercise in black, so that the first lesson of the new calendar plunged you into instant anxiety and gloom. His bedroom was always in perfect order, even before the cleaning lady had made the bed. It was as if he could sleep only under a completely smooth quilt with his head on a pillow without a single dent in it. In Kalmár's and Miss Gigus' rooms a more natural and reassuring disorder prevailed, but in Kőnig's it was all very impersonal. It was as if he never actually used the things he had. He seemed to do very little in there except gaze out of the window and listen to music – they had found a gramophone and a large pile of records. And he was the only one who always locked his drawers. They would have loved to see if he kept a diary. He was the sort of person you could imagine writing long meditations on the full moon, or the charms of an especially good dinner. Generally, none of the teachers were in their rooms when they came to dust; they appeared only at mealtimes. The girls could never discover what they did during the day, except on one occasion when Miss Gigus' coiffure revealed that she had spent the morning at the hairdresser's. It was Kalmár they saw most of, prowling around hoping to bump into Susanna. Kőnig and the Director they hardly ever encountered other than in the refectory and at prayers.

Gina felt she had been given far too little to do. She asked to be given more, pleading that as she was confined to the premises she would prefer even to have too much, to keep her mind from dwelling on the holidays the others would be enjoying. Susanna's response was that the two of them should get out into the fresh air more often, read more, play games and try to enjoy the break; she took them out walking more frequently than she did in term-time, and on some completely new routes. She had already given them the pocket money they were due before Christmas; normally she would do this only for purchasing stamps and giving to charity. Torma's allowance was passed to the Prefect every month by her uncle; Gina found that with hers there was an additional envelope that her father had left with Susanna on his last trip to Árkod, for her to buy herself something if they were unable to spend the holiday together. Susanna gave her a stern warning: she should spend it wisely. The General had left her a very large sum, but if she wasted it on things that brought only fleeting pleasure she would later regret it.

One morning she took them out shopping. Not wanting to spoil their enjoyment by trying to influence them with her inevitable looks of disapproval, she declined to go with them into the shop and stayed outside in the street, a loyal figure in the drifting snow, peering through the window from time to time to try and make out what they were doing. Seeing her standing there, Gina realised that she had begun to love her again, almost as much as she had before the Bishop's visit. Torma had made a special book cover for her uncle, so she already had her most important present, but, she told Gina, she thought that everyone who was staying on for Christmas with them should be given gifts and they should buy some small things for the teachers and the two deaconesses. She chose diaries, cheap pocket diaries for 1944, that she planned to wrap in attractive, brightly coloured paper with their initials cut from shiny cardboard and glued on. She advised Gina to look for needles and thread, and some men's shirt buttons, because the teachers would not accept anything more expensive from a pupil; there was still time for them to sew pouches to keep the buttons in, using the pattern for the cubes they had once made from cardboard lower down the school, but with an extra button on the flap and a little loop of string to open and close it with. For the ladies they would make pin-cushions, but not shaped like people or the Director would yell at them. In his opinion all human images, even dolls and statues, were idolatrous, but theirs would be more respectable. They would look like miniature sofas, with threaded needles sticking out of them.

But once she began shopping Gina found that needles were very hard to come by. It was hardly surprising. Ever since the war had started even the most ordinary everyday things had been steadily disappearing from the shelves. She wanted Torma's advice on whether she should take something that did happen to be available, a set of the thicker variety used for sewing sacks; but when she turned to look for her friend she found that she had sneaked off to the glass and ceramics counter and had just asked the assistant to wrap up a little plaster dog with a sad-looking face. She's buying it for me, Gina thought, and a warm glow filled her heart. It was hideous, and its muzzle was tied with a bright red cloth handkerchief that made it look as if it had toothache, but it seemed to her as wonderful as any of the porce-lain they had at home. Torma had so little money, a few fillér at the very most, and to pay for it she had had to dig in the bottom of her bag to find the very last one.

Gina moved on to the women's fashion department. The things she had bought so far had all cost very little. She still had most of her pocket money left, and there was also the hundred-pengő note in the General's envelope. She looked for something she could buy without a coupon and found an astounding night-dress. It was low cut and extremely provocative, just the thing for a shapely young woman of spirit to wear. It was very expensive, but she bought it all the same. Torma, having grown up in the gloomy and repressive fortress, would never have owned anything like it in her life. Where she might keep it and when she might get to wear it were questions still to be considered, but at least she would be the proud possessor of the sort of nightdress you saw on the posters outside theatres. Gina knew she would love it.

Both girls tucked their parcels out of sight before they rejoined Susanna. Torma told her she had not a single fillér left, and Gina handed back her remaining ten-pengő notes. The Prefect looked at her sternly, convinced that she had spent far more than she should, so Gina whispered in her ear that she hadn't bought it for herself, it was for someone else – and not for a member of staff either, she added, so that Susanna would realise that it was for Torma, who was after all an orphan, and not think she had planned to buy something for her too. "But please don't ask me what I bought," she pleaded. "Promise me that for once you won't ask me to show you what it is. Just let it be." Susanna took them back to the school without saying another word or asking a single question. Gina breathed a happy sigh. What a wonderful day! Susanna had done a rare thing: she had shown that she was human after all, because it was Christmas.

The days flew by in a fever of activity, racing to get the diaries and button pouches finished in time. Susanna kept coming into the sewing room to tell them to go outside into the snow, where they threw snowballs at each other like first years; sometimes they were allowed to listen to music on the school gramophone, in constant terror of damaging Hajdú's antiquated records: that would certainly have been the end of them! The morning of the twenty-fourth brought a particularly heavy snowfall, and the kitchen corridor began to fill with the aroma of cloves and vanilla. It brought tears to Gina's eyes: it was the smell of Christmas itself. What was happening at home? Where was her father? When would she see him again?

Their Christmas Eve was not so much a Christmas Eve as a Christmas afternoon, but they did have a tree. It had been set up in the refectory, a plain and simple tree, all the lovelier and more touching for that, and Sister Erzsébet lit some candles. Staring into the tiny flames Gina realised it would be a mistake to post the bookmark, especially from Árkod, and she told a doubtful and non-committal Susanna that she wanted to deliver it in person. They sang the hymn "Christ our Lord is born", and Susanna read the passage from St Luke's gospel describing the birth of Jesus. A prayer followed, then Kalmár switched the lights back on and Susanna blew out the candles. Everyone who had stayed on was now together in the room. The teachers were all in their Sunday best, and Miss Gigus' dress was one they had never seen before. It was extremely elegant, with fur lining around the collar and cuffs, and Susanna had subjected it to a long and hard stare. The cleaner and the porter and his wife joined them for the prayers, but the moment they ended they asked permission to leave: they always spent Christmas Eve in their own homes, and they had invited their children and some relatives who lived in the town.

The presents had been arranged at the foot of the tree, each with its own white label inscribed in Sister Erzsébet's tiny hand-writing. Gina saw that for the very first time they had used the familiar form of her name, "Gina". The informality touched her deeply: in the Matula the diminutive and affectionate forms were never normally used – Torma was "Piroska" only at Christmas, as now written on her card. Gina looked for the little plaster puppy, without success, then it struck her that Torma probably wanted to keep her present a secret just as she was doing with the nightgown. As it turned out, Torma had sewn a pincushion for her and she had chosen a diary for Torma. Susanna, super-vising the distribution, made no comment to either of them, nor did she ask what they had bought in the shop. She was making it clear that she knew they would have preferred a very different Christmas for themselves, and she fully understood why.

Gina was given a new Bible, much grander than the one she had brought with her from Budapest. It was inscribed: "For Georgina Vitay, from the Director and school staff, Christmas 1943", and everyone present had added their signatures, Gedeon Torma at the top and Susanna at the bottom. Gina was aston-ished at the pleasure it gave her, though she also suspected that it had been chosen as a hint for her to do rather better in next year's competition. Torma too was given a book, a particularly fascinating work, chosen no doubt by her uncle, entitled *A History of the Lutheran Order of Deaconesses* and signed like Gina's. The Director and the teachers voiced their appreciation and thanked them for the button pouches, the book holders and the "beautifully wrapped" diaries, and the ladies did the same for their pincushions. The teachers and deaconesses gave each other books, each with a title more boring than the last.

With the Christmas dinner Sister Erzsébet surpassed herself. Gina laid and then cleared the table, and Torma acted as waitress. The Director left soon afterwards, taking his niece with him. She went off with a gloomy face, to spend the start of her holiday in his apartment: the entire evening would be taken up listening to his endless comments about what this or that relative (none of whom she had ever met) was like, until he had exhausted his limited reserves of affection. The other teachers stayed on, Kalmár sitting close beside Susanna and Kőnig trying to entertain Miss Gigus, clearly without much success. She kept glancing at her watch, then suddenly excused herself and said she was going to the night-duty room because she was expecting an inter-city telephone call. Everyone stared after her in wonder: her face was lit by something that was certainly not very Matula. Kőnig suggested they play a few games and called Gina over to join them. She had been musing on her misfortunes next to the Christmas tree and envying Torma. At least a relative had spoken to her that evening and she had not been left there standing around on her own. But Sister Erzsébet shook her head. Games were for New Year's Eve, not Christmas Eve; they would have plenty to amuse themselves with then. The Director always gave permission for any staff who were not on night duty to go to Mitsi Horn's: it was very jolly there and very good fun, even if they didn't stay until midnight. They went there on the last day of the old year, as soon as the afternoon service finished, and stayed there until ten, which was quite long enough to have a really good time.

Gina's memories of Mitsi Horn were still raw, Erzsébet bored her, she could hardly bear to look at Kőnig, and Kalmár was sitting beside Susanna explaining something of apparently great importance. There was no point in hanging about where she was totally superfluous. She asked permission to go back to her room and read. To her surprise Susanna also stood up and said that she too was tired and needed to rest, if not actually go to bed. That put a sudden end to what little was left of the festive mood, and now that the Prefect was leaving, everyone else got to their feet and prepared to follow her. Kőnig muttered something about having to be somewhere else, Kalmár seemed suddenly upset and anxious, and Erzsébet suppressed a yawn. Kőnig was the first to disappear, in the direction of the teachers' quarters; Erzsébet set off towards the porter's lodge, saying she wanted to have a word with the porter and see how their party was going, then she too was going to bed. Gina followed a short way behind Kalmár and Susanna. The class tutor was trying to speak as softly as he could while avoiding the suggestion of whispering, which was forbidden in the Matula, but Gina could tell that he had said something to Susanna to which the answer was a decided "no", whereupon he bade the two of them goodnight and went off to the staff common room. He'll be spending his Christmas Eve in there on his own, Gina thought. He'll be listening to the radio or the gramophone. He must have had something very particular to say to her – probably asking if he could go back to her room with her. But she obviously isn't the least bit interested in him, and anyway, she would never receive a man in there. This Kalmár must be very much in love to be so utterly blind.

So now it was just herself and Susanna making their way down the corridor. The Prefect had put on leather-soled shoes like Gina's for the occasion and they clattered loudly on the hard floor. Going back to her temporary abode Gina had the feeling she sometimes had at home, when the fire was put out and the heat seemed to drain from the walls. She was oppressed by a consciousness of living in a world of strangers, subject to rules that constantly disrupted the rhythm of her life, and where everything that belonged to her, everything that was part of her, seemed far away. In truth she had felt close to none of them that evening: she was an orphan, just like Torma. As she walked along beside Susanna her head drooped, then came up sharply as Susanna let out a cry. It was a very small cry – she always expressed her joy and her distress with equal restraint – and it was a cry of surprise. Gina looked for the cause and discovered what it was. Suspended from the handle of Susanna's door was a small packet. Gina had been given these jewellery boxes so many times, both by her father and Auntie Mimó, that the familiar shape declared itself at once through the shiny paper.

"Oh my God," Susanna gasped and instantly blushed at the word one should never take in vain. "Someone's paid me a secret visit."

Marcelle would have been well pleased with Gina. She took her leave at once and went off down the last of the corridors, leaving the Prefect to deal with her Christmas surprise alone. Who it had come from, and what it might contain, was clearly a greater mystery to her than it was to Gina. She had pictured Kalmár's engagement ring adorning the Prefect's busy hand so

323

many times that the moment she was back in her room she forgot her unhappiness and her longing for home and wrote, on the two middle pages of her exercise book, the ones you could tear out: *The engagement of Mr Péter Kalmár and Miss Susanna Molnár*. It was such a shame Torma wasn't with her. They could have talked about it at length, then sneaked over to eavesdrop outside Susanna's room. She found she could not bear to be on her own a minute longer. She went back to the teachers' residence and stood outside the barred gate waiting for the Director to grow weary of family life. But Torma did not appear, and there was no sign of Susanna. The only sound came from the staff lounge, where the strains of "Stille Nacht" were playing quietly on the radio. Her sense of excitement and curiosity drained away, and she lost interest in both Susanna and Kalmár. It was Christmas Eve, the others were all getting on with their own lives, their private joys and griefs, while she floundered around, abandoned, alone and desperately missing her father. If only she could hear his voice! She was as lonely and bereft as only an adult could be, beyond tears, enveloped in a sadness like that of old age.

Hearing someone approaching from the direction of the night-duty room she spun round. Miss Gigus must have finished her conversation on the telephone because she was on her way to the staff quarters. She could have been any one of Auntie Mimó's friends, a slim, attractive, dark-haired young woman smiling a secret, happy smile. She had spoken with a man, Gina was sure. Miss Gigus was going to get married. Only spinsters and bachelors were allowed to live in the wings for the teachers and the deaconesses, so she would be moving out in the new year and going to live in town . . . and all this had come about because she had spoken to someone on the telephone that evening. Did the operators have any idea how much happiness they spread?

The moment it struck her the thought became an impulse. The duty room, the room with the inter-city telephone line, was standing there empty. Susanna would be contemplating her engagement ring, Erzsébet had gone to bed, Kőnig was probably no longer in the building, Kalmár was waiting in the lounge to hear what the Prefect thought of his gift and the Director was playing at family life. No-one was anywhere near. She stepped inside.

Her fingers were trembling with excitement, and she had difficulty finding the light switch. Next to the telephone there was a board bearing the most important numbers: Emergency Services, Police, Fire Brigade, Inter-City, Telegrams. She dialled the central post office and asked for a connection between the Matula Academy and Budapest 557 599, then sat down beside the receiver and prepared for the call. My dear father, she said in her head, in a sort of prayer, I know it'll be you who picks the receiver up. The staff will be having the evening off, and you'll take this yourself. I promise you I won't chatter away. I won't say anything. I won't even speak, or give my name, or say who I am. I just want to hear you breathe, and clear your throat, and say "hello". As soon as you do that I'll put the receiver down. The silence at this end will make it seem like a wrong number. It's Christmas Eve. I know you'll understand.

She waited. The minutes ticked by. She heard footsteps coming down the corridor, then falling silent just outside the door. Oh my God, she thought in terror, there's two of them out there. They came from opposite directions. Please let them go away; they mustn't start talking here. What if one of them wants to use the telephone? That would be just my luck.

One of the pair spoke. She could hear every word.

"Was it from you?" Susanna asked.

"Was what?" Kőnig asked.

There was no reply. If she had not been so agitated and so focused on what she was waiting for she might have taken more in, but she had been thrown into total disarray by their stopping to talk where they had, and she felt utterly ashamed of what the Prefect had just done. She would have expected rather more from her: how could she ever imagine that Kőnig – Kőnig, who she must have realised had been avoiding her ever since the harvest-gathering and the Bishop's visit – would have given her such a present?

Silence. What on earth were they doing now? Susanna had still not answered his question. Surely she wasn't still showing him what was in the box?

She was. This was clear because he laughed and said, "An engagement ring? Me? I gave this to you, Susanna?"

This was pure torture. Here she was, witness to an exchange that would never have been allowed to take place in the presence of a pupil, but in circumstances that made it impossible for her to exult in. She knew she should have turned her attention elsewhere and not stayed there eavesdropping so avidly; she should have been praying to be left alone to wait for her telephone call, and for them to take themselves off.

The Deaconess had still not replied. Gina could imagine her face turning red with shame and embarrassment, and it served her right. Kőnig, that cowardly sentimentalist, now showed he could also be brutal and rejecting. Hadn't she learned that lesson when she followed him on the train?

"The only woman I could ever marry is Mitsi Horn," he told her. "Sadly, she isn't interested. I'm off to see her right now; we're going to light her Christmas Eve fire. Go to the staff lounge, Sister, and comfort Péter Kalmár. He's the one who had this ring made for you: I saw him going into the jeweller's. You should be impressed that he found enough gold to make a ring."

Something was murmured, so softly that she failed to catch it, but she gathered what it was from his reply. "No, I'm not in the least put out. I'm not even sorry about the misunderstanding. It's given me the chance to say something to you. Let me be, Susanna. Don't keep running after me and being so very kind to me. I'm not worth bothering about, so there's no point."

No answer was possible to that, or rather not in words. There came only the clatter of Susanna's receding shoes. As full as her heart was with her own concerns and problems, Gina turned white with rage. The wretch! The nonentity! The clodhopper! How dare he talk to Susanna like that! And what could he possibly have been thinking – that anyone would ever want to marry him? What a disgrace! She listened again. The silence seemed to go on forever. Was he still there behind the door? "Please let him go away," she murmured. Her heart was beating wildly. "Let

327

him go to the bosom of his chosen one, Mitsi Horn, and may we never set eyes on him again!"

At long last he set off down the corridor. Why he had stayed there so long continued to puzzle her. Was he trying to gather his thoughts, or summon up the strength to take himself off? At that moment the telephone burst into life, and her heart jumped. The noise was even more strident than she had expected, and she picked up the receiver in terror.

"Matula?" a voice enquired. "Is that the Matula Academy? I have your connection to Budapest. Please speak now."

The line started to buzz, and there was a loud ticking noise. She had no idea when he had entered the room because the door was closed behind him and she was completely engrossed in the call. She became aware of him only as he lifted the receiver out of her hands and replaced it on its cradle. Years later, when the two of them recalled that episode, he told her that, though she might not believe it, she had screamed at him as if he were attacking her.

"Ahem," he coughed. "What's all this about? Go back to your room like a good girl, Vitay."

She began to wrestle with him, like someone in a frenzy. She was strong, and she surprised him. He had not expected her to resist, least of all because he was holding a bunch of flowers in his left hand. Even in that surreal moment she spotted the white violets peeping out from the silky wrapping paper and fell on them in a rage, tore them from his hand and hurled them to the floor. He stooped to pick them up, and she immediately grabbed the receiver again: it was now ringing non-stop, as if trying to make out what was going on. Kőnig threw the flowers down to free both hands, then seized her with his right and the receiver with the left. Then, as calmly and naturally as to someone present in the room, he spoke into it: "Would you kindly terminate this call. No-one here wishes to speak to anyone." Only when it had gone completely silent did he release the girl.

Neither of them had noticed, but Susanna had also responded to Gina's screams and was now in the room. She took Gina outside at once. Gina allowed herself to be led away without a word of protest. Her hatred of Kőnig was so powerful it propped her up like a walking stick. He trotted along beside them explaining to Susanna that poor little Vitay had apparently wanted to telephone Budapest, but the pupils were not allowed to make such calls, it was a school rule. Susanna took her back to her room, sat down beside her and took her hand. She immediately began to calm down, and soon she was able to feel something other than her own rage. She was thinking how very cold Susanna's fingers were.

The first words she managed to utter were not "Forgive me, I am so sorry", but "How I hate Mr Kőnig!"

"A good Christian hates no-one," Susanna replied, and immediately let go of her hand. Her speech became cold and impersonal. "Pull yourself together. This is no way to behave."

"I can't bear it." Gina sobbed, forgetting that it was foolish to try to explain and that it would have been far better to say nothing. "I can't bear anything to do with the Matula."

"But you will have to bear it, or it will be even harder for you to wait for the holiday to end. I shall have to punish you for trying to use the telephone, and for the way you behaved towards your teacher, so don't raise your hopes, Georgina. He can do nothing for you after this. Don't expect him to forgive you, as he has so many times before. For the rest of the holiday I shall not allow you out of school, and you will not be going to Auntie Mitsi's on New Year's Eve. You will remain here with the night-duty staff. You must learn to control your temper once and for all."

"I shall hate Mitsi Horn as long as I live," she sobbed, "and I don't care if Mr Kőnig forgives me or not. He needn't bother. I will never forgive him."

"Go to bed, Georgina. It pains me very much that this should have happened on Christmas Eve. It pains me too to have to be severe with you, but it is for your own good. I feel very sorry for you, but I have good reason to feel the same for myself." And she stood up to leave.

The thought of being left alone even for a second was unbearable to Gina, even more than the recriminations and the punishment that awaited her. Torma was elsewhere, she had no-one. If she had managed to make that telephone call then at least the punishment would not have been for nothing. But it had all been pointless, because of Kőnig. And Susanna's words were hollow. If she really did feel sorry for her she would not be leaving her alone; she had no such feelings; all she could think of was Kőnig; she was a hypocrite. The hatred she felt for Kőnig flooded through her like a poison, and she no longer knew what she was saying.

"Why should it bother the Prefect if I hate Mitsi Horn or my teacher? She has her own reasons for hating both of them, so why is she protecting him? It's Mitsi Horn that he is in love with, not the Sister. He was taking her flowers, only I smashed them."

Susanna froze in the doorway and looked at her. Her face was expressionless, as if she had not heard. But she had taken everything in. She nodded her head, then said very quietly, "I forgive you for that, Georgina, with all my heart. But what is coming to you in the next few weeks and days is something you will have to endure with the same degree of courage you have shown in giving offence to grown-ups whose lives you know absolutely nothing about."

When Torma came in she found Gina lying in darkness. She had been struggling the whole evening to find answers to her uncle's questions that would not make him even more irritable, and she was exhausted; finding the lights off made her look around in surprise. She turned them back on, and when she realised that Gina was still awake she set the little plaster dog down on her bedside table. Having sobbed her heart out, Gina had calmed down and was able to speak again. She greeted Torma, and told her to look under her quilt where she would find something that Father Christmas had put there for her. Torma pulled the cover back, took one look at the nightgown, knelt down beside the bed and rubbed her loveable round face in the silk. Unable to say a word, she breathed heavily and stroked the soft material. Gina looked at her the way Susanna had so recently looked at her, like a sorrowful adult contemplating a child. She would have given years of her life not to have humiliated the Prefect by making it clear that she had overheard that conversation outside the door, and she wished even more that she had not succumbed to the dangerous charms of Christmas and broken the promise she had given to her father not to try to contact him. Her hopes for the rest of her holiday and for everything else could be put to one side, but there was one thing she was certain of, that she would never, ever, forgive Kőnig. Torma heard her through to the end, and was horrified. What had Gina got herself into again? But she could only agree with her about Kőnig's barefaced cheek.

She tried the nightgown on immediately. It was a bit too long, but otherwise fitted her well. She raised the hem with a piece of string tied round the waist and sauntered around in it as if it were an evening dress. If there was one thing Gina took away from that Christmas Eve, something she could hold on to and cherish, it was the radiant joy on Torma's face.

They considered where to hide it. Torma decided she would first raise the hem properly by tying a bootlace around the waist, then she would wear it under her school nightgown for the rest of the night and keep it in the art storeroom thereafter. Gina had kept her own things in the washroom flower box? That would never have occurred to her, it was such a risky place! But of course, having just arrived and having so little time to act she would not have found anywhere better. In the art cupboard there were some geometrically shaped wooden boxes that had removable panels. Mitsi Horn had once used one of them to hide a silk scarf her fiancé had given her; they were an excellent place to keep anything that wasn't too heavy. The nightgown weighed nothing at all, the material was so fine, and it would fit very nicely into the rhombus. Gina envied Torma in her happiness; she herself felt only a leaden, impotent grief.

The next morning Susanna put a stop to her dusting round and her work in the kitchen. She was now sentenced to spend the rest of the holiday like a prisoner condemned to a life of enforced inactivity. She could read and play the piano for the whole day if she chose, but she would take no further part in the life of the fortress and its cares and concerns. She could go out into the courtyard but not into town. Erzsébet took Torma twice to the cinema and once to a concert, but she took Gina nowhere, and it was through Erzsébet that Torma learned that Kőnig had asked Susanna to forget that "unfortunate episode" when Vitay had broken yet another school rule. "So he obviously didn't tell Erzsébet any more than that. He told her that I tried to use the telephone but probably not that I had overheard his conversation with Susanna. He greets me amiably enough, and he obviously bears me no grudge, even though I have never apologised to him. And he's the one Susanna loves: he and not Kalmár!"

Kalmár hardly ever showed himself, and when he did he never spoke to Susanna. Neither of them wore an engagement ring, which said all that was needed about their relationship. He seemed at long last to have accepted that he had nothing to hope for as far as the Prefect was concerned. Gina generally held her tongue. She never complained about her situation, not even to Torma, went nowhere near the telephone, asked for nothing and passed no comments. On New Year's Eve it was Erzsébet who took the invitees to Mitsi Horn's. Gina spent the evening with Susanna, who sat beside her reading in total silence.

Torma came back in a state of high elation, bearing a parcel for her from Mitsi Horn. The party had been amazing, and even the Director had joined in the games. Gina gave her back the pastries she had brought, explaining that she hated Mitsi Horn so much she would never accept anything from the woman. Torma sat down beside her, her happiness destroyed, and did everything she could to cheer her friend up. She did not succeed. She kept trying whenever it was just the two of them together, but with no more success. Gina accepted her well-meaning efforts with good grace, but always with the detached calmness of a disillusioned adult. She did manage a smile from time to time, when Torma put on her nightgown and did an oriental dance for her, but her attitude was that of an older sibling towards her much younger sister.

When the class returned at the end of the holiday they found her a lot more solemn and serious, and no longer the amusing companion she once had been. Bánki came back on the last train on the afternoon before lessons began. It was a very cold day, and her face was bright red. She fell on Gina's neck and asked her if she had received the present. Gina told her she had no idea what she was talking about. Bánki's face made it clear that she had made the surprise gift she had promised, and she was astonished that it had not arrived. It must have been lost in the post, Gina said to herself. Either that, or Susanna didn't give it to me. Another failure. But why not? Everything else seems to be going wrong at the moment.

The year was drawing to its close and there was still no news from the General. In his lessons König hardly ever questioned her, as if he were afraid of provoking another scene, but she had resolved to be far more guarded in her conduct and never again show how she felt about him. Her face became thinner and more watchful, as if she were always listening out for something – a far-distant voice perhaps? But there were no more Saturday afternoon telephone calls, and nothing came either by post or word of mouth. Susanna sent her off for an X-ray; the doctor examined her several times but could find nothing wrong and told her she was too thin. She prescribed iron tablets and more exercise, especially walking. Her classmates were always sympathetic when she failed to respond to their queries about how they could help her cheer up, and Bánki started making strange remarks about the shocking infidelity of men. Mitsi Horn had become a regular visitor to the school. One day in February she stayed for lunch, sitting at the high table with the teachers and the Director, and the girl on duty had overheard the staff talking about the dissident of Árkod. Perhaps he could give her some news, Gina wondered, even if her father hadn't? But no news came. There were occasional messages from Abigail, but never for her; she heard the others talking about who they had been sent to, but it was always someone else. By the end of February she was completely crushed. She was sure now that she would never see her father again.

Kalmár, a now more reserved and serious-minded Kalmár, became a real help to her. He had obviously given up on Susanna and seemed to be paying special attention to Gina because of the repeated scenes involving Kőnig. His hostility to his colleague was undiminished, but there was no contact between the Latin teacher and Susanna beyond what was strictly unavoidable, and Kalmár could not bring himself to see him as a victorious rival. He was constantly giving Gina missions to carry out, including some tasks that were really more suitable for a colleague. She was immensely grateful. He became the one she tried to befriend, rather than Susanna, whose behaviour towards her was now one of cold formality. Her urge to love someone, and her need to feel that she mattered to at least one of the grown-ups around her, were very strong.

Spring arrived early that year. On March 15 they put on their summer coats and went to lay flowers at the Cenotaph and on Petőfi's statue. In the military cemetery the violets were already out. Mari Kis pointed out to Gina that the place was surrounded by police. "Look at them standing there. They're in mourning clothes but they look so out of place you can easily tell who they are." The older Aradi girl had had it from Suba that the dissident had found a new source of amusement, hanging collars around the necks of statues. The day before he had hung a truly horrifying report from the battlefront around the mane of one of the lions in the cemetery for war heroes. Gina looked long and hard at the bronze statues, thought of her father and did not cry.

On March 19, a Sunday, they attended the usual service. In the morning of the twentieth there was a new development. The Director had summoned the teaching staff during break and in the fourth lesson of the day Kalmár came into the room with a look on his face that told everyone that he brought important news. He had not been so buoyant since Susanna had rebuffed him.

"From today our German allies will be based inside our borders." He beamed. "This way it will be easier for us to defend ourselves. It is most reassuring. We are entering a new phase in the war!"

If that is the case, Gina thought, then something really important must have happened. The Germans wouldn't be here without their reasons. Surely now there would be some news from her father. Something was about to happen, or had already started, and for the first time in months she could hope with more certainty. There would be an end to all the silence and lack of movement.

She was right. On March 26, a week after the German occupation, the Chaplain gave one of his finest and most inspiring Sunday sermons. Gina sat listening with only half an ear, opening and closing her fingers in boredom, when she suddenly had the feeling that someone was looking at her. There was no obvious reason for it: in her Matula uniform she was not so very alluring that some unfamiliar guest should be unable to keep his eyes off her. She had the feeling that someone was staring at her from the raised gallery in front of her. She glanced up, and her whole body started to tremble. Sitting next to the hymn number board, with his eyes trained on her, was Lieutenant Kuncz.

Midnight rendezvous

The face whose contours she had conjured up so many times in her mind's eye was now before her in reality. She had talked about him so often that the thought flashed through her mind that any member of the class who saw him would surely know who he was. She had told them everything about him, the exact colour of his hair, his eyes and his figure, and there was not one of them who did not know that Lieutenant Ferenc Kuncz of the Royal Hungarian Army was twenty years old and lived in Budapest, not far from Gina's auntie Mimó, at 44 Zápor Street.

How wonderful it would have been to let out a great shout, run across the chapel and up the stairs to the balcony and, as she could never do with her absent father, fling herself into his arms. Be careful! her racing heartbeat warned her. Don't take any risks. The whole of the Matula will be watching you, even if they don't make it obvious. She knew that she should not, by so much as a flicker of an eyelid, show that she had recognised him. She would have to leave it to him to arrange a meeting: there could be no doubt that he was there in the white church only because of her. How he had got there, and whether he was now permanently based in the town or had come there simply to speak to her was of no consequence. If he was in the church then he knew that she was at the Matula, and that was something he could have known only through her father. He's bringing me news of him, she decided. The line-of-sight connection that had been broken after her father's last visit had been restored, and life could begin afresh, charged with hope.

In obedience to responses drilled into her since the autumn, she stood up and sat down as the order of service dictated, and she sang, as Susanna and the Chaplain insisted, keeping her eyes on the text. But she heard not a single word of the sermon, and while she mouthed the words along with the rest of the congregation, the meaning of the Lord's Prayer passed her by completely. Her eyes were fixed on Lieutenant Kuncz, who gazed back at her in turn, so short was the distance between them.

It was the first time she had seen him in civilian clothes. She spent some time wondering why he was not in uniform and decided that it must be to avoid attracting attention to himself as a non-local person with an unfamiliar face. She had come to know, at least by sight, all the regular outside attendees at the Matula services, and there were some other people present whom she had never seen before who were also paying her close attention. Feri's face gave nothing away. He too was taking care not to let anyone notice that he was gazing steadily down at her. His eyes never left her, but they held no message. Still staring at him as if awakening from a long superstitious dream, she gave a deep sigh and sat back in her pew.

She was careful not to look at him all the time. Every so often she lowered her eyes and studied her hymn book, happy in the knowledge that she would be seeing him again a few moments later. But how hoarse the poor Chaplain's voice was! All that speaking must have worn it out. She had no idea what he was talking about, and she sat there half-listening to phrases that had no meaning and registering only what a dreadful state the man was in. The Director sitting there, with his large round face – why on Earth was he so afraid of this man, this bustling, officious pedant, this offensive, thick-set, dark-haired little person? There too were those lesser mortals the form tutors, and hark at Susanna trilling away! Poor, simple-minded Susanna, poor humiliated Susanna, who had such weak judgement that she was still running after Kőnig even though he had made it clear that his interests lay elsewhere. Compared with Feri even Péter Kalmár was no more than an elegantly dressed provincial, a rather less than imposing young man. And Hajdú, with his bombastic eloquence, cynical Éles, and Kerekes, the fanatical guardian of the school paintings . . . were they people to be feared? Had she really disliked them so much when she first arrived? She did something she had not done for a very long time: she took a close look at Kőnig, as he sat there following the sermon with furrowed brow. You doddering old coward, she thought, you buffoon, grabbing the telephone from a young girl's hands and dreaming of marrying Mitsi Horn who wants nothing to do with you, you utter, you total, nonentity! She moved on to the rest of the teachers and deaconesses, those observers of and companions in her life, and she began to pity them. Sooner or later she would be gone but they would remain. There they would grow old, hemmed in by the black-and-white rules of the fortress, without hope of change or escape, while for her the one fact she could be sure of was that

Feri was there, looking at her. If he had known where to find her, then the General must have entrusted her fate to other hands than his own, and she would soon know the reason why.

The closing canticle had been sung. Gina's voice had never rung out so pure and untrammelled in all her life. Feri too had a hymn book in his hands, though he obviously had not been following it, and the moment the final blessing ended he stood up and left. Gina was not concerned: she knew she would see him outside.

The crocodile found itself temporarily stranded outside the entrance as the form tutors and deaconesses lined the girls up with their backs to the raised traffic islands, on one of which Feri was now standing. Gina heard Torma say something to her, but she was too busy watching Feri and did not answer. He made no attempt to greet her. No doubt he had his reasons for that, as he must have had too for what he did next. He suddenly raised his hymn book and waved it at her. The message was unclear. Perhaps he meant to tell her that they would meet again in the church the following Sunday? If nothing happened before that the week would seem a very long one, and she wondered how she could ever wait all that time. "Have you gone deaf?" Torma hissed at her. "I've asked you three times if you've noticed that young man who's been staring at Mari Kis." Mari Kis! What a joke! She was dying to say that it wasn't Mari Kis he had been looking at, it was her, standing next to Mari Kis. But she knew she should say nothing if she wanted to avoid putting her hopes in jeopardy.

The procession set off, and Feri with it. When they reached the main road and turned into János Matula Street he was still there beside them. He never once glanced in their direction, he just maintained a steady pace beside the row that included Torma, Mari Kis and Gina. Susanna, walking just behind them, had noticed him but had not given him a second glance – he was clearly just an innocent passer-by carrying a hymn book, no doubt on his way home, and not bothering the girls with importunate glances. He seemed suddenly to decide that he needed to cut through the line and stepped, rather rudely, straight into its path, as if on his way through towards the next side street, trod, in his apparent haste, on Torma's foot and knocked Gina's hymn book out of her hand. Torma let out a scream, Susanna glared at him, Gina came to a halt, blushing crimson, and Mari Kis put on a face of transcendental dignity. Feri raised his hat, picked up Gina's hymn book, excused himself (not to Gina but to Susanna) for his thoughtless haste, said that he was late for an important meeting, returned the hymn book to her, apologised a second time for his boorish absent-mindedness, put his hat on again and hurried off down the street without looking back.

Gina's eyes followed him in amazement, until Susanna called out to her: "Don't stare at men you don't know! Keep moving, and keep your eyes to the front." Gina was in a complete daze. None of it made sense. He hadn't tried to approach her, he hadn't said a single word to her, even to greet her or show that he recognised her. So what did he want? And how were they supposed to meet? She was quite sure he had deliberately bumped into her and knocked the hymn book out of her hand. It had looked perfectly accidental, but he must have had something in mind, though she could not for a moment think what it might be.

Of course, the hymn book! All this time she had been engrossed in her thoughts of Feri, but she had not entirely forgotten the rules of the Matula. If her hymn book was dirty she would be in trouble. She held it up for a closer look, then immediately lowered it again and pressed it against her coat, as firmly as if it were Feri's hand itself, the hand that would be taking her to her father. It wasn't hers, it was a different one, and there was a sheet of paper inside the back cover. He had swapped the two, and the piece of paper with the corner turned down contained not a list of hymn numbers and pages but a message. Mari and the others around her were whispering away, she had no idea what about. The moment they were back in the school she dashed into the washroom without waiting to hang up her coat and opened the hymn book.

Gini, she read (no-one had called her that since Marcelle had left)

The General is very ill, and I have come to take you to him, but it won't be straightforward. For some days I have been trying to get to see you in this accursed Lutheran nunnery, but they won't let me in. I shall try again this afternoon, but if they don't let me speak to you, then you must come at midnight to the garden gate, the one that has no key. I shall be waiting for you in the street outside. I kiss your hand,

   Feri

She tore the note into tiny shreds. It broke her heart to do so, but she knew enough about the ways of the Matula not to take any risks. What schemers they were, and how they loved to keep you in the dark! No-one had said a word about the fact that he had been trying to see her for days. And her father? What was happening to him? If he were seriously ill, then it was not his dangerous project that prevented his coming to see her but some simpler and more sombre circumstance. If he had asked Feri to take Gina to see him, then clearly his old injunction to stay where she was no longer applied. But how could she make these pig-headed saints understand that she absolutely had to leave, and leave at once, to be with a man undergoing Lord knows what suffering without his only child at his side?

So, how to get to him?

Feri did not know the Matula. These people weren't human, they had no souls: they had precepts and books and a collection of school rules instead. The Lieutenant had promised that he would try to reach her again that afternoon, but she had little hope of their meeting. She told Susanna that she was feeling dizzy and asked if she could miss the usual walk. The Prefect sent her off to the doctor, who diagnosed nothing beyond the usual problems of puberty, and Susanna reluctantly allowed her to stay behind. The afternoon walk was always an eagerly antici-pated event in the girls' week and it did not occur to Susanna that she might not have been telling the truth.

Gina sat in the day room looking through her lesson notes; or rather, her schoolbooks were in front of her but she was staring out of the window. Almost every one of the teachers looked in on her at some point, even the Director. The telephone in the duty room rang almost continuously. No-one came to call her, and no-one summoned her to the sitting room where visitors were received. When the class came back Mari Kis could not stop talking about the young man they had seen that morning. This time he had been standing on the pavement across the road from the school and ogling her again. Wasn't it amazing that someone should have fallen so completely in love with her?

So his attempt to visit me failed, Gina thought. Now it was up to her to make the final move in this complicated game of chess: she would have to be there at the garden gate at midnight, the gate that had no key.

It seemed a thoroughly impracticable idea. The Prefect was likely to come into the dormitory at the most unpredictable times, and indeed anything could happen – another air-raid practice, for example, or this time an actual attack. And even if it did prove to be a perfectly normal night, how could she possibly slip out of the dormitory at twelve and wait in the garden for perhaps a quarter of an hour without being spotted, or even get past the locked door at the end of the corridor? If she climbed out of the window she would be unable to close it behind her or climb back in. If anyone noticed it and thought it had been left open by mistake and shut it, she would be trapped outside and have to hunker down somewhere in the garden until the morning.

But the thought of having friends who would do anything for her, at whatever risk to themselves, first calmed her nerves and then banished them altogether. When Susanna allowed them some time to themselves she took Torma, Bánki and Mari Kis to one side and asked them, very quietly, if they would help her: she had to be in the garden at exactly midnight to meet some-one. The effect those words had was electric. The garrulous Mari Kis was reduced to speechlessness and stood there gulping in wonder. Torma began to shake and stammer, "Who with? Who is it?" The person least surprised was Bánki. She did not exclaim. Instead she asked, very calmly: "Could it be that your Feri Kuncz has turned up at last?"

Gina was astonished. True, she had talked a lot about him, but it was hardly self-evident that her night visitor would be the Lieutenant. It could have been Auntie Mimó – she was certainly romantically-minded enough for it – or one of her girlfriends from Budapest, or even the General himself. So why Feri? Where did she get that idea from? Yes, they had all seen the young man, but everyone thought he was looking at Mari Kis and none of them had seen him swap the hymn books. Bánki did not leave her to wonder for very long. "Then he must have got my letter."

All was revealed. Mari Kis and Torma were now transported by the unexpected drama. Gina-Juliet awaiting her Feri-Romeo whose welcome in the Matula, once it was realised what he was there for, would be no warmer than Romeo's had been in the house of Capulet . . . and Bánki, the Nurse and go-between, taking pity on the unhappy girl who had to spend her Christmas holiday alone. The moment Bánki had got back with her mother to the little town where they lived she had immediately written to Lieutenant Feri Kuncz, at 44 Zápor Street in Budapest. This is what she said:

Respected Lieutenant,

I am writing to tell you that Georgina Vitay is in the Matula Academy. She is very unhappy there, because she is not allowed to correspond with you and because she will not be going home for Christmas. It would cheer her up very much if she could see you.

From a well-wisher

She had not dared put her name to it, Bánki said, because she was afraid that this Lieutenant Kuncz might be indiscreet and pass it on, and if the letter were traced back to her the Director would almost certainly expel her. But she really hoped that it would persuade him to come. It was the special Christmas present she had promised Gina, and she had been so disappointed when she came back from the holiday. She hadn't mentioned that the present had been a letter because she had thought it was just the fickleness of men and that he had found someone else, or even worse – she apologised for the idea – that it had been all talk on Gina's part, while he just saw her as a silly schoolgirl and was merely toying with her. But she now saw how serious the relationship was, and hadn't she done well to bring the two lovers together?

Torma thought the ruse both ingenious and extremely touching, and the selfless Mari Kis, apparently not in the least downcast by the revelation that it was Gina and not herself that he had been staring at in the church, congratulated her with genuine delight. Gina told them what Feri had written and how he had passed his message to her, but what privately pleased her most was that he had come to take her to her father, and that he had written because the General had asked him to and not in response to the letter. So there was no need for soul-searching: true, Bánki, in the goodness of her heart, had given away the secret of her hiding place, and yes, she herself had been forbidden to reveal it to anyone, which of course included Feri, but his visit had nothing to do with her letter. The Lieutenant had asked her to meet him in the garden at midnight, she told the others.

But she would not be able to do that on her own. She needed their help.

Years later, when the events of that afternoon were no more than a memory, she often thought of her precious friendship with the three of them: the fair-haired Bánki, with her proud, smiling face; spirited Mari Kis, who was game for anything; and Torma, with her big blue eyes and her timid little mouth widening in terror at the thought of what they were going to do, but still ready to play her part. Together they cooked up a plan that seemed both feasible and simple. Torma was the most nervous of the three, so her role was to pretend to fall sick during the evening. At 11.30 p.m. Bánki would summon Susanna, tell her that Torma was unwell, and Susanna would help her down to the infirmary. There, she would moan and scream in agony for a good half-hour, to make sure that Susanna and the doctor remained by her side. She had until the evening to decide what her ailment might be, ideally something not readily detected like a sore throat. Best would be a stomach ache, with a suggestion of appendicitis, Bánki advised, having had the operation herself. At a few minutes to twelve Gina would climb out through the corridor window, Mari Kis would close it behind her and then stand guard by the dormitory door. Bánki would meanwhile have stationed herself at the start of the infirmary corridor to signal when Susanna was on her way back or, if needed, to delay her by pretending that she too had stomach pains and throwing herself to the floor as if in the throes of some hideous ailment. At 12.15 a.m. Mari Kis would open the window again and let Gina back in from the garden. Gina would have to be there exactly on time: any longer and the risk would be too great.

Once they had decided on their plan the usual pleasures of gossiping and giggling seemed to pale, and even the eternally smiling Mari Kis became serious: it was as if the plotting had made them aware of something else, something beyond the excitement and the secrecy of their enterprise, something to which they could not put a name. None of them had any appetite, and they could barely swallow their supper. Susanna studied them with particular interest during prayers. All the girls involved themselves in the service the way they should, but this group of four went at it with such intensity and fervour that Bánki had tears in her eyes.

The lights were switched off at 9 p.m., but the class took a long time to calm down and fall silent. As always on a Sunday, seeing people from outside the school and spending so much time in the company of outsiders, even if only in the constrained atmosphere of a religious service, had left them more than usually excitable. Nonetheless, with the exception of the four conspirators, they were all sound asleep by eleven. At 11.30 p.m. Bánki went to Susanna and told her that Torma had been taken ill. Susanna, still in her day clothes, came to the dormitory straight away, beckoned to the anxious Torma to follow her and made a sign to Bánki to tell her to be careful not to wake the others.

Gina and Mari Kis lay waiting under their quilts. Everything depended now on Torma and how she performed her role. A few minutes later Bánki slipped out and returned shortly afterwards to report that she had been to the infirmary: Torma was now uttering terrible cries; they were probably trying to make her vomit. Tense as she was, Mari Kis had to chuckle: poor Torma, it was the story of her life. Now she was having to put up with some disgusting laxative, and the three of them lay huddled up giggling together on Gina's bed while everyone else slept – luckily no-one had been disturbed by Torma's departure. They kept glancing at their watches in the dim glow of the nightlight, and at precisely 11.58 p.m. they rose. There was no chance, and no time, to get dressed, but Gina had kept her underwear and her stockings on under her dressing gown, and Mari Kis gave her her own as well, to help her keep warm in the chilly garden. They crept out of the dormitory, Bánki took up her position at the bend in the corridor, Mari Kis opened the window and Gina clambered up onto the ledge. She leaned down with her arms behind her back, the two girls exchanged a kiss, and she was out in the garden. The window, in its wartime covering, closed gently behind her. She reached Abigail's statue just as the garden clock began to sound twelve.

It was a bright, moonlit spring night and she had no trouble seeing her way. When she reached the gate she was at a loss what to do, so she waited for a signal. She did not have to wait long. As the chimes came to an end she heard a gentle knocking on the metal door. Not daring to speak, she knocked back. She felt as if her heart were about to explode.

Someone on the other side was fiddling with the lock and lifting the little iron tongue that covered the keyhole. Gina did the same on her side and put her ear to the opening. She heard a voice whisper: "Gini, my little Gini, is that you? Can you hear me?"

"It's me," she breathed into the keyhole. Her whisper sounded alien and strange; it was as if someone else were speaking. "What's the matter with my father?"

"It's his heart," the voice replied. "There's no need to worry. He's already out of the worst danger. But he very much wants to see you, and he's asked me to get you out of the school and take you home."

His heart? He had never had trouble with his heart . . . but if her father had asked Feri to come and fetch her then the Lieutenant must also be in the resistance. What joy, that he too should be working with her father! Great as was her respect for the Árkod dissident, it would be even better to make her escape with Feri. But perhaps he would go with them? Perhaps he too was out there, standing next to Feri, though she of course couldn't see.

"Are you alone?" she asked.

"Of course. Who else would be here?"

"My father told me that if he couldn't come himself he would send the man they call the Árkod dissident. I thought he might be here with you."

"The Árkod dissident?" the voice whispered.

"The man who changed the hymn boards in the white church and hung up those placards. My father told me I should leave the school only with him."

"But that was me," the voice breathed back.

She did not know how to reply. There were a few moments of silence on the other side, then the whispering began again.

"I've been here in Árkod for some months now. Your father had me transferred to be nearer you and to take care of you. I'm doing the same work here that he is in Budapest. Have you not noticed my presence?"

She placed her two hands on the iron door; her legs could barely support her. Her father had told her that she would recognise the dissident of Árkod when she met him, but she had not realised it would be Feri himself – that it had been Feri all along! So then, if he had been stationed here for some months he could not have had Bánki's letter, and even if it had been forwarded to him, it would have told him nothing he did not already know. She had always believed that the heroic dissident, that incredibly brave man, must be a soldier . . . and it was her Feri! Everything was now clear, and how wonderful it was. All it needed was for her father to get better, as of course he would. Feri had just said that he was over the worst.

"I haven't seen him since November," she whispered into the keyhole. "At first I wasn't too worried, because he had said he wouldn't be able to come for a while. But then I started to think that there must be something wrong, something to do with the work he was doing. But that's not the case, is it, Feri?"

"Not at all," the voice returned from the other side.

"Is the work going well?"

"Of course," came the reply.

"Why are the Germans here?"

"They aren't here to stay. They'll be leaving soon. Don't you worry about it."

"They won't be here long? So there's no danger?"

"Listen, Gini. I'll be back here tomorrow night. You must be ready to leave immediately. I'll have a key made for this door, I'll open it from this side, and by the morning we'll be with your father in Budapest. I have to do things in this rather romantic way because these lunatics won't speak to me. They won't even let me see the Director. I told the porter that your father had sent me, and he said it was no concern of his. Never in my life have I seen a school like this one. It's not a school, it's a prison."

How true that was! As someone who had lived in it since September well knew.

"The car will be waiting for you here, outside the gate. The moment you step through it we'll be gone. After fifteen minutes you will have forgotten you were ever here."

I shall never forget that, she thought, and she was filled with wonder that even at that strange hour, standing in that chilly garden bathed in frail moonlight and filled with the scents of spring, she should find herself thinking that she would never forget the Matula.

She waited for him to say something. Though she was ashamed to admit it, she was hoping he would say something personal, something other than what her father had told him to say or to do with his orders. But perhaps these young men working in the resistance and busying themselves with heroic deeds never spoke about such personal things as love as they went about their business.

"Same time tomorrow, Gini. Be here on time," the voice breathed. And he left without a word of farewell; all she heard was the sound of his disappearing footsteps. She waited a while for him to come back, but he did not appear again. She soon understood why. There were more footsteps; someone was walking round the perimeter fence, some late-night passer-by with a heavy tread. His approach must have alarmed the Lieutenant. Never mind, they had talked about what mattered. She ran back through the garden and knocked on the window. It opened immediately. Mari Kis reached down and helped her climb inside the corridor again. In a few seconds they were back in the dormitory.

They did not go straight to bed; they were still waiting for Bánki. Gina stood there shivering from excitement and the freezing air of a night in March.

"Did he kiss you?" Mari was desperate to know, and was immediately covered in embarrassment. How could they possibly have kissed with the wall between them? "Did he get Bánki's letter? Does he worship you? Did you get engaged? You must tell us everything!"

Gina did not dare reveal that he had said not one word about love, only about her father and the resistance, and that Bánki's letter had been irrelevant because Feri had been based in Árkod almost as long as she had but had obviously not been allowed to let her know. As for the outrage in the church, she might not have seen him among the members of the local garrison, but he could still have been the person who tampered with the hymn boards. She decided to go along with the idea that Bánki's letter had reached him after all, so that her friend could at least have that satisfaction. Tomorrow I shall be leaving these people forever, she thought, but I won't tell anyone or get them involved. I don't want them to get into trouble when it all comes out. Tomorrow at midnight the gate will be open, and even if Susanna does come out of her room while I am climbing out of the window she'll be too slow to catch me once I'm in the garden: she'll be in her long nightgown and she won't be able to run as fast as I can.

At 12.30 Bánki came back from the infirmary to report that all was now quiet there. Torma had stopped groaning, but Susanna and the doctor were still at her side. To spare her the feeling that she had been standing all that time in the corridor for nothing, Gina felt she had to offer her the fiction that she and Feri had talked of love, and that it was all thanks to her. The girls couldn't have enough of it. They had to hear over and over again the tender words that she and Feri had never exchanged. After all the risks they had taken for her that night she felt she owed them that pleasure. When they were at last in bed she lay there, wide awake, thinking about the strange and unexpected way important events in our lives come about – never as we imagine them beforehand, always in quite other ways, in very different circumstances and seemingly by chance. One fine day a young man appears on a balcony in a church, two people exchange glances, and life is transformed forever.

It was her last night in the Matula. The next day its occupants would still be there without her, caught up in their dreams and their black-and-white rules, and she would be spending it with her father. The moment he saw her at his bedside he would get better, she was sure. He had said that if he couldn't come for her himself the person he sent in his place would be someone she had known a long time. How had she not realised that it would be Feri, the man she loved? All this secrecy and mystification surrounding her father's work! To keep up the illusion he had even gone so far as to let her believe that he disliked the Lieutenant and would not even have him in the house, when all the time the two of them were the best of friends, and, obviously, since he had placed his beloved daughter in his care, the most trusted of colleagues.

The door opened a crack and Susanna peered in. Gina watched her through half-closed eyes. The Prefect satisfied herself that everything was in order, closed the door behind her and disappeared. Now Gina really felt herself to be the more adult of the two. Susanna was the child, the pupil, bound in by her monochrome rules and regulations. Never mind: the days of exile were over. Tomorrow the world would open to her once again. She would be out there in it, while this child, this simple-minded Susanna, would remain a prisoner in the fortress forever.

The Árkod dissident

When they were concocting up their plans for Gina's meeting with Feri, the four had debated long and hard whether to let the rest of the class in on what they were doing. Mari Kis was the strongest in favour. No-one would give them away, she was quite certain. For five years they had lived together like sisters; now Bánki had found a way to bring Feri Kuncz to the school and they were preparing a romantic rendezvous with him that night – it was such a sensational thing that they really had to be told. Torma, apprehensive as ever, was against it: to help one of your classmates meet someone from outside was a serious offence and it would be most unfair to make them accomplices. Some of them had sisters in other years, and if they told them, the news would be out and what would become of the four of them then? They had to keep it secret. There was no need to involve anyone else. Bánki agreed, and things stayed as they were.

The next day began with yet more deception, and not only because they were keeping the class in ignorance of what had happened. Gina's fellow-conspirators wanted to hear about the romantic assignation all over again, and Gina had to keep making things up: they had sworn to love one another forever; the Lieutenant had said he would wait for her because he loved her, but she would have to be patient because they would not be able to meet again soon; he was being transferred from Árkod and would not be allowed to write to her. When he did come again it would be on another Sunday. He would come to one of the Matula services, as he just had. During lessons that day Bánki and Mari Kis kept exchanging excited glances to remind one another of the sensational events they had been party to the night before.

It had often happened in Gina's childhood that she would get in a rage with Marcelle or her father because, inevitably, there were times when they had had to be strict with her, but when it had all blown over she would be filled with a burning desire to be especially good and kind to everyone. She would go down to the kitchen, ask who would like some help, dash off a bit of cleaning, tidy up the display cabinets without being asked or dust the contents of the bookshelves. Sometimes – the noblest sacrifice of all – she even offered to visit the aged aunt her father was so very fond of, a woman she found utterly boring and whom she could hardly bear to call on, because she would have to endure sitting for ages in artificial light in a drawing room filled with strange smells.

She knew she had sinned against the Matula rules, and even though she did not for a moment believe in the legitimacy of those rules, and felt that what she had done and what she was planning to do were both necessary and inevitable, the urge to be nice to everyone possessed her once again. It was already strong in the first lesson of the day, when they were set a piece of French translation. As usual, Miss Gigus made her sit on the dais, to stop her helping the others. Gina had the supreme audacity to slip the crib she had prepared for Szabó, who always struggled with languages, into the teacher's pocket while her friend watched, her eyes following Gina's hand like the movements of a snake charmer. Miss Gigus wandered dreamily down the aisles, bringing the crib ever closer. When she reached Szabó she leaned over, as she always did, to see how she was getting on, and with trembling fingers the girl plucked it out of her pocket. Gina's own translation that day was full of the most stunningly apt turns of phrase: her French, learned from Marcelle, was far more immediate, colloquial and natural than the classical tongue dunned into the Matula girls, even the best of whom would try to write in the language of the *ancien régime*. The crib Gina had sent mimicked this antiquated style so well that Miss Gigus might have written it herself.

However it was in Kőnig's lesson that this urge for universal benevolence reached its height. She did not misbehave once. She scribbled no secret messages. She did not draw or doodle, or sit there yawning or staring out of the widow; for the first time in her life she listened carefully to everything he said, and once again she was astonished by how very interesting, and how lively and persuasive, his arguments were, and, though it was also a source of private amusement, she rather regretted that she would not be there the next day to hear how the topic ended. Kőnig noticed how attentive she was, especially as, again for the first time ever, she volunteered for extra work as part of the team selecting the passage for the next day's lesson. Latin had always come easily to her because of her French; the similar vocabulary helped her learn new words instantly. Kőnig congratulated her, and kept giving her thoughtful glances, as if he were wondering what had happened to the Vitay he thought he knew.

The next lesson was music. She sang her heart out and rendered hymn 186, the subject of her preparation work, with such grace that Hajdú gave her the top mark. Bánki and Mari Kis, however, were sent to the corner of the room because they could not restrain their mirth during the performance, and Hajdú "failed to see the joke". Gina had taken the song seriously, even though she too could see the relevance of the words to what had happened the previous night. "The sun is down, and darkness fills the sky, / Deep silence reigns, and nature lies at rest. / I too have found repose for weary limbs. / My dream awakes, my soul prepares to fly."

The teacher almost had a fit when he realised that that reprobate Mari Kis and the shameless Bánki were still giggling and smirking in the corner for all the world to see. What was so funny about the fact that, for the first time ever, Vitay had properly mastered this beautiful hymn to the night? But her friends knew only too well what had gone on in the garden when the sun went down, and that her body and soul had not exactly been "at rest" around midnight, and not only hers but theirs too, with Bánki standing guard in the infirmary corridor and Mari Kis at the window in her nightshirt, because she had lent her nightgown to this person now warbling away like an intoxicated nightingale when a few hours earlier she had been exchanging whispers with her lover through the garden gate.

The fourth lesson was with Kalmár. Gina was still in her

mood of wanting to be good and helpful to everyone, but he failed to ask her any questions and she was given no chance. In fact he addressed not a single word to her; he simply talked non-stop until the bell went. All she could do was behave impeccably, pay constant attention throughout, and slip his piece of chalk into her pocket as a memento when he left.

Kerekes appeared for lesson five. Ever since their first lesson in September he had criticised Gina for not writing her number four properly. She had never bothered to change it, because she found it both incomprehensible and exasperating that someone should have nothing better to think about than the shape of some insignificant digit. This time, when it was her turn to go up to the blackboard, she produced the most beautiful four ever seen. Kerekes looked at her incredulously, reached for the comments book and wrote: "Today Georgina Vitay wrote the number four correctly. I congratulate her, András Kerekes." He rarely praised anyone, and in other circumstances this would have given Gina no small pleasure, but now she found herself blushing with delight. How very strange, considering that it was all now so meaningless.

The fifth lesson finished and Kalmár came in promptly, as he always did, to ask who had done best that day. He was told it was Vitay. It was the first time this had happened all year. He looked through the notes in the class register and the duty report, nodded twice, and Gina knew that her name would be read out by the Director at the end of lunch, when the names of those who produced the best results on the day were announced. Naturally Gedeon Torma, in his blackest of voices, would also be revealing those who had been in trouble. How often had she herself been shamed that way! But this was the very first time she would be among the praised. It was both highly amusing and rather sad.

With just a few hours to go she had the urge to leave a few remembrances of herself. She wanted everyone to think of her as a clever, cultured, thoroughly pleasant person and a good friend, always kind, polite and generous. Just before lunch she knocked on Susanna's door to ask if she could take time out during the afternoon walk to buy some presents for her class-mates from the money she had left over from Christmas, and to be allowed to visit poor Torma in the infirmary afterwards. With-out a word, Susanna pulled open a drawer and handed her what she wanted. As she did so Gina spotted several other envelopes with her name on them, and she realised that when he had enrolled her in the autumn her father must not only have paid the full boarding and tuition fees but also left her monthly pocket money for the rest of the year. Susanna gave permission for the visit to Torma, but only for a few minutes, because her condition was being closely monitored. If she had improved by the evening it was probable that she had been suffering from some mild liver complaint during the night, but if she was worse she would be taken to the hospital for a stomach X-ray in the morning. She was not to be tired out: she had had a very bad night and had been given several powerful and rather unpleasant medicines.

At the end of lunch the Director did indeed read out Gina's name.

The practice was that the named girls would leave their seats, walk towards the teachers' table and bow, first to them and then to their classmates. In her early months in the school Gina had found this ridiculous, but as she grew accustomed to it, it seemed less so, and rather an honour to be envied. Going up between the tables she was again surprised to find just how much the congratulations meant to her, and when she made her bow to the Director's table and noticed that Kőnig was again paying her particular attention she smiled back at him without a flicker of irony or ill-will.

It was a day of real happiness. She was feeling self-confident and liberated, and the air around her was filled with radiance. She knew she would soon be free, Feri would be taking her home, and everything there would be well: her father was over the worst of his illness, and the German occupation obviously wasn't too much to worry about – in fact it would bring an early end to the war. She felt as charitable, gentle and serene as only a perfectly contented person could be. But always she was aware of Kőnig's eyes on her: he never seemed to look anywhere else. No doubt he was still astonished that there should exist another Vitay who smiled and could be found worthy of praise.

That afternoon the class waited patiently while she made her purchases at Hajda's patisserie, and then again at the flower shop next door to it, where she spent her last few fillér on a little pot of hyacinths.

"You're in a good mood today!" Susanna commented, when they were back from the walk. By then the class had all been treated to Mr Hajda's delicacies and the Prefect had found her usual place adorned by the pot of pretty white flowers. She lifted the hyacinths to her nose and breathed the perfume in. "You have every reason to be happy, Georgina. You have now joined the ranks of the very best pupils, so naturally you want to give presents to everyone. But I cannot accept these flowers from you. I have done nothing to deserve them. They would, however, make a very good present for the Director, especially if you offered them to him on behalf of the class for his name day. His first name is Gedeon, and tomorrow is the twenty-eighth."

There was something exhilarating, even intoxicating in the idea. Susanna had forgiven Gina, as her faith required, but she had also made it quite clear, however gently and tactfully, that she would never accept a gift from her, not even a miserable little pot of hyacinths, so how perfect it would be to visit the man in black, present him with them and then vanish overnight. When they started to look for her the only clue would be these white flowers on the Director's desk. And when she had finished in the teachers' residence she would call on Torma. Torma, she decided should be her heir. She loved her even more than Bánki, not because of the little plaster dog, or the fact that they had spent the winter holidays together: what bonded them so closely was that they were both orphans in the fortress. Watching Gina tidying her hair and putting on her going-out uniform (nothing else would do for the occasion) Bánki and Mari Kis almost fainted with laughter. That she should have the cheek to call on the Director after all that had happened the night before! If he knew about that it would strike him dead in his chair. Arranging her locks in the tiny washroom mirror made her think of the curlers she had left in the drawer of her bedside chest at home. It was so long since she had last done her hair with them she would have to learn how to use them all over again.

On her way to the teachers' quarters, with the flowers, freshly and prettily re-wrapped, in her hand, she found herself humming a little tune. The barred gate was locked, as always, but she did not have to ring. Gertrúd Truth happened to be standing in the corridor on the other side, spotted her and let her in. She found the Director in his sitting room. Kőnig, Kalmár and Miss Gigus were with him. The meeting did not seem a very happy one. They were all poring over open registers. How typical, she thought. So this will be the final image I take away of them: the Director disciplining his staff. Miss Gigus and Kalmár regularly forgot to sign off her lessons in the record book, and Kőnig was so absent-minded he almost always wrote his name in the wrong subject column.

She looked at them as an adult might look at three little boys and a girl found playing with marbles. The Director stared at her blankly as, without the slightest trepidation, she wished him a happy name day on behalf of the class. He stood up and offered her his hand. Gina noticed to her surprise that his face had turned bright red. She had long seen him as merely the gloomy source of impenetrably stupid prohibitions. Who would have thought he would have been so affected by someone simply wishing him a happy name day and giving him a pot of flowers? Nor would she ever have thought him capable of asking her to sit down, as he now did. She replied that she did not wish to intrude, she had come only to congratulate him, and she was in a hurry to go and visit his sick niece.

Every morning the Director was sent a report on anyone who was sick, so he knew that Torma had been taken ill in the night and had sent a message that he would come and see her at some point during the day. But he had also expressed surprise. This was a girl who was never unwell. She had not missed a day's school since she had been in the Matula; she had a constitution of iron. He bade Gina goodbye and then, surprise of surprises, offered her his hand again. Gina took one last look around the black-and-white room, and at the teachers sitting there gloomily among piles of exercise books, bowed, as Susanna had taught her, and hurried off to the infirmary.

She found Torma alone. She had been lying down, but as soon as she saw Gina she sat up and asked her if she had brought her anything to eat: she was being systematically starved and was dying of hunger. Gina had a cake with her that she had asked Mr Hajda to wrap separately for her friend, and she gave it to her.

The poor creature, so grievously afflicted with stomach pains, wolfed it down without even pausing to chew it. Her mouth was still full when she demanded to know for the love of God what had happened to Gina during the night. Mari Kis and Bánki had been to see her but they had exploded in fits of laughter as soon as they came in, and when they did finally start to tell her the nurse had come in and sent them away. Gina gave her the same story she had concocted for Mari Kis and Bánki, about the wonderful romantic conversation she had had with the Lieutenant. Torma breathed a great sigh. She was glad that she hadn't endured those emetics and laxatives for nothing, though she certainly had suffered.

Gina looked at her, at the drained, weary face, that kind and gentle face that had become so much more dear to her over the last weeks and months than that of any of her friends at home. Inside her bag were all her personal treasures, the things she had hidden under the flower box and the ones her father had brought for her on his last visit, including the presents from Auntie Mimó. They had all given pleasure to the rest of the class, but of course they were Gina's and the others had not felt free to make use of any of them, not the bottle of perfume, which they had held up to their noses without daring to put any of the contents on their skin, nor the squirrel brooch with the wonderful marcasite eyes, which the General had brought even though he knew she would never be allowed to wear it, or even (the two things they had most universally admired) the stick of rouge and the special pencil that could write in different colours, blue, green, red or black, depending on how you set it up. What a joy that would have been to try! But of course such a thing would never be allowed. No distinction was to be made between the richer pupils and the poorer, and that principle applied even to the pencils they drew with: everyone made do with the same Hungarian-made items, low-quality wartime goods that produced unreliable colours.

Torma stared in wonder as each of these splendours was laid out on her quilt. She had no idea what Gina wanted to do with them. The infirmary was no place to play with them. They would be confiscated the moment anyone popped in to see how she was.

"I brought them to give you," Gina explained. "Everything. For you to keep, forever."

"Are you feverish?" Torma asked in astonishment. "Or have you gone mad? All these lovely things? What would you have left for yourself?"

She could hardly reply, "Freedom, Budapest, my father's love, my old home," and she kept silent. She was so glad that even as she was about to escape she had thought to give her most precious things away, knowing that they would be in good hands, the hands of an orphan whose only possession in the world was a provocative nightdress.

"I don't need them anymore," she said at last. "I don't need any of them. I'm giving them to you."

If Torma, usually so timid and circumspect, had not been swayed beyond reason by the comb with the silver handle, the lipstick, the four-coloured pencil and all the other treasures, indeed almost intoxicated by the sight of them, she would never have agreed that they should wrap them in a large handkerchief and that Gina should hide them with the nightie in the wooden cube in the drawing supplies cupboard. Gina had brought them to show Torma what she was leaving her, to see the delighted look on her face and then hide them promptly again, but all Torma wanted to do was to revel in her wonderful new possessions, and they were so engrossed in their discussion that they failed to notice as soon as they should have done that the door behind them was now wide open. It was only when he cleared his throat that they realised that Kőnig and the nurse were standing behind Gina. Torma looked up and Gina turned round. Kőnig was holding a plate in his hands, with an apple on it. The nurse had a face of thunder.

"I've brought you a nice red apple," he said. "Very good for an upset stomach, they say. How are you feeling, Piroska?"

Torma was speechless. Utterly bereft, she put her hands over the contents of the oriental bazaar that lay glittering on the quilt. The myopic Kőnig came closer to the bed, picked up the bright red stick of rouge, sniffed it, reached for the comb and ran his nail along its white teeth in admiration. Once again Gina had the feeling that this man had been put on earth only to make the lives of other people hell. The nurse stood there, breathing heavily.

"Please don't take them from me," Torma pleaded. The sound of that tearful little voice would often echo in Gina's mind as an adult, when her own daughter pushed away some really valuable object that did not especially appeal to her because she had always been allowed to have whatever she liked. "Please don't take them away, sir, I beg you! Please don't take them away, Sister!"

His hand shaking, Kőnig put the comb down, and the rouge after it. With her lips clamped tight to stop her uttering words that might displease the Lord, the nurse picked up a towel from the side of the bed and, disregarding Torma's protests, wrapped everything in the towel and left the room.

She's taking them to Susanna, Gina realised. Now they are neither mine nor Torma's, and once again I am in deep trouble. If they are going to punish anyone it must be me. There's nothing they won't be able to stop me doing now.

Torma pulled the quilt over her head and buried herself inside it to weep. Kőnig stood with his eyes fixed on Gina. She waited for what would happen next; she was almost exultant, but she felt desperately sorry for Torma. The poor thing had had such a brief glimpse of what might have been hers and then lost it before it had been of any benefit to her.

Susanna did not take long to arrive. She had brought the offending objects back, now wrapped in the towel. She glanced at Kőnig, as if to tell him to leave, but he failed to take the hint, and stayed where he was, loitering about, most unsuitably in terms of the Matula ethos: a man, even if a member of the teaching staff, did not moon around in a sick room occupied by one of the girls.

Susanna began by trying to question Torma, but the girl refused to answer her and simply huddled deeper under the quilt. Gina replied for her. She told Susanna that the things belonged to her, and she had brought them for Torma to enjoy; Torma was completely innocent. Susanna was shocked. She demanded to know why she had never seen these baubles, this ungodly merchandise, before, and Gina explained that she had been keeping them in a special hiding place. Kőnig was visibly struck by the calm and supercilious way she had spoken to the Prefect. Knowing that she had been deceived always made Susanna angry, and now she was furious. She told Gina she had no idea what sort of punishment she would give her, but she would make sure it was something that she would remember for a very long time. Gina nodded serenely, as if this were a compliment. Kőnig's eyes never once left her face.

Susanna was about to leave when Torma, outraged by the idea that her friend should be punished for her act of super-human kindness – the friend who had given her first a wonderful nightdress and now, however briefly, her entire collection of treasures – mastered her natural timidity for the first time in her life. She pulled her head out of the quilt and declared, between gasps for breath, that Vitay had taken the blame but it wasn't right. She was the kindest and most unselfish girl in the whole school, she had just given her everything that she had, these treasures were now her property and she was the one who should be punished, not Vitay who had given them to her.

The Deaconess was now so angry with the two of them she could barely contain herself. She told Torma that she too would be included in the punishment, she could be quite sure of that, and she gave Kőnig another of those looks, so that he finally took the hint and turned to leave. Susanna signalled to Gina that she should go too, but she just stood there gazing at Torma. Realising that she might never see her again in her life, she leaned over her, put her arms around her neck, covered her in kisses – something that would have been scandalous in the day room let alone in the infirmary – and said, "God bless you, my love." Susanna was beyond speech. She pointed sternly to the door, and Gina sailed out as calmly as you might wish, not forgetting to take her leave of everyone in turn and executing the most graceful and Matula-worthy bow she had made in her life.

She went back to the day room and began to go over the day's lessons, though she knew she would not be there to be tested on them in the morning. She kept glancing at her watch and noting with surprise how quickly the time seemed to be passing. She would have no chance to tell her classmates about the saga of the sickroom, but, in any case, she had no desire to explain what had happened. Susanna was going to announce her punishment in the morning, but by then she would be over the hills and far away, so what was the point of upsetting her friends by revealing that she had given everything to Torma alone? They would simply wonder what had brought on this sudden fit of generosity that left her with nothing.

In their free time Mari Kis and Bánki nagged her yet again for the story of the night's doings. She had grown tired of endlessly repeating the same lies, and it was a relief when suppertime came. Again she felt Kőnig's eyes on her throughout the meal, and she returned a look that verged on the flirtatious. Of course, you're now wondering why I'm not more worried or upset than I am about the fact that I'm going to be punished, she thought. Well, tomorrow you'll find out what gave me strength and put me in such good spirits.

During prayers, however, the realisation that this was the last time she would be taking part moved her in a way that surprised her. Her visceral hatred of the black-and-white world and all its constraints had begun to melt away. Susanna was looking her loveliest that evening, both beautiful and sad, and it made her think of the months that had passed since the autumn – and what months they had turned out to be! Far from unrelieved bitterness, they had brought her light and joy and love and laughter. It was only years later, when Árkod and the massive bulk of Matula loomed up in her memory like rocks surfacing from under the retreating tide, that she came to understand exactly what she had felt that evening.

Once they were in bed she did not have to talk for long. The whole class were heavy-eyed, Bánki and Mari Kis especially so. By ten everyone was sound asleep, and she was able to begin getting ready. She was not in the least bit nervous. She trusted Feri so much that she had not a moment's doubt that their plan would succeed. While the other girls were finishing off in the washroom she had hidden her school uniform and her coat under the mattress: this time she would have to wear proper clothes – she could hardly travel to Budapest with Feri in her dressing gown. At a quarter to twelve she put her uniform on. Lacing up her hideous long black boots she smiled to think what Feri would say when he saw her in her everyday school uniform.

Before she stepped out into the corridor she took a long look around the room in the dim glow of the nightlight at the faces of her sleeping companions. She longed to say goodbye to them, to kiss them all for the last time, because she loved them so very much. But she could not put her chance of escape in jeopardy.

She peered down the corridor leading to Susanna's room, and then along the one to the teachers' quarters. Nothing moved. Sometimes we just know when an enterprise is going to succeed. Gina was quite sure that nothing would stop her getting out into the garden. She opened the window, climbed out and pushed the shutters back as best she could: that way less light would fall into the garden, and they would not betray to a casual glance that something was amiss. When the staff realised that she was not in her bed they would look for her in the building first, and it would not occur to them that she might have gone out into the garden. Why would anyone want to be out there in the freezing cold, with the church bells tolling midnight?

And toll they did, with a deep, ceremonial boom, as she ran across the moonlit garden and reached the statue of Abigail. She was not in the least afraid. Her feelings were very different from those of the night before. Then, she had had no idea what was waiting for her. This time she was going back to her old existence – her home, Auntie Mimó, Feri and her father. She was going back to life itself.

She reached the iron gate and waited for it to open. All was silent on the other side, but she had a strong sense that she was not alone. The last notes of the bell were now fading away. She glanced back over her shoulder at the sleeping building, and at the garden filled with the chilly scents of March – the smell of raw earth and the cold breath of violets. As she stood waiting at the gate the moon lit up her face and figure.

Someone knocked on the other side. She replied with a gentle tap, tap, tap.

"Gini," Feri whispered. "We'll have to wait a moment. Someone's coming down the street. Can you hear me?"

"I can hear you," she breathed back.

"There are two men standing talking on the other side of the road, opposite the school entrance. Thank God there are no lights on."

She made no reply. She was now anxious and tense. Her brain was telling her to wait and not to move, but instinct made her desperate to get out through that door and away.

"The car's waiting in a side street. I didn't want to park it here, where people would notice. Cars aren't usually parked here. I've done pretty well, as you'll see. What a place this Árkod is!

I've never seen the like. How on earth have you put up with it for so long, you poor thing?"

"With difficulty," she whispered back. "Can we go yet?"

"Soon. Now they're saying goodbye, I can hear their voices clearly. I would never have thought anyone would be out at this time of night in a provincial town. Right, they seem to be on their way. Mind out, Gini, I'm going to open the gate!"

She had flattened herself against it. Now every breath was painful and made her feel ill. She heard the key moving in the lock, and then back again. The mechanism seemed unwilling to budge. She pressed with her whole body against the gate. Still nothing. It must be double-locked. The key was tried again, this time with greater force, but the final turn that should have freed it stuck solid. She pressed herself against the gate even harder. There came the sound of footsteps in the street, of people running from opposite directions, and a light flashed.

"Hey, you!" someone shouted. "What's all this? Stay where you are! What are you up to with that key? Why are you trying to open that gate?"

"Get that light out of my eyes, you fool. You'll have the Civil Defence people here. Put that torch away!" Feri hissed. "What are you doing here?"

"What are we doing here?" the unknown voice said indignantly. "The question is what are you doing here? Who sent you? Who are you? Are you one of the Cock-a-doodle-doos? Or a burglar? Just you wait. We've sent for the Director. So you want a fight? Right, chum: you stay right where you are while I call the Matula!"

The alarm bell, the bell no-one ever used, the bell that had hung for centuries next to the iron gate that had no key, started to clang. Gina stood there petrified while it sounded, then someone swore. There were more running footsteps, followed by some new ones, obviously in pursuit, and all was silent again, an unnatural, deathly silence. For a moment her brain was numb with fear, then her survival instinct kicked in and she ran – back past the smiling statue of Abigail, back to the window, where she had to climb in without the help of Mari Kis, and found herself standing in the corridor once again, totally out of breath. Susanna's door stood wide open, her light was on: she must have dashed off somewhere, perhaps to the main entrance, or the teachers' quarters. What if she were in the dormitory? And if the other girls were awake?

They were all asleep. She tore off her clothes, pulled on her nightdress and threw her uniform and her coat under the bed. As she huddled down under the quilt she found herself trembling all over. Something seemed to be rubbing against her back, but she took no notice amid her floods of tears. Feri had been caught red-handed and chased away; now she did not know if she would ever escape. Because he had tried to get into the garden that gate would probably be kept under watch from the morning onwards, or they would put a steel bar across it with a padlock – anything was possible in this place. She wept bitterly, and her sobs grew louder. Sounds of movement came from Mari Kis' bed, but she was so deeply asleep she just coughed and mumbled a bit and turned onto her other side. But someone had heard Gina's sobbing from even further away and she soon appeared. It was Susanna.

She was fully dressed: you would have thought it was broad

daylight. She straightened the chair beside the bed, sat down, and put a hand on the weeping girl's brow. Her fingers smelled of soap. They were cool and comforting.

"I'll find a way to make your life easier here," she said softly. "I'm afraid I often lose patience with you, because you are so different from anyone I have met here – so headstrong and rebellious. And today that collection of forbidden objects! You really must try to be more sensible. I was very, very angry with you, but I'm not any longer, and even if the Director also punishes you it won't be so very bad that you should lose sleep over it, or be so afraid that you need cry."

You still imagine I'm afraid of that man, Gina thought, as her eyes ran with tears. But what has happened to Feri? And what will become of me?

As if she had heard what the girl was thinking, Susanna spoke again.

"Did you hear the alarm bell ringing? Mr Mráz sounded it because someone tried to break in through the garden gate, a burglar no doubt, but he was seen off by the glazier's assistant and his friend. He left his key in the lock and ran. You mustn't tell the younger girls, because they are little and they will be afraid, but nothing can happen to us here. The men are very good, and they take good care of us."

She paused briefly, thinking that Gina might want to say something, perhaps to thank her for forgiving her, or for coming to be with her. But Gina remained silent. She was weary to death and filled with despair. Susanna stood up, told her to say her prayers, and left the room.

Eventually the flow of tears stopped and her strength began to return. She got out of bed and went to put her coat and uniform in the wardrobe outside, not wanting to find them creased when the bell rang in the morning. She hung them up on the hooks and made her way wearily, with bitterness in her heart, back down the corridor. She picked up the quilt to straighten it before she lay down, and began to tidy the bed. Earlier something had been pushing into her back. Now, by the dim glow of the night-light, she saw what it was. She stared at it for what seemed hours, in total disbelief. What she found was no less astonishing than if a star had fallen onto her bed. There, glittering faintly, was a silver ashtray. It was the one she had bought for her father on their way to Árkod. Beneath it was a note, printed in the now familiar capitals. She read it, then stood staring dumbly ahead of her. What she felt was beyond anything that could be expressed by tears or the wildest howls of grief.

THIS ASHTRAY, WHICH YOU BOUGHT FOR YOUR FATHER IN A JEWELLER'S SHOP IN SZOLNOK IN RETURN FOR A MOON PENDANT, WAS GIVEN TO ME BY HIM. IT IS SOMETHING FOR YOU TO REMEMBER HIM BY, AND TO LET YOU KNOW THAT HE SPOKE WITH ME AND ENTRUSTED YOUR LIFE TO ME. WHEN THE GERMANS INVADED ON THE NINETEENTH HE WAS AMONG THE FIRST TO BE ARRESTED. LIEUTENANT KUNCZ CAME TO ÁRKOD THE FOLLOWING DAY TO LURE YOU OUT OF THE SCHOOL AND USE YOU TO FORCE YOUR FATHER TO BETRAY HIS COLLEAGUES. IF I HAD NOT BEEN KEEPING A CLOSE WATCH OVER YOU YOU WOULD NOW BE A

HOSTAGE TO BLACKMAIL HIM WITH. WHAT HAPPENS TO YOU FROM NOW ON IS FOR ME TO DECIDE, AND ANY MESSAGE I SEND YOU IS TO BE TREATED AS AN ORDER FROM HIM. STAY WHERE YOU ARE AND TRY NOT TO WORRY. I SHALL TAKE CARE OF YOU. KEEP CALM UNTIL YOU HEAR FROM ME AGAIN.

ABIGAIL

Feri Kuncz in the Matula

The day began much like any other. They rushed about getting themselves ready, queued up for the showers and chivvied one another along, and no-one had time to notice the expression on Vitay's face. What with everything they had to do and their worries about work, probably no-one would have done so before lunch; they only did so after the doctor had spotted her in the corridor on her way to prayers, stopped, taken her pulse, examined her throat, asked her if she were ill and told her to come to the infirmary at break for a proper examination. Gina simply shook her head and said no, she didn't feel unwell, and it was then that Mari Kis and the others realised how pale she was. When they pressed her, she just shook her head, gave them the same answers as she had the doctor and repeated that she was fine. The doctor began a separate conversation with Susanna, during which Gina was dismayed to hear that Torma had become ill again during the night: it was difficult to say what the problem was, because she had had nothing all day but tea and had been feeling extremely well, and then this second, even more acute, attack of stomach pains had occurred. There was no chance of her being allowed to attend lessons.

Gina suppressed a smile as she listened to the adults discussing this mysterious relapse; only she knew that Torma had bolted down Mr Hajda's cream cake on an empty stomach. But it all felt very distant from her now, as did the fortress in which she was still compelled to "live, move and have her being". These grown-ups seemed to her no more than shadows. Susanna made no reference to their conversation of the night before, or to what had happened earlier at Torma's bed, and Gina gave no thought to them either, so insignificant did they seem beside her current problems.

It was only after prayers, when the nurse went up to the Director to tell him something and the man in black turned towards her with a look of astonishment, that she started to wonder again what sort of punishment lay in store for her. She now realised that Susanna had chosen to keep what had happened a secret, or at the very least wait to tell him at some other time, or even to present it in a rather different light. But the Nursing Sister had been mortally offended, and her sense of justice called for instant retribution, so the day would almost certainly begin with some sort of punishment. When she was told after prayers that she was to miss the first lesson and go unaccompanied to the Director's office instead, she was almost glad. Anything was better now than being left alone to her thoughts, to the task of sorting through the mass of fragmented memories and trying to make sense of things she had never before considered problematical or felt a need to resolve.

She had no opportunity to take her leave of her classmates, or even to explain what had happened to her this time, and they followed her with looks of alarm as she set off for the office. She gathered that Gedeon Torma intended to summon Kalmár between 8 and 9 a.m., when he was free, and that he would be there when they decided what the punishment would be. It mattered little to Gina. Indeed, the thought was almost welcome, a concrete detail in the miasma of horrors swirling about in her mind.

As she waited to be called in she gazed at the Director's door with an affection she had never felt before. Kerekes' mania for the correct shape of her number fours, Hajdú's fanatical insistence that they pace their canticles precisely, the order and regularity observed by one and all, the rules that were never to be transgressed, in short the whole daily life of the fortress, now appeared to her benign and comforting. This world of black and white, with all its severity, was a universe away from that outer world of deceit and betrayal, of base conduct, danger and death. At that moment she was merely Georgina Vitay in year five, awaiting her well-deserved punishment. She had hidden banned objects in the building in defiance of the school rules; she was a thoroughly disobedient little girl, who would be dealt with severely. When she behaved well they praised her, when she was naughty she was punished, and she could forget about Gini, that spoiled niece of Auntie Mimó, that silly, arrogant little girl who had imagined that she was an adult because she had mixed with adults, and the moment the Internal Security department of the Ministry of Defence sent a personable young lieutenant to woo and flatter her, in order to tighten the net around her father and force him to reveal the names of those who fought with him on an invisible battlefront in his attempt to end a murderous war and save the lives of soldiers and prevent the total destruction of the country, that same Gini had believed that he genuinely admired her English-style tresses and was sincere in his pursuit of her, had instantly fallen in love with him and yearned for nothing more than to become his fiancée. Her father had realised that he was under surveillance, had feared for her life and sent her to Árkod for her own safety, and she had put everything at risk by her foolish attempts to escape. Her behaviour had been incredible. The luckless Bánki had betrayed her secret, and had Abigail not stepped in to save her she would have been captured by Feri Kuncz the night before.

When they finally called her in, the first thing she saw was the towel lying on the table spread with the evidence of her guilt. The Director had spaced out the different items so that Kalmár could see them. The class tutor was standing at the window, looking solemn and aggrieved, but not because of the trinkets. What upset him now was that once again Vitay, his favourite, would have to be punished. As she entered the room he shook his head reproachfully and lowered his eyes in the approved manner.

The Director picked up the silver-handled comb, threw it down in disgust and launched into one of his sermons. It began with a brief account of the character of his niece, a girl difficult to control because of her weak nature. What made him especially angry with Georgina Vitay was that she had exposed this impressionable child, with all her love of vanities, to worldly temptation, and for that he intended to hand out a more severe punishment than he otherwise would have. He had reached this point in his

Ciceronian peroration when the telephone rang. Kalmár went to pick it up, but the Director stopped him with a shake of the head: he did not like being interrupted in full flight. But the instrument refused to stay silent. It rang again and again. He kept trying to press on with his suitably eloquent description of what the future might hold for someone as devious, untruthful, hypocritical, prone to hiding meretricious baubles and ungovernable as she . . . until he finally gestured to Kalmár to pick it up and silence it that way. Kalmár held his ear to the receiver for a few seconds, said, "Yes, of course, straight away," and handed it to the Director.

"I'm busy," he snapped. "Tell them to ring some other time. I've already told you that."

"It's Kázmér Szenttamássy," Kalmár whispered. "He wants to speak to you personally."

The Director, muttering something about there being no question of installing a first-aid centre in the school as the Pál Kokas secondary was not a religious institution and it would be much better to put it there, reluctantly took the receiver. Gina gazed at her possessions spread out on the table. She was thinking that, centuries before, when the students in the school were all seminarists, there was an underground cellar where they shut miscreants up as a punishment. It was still there, but no longer used as a prison; they grew mushrooms in it that were sometimes used in preparing meals. They could do worse than lock me in there for my crimes, she mused. No-one would find me down there. I'm sure I would be frightened, but the girls would work something out and Abigail would think of a way to visit me. At least I would be safe from Feri.

How strange to find yourself thinking of a cellar as somewhere you would actually want to be!

The Director was now speaking in monosyllables. Gina could not make out what the two men were talking about except that they were agreeing about something. It didn't seem very interesting; she had other concerns and worries than who might be on the line to Gedeon Torma. When he finished, he pushed her hapless treasures under her nose one after the other, and demanded to know the story behind each – where, when and how it had been smuggled into the school, whether she had brought it when she first arrived or had it from her father afterwards, and where she had hidden it all this time. She told him about the flower boxes but not the wooden dress model in the art storeroom, so that Torma could continue to keep her nightdress in there. He asked repeatedly about the role of his depraved niece in all this, and it was now abundantly clear that that was what was driving him. Kalmár watched gloomily and asked no questions.

The Director was ranting on about the squirrel with the marcasite eyes when the telephone rang again. Again Kalmár took the call. It was from the porter. The Director growled, "Yes, yes, let him in," and sent Gina out of the room. He told her that he would have to suspend the interview as he had to receive a visitor. She should wait outside in the corridor and not go back to the classroom; he would call her back when he had finished his meeting.

Off she went. Kalmár stayed in the room. Once outside, she leaned back against the wall and gazed at the rows of faces under the school crest in the framed photographs. Everything that had been boring, childish and indeed hateful the day before now seemed wonderful, reassuring and comforting. She wondered who it was that the Director had given up his time to see: it must be someone very important. That was a disturbing thought. If it were a member of the school's governing body, the first question he would ask when he reached the top of the stairs would be, who is this girl standing in the corridor and why is she not in her lesson? She moved further away from the office. There was a swing door closing off the section of corridor that led to the storerooms. She stationed herself behind it and opened its two wings a crack so that she could watch what went on outside. From there she would hear if anyone called her and would be able to get back quickly, but the visitor would not be able to see her, and she would not have to stand before him in disgrace.

The person arrived at the second floor. When she saw who it was she was so horrified the doorknob nearly slipped from her hand. This time Lieutenant Kuncz was in uniform. He stopped to adjust his belt, then knocked on the office door. He glanced to neither right nor left.

Had she not had Abigail's message she would have run to him, clung to his arm, and nothing would have dragged her away from him. Given the chance, she would have gone with him anywhere, in complete trust. She drew herself back, waited until he had disappeared inside, then went and stood at the door and pressed her ear to the keyhole. Her heart was beating wildly. She could hear every word as clearly as if she were in the room herself.

They must have got beyond the initial introductions because the Director was speaking.

"Yes, Commander Szenttamássy did tell me that he was sending you here, Lieutenant. I would like to draw your attention to the fact that the Matula Academy is a listed historic building exempt from all forms of requisition, whether for housing personnel in the short term or for any other purpose, and I must regretfully inform you that although I am aware that in the interests of national defence I am obliged to give the security forces every assistance, our institution is specifically exempt from billeting under an order signed by the Minister himself."

"You have nothing to fear, sir," the voice replied – the same voice that the night before had been whispering, "Gini, little Gini, can you hear me?" "This is about a different matter. My orders refer to one of your pupils, Georgina Vitay. I have come to take her to her father, who is seriously ill."

My God, she thought. His smiles, his very breath, are nothing but lies. What will become of me if the Director believes him? She was terrified. That Gedeon Torma, a man in whose eyes the lowest form of human depravity was represented by a hidden stick of rouge, would understand the kind of game he was being drawn into, seemed completely improbable. Why should he imagine for one moment that the Lieutenant, a military officer who had come bearing an official directive, should not be telling the truth? In his little universe it was only pupils who told lies.

"I am sorry to hear that," she heard Kalmár say. "What exactly is wrong with the General?"

"He has had an accident," replied Feri Kuncz. "A car accident. His situation is serious. You might say critical."

For once he speaks the truth, Gia thought. Every prisoner is in a critical situation. Yesterday it was a heart problem, today a car accident. I wonder what it will be next time.

If the Director believed him and handed her over, she was lost. If she hid herself away somewhere in the building they would eventually find her. There was nowhere in it that Gedeon Torma did not personally know, and if she couldn't hide there, then where could she? In Árkod, if they let her out? She could no longer count on Abigail. Did Abigail know where she was at that moment, or what she was doing? She probably did not even realise what danger she was in; she certainly had not been there to help her the night before. At any moment the Director was going to say, "The girl you want is outside in the corridor. I'll send for her." If she went into the room and shouted in the Lieutenant's face that he was a liar and her father had been taken prisoner, how could she prove it? With the note from Abigail?

"I'm afraid that will not be possible," Gedeon Torma said. He always spoke more slowly than anyone else, but never as slowly as now. "General Vitay made it clear that I was not to hand his daughter over to anyone. It was a binding condition of our agreement. And at the moment it would be impossible anyway, because it is termtime and it is not our practice to grant exceptional leave."

"But if the General is so very ill . . ." Kalmár interjected.

"Seriously ill," Feri Kuncz added. "So ill, I must repeat, that he is unable to come for her himself. Director, sir, I think you would not wish to be responsible if the girl never saw her father again, should he fail to recover."

"That would be sad indeed, if it were to happen," Gina heard the Director say. "But in that case I should be answerable to the Lord's Judgement Seat. General Vitay gave me precise instructions not to hand his daughter over to anyone other than himself. He also stipulated that if news came of his death the girl should not be given permission to attend his funeral. Those were his wishes, and that is what was agreed between us. The girl is not allowed to leave the premises without her father for the next three months and three years, when she finishes her school-leaving exams. Her fees and boarding charges were calculated for that period."

So, my dear father, Gina said to herself, overcome by the realisation that she was thinking of him for the first time as a deceased person whose last wishes she had just heard, you have taken good care of me. You made sure that I would have some means of support if our home were blown away in the storm.

"The Director appears to have forgotten that I am under orders to take General Vitay's daughter to Budapest."

"I certainly have not," Gedeon Torma replied. His voice, which at various times had made her both tremble with terror and shake with mocking laughter, and had so often struck her as either boring or simply ridiculous, was now deadly serious, rock-solid as the city of Árkod, as the Matula itself. "I have not forgotten it in the least, Lieutenant. But this order of yours does not apply to me. My unquestionable superiors are the Bishop of Árkod, the Reformed Protestant Church and the Minister of Education. My invisible superior, to whom I must render my final account, is Christ the Redeemer Himself."

"Consider this," returned the voice, so soft and ingratiating beside the garden gate at midnight, now so harsh and filled with an anger that verged on contempt, "I would be reluctant to resort to stronger measures, but I am required to remove General Vitay's daughter whatever the consequences."

"You certainly will not remove her," Gedeon Torma replied, and from the accompanying noise Gina gathered he had risen to his feet. "You will not, because my school and I have given her father our word that we would hand her over to no-one we did not know, and we are even less likely to do so at the moment. There seems to be an unusual degree of interest in the girl right now, and the porter's lodge has been under siege on her account. Unfortunately, I am rather busy at present. We are in the middle of a disciplinary matter. Allow me to ask that we put an end to this pointless conversation."

"Be well advised, Director, sir, you will hand this girl over to me. And I cannot promise you that this institution will not feel the consequences of the fact that its Director has wilfully obstructed the work of the national army."

"I understood that it was simply a question of my keeping a pupil away from her sick father," Gedeon Torma said. "If by doing that I am obstructing the work of the national army that is a rather different matter, and one to be regretted. Nonetheless I shall not let you have the girl, because I cannot, and if you tell me that I shall be held responsible for the consequences, so be it. I accept that responsibility. I know that the future holds for me only what the Lord intends. I am delighted to have met you, Lieutenant. Oh, and one other thing . . ."

She was about to take refuge behind the swing door again

when this last sentence stopped her. She was almost whimpering with joy and relief, and a fountain of warm love welled up inside her for Árkod and the man in black – something she would never have thought possible.

"I should just like to add, Lieutenant, that I would have been only too delighted to let you have this girl. She is the most difficult, the most incorrigible pupil I have known in the thirty-five years of my career. It is simply that I cannot do that because I gave my word to her father. I wish you good day."

She did not hear Feri's reply as she fled back to the bend in the corridor. She saw him come out, adjust his belt again, this time in a rage, and hurry off down the corridor. She stared after him in fear and trembling, as at a complete stranger, a man she had never known. When she heard the steel grille clink shut she went back and stood outside the office door. It opened immediately. Had she not heard for herself what had gone on inside she would never have believed that anything had happened at all. Kalmár's face was rather more flushed than usual, but the Director was every bit his habitual self. He pointed a stubby finger at the incriminating items spread out on the desk.

"Have you reflected on how you can atone for what you have done?" he asked. He studied her with the fierce interest of a man obsessed with sin and sinners, as if his only concern in the world was that Georgina Vitay had hidden, Lord knows where, a squirrel brooch with marcasite eyes. "No, of course not. Typical. Mr Kalmár, until I tell you otherwise, Georgina Vitay must not be allowed to leave the premises again, and, what is more, as the most severe punishment a pupil can incur, I shall prohibit her from going to services in the white church. She is to be a prisoner here."

I see what you are doing, Gina thought. You have no idea how well I understand you. I will be safe as long as I remain inside the school. If only you would lock me up in that cellar, however deep and dark it may be! Better mushrooms for company than Feri Kuncz.

"Now clear out of my sight and go to your lesson. I am lowering your conduct mark. Mr Kalmár, please note that, however well she does from now on, until the end of the year she is not to be listed among the outstanding pupils in her class."

Kalmár nodded in acknowledgement. He did not look at Gina.

"Now take yourself off. I can't stand the sight of people like you." He swept up her treasures and threw them and the towel into the waste paper basket. "It's a pity we don't have an open fire in here. I would have stood over you while you burned them yourself. But they will still end up in the boiler, you can be sure. Mr Kalmár, kindly stay behind for a moment. Now who is that on the line?"

The telephone was ringing again. Kalmár lifted the receiver and the strident tones of the porter could be heard as clearly as if he were in the room.

"Director, sir, that lieutenant asked me where his excellency the Bishop lives, and to tell him the shortest way to get there."

"I hope you told him," Gedeon Torma growled.

As she left, Gina heard him telling Kalmár that the Bishop was away on a tour of the rural parishes in the neighbouring county and would not be back for another two days; but they would be able to follow him from one village to the next as he had left his itinerary. She went on back to class without waiting to hear the reply.

In the classroom she found a paradisal calm. She had interrupted the lesson, and Miss Gigus gave her a look of reproach. She asked her why she was late. "I was with the Director," Gina said. "He has banned me from all afternoon walks and from going to the white church."

"How stupid," Mari Kis whispered to Bánki. "This obsession with punishing people has affected his brain. Nothing would please her more than to have the old black tom cat play another trick like that on her."

St Gedeon's Day

She had intended to be especially attentive during lessons, but she found it impossible. She kept wondering whether she should write to Abigail, and whether she could even assume that it was Abigail who had saved her from the Lieutenant. She had more or less decided what to put in the note she would slip into the stone pitcher when it occurred to her that writing would be pointless. During lunch Kalmár had obviously made every adult in the school aware of who had come for her and why, because all through the meal the teachers at the top table had kept giving her anxious looks of concern, as had the deaconesses sitting with their pupils. It was now the afternoon when she was due to stand in front of the whole school with the other delinquents. The Director announced that Georgina Vitay had committed a very serious offence, that of hiding forbidden objects in the school. She listened in silence. It meant little to her now. It was as if the accusations referred to someone else. It was only after supper that she had a chance to tell the rest of the class what had happened in the infirmary the night before, that she had been caught giving her personal possessions to Torma. Half of the class felt desperately sorry for her, and were full of condolences for the beautiful things she had lost; the other half condemned her even more roundly than the Director had. She had gambled with the secret pleasure they themselves might have had in them, to give everything to Torma was just stupid. And to take them into such a risky place as the infirmary!

The others went off on their afternoon walk and Gina was left alone in the day room, with a lesson to prepare. Silence reigned in the Matula, a peaceful, blessed silence. She read through the set text but took very little in. She kept thinking of her father and trying to decide what he would want from her, far away as he was now: she was every bit as conscious of him as she was of the heat from the radiator. Be strong, she seemed to hear a voice telling her from that unknown place – possibly from outside the country. Be strong, my dearest love in all the world. Be strong, so that I too will have the strength for what I must do. Show your strength not by being stubborn and recalcitrant, by protesting and complaining, or making unrealistic plans, my child, but by mastering yourself and listening to wise counsels, so that those I have entrusted you to will be able to help you. If you simply dissolve in tears or break down under pressure like a crushed pearl, then we shall have loved one another in vain. And don't be sad. Don't let it spoil your appetite. Be brave and be happy! Perhaps we shall see one another again, so please do nothing to tarnish the joy of that meeting, and give me strength by allowing me to know that I can trust you!

When they got back from their walk Mari Kis and the others told her that in the boutique next to the Hajda patisserie there had been the most amazing scarves for sale, so amazing in fact that it was hard to believe there was a war going on. She listened in silence, nodding her head from time to time, which they decided was simply the result of having suffered all that bad luck. That afternoon there had been constant comings and goings. The teachers and the prefects had been disappearing by turns into the residential quarters. Szabó explained that this was because it was the Director's name day. On March 29 everyone went to congratulate the ogre in black. If he were in a good mood he would be with them longer after supper, and prayers would happen later than usual; if he were especially moved he might even read them some of the more successful pious effusions from the older pupils' creative writing group, but of course it was impossible to say beforehand what he would decide to do, because all through supper he had worn a face of darkest gloom, and the sight of Gina's oriental bazaar hadn't exactly brightened his mood: on these name days their principal amusement was trying to work out how to avoid doing anything that would destroy his goodwill, and the revelations in the infirmary would not have made his mood any the merrier. The mere fact that he had set eyes on a stick of rouge would be enough to depress him for several days.

The meal progressed in an atmosphere of orderly calm. There was no sign that the evening would soon take on a more festive character. The Director said barely a word other than to issue an irritated rebuke to the seventh-year girl who was doing the reading, very badly, in a dull monotone. That was about all the conversation that took place.

There was a sudden flurry of activity and the refectory door burst open. Like the scent of a spring breeze wafting into the room, laughter rang out and everything sprang to life. The girls jumped to their feet and stood to attention, their eyes shining. The custom was that if the reading was interrupted by an unexpected visitor only the reader herself should welcome him, and now, speaking for everyone, she squawked out, her voice suddenly alive and expressive: "Good evening, and God bless you."

In the doorway stood Mitsi Horn, clutching an armful of branches. Behind her was the old lady Gina had met once before. She was holding some large boxes and a huge demijohn. "Sit down, Matula!" Gedeon Torma barked, then suddenly relaxed and rose to his feet with the male teachers to greet her.

"May God preserve you," the guest called out, and pushed the huge bunch of branches into his arms. "May you live till the seas run dry. I've come here to enjoy myself! I'm in a merry mood tonight."

"I'm afraid I am not," the Director replied. "I do not celebrate my name day, Mitsi."

"But of course you are." She laughed. "I've used up the last of my flour to bake for the girls. It's all going to be happening tonight, Gedeon. The whole school will dance and eat fine pastries and enjoy themselves. I'm inviting myself to supper."

Before he could utter a word of protest she had run the length of the refectory like an unruly first year and rapped for attention on the wooden panel closing off the kitchen. The cook opened it, peered out in alarm, and Mitsi Horn declared, "I haven't had my supper. Can you give me something to eat?"

Hordes of people dashed around looking for a knife and fork for her, and the prefects had their work cut out to keep the girls in their seats. It was Susanna who went off, at the dignified, decorous pace of a deaconess, to fetch a tablecloth. Chairs were moved around the Director's table to make room for the guest; Hajdú moved from his seat beside Gedeon Torma and went to sit at the far end, leaving a space free between him and Kőnig. Susanna returned with the place settings; she kept her eyes not on Mitsi Horn but on Kőnig, though he did not seem to notice. There was something quite extraordinary, as even Gina, in her own rather unusual state of mind, observed, in the way he kept watching Mitsi Horn . . . and now he was whispering something in her ear. By the time Susanna got back to her seat her face was as scarlet as if she had been slapped. She really does not like this woman, Gina thought. She's jealous of her, and obviously ashamed of that. She's trying to get the better of it, but she can't.

The next moment all semblance of order collapsed. Mitsi Horn called out to the reader: "You must join in too. Put that sanctimonious book down and go and help in the kitchen; they're about to share out the pastries. But not the cake I cooked specially for the Director. Bring that here first." The girl dashed off happily, and the Director turned to stare at the guest in astonishment. He was like a lion bewildered by a humming bird hovering at its face and singing that the beast held no terrors for it; life, for all its horrors, was wonderful, and of all those wonders the most precious was youth. And then a miracle happened. Gedeon Torma twice opened his mouth to tell her to call the girl back to continue with the improving tale, and twice instantly shut it again. He had succumbed to the blessed joy filling the room with its warmth; he had seen in the rows of shining eyes how happy everyone around him was feeling. Even the rouge-smuggler Vitay had lost the look of someone bowed down by her cares. This Mitsi Horn was a magician. Now she had risen to her feet to make a speech, like a man. And the old lady who had come with her was going round behind the tables with the demijohn filling glasses with wine. Even the pupils were given a finger.

"May God bless you, Director, sir, and send you a long and happy life. May you preside over this school to the end of your allotted span, this school that gives so much to everyone raised in it. They will surely treasure the memory of their time here to the end of their days."

She must indeed be a magician, Gedeon Torma told himself, if even I can feel like this! But "to the end of my allotted span"? That's going a bit far. How long will I be in charge here if I don't let them have Georgina Vitay? He raised his glass, thanked Mitsi Horn, nodded towards the form tutors and even the pupils, and the whole school emptied their glasses as one, then stood in silence. Not even the youngest girls were smiling. The flood of emotion lasted until Mitsi Horn called out again to tell them to hurry up with their meal because she had prepared all sorts of entertainments for the evening, and the girls started to wolf down the pastries at such speed that the prefects had no hope of stopping them. She egged them on, like a sports commentator: "Faster, faster!" By now even the doctor was almost choking – she who always talked about the importance of eating slowly and giving your stomach food that had been thoroughly chewed. It was an astonishing sight: the guest beating the time with her hand, and the teachers all tucking frantically into their supper.

Kőnig was making no attempt to conceal his feelings, murmuring non-stop into his beloved's ear. Susanna could not bear to watch; she kept her eyes lowered to avoid catching sight of the teachers' table. Gina, who was being a little more sensitive than usual that evening, longed to stroke her arm and tell her that her own heart was also sad and that she felt truly sorry for her. But a pupil should never touch a teacher, and besides, what would the Prefect think of being consoled by the reprobate Vitay? Mitsi Horn listened to something Kőnig was whispering, then turned to the Director and the whole table exploded into laughter. She must have said something truly hilarious – she was such good fun, and so very amusing. Naturally she got what she wanted; when did she not? Susanna, still keeping her eyes averted, helped pull the tables to the side as requested; Hajdú, clearly in thrall to the same ungodly spell, went and fetched the gramophone, and Miss Gigus lent him her records of dance music, leaving the Director staring at her speechless – he had no idea she had been harbouring anything like that in her room. Mitsi Horn called out again: "There is a war on. Who knows what future lies in store for the poor things!" To which there was nothing to be said, and in no time at all the sound of profane music filled the room, very different strains from the classical and religious tunes they were accustomed to. The deaconesses and teachers were astonished by the proficiency the older girls now displayed. It was a different matter with the little ones. They were all at sea. They stumbled around, blushing furiously, until Gertrud Truth took them off to their day room to play while the older girls danced. Reaching the door, she turned and told the dancers to find the girl they were usually paired with in the gym, or there would be chaos. Gina's partner there was Torma; she had recently replaced Bánki, who had grown too tall for her. But Torma was not there, which pleased Gina, who was in no mood for dancing and had retreated into a corner to watch the others. She did not feel envious of them and she did not want to join in anything. So there were now two of them standing apart from the others; they had moved away from the tables and were standing next to the chairs, like two waifs shut out from life without any hope of getting back in.

"That girl over there isn't dancing," Mitsi said. "The little one from Budapest. Where is her partner?"

"Her partner's ill," replied Gedeon Torma, suddenly grave again. "But even if she were well she would not be dancing. She is being punished."

"You can punish her tomorrow," Mitsi cried. "Today is a holiday! Shut your eyes if you don't want to watch – I'll dance with her myself if she can't find a partner."

I don't want to dance this evening, thought Gina. She too could feel the powerful attraction of the woman, but she refused to surrender to it. I don't want her to touch me, or try to cheer me up.

Gedeon Torma said something in reply, but no-one heard him. Mitsi darted down from the teachers' table, made an elaborate comical bow before Gina and asked her to dance.

"She is not allowed to dance," Susanna said quietly. "You heard that, Mitsi dear."

"Oh, my word. Why do you have to be so much stricter than Jesus himself?" Mitsi replied. "I only want one dance, for just a few minutes. Come, little girl from Budapest."

And she led Gina away. She was strong, and an accomplished dancer, and the two of them drifted slowly away from the inner circle. Gina did not once look at her. Let the woman amuse herself, she thought. She was playing with everyone and everything, as if they were dolls.

"Tonight you are going to make your escape," Mitsi whispered. The smile never left her face. With her left hand she made a gesture towards the teachers' table. "Tonight, while the rest of us are partying here. At nine o'clock, just before the start of prayers, go to Susanna's room and put on her going-out clothes. Don't leave the school through the main gate; you must use the one in the garden where you waited for the Lieutenant the day before yesterday. The gate will be open. Once you are out in the street, walk slowly and keep away from the light. Now don't just stand there, dance! And don't look at me like that. Smile!"

Gina was incapable of smiling. She just stood there with her mouth open.

"These wonderful people will be able to protect you from Lieutenant Kuncz for only a few more days. After that the local Commander will force the Bishop to open the school gates. There is a war on. They will insist that handing you over is in both the military and the national interest. The Germans who took your father away will not take no for an answer. If you do fall into their hands, and the school has tried to obstruct them, it will be the end of the Matula. They will arrest Gedeon Torma and send the teachers elsewhere. Now smile!"

But all Gina could do was stare at her in shock. Hajdú was busy changing a record on the gramophone, and soon a husky female voice started to croon, "Goodbye, Lieutenant, goodbye. Think of me sometimes, when you get to the front."

"We cannot let you fall into the Lieutenant's hands. That would only add to your father's troubles. You must disappear immediately, and not put Gedeon Torma's life in danger. If you escape and they never find you, no-one can be held responsible – you always were a notorious misfit and rebel. Go to my house. You will find it empty. I live there on my own with the old lady, and I'll cover your escape. You will have to unlock the door yourself. This is the key. I've just slipped it into your hand. Can you feel it?"

Gina nodded her reply.

"Be very careful. It's not just your safety that depends on it, it's other people's as well. A few minutes before nine you must slip out of the room. I'll make sure no-one notices. Susanna's door is never locked. Do everything I tell you. Tuck your clothes under the bed so that she doesn't realise that you've taken hers. And don't keep staring at me!"

"Are you Abigail?" the girl whispered.

Mitsi Horn laughed so loud that everyone turned to look at her. Gedeon Torma swallowed his shame. This was a woman they had raised themselves, on exactly the same principles as the current intake, and look how she was behaving! She was forty-eight years old and she still wore lipstick. Mitsi ignored Gina's question. She said they had danced enough and led her back to the line of chairs. Barely able to stand, the girl had to lean on one for support. The guest returned to the teachers' table and tried to persuade someone else to dance with her, but the Director put a firm stop to that. She laughed the matter off, had a brief conversation with the teachers, then clapped her hands loudly and brought the dancing to a halt. She had a fresh announcement to make: that was enough exercise; now it was time for games.

"Arrange the chairs into two large circles. One of you go to the duty room and ask for writing materials, enough for half those present, and some slips of paper for the other half to write on. But be quick, it's getting late." Murai dashed out. The Director was about to call out to her that they didn't need any paper, the party was over, but the girl was gone before he could open his mouth, naturally leaving the door wide open behind her.

Gedeon Torma rose to his feet and bellowed for silence. The familiar terrifying voice worked its effect, but the laughter instantly gave way to a rather different sound. To relieve her boredom the sister on night duty must have been listening to the news, and the fact that the ever-impatient Murai had left the door open meant that the words carried into the refectory. "Our troops have regrouped and reorganised the line at the front." Gedeon Torma inspected his fingernails to avoid looking at the teachers. He knew as well as every other adult in the room what that meant: the army was in retreat; the line was coming ever closer. "Time for some games!" he called out, almost despite himself. The faces around him brightened again and he lowered himself slowly back into his seat. Mitsi Horn gazed at him with a new light in her eyes, not of laughter or of gentle mockery but of heartfelt compassion. He was no longer simply someone to be opposed. She knew that when the front reached Árkod no wall in the Matula would be thick enough, no cellar sufficiently secure. Good old Gedeon, that was very well done, she thought. But she said nothing.

She arranged and oversaw the formation of the chairs into two circles, and assigned the two senior years to one and the sixth and fifth years to the other. Then she took up position at the centre of the first and asked Susanna to take her seat in the second as leader of that group. Susanna went to the appointed chair with the joyless face of someone practising stern self-discipline. She's making it an exercise in humility, Gina thought, to fight down her feelings of jealousy. She thinks Mitsi Horn is giving her these orders to parade her superiority. She will never know that Abigail has asked for her to be put in charge so that she won't be able to leave her seat when she notices that I'm no longer here.

Mitsi had come well prepared for the evening and had brought a large book of games, which she handed to the Deaconess. It contained a great number of distinctly un-Matulan activities. Susanna's task was to play questions and answers with her group. The book had a list of questions with a hundred possible answers, each one numbered. The leader posed a question to which the answer was a number, which was then read out. It produced some surprising results. To the first one, "How can I win your heart?" the elder Aradi responded with the first number that came into her head: "Nineteen," (the age of her Kutyó).

Susanna ran her eye down the list and read out, "With sorrel sauce." The eighth-year girls put their hands over their mouths to stop themselves laughing out loud, but the presence of the cook, who was standing at the service window, added to the general hilarity: there was no-one in the school who did not know about Aradi's aversion to spices.

"And how can I win your heart?" Susanna now put the question to Aradi's friend Tenk, in a quiet, rather sad-sounding voice. "Nine," was the reply. Susanna looked up the answer: "With a goods train." The teachers watched in surprise as Tenk's face turned scarlet and her classmates wriggled about in their seats with more suppressed laughter. What was so funny about that reply? The fifth year were also totally at a loss – the older girls had not confided to them that in that other world outside, the one in which young men existed, there was a railwayman who was courting her.

Mitsi then joined the combined fifth- and sixth-year group as a playing guest. Murai came back with the paper and writing implements. She also had a message from the duty sister, Sister Erzsébet: would she please call the Director to the telephone, that evening, if at all possible? She was sorry to say that Mr Ruppert was on the line. Murai had spoken very quietly, but everyone at the staff table looked at her as if she had announced a meteorite. Ruppert was the Director of the Cock-a-doodle-doos. Whenever he called the Matula the consequences were always dire: it was invariably to object to something, announce this or denounce that, or to complain that yet again a Matula girl had shown insufficient respect. Ever since the state school had been opened there had been this constant friction between the two institutions. Murai was sent back to say that the Director was not available that evening but would ring back in the morning. "This evening must run according to whatever the dear witch has planned. I want nothing to disturb or upset me."

The game Mitsi had proposed was so amusing that the adults asked if they could join in. To prevent Susanna's group feeling slighted the staff were divided between the two groups, so that all the girls could have teachers with them. The only exception was the Director, who remained on the dais looking on, with a certain shamefaced affection, while his colleagues and pupils roared with laughter. Kőnig was in Susanna's group, along with Éles and Kalmár; Kerekes, Hajdú and Miss Gigus were with Mitsi Horn. Their game was a clever one. A sheet of paper was passed from hand to hand; the first person wrote down a phrase and passed it to her neighbour, who had to draw an image of what she had read; the paper was then folded to conceal the original phrase, and the third person had to write down what they thought the illustration depicted; the fourth drew a picture of what the third person had written; the fifth had to say what they thought their drawing was about, and so on. "At the end of the round," Mitsi promised them, "you'll see what the last drawing has made of the original phrase."

She handed the paper to Gina for her to start. Gina wrote: "A small column of soldiers marching below a lofty citadel." This went to Mari Kis, who sketched a mountain topped by a castle, with some tiny figures walking below, done the way children draw them, with matchstick arms and legs. She folded Gina's text down and passed the drawing on to Bánki, who studied it for what seemed ages and, when she finally thought she understood it, wrote: "We are on an excursion to the hills." Szabó now had to illustrate this; she drew two girls with oversized heads, to make it clear that they were wearing regulation Matula hats, and, to avoid any further possibility of error, added a railway line at their feet and a sign saying "To the Mátra Mountains". Salm likewise thought for a long time, then her face lit up: she had remembered that once, in their early years in the school, Cziller and Gáti had been punished in a geography lesson for not knowing enough about those same mountains. Beneath the two large-headed girls she wrote: "Cziller and Gáti gave the wrong answers." Miss Gigus, who was next in line, found this very hard to illustrate. But she had a good eye, and spent some time studying the two girls intently to try and create a good likeness.

That particular group was relatively calm, because its members were busy drawing, or trying to work out what they had to draw. By contrast, the circle around Susanna kept exploding with laughter. Susanna had now arrived at Kőnig with the prescribed question. It was, "What can I do to win your heart?" "Fifty," he replied. Her voice did not waver as she read out the answer, "Nothing, ever."

At that point Sister Erzsébet put her head around the door and announced that Mr Ruppert was still on the line. He was insisting that the Director should stir himself and come to the telephone. The man in black puffed his cheeks and told her, "Tomorrow," and Erzsébet disappeared.

The scene stuck in Gina's memory for a great many years: it

was exactly twelve months later to the day that she sat down again in her old seat in the classroom between Mari Kis and Torma. Some of those present that night she would never see again. Their idol and favourite, Kalmár, was called up a few days later and died in the Carpathians. The older Aradi, who carried the school banner with such flair, was killed in a bombing raid in the summer. Sister Erzsébet, who had cooked that special Christmas feast for them, perished during a fire in the east wing trying to save the library. In her mature years Gina often thought back to that last evening, not only because it marked the beginning of her freedom but because her adult awareness allowed her clearly and finally to see the two contrasting sides of the occasion – the gaiety and laughter, the flow of high spirits inside the massive walls, and the darkness outside, including the full dangers faced by a girl out on the streets who desperately needed to get to Mitsi Horn's house.

Susanna had now moved on to the second question: "What would most make you happy?" Igger in year seven answered, "Forty-one," and Susanna read out, "Winning at roulette." In Mitsi Horn's group Miss Gigus was still working on the two, now very tolerable, portraits, which Szabó naturally failed to recognise: she thought they represented two girls' heads in the Árkod museum. I'm actually very frightened, Gina thought. I am terrified by what I have to do, even if Abigail is there to help.

For her, time had never flown so quickly. It was now 8.30 p.m.; soon it would be 8.45. But there seemed little cause for worry. The others were all so caught up in the game that probably no-one would notice if she were fidgety and restless, or even realise she had gone. Her phrase about the "lofty citadel" was now long in the past, and a new sheet of paper and words had reached her. It had been started by Salm and it was her turn to draw the picture. She dashed off something that was neither well-executed nor convincing and passed it on. She and the Director had been the only people not following the game but rather viewing it from the outside, and they were the only ones to notice that someone had appeared at the door. The staff realised what had happened only when the Director rose to his feet, mastered his dismay with his customary self-discipline, and went to greet the man. Gina had no idea who this emaciated person standing in the threshold might be, but she could see from the look on the Director's face that it was someone important. Her heart beat wildly in terror: had he come for her?

"Matula, stand to attention!" Gedeon Torma barked, with all the bitterness of a man who lives to rule his domain with a rod of iron and who, for the first time in his life, finds himself face to face with his arch enemy – Ruppert, the Director of the Cock-a-doodle-doos – at precisely the moment when this witch Mitsi Horn has turned his house upside down, demijohns of wine shame him from every corner of the room, and the deaconesses and pupils are given over to frivolity. He had to call out twice before the games finally subsided, everyone came to their senses and stood up. Mitsi Horn was gazing at the new arrival with bright, intelligent eyes.

"Good evening, Director," said Ruppert. "What a jolly and pleasant atmosphere you have in here, a real Isle of the Blessed after the darkness outside. I see you are already aware of what has happened and have arranged a farewell party, so I have troubled you needlessly. Your secretary or whoever it was asked me not to bother you when we spoke, but I truly believed you knew nothing about the matter and would find out only tomorrow. So I thought . . ."

He stopped. There was no fifth-year girl, however generally unaware, who did not understand what he had failed to say. He went on: "I thought that in the circumstances it no longer matters that for generations our two institutions have been at loggerheads, with us being a state school and you a religious institution."

"Do come in," said Gedeon Torma. "Can I offer you something to drink? Have you dined?"

"No, thank you, I don't want anything. If I still had my school I would be glad to return your hospitality. It would give you a chance to see what very good order we keep. Especially in all this . . ."

He fell silent again, and once more what he had not said was perfectly clear. He continued: "This hostility between our schools is really absurd, Torma. Can you even remember how the whole nonsense started? It was so long ago I certainly can't."

"What did you mean, if you still had a school?" Gedeon Torma asked. The silence in the building was like the silence during prayers.

"Well, if you're holding a farewell party, then you must have heard the news from Budapest. The Minister has announced that from March 31 every educational institution in the country will be closed. That's two days after the end of the school term.

The pupils will get their results on April 4 and all boarders will be sent home. Only the final year will stay on, for their leaving exams."

The Director took him by the arm and led him in silence out of the refectory. He did not take his leave of the assembly and the girls did not say goodbye to him. No-one had told them to. They stood where they were, stock-still. All year they had been dreaming of being allowed to go home; now they could only stare in stunned dismay as the two men vanished from the room.

That's it, Gina thought. It's now 8.45. I really should be gone by now. But the games have stopped, everyone is standing up and no-one is talking. They'll all see me. How will I ever get away?

"Shame on you all!" Mitsi Horn called out. "I don't know what to make of you! Won't you be pleased to be at home with your mothers? What silly girls you are!"

All eyes turned towards her – unsmiling faces, edged with fear.

"You'll be so glad to be back home!" she went on. "So why all the glum faces? If we are going to have to leave soon, let's at least enjoy ourselves for a while. You won't have a chance tomorrow, because by then the Director will be back to his usual self. So do carry on!"

She looked at the teachers, the pupils and the deaconesses in turn, and every adult understood her message: "Help me. We must do something to stop them being afraid!"

"Next question," Susanna called out. "What do you love most in the world? Mr Éles."

"Number thirty," the science teacher replied. Susanna read

out, in all earnestness, "Embroidered underwear," and blushed furiously. Almost no-one laughed.

"What a dreadful lot you are!" Mitsi Horn exclaimed. "In my time, if anyone had said to us, 'School's over, no more exams, no more reports, because there is no alternative in the circumstances,' we would have been beside ourselves with joy – and there would have been none of these long faces. Talk about degenerate youth! Isn't it better to be enjoying yourselves at home than sitting around here praying all day?"

The worst of it was that not one of the teachers said, "Come on, Mitsi, you're talking nonsense."

She's wasting her time, Gina thought. The mood for games has passed. Everyone's too awake and aware of what's going on. I can't do what you want me to, Abigail. I'm done for.

Heads were put together and the girls began to whisper among themselves.

"Stand to attention, Matula!" Hajdú bellowed. "Who gave you permission to talk?"

That certainly helped: something familiar, reassuring. Hajdú's squeaky voice, the commanding tone, the old severity. The girls rose to their feet and stood to attention. Hajdú scowled at them the way he did at anyone who sang their psalms badly. Gina, thinking now like an adult, understood what he intended: at that moment anything would be better than panic. Better by far to put on a show of anger, however pointless or rude, to stop them being frightened and confused.

The girls stood in numb silence, and the book of games slipped from Susanna's hands.

"Well, you do get bored easily," Mitsi Horn said. "Look at Vitay standing there as if her feet were glued to the ground. But she's a fast enough runner when she's up to no good. But alright, if you aren't enjoying these two games, let's find something else."

"Go on, Matula: get on with it!" Kerekes ordered in the voice he used in his maths lessons.

Mitsi Horn went from one group to another explaining the next game: they had to stand with their faces to the wall and turn their backs on her. One of them would be blindfolded and have to feel her way along the line. Any person she touched would have to make a noise, any noise, and the blindfolded girl would have to guess who it was. If she guessed correctly, the two of them changed places; if she was wrong, she would have to carry on until she got someone right.

No-one seemed very much amused. Miss Gigus asked why they had to face the wall, because if the person were blindfolded they wouldn't be able to see who it was anyway.

"She might recognise the person from the shape of her nose or her forehead," Mitsi Horn explained. "Touching the back or the shoulder makes it harder to identify the person."

"Line up, Matula, and face the wall!" Éles bellowed. It was back to school again, no longer a celebration: Ruppert's visit had totally destroyed the buoyant mood and the spirit of fun. The classes went to their places in silence, with Mitsi Horn darting here and there to sort out the line and to persuade the teachers to join in. Which they all did. Gina turned round and looked hesitantly back at Mitsi Horn, who promptly called out to ask why the girl from Budapest wasn't facing the wall; time was running out, it was almost nine o'clock. Gina translated this in their new shared secret language to mean: "I'm doing this for you. I've made them put their faces to the wall so they won't see you going. Your time's up. Go as quickly as you can."

But Gina stayed where she was, staring at the wall, as she had been told. She had no idea how she was going to get away. There were girls on either side of her, Bánki on her left, in Torma's absence, and Mari Kis on her right. They would certainly notice if she left.

"And who is that dark-haired girl standing next to her? What's your name?" Mitsi went on. "Give her the blindfold."

Mari Kis turned round and presented herself. She was furious. She detested this game! Only the little ones played it, and she loathed the idea of going around touching people. How could you possibly tell who was meowing or heehawing just by putting your hands on them? This Mitsi Horn could go to the devil. She should just let them get on with the usual prayers and bedtime. The class had a million things to talk about; the school year would be over in two days' time and they would all be separated. And she stayed where she was, hoping she would somehow be passed over.

"Well?" asked Mitsi Horn. "How long will it take you to do us the honour?"

"Off you go, Mari Kis!" Kalmár barked. "What do you mean by this? You're holding up the game."

"A fine game this is," Mari muttered angrily, as she went across to Mitsi Horn. Gina could see what her plan was: with Mari gone there would be no-one next to her. Centimetre by

415

centimetre, she edged away from Bánki. Mitsi Horn announced that to make it more fun she would join in herself. She went over to Éles to borrow his handkerchief, then covered Mari Kis' head with her scarf and tied the handkerchief over her own eyes. "Off you go, then," she said, and sent Mari Kis on her way. Mari stumbled towards the line; Mitsi went straight to Bánki (so unerringly that she clearly hadn't covered her eyes properly) and started to tug her pigtails. At that point Gina stepped back from the wall, and the space next to Bánki was now blocked by Mitsi standing there and pulling her hair. The girl responded by making a series of cackling noises, trying to disguise her voice. Mari Kis had reached the other end of the room and began to prod a girl, who just giggled. During the shrieks of laughter that ensued Gina was able to open the door without being heard. Her last glimpse of them all was of Mari with her head completely covered and the others standing with their backs to her. At that moment the giggler finally found utterance and grunted. Gina was still too young to take in the full horrifying ambiguity of the situation. Her heart beating wildly, and almost choking with fear, she fled down the empty corridor, taking care to avoid the duty room, whose door was still standing slightly open. "Matula, stand to attention! Get on with it, Matula!" War. Death. Grunt, grunt.

Ruppert and the Director should by now have been either in Gedeon Torma's office or over in his apartment. If she ran fast enough she might be able to avoid them – unless of course the Director was escorting his visitor through the garden on his way to the gate and they spotted her climbing out of the window. But she made it to Susanna's room without any problem. Inside, a fastidious orderliness reigned, and there was a slight hint of fragrance. The wardrobe key was still in the lock. Her fingers were stiff and numb with fear and she had difficulty controlling them, but she managed to tear off her jacket and dress, kick them under the bed, and take Susanna's gown and pull it over her head. The dress went on easily, but the bonnet resisted her best efforts. Overcome by helplessness she burst into tears. She had never seen Susanna putting it on and could not work out how to tie it. In the end she found two hairclips attached to the stiff material and used those, but she had great difficulty squeezing her hair under the bonnet. The dress was too long for her, and too big; there was no mirror in the room and no opportunity to see how she looked.

Now that she really had to be going fear drained what little was left of her strength; her legs started to shake, and she had to sit down. She collapsed on the chair beside Susanna's bed and wept. She knew that by then she should already have been in the street, but she simply could not bring herself to step out into the corridor in Susanna's clothes. What if anyone had turned round and noticed that she wasn't there, and they were already looking for her? She tried to say the Lord's Prayer, but she couldn't remember how it went after "Blessed be thy name". That shocked her so much that her hysteria began to subside. She got up and went to the door, determined to do everything Mitsi Horn had told her.

There was no-one in the corridor. Every door into the garden was of course locked: she would have to go out through the window again. It would be much harder this time, in Susanna's bonnet and gown.

For the third time she found herself running across the lawn, in the cold, violet-scented air of late evening, passing the statue of Abigail, and arriving for the third time at the gate behind which, two nights earlier, that voice had so entranced and deceived her. What would she do if the door were not unlocked, as Mitsi Horn had promised it would be? Or if someone had noticed that it was open and had locked it again, and she couldn't get out? The bell in the white church tolled the hour of nine, in deep, masculine-sounding tones: bo-ng, bo-ng, bo-ng. She pushed carefully on the metal door. It moved instantly to her touch and opened without a sound. She went through . . . and froze.

A man was standing next to the gate, on the street side, barring her way.

She burst into tears and tried to turn back: better to let whatever might happen to her in there take its course, however implacable, than be caught by Feri Kuncz and his associates. But there was no escaping him. He grabbed her by the arm. The sense of failure, of yet another disaster, the feeling that once again it had all been futile, stemmed the flow of tears. Now it was all one. Nothing could matter anymore. She stood stock-still, incapable of speech, waiting to be taken off and put in a car, or marched off to the barracks, and to Feri.

"You mustn't go back, Sister," the man whispered. She had never seen him before, or heard his voice. "Now why should a god-fearing deaconess be so very afraid? I'm only the guard. You'll have to go by a different route to get to Mitsi Horn's. The

Lieutenant's people are patrolling around the school. They've just left Teleki Street, the way you will have to go. Carry straight on ahead. In the first side street on the right you'll see a pub. My friend will be waiting for you, and he'll direct you on from there. Good luck!"

She went up the road to the side street, as instructed, not realising that she was as unsteady on her feet as a chronic invalid. The man, Wallner from the wagon factory, watched her with a smile, then set off towards Teleki Street, singing loudly and bitterly, "Heigh-ho, the clock's struck nine, and night has fallen." Lieutenant Kuncz shrank back in disgust, thinking what a pity it was that ordinance couldn't be produced entirely by machines, and how disgraceful it was that with a sacred war going on there should be drunk workmen racketing in the silent streets.

Abigail

Gina was familiar with the way to Mitsi Horn's that went past the monument to The Sorrows of Hungary, but this was a very different route. As far as her fear allowed her to think at all, she realised it involved a long detour. She had no difficulty finding the pub. A young man was leaning against the door, smoking a cigarette. Looking not at her but into the darkness beyond, and seeming to address the shadows rather than anyone in particular, he murmured, "Straight on to the pharmacy, and walk more slowly – much more slowly." That was the hardest thing to do, to fight down her natural instinct, to reduce her pace and glide serenely along in Susanna's costume so that no-one seeing her would give her a second thought.

The pharmacy shutters were closed; only a tiny illuminated plate indicated what was on sale inside. She approached with some trepidation; there seemed to be no-one there. She was too frightened to stand and wait in front of the window for something to happen, but the problem resolved itself. Just as she arrived, someone, a figure undetectable in the dim lighting – a mere voice in the darkness – spoke from inside the doorway. It was not the ingratiating tone adopted by Feri Kuncz. "Turn left at the second crossroads and carry on to the end. The house facing you will be Mitsi Horn's. And don't run!"

She did her best to walk even more slowly. The second road proved much longer than any of the others, but at last she reached the end and caught sight of her goal. Its gables and narrow windows glittered in the moonlight.

When I get there I'll wait a few minutes, she thought, to make sure there's no-one about. Then I'll do what Mitsi said. I'll open the gate, take a few steps up the covered walkway to the front entrance and let myself in . . .

She froze in horror. She felt so weak she thought she was going to collapse. The key! Mitsi Horn's key, with the laughing jester's head on the end! She had left it behind. It was still in the pocket of her school uniform, under Susanna's bed.

The bell in the distant white church rang again. It was now 9.30 p.m. She leaned against a wall and gazed up at the sky, at the wisps of cloud playing hide-and-seek with the moon. The only thing that surprised her now was that she felt so much less sorry for herself than she did for Mitsi Horn and for everyone who had tried to save her; despair had given way to a kind of clear-eyed bitterness. All certainty of rescue was slipping away, everything was at risk again, with no clear prospect of a way out. If only she had kept her head, had been more sensible, had paid attention, she would not have forgotten the key and would now be safe with Abigail. What could she do?

Walking around the streets at this hour in Susanna's formal gown and bonnet she would be as conspicuous as if she were dressed for a ball: deaconesses did not loiter outside on their

421

own at 9.30 at night. But where could she go to wait? The older Aradi had told her that soldiers were now regularly on the streets after dark; according to the porter they were looking for the people who hung placards on statues and they took an interest in everyone who came their way. If one of them found her and flashed his light in her face it would be obvious that she wasn't a grown-up but a girl in someone else's clothes. She had no papers and she would be unable to give convincing answers to their questions. What would become of her then? In this town only staff from the Matula would be seen in deaconesses' robes. In fifteen minutes she would be standing in front of the Director again.

She stood stock-still, unable to move. The windows of the house behind her were blacked out according to the regulations and she had no way of knowing if there was anyone inside. Taking a risk, she slipped in through the gate. There was still no-one in the street, and no traffic; she could hear the roar of a motor somewhere in the distance, and from time to time the blast of an engine issuing steam in the nearby station. She thought of going and standing on the platform to pretend she was waiting for a train, then remembered that it was now under military control and one of Feri Kuncz' agents might be looking for her there. It was far too risky. She remained where she was, still barely able to move.

Footsteps sounded in the direction that she had come from. Someone, a single person, was approaching; from the heavy tread it sounded like a man. She flattened herself against the gate. He drew level with her and stopped, went back a short way, stopped again and looked around. He can't have heard me breathing, she thought. It would be impossible at that distance. She found herself torn by contradictory longings: for him either to vanish and never be seen again, or to come back, find her, and just kill her. The fear and the hope were both now more than she could bear.

The man bent down and picked something up from the ground. In the fleeting light of the moon she saw what it was, and she almost fainted. She raised a trembling hand to her forehead, then lowered it again: she now knew what the stranger had found and why he was studying it with so much interest. Susanna's badly tied bonnet was no longer on her head. It had fallen off in the street, a little way back.

He was now coming towards the gate again. She knew he was looking for her, that he would be there in just a few minutes, but meanwhile he was stopping to peer carefully and systematically behind each of the others. At last he stood before her. She neither called out nor tried to run away; she simply allowed him to take her by the arm and lead her out into the street.

"Are you out of your mind, Vitay?" he asked. The voice was one she had heard before, but she could not remember whose it was. "Did you drop your bonnet so that it would be found in the morning and taken as a present to Gedeon Torma? Why on earth didn't you go into Mitsi's house?"

He was now leading her by the hand and she caught a glimpse of his face in the moonlight. She still could not think who he was, but she knew from what he had said that she was in safe hands once again; the stranger was a friend, not an enemy. But she was still too terrified to speak or ask him who he was. At the crossroads he made sure that no-one was approaching from either side, then led her down the street to the house with the gables and opened the door. So he too has a key, she thought. How many keys are there to Mitsi Horn's house?

They went inside. He insisted on knowing why she had not gone in earlier. She did not dare tell him the truth, she just said that she had been too frightened. "You were afraid to come in but not to wait outside in the street?" He shook his head. "That was pretty stupid, let me tell you. So when would you have done us the honour? When Mitsi had come back and fainted with the shock of finding that you weren't here? Anyway, these are your new papers. Have a look and see who you are."

He thrust them into her hand and she studied her new birth certificate. She was now Anna Makó. Her birth year was unchanged, but the day and the month were new. Her father was Antal Makó, her mother Rozáli Tirpák; father's occupation, locksmith; mother, none. Both were Roman Catholics, born in Bolita, Csongrád County.

He opened Mitsi Horn's drinks cabinet, took out a bottle of cognac and poured himself a glass. Later, many years later, when he was an old man with a bent back and she still an attractive young woman, Mráz the glazier's assistant told her that nothing had ever moved him so much as seeing her sitting there hunched over in Mitsi Horn's drawing room, her eyes brimming with tears and her dark-brown tresses tumbling onto the severe shoulders of the Deaconess' formal gown.

He had left the door into the hallway open, and every now and then he cocked an ear in that direction; suddenly he made a sign with his hand, and she heard someone moving about at the front entrance. He closed the drawing-room door and gestured again, this time for her to be silent. Voices sounded in the hallway. Mitsi Horn and the old lady had returned.

"That's everything for today," they heard. "You must get to bed straight away, Auntie Róza. I don't need anything more tonight. Thank you for all your help. It was a nice evening, wasn't it?"

"It certainly was," said the old lady. "We always have a good time at the Matula. But the girls aren't what they were in your day. Now where could that naughty little thing from Budapest have hidden herself?"

"Oh, in the attic, or perhaps the cellar. She'll show her face once she's had a good cry. You know, life isn't so easy here for these girls from the capital. It takes nerves of steel to adapt to the Matula. Good night, Auntie Róza."

"Good night, Mitsi dear."

They heard the old lady going down the stairs to the cellar. Mitsi Horn stayed in the hallway for a few minutes longer, then came into the drawing room. Her cheeks were flushed and her eyes were shining.

"Good evening, Mráz," she said, and at that moment everything came together – the fish on the floor, the smashed aquarium, the forged papers for Bánki, Kun, Zelemér and Krieger, and the glazier's assistant stepping into the room as she dabbed her towel at the wet carpet. "And which of you got here first? Was it you, Sister? Good evening, my dear."

"We arrived together," said Mráz. "The sister was scared as a rabbit. I had to open the door for her. She was standing shivering behind a gate at the end of Árpad Street, and she had lost her bonnet."

"Not everyone is a wily old conspirator like you and me. Now come this way, dear."

Gina had struggled many times to resist the attraction she felt towards her; she had even persuaded herself that she hated the woman. Now she ran to her and buried herself in her arms. Mitsi felt her trembling and held her tight, while Gina silently mouthed the words she did not have the strength to utter: "Abigail, my thread of gold in the maze of all that we can and cannot do; Abigail, preserver of my childhood treasures, Abigail, brave dissident and colleague of my father, dear, wonderful Abigail, thank you!"

"When will you take her, Mráz?" Mitsi Horn asked.

"Probably tomorrow evening, once everyone knows that she's run away, including the police and the Lieutenant. Wallner's daughter should be at the station by now. She'll be leaving shortly for Budapest. I told her to make such a show of panic at the ticket office that the cashier wouldn't forget her in a hurry. She promises she'll try to cry. It'll be quite an effort for her, she's only too happy to be using your money to go and see her god-mother, and Budapest, for the first time in her life. But she has the same grey eyes and dark hair, and she's now over fourteen, so I'm sure Kuncz will go flying back to the capital after her. I'd love to see his face when he finds she isn't in the family home. As soon as I'm told that he's left Árkod I'll set off myself with Anna Makó."

"Now I must get her to bed," Mitsi Horn said. She took Gina up to a floor she had never been on, where the bedrooms were. She was put in what was clearly a boy's room. There was a row of fencing gloves on the mantelpiece, a large glass case with colourful stones and minerals such as you might see in a museum, and an enormous globe of the world held up by a copper band like a goblet on a table, surrounded on all sides by chairs with clawed wooden legs.

"You have your own bathroom," Mitsi told her. "If you move around no-one will hear you down below. We never heard my son."

There was even a dressing gown on the bed, and a nightdress. It was rather like the one she had given Torma.

"Take those robes off and have a good rest. I'll call for you in the morning. Don't go downstairs before I come for you. I'm sending Auntie Róza to the vineyard early and she'll be there all day. Once she's gone you can move around freely. Good night."

Gina stood and looked at her. Mitsi said softly, "Don't say anything. I know." And she was gone.

Gina collapsed into one of the chairs beside the map of the world and sat staring at it. Her thoughts were muddled and disordered. The only thing she realised with any certainty was that it was going to be very difficult being on her own. It was not enough just to feel safe: she was now missing Abigail horribly. And there was something else too. She had eaten only half her lunch, the mere thought of opening her snack box had revolted her, and she had barely touched her supper. Now that she felt herself out of danger she was ravenous. She smiled to think that the kind people who had helped her escape had given thought to every smallest detail but had not given her so much as an apple. "In any work of literature the most interesting bits are in the detail," Kőnig had often said in his lessons. "Be sure to attend to them closely." Kőnig the coward, the bumbling incompetent: if only he knew the woman he loved, and how little chance he had with Mitsi Horn! Abigail could marry only a hero, never a clownish sentimental schoolteacher. But he had been right about the details: she saw exactly what he meant. Her hunger was a mere detail, simply nothing in terms of what had happened and all she had been through, but it was enough to make her tiptoe down the stairs and tap sheepishly on the drawing-room door, which was once again open. The conversation inside came to a stop. Mitsi Horn came to see who it was, and Gina stammered out, in extreme embarrassment, that she had had almost nothing to eat and could she please have a bit of bread? Mitsi pealed with laughter and took her into the drawing room. A table had been set out before Mráz for him to have his supper, and Mitsi laid a second place for Gina.

"Now eat up, you poor starving creature!"

"You're going to have another visitor," Mráz warned her. Mitsi said she knew, it was why she had sent her up to bed, but he could see how hungry the girl was, and her day had not exactly been a picnic. If she had a bite to eat with them she would sleep all the better. Mráz said they ought to be quick about it, but Gina was devouring her food at such speed she was barely taking time to chew. The last morsel was in her mouth when Mráz gestured for them to be silent. Through the still open door into the hallway he had heard someone coming along the covered walk-way from the gate.

"As I said. I've been expecting them. Off you go, girl!"

"And quickly," Mitsi added. Gina dashed up the stairs.

As she reached her room she heard someone come into the hall and Mitsi uttering a scream. She was so frightened she was unable to budge from the door and stood there listening intently. If Mitsi had screamed at the sight of her visitor then it must have been someone very unexpected. But whoever it was, the question was how would Mitsi deal with him? Mráz was in the drawing room, and she was upstairs.

At last Abigail spoke. She said: "How did you get hold of a key to my house?"

"I found it in the pocket of a girl's uniform," Susanna replied. Her voice was as cold and calm as ever. "A uniform someone had pushed underneath my bed, with some other bits of clothing. Would you be so kind as to return my clothes?"

"Have you been drinking, Susanna?" Mitsi asked. And again she laughed. "What sort of clothes do you mean?"

Oh my God, I never told her about the key, Gina thought. And I didn't tell Mr Mráz because I was afraid of him. She doesn't know that I didn't bring it with me. What have I done now?

"I knew you were up to something! I spent the whole evening wondering what it could be. I couldn't think why I was supposed to stand facing the wall, and when we realised that Vitay had gone you kept saying there was no need to look for her because she would be back soon: that was a real help. It's thanks to you that she got away; you were pulling the strings. You came

429

to celebrate Gedeon Torma's name day. Well, you certainly gave him a good one."

"You *have* been drinking!" Mitsi Horn replied. "You're such a clean-living girl the tiniest drop of wine goes to your head. How can you say I helped Vitay run away when I was with you playing games not fifteen minutes ago? And if you found the key to my house in her pocket, she couldn't possibly have used it, even if she had stolen it from me."

"I have no idea how she managed to run away, but run away she has," Susanna replied bitterly. "Someone in the Matula found a way for her to do it. I know only too well what Abigail is capable of."

Mitsi Horn was silent for a moment, then she laughed again.

"She must have put down her pitcher – she was tired of carrying it anyway – stepped off her pedestal and led Vitay out of the school by the hand. Well, well, Susanna. I had no idea you knew about these juvenile superstitions. Perhaps you really believe in them? How does that square with your religion?"

"I have known for eight years that there is someone operating behind that statue," Susanna said. "In my third year Gabi Sarkadi, who left last summer, was in the first form. I nursed her once when she was very ill. I was with her all night. The next morning she was in floods of tears. She asked for some paper and a pencil, scribbled the words 'Mummy, Mummy,' and begged me to drop it into the pitcher because Abigail would bring her mother to see her. There was no reason to alarm her parents, the doctor had told us that she would recover, but she was very unwell, with such a terrible fever, and so frantic. I felt thoroughly ashamed of myself, but I did what she asked; it calmed her down and she immediately fell asleep. The next evening her mother arrived. She had had a long-distance telegram from the school telling her to come at once because her daughter was ill. The Director was convinced that I had sent it and I accepted the reprimand because I thought his anger was justified. If I had not been so weak the message would never have gone, whoever sent it."

Gina thought she would die if she were unable to see the two of them at that moment, when her fate, and the rest of her life, was being decided. And not just her own – Abigail's too, and perhaps even Susanna's. She opened the door a crack. Mitsi Horn was standing with her back to her and the Prefect was facing towards her. Her face was scarlet.

"I won't give Abigail away, you can be sure of that. Just let me have the girl I am responsible for and I'll go. How can I deal with this matter if I haven't got my formal costume?"

"You are a child," Mitsi said, in almost the same tone she had used with Gina. "You hate me so much you're out of your mind. I may be frivolous by nature, but coming here with your story about the statue and the Sarkadi girl is too much. And as for this Abigail! You should be ashamed of yourself, Susanna. Your clothes are not here, I have told you that, and nor is Vitay. I know nothing about this. On the other hand you seem to have found my key and I would be grateful to have it back. My handbag was lying on a chair in the refectory the whole evening; anyone could have dipped their fingers into it if they wanted to, though why they should I have no idea, and I have even less idea why they should have thrown it under your bed inside the pocket of a girl's uniform. So go back home. A pious young maid shouldn't be out on the streets at this time of night."

Susanna slammed the key down on the table. Her face was clearly visible through the crack in the door, and Gina watched as she twice opened her mouth and closed it again, then pulled her bonnet over her head and made to leave.

"Susanna!" Mitsi called after her.

The Deaconess stopped in her tracks. Once again Gina could see her face, but not Abigail's.

"I have not set eyes on Vitay since that game in the refectory. I would like to forget this ridiculous business of the key, and the harsh words that have been said here tonight – that was all nonsense too – but there is something I have meaning to say to you for a long time. There is nothing going on between me and the person you think."

"Good night!"

"Just a moment. Nothing personal, do you understand? He has loved you for years. If he has let you believe otherwise, it just isn't true. Ask him to marry you. He feels so diffident towards you he simply doesn't dare ask you himself."

Once again Susanna was silent. She stood and stared at Mitsi in astonishment, then suddenly flinched, as did Gina standing behind the door. From outside came the sound of shooting.

"I really must go," Susanna said. "It's very late. But how can I get back now? What's going on out there?"

"That was gunshot," Mitsi said. "Perhaps it's the night patrol. I really don't like the thought of letting you go, though I suppose no-one would molest a deaconess. But if you don't want to stay the night, I'm afraid you will have to."

"You know I am not allowed to sleep outside the school premises," Susanna said. "I'm quite sure I'll get back safely. God will protect me."

"I know He will," Mitsi said. Gina noticed that the voice that was usually so full of laughter was now deadly serious. "And don't forget what I told you. Bear it in mind. There is nothing between me and him. Have you understood that? And if you have to tell people in the school that you lost your gown and bonnet, please don't tell them about the key. You would get me into serious trouble, and Gedeon would be very upset. See, I am putting it here. It can't fall into the wrong hands again. And don't make Vitay's life difficult when she comes back."

"I'll tell them only if they ask me if I found anything in the girl's clothes. If they do, I will have to. I am not allowed to tell lies."

The Prefect went towards the door, and Mitsi followed her to open it for her. It proved unnecessary. As they reached the top of the steps it swung open. Kőnig was standing on the threshold. In his hand was the key he had used to let himself in. The moment he saw Susanna he froze.

Abigail was lying! Gina thought, and was surprised at how much the idea pained her. Abigail had always come to her aid, had even helped her escape, while Susanna had only ever punished her, and now she had told a lie. It upset her so much because for once Susanna had not been making difficulties for her by asking questions. And what a pity she had told her that she was not in love with Kőnig – when he even had a key to her house! This Abigail was incredible. Wasn't she afraid that Kőnig would betray both her and Mráz, and everyone else? The man was so soft he cried if you shouted at him. That she should be so fond of Kőnig that she could think of him as someone who could come and go in her house at any time of day or night! It was utterly shameful.

For a few seconds they stood looking at one another in silence. No-one moved. At last Kőnig shut the door behind him. His face was scarlet. He was not wearing a hat and his thick, greying hair spilled over his forehead. Susanna had so far kept her eyes on the carpet; now she looked at Mitsi Horn and said, "It's alright, Mitsi."

"What are you doing here?" Kőnig asked her, and stood in her way to stop her leaving. "You can't go out there now. Someone's hung another of those placards around the neck of the Kossuth statue. He was seen by the night patrol when he jumped down from the plinth and they shot at him. What on earth made you leave the school? Torma said that only we men should look for Vitay."

"I was looking for her too," Susanna said. "I am her prefect. Please stand aside, I can't bear to be with you a minute longer. Stand aside, I say!"

"No."

"For God's sake, let me out!"

And she began to sob like a child. Mitsi Horn shrugged, felt around in her pocket, took out a cigarette case and lit up. Kőnig did not move, but Gina saw him asking her something with his eyes. She gestured with her chin towards the stairs and then the drawing room, and a wave of fear passed through Gina. Now he knew everything. She had told him there were other people in the house, including her. "In that case it's of no consequence," he said. He took the cigarette from Mitsi and inhaled. Before anything more could be said the doorbell rang again. Oh my God! thought Gina. What if it's Feri? What will become of me if they find me? And not only me, all of us. Including Abigail, who has been hiding me.

"Open the door," Kőnig said to Mitsi.

She went down the two steps and opened it. Soldiers burst in. Their leader was not Feri. It was an older man, of lower rank, an acting corporal in the reserves.

"I am sorry to disturb you, madam, but, with your permission I shall have to search this house. My colleagues saw a man running away after tying one of those cowardly placards on the Kossuth statue outside the station. It's our job to protect that monument. We nearly caught him, but we lost a few minutes and he got away. He ran off down this street. We heard his footsteps for a few seconds and then they faded away. He must have taken refuge somewhere close by, in one of the houses on this street. Do you mind if we look around?"

"Not in the least," Mitsi said with a smile. "It's no trouble at all. No-one has come here. Mr Kőnig the teacher, Sister Susanna his colleague and I have been standing in this hallway for some time, talking and commiserating with one another. They are looking for someone too: a girl has disappeared from the Matula. You didn't happen to see a girl in Matula uniform on your way here?"

"Only the man who ran this way," the Corporal said. "How long have you been here, Sister?"

"At least fifteen minutes," Susanna whispered.

"And the teacher?"

She was silent for a moment, then replied: "He came with me."

"And you were all here in the hall? Standing talking, next to the door?"

"Right here," Susanna said.

"We noticed a large window in the cellar. May we go down?"

"But of course," Mitsi replied. She went to the top of the stairs and called down: "Auntie Róza, you mustn't be worried, but some soldiers have come to visit us. They're looking for someone. If they ask to see inside your room you must let them in."

Susanna leaned against the wall and closed her eyes. Kőnig yawned; he seemed suddenly very tired. Gina could not see Mitsi Horn's face, only her back and the nape of her neck. Her heart was pounding. What will happen to me when they come upstairs? What will I tell them? What shall I do? Save me, Abigail!

The soldiers were soon back from the cellar. They reported that there was no-one down there, just an old woman who was getting out of bed. But the Corporal showed no signs of wanting to leave.

"I do apologise, but we will also have to inspect the attic and the other rooms. The person we are looking for is a tall, fair-haired man, like the teacher here who came with the sister."

"Do whatever you wish," she reassured them. "You will find my brother-in-law in the dining room, having his supper, but he is rather short and his hair is dark, not fair. On the upper floor you will find another deaconess. Sister," she called out, "did you hear that? There's no need to be shy; come down from your room. These gentlemen have to check all our guests. I promise they won't try to flirt with you!"

"Excuse me!" the Corporal said. He was visibly offended. "With a deaconess! I would be ashamed. What is she doing up there?"

The question was addressed to Susanna. She licked her lips. I must never tell a lie, a voice from the past whispered in Gina's ear. Now it really is all over! she thought. Susanna will never tell a lie, for any reason.

"She went up to rest," the Deaconess whispered. "She is very young. She finds the long hours hard to cope with."

Gina stepped forward and stood in the doorway. Everyone turned to look at her. Good God, the Corporal said to himself. She's almost a child. What sort of person would make her wear that hideous black uniform? He was no happier with the brother-in-law. The gentleman was in the middle of his supper, accompanied by a large bottle of cognac, and wearing what appeared to be a silk housecoat – and as if that were not already absurd enough for a grown man, you might have mistaken it for a negligée. But he was undoubtedly short and dark-haired, and not in the least like the man they had shot at.

He took his leave and went off with his men. Gina heard him knocking on the next house as vigorously as he had on Mitsi's. As he watched them go König said that there were soldiers outside all the neighbouring houses and at the crossroads. Her sense of relief made Gina almost too weak to stand.

But no-one was interested in her. Kőnig and Mitsi were looking at Susanna, and, strangely enough, both had the same expression on their faces, at once amused and profoundly touched.

"Welcome to the club," Mitsi said to her, though it made no sense to Gina at the time. "It took you a while, but you got there in the end. You're in it up to your neck now, and he won't have any more dark secrets to tell you when you are married."

Susanna was trembling so violently that even Gina could see it from her position behind the door to the attic. Mráz pulled on his coat and joined the other three in the hallway, with a full glass in his hand. Kőnig took it and gave it to Susanna to drink. She took a sip and immediately spluttered.

"It's a good cognac," Mráz said. "It goes down especially well when you've told a lie. That's something for you to mention at your next holy communion. I'm sure when you get back to the Matula you'll wash your mouth out for taking the Lord's name in vain. I just hope those virtuous people don't smell your breath before you do, or they'll faint."

"Come," Mitsi said quietly, and took both him and the bottle into the drawing room, shutting the door behind them. Gina now felt she should follow Abigail's example and leave, but she could not bear to: it was all so beautiful, so wonderful and so moving. Susanna loved her so much that she had told a lie to save her and not betray her. The Prefect clearly had no sense of time – Kőnig had arrived barely a minute before the soldiers, and he certainly had not come with her – but it really didn't matter. The important thing was that she had not given her away. Good, kind Susanna! But neither of them seemed to see her; they were not interested in her now. They had eyes only for each other.

"I knew about half of it," Susanna said, in a voice Gina simply did not recognise. She had never imagined that the Prefect could speak that way. "And for many long years. It was obvious that someone was operating secretly inside our walls, and whenever that person acted the tears stopped. I've known that much for a very long time."

She was speaking about Abigail, about Mitsi Horn.

"And now you know the other half," Kőnig replied. "That side of it began as a game played with your sacred rules and restrictions. It started in my first year as a teacher. I was twenty-two, and it was my first job. Mitsi was then in the eighth year, and she kept begging the statue to help her. She was desperate. Abigail was her idea and it deserved to be made a reality. Later, of course, her field of action went beyond the needs of the girls, and the risk involved a great deal more than upsetting Gedeon Torma. Sister Susanna was not let into the secret because Abigail loved her far too much and had done so for far too long. She was afraid to put her in the same danger, and afraid too of her own feelings. Why did you think I came here tonight?"

Susanna looked down at her feet and made no reply.

"You should be ashamed of yourself. You will have to do penance for the rest of your life." He gazed at her for a moment, then went on, "Since neither of us has managed to find Georgina Vitay here, we should be on our way. Sister Susanna, I shall escort you back to the Matula. Goodbye, Mitsi."

Mitsi had returned with Mráz. He was now properly dressed

439

and wearing a tie. He too was about to leave.

"We'll go part of the way together," he said. "We've all three of us been through their checks. I'll come back tomorrow evening with the Wallner girl's clothes."

"Quick, Vitay," Mitsi called out. "Take the Sister's gown off, she wants to take it back with her. My dressing gown is on the bed. Put it on quickly, then come and say goodbye to her and to your teacher."

When Gina came in with the Deaconess' robe her eyes were shining with admiration for Mitsi.

Abigail, Gina said to herself, you who see everything, who find a solution to every problem, who can make anything happen, you have even managed to make something of the impossible Kőnig. Thank you, and thank you, Mr Mráz, and Sister Susanna, and you too, cowardly Kőnig, for standing by me and saving me from Feri Kuncz.

For the first time in her life she said a properly respectful goodbye to him. He bowed to Mitsi Horn, kissed her, and went to open the door. Susanna kissed Mitsi Horn, as did Mráz, and they all went off. At last Gina was alone with her Abigail.

Mitsi Horn pushed the latch back on the door and collapsed in a chair. The merriment had vanished from her face, and she looked every one of her forty-eight years. She was exhausted, and had no doubt been very frightened that evening. Gina buried herself in her arms and tried to say how much she loved her, but as she fumbled for the right words Mitsi spoke.

"First I lost my husband, then my son. I don't want anyone else to lose theirs in such a pointless war, fought for such alien principles. It's quite enough that I should be alone and unhappy."

The evil witch's face was now bleak and bitter, the face of a stranger. Gina put her hand on her arm.

"Abigail isn't alone, even if her husband . . . her son . . . even if she doesn't have a real family. Everybody loves Abigail, I more than anyone."

Misti turned her big green eyes on Gina and laughed out loud – that same mocking laugh that had so alienated her at first.

"You more than anyone? Are you so sure of that? You can only love heroes, little Vitay, dashing young lieutenants and showy, high-spirited women who like to dance and say cheeky things to the Director and won't submit to anyone. Susanna loves Abigail, Vitay: Susanna. She knows what he really is, and she absolutely hates it when people are taken in by his play-acting and think him a sentimental old donkey."

She stopped, too upset to carry on. The girl stood before her, stupefied. What she had just understood was so much more astonishing and shocking than anything that had happened to her in the last dreadful and wonderful seven months.

"*You* love Abigail?" Mitsi went on. "Until this moment you thought that I was her. I, and not the bravest and most noble-hearted man I have ever known."

She stood up, stretched her arms out and walked a short way around the room, as if to release the tension that had built up inside her. Then she smiled again and looked at Gina.

"Go to bed, Anna Makó. It's been a difficult time. And not only for you. For all of us."

She led her up to her room, as she had done once before. As

she was about to leave, Gina blocked her way. She was trying to think of words to express what she wanted to say.

"Don't say anything," Mitsi Horn said, with a shake of her head. "Not everything has to be put into words. Try to get some sleep."

As soon as she was alone, Gina turned the light out and opened the window a crack. The chilly, violet-scented March air came flooding in, just as it had at home (at home?) in the Matula garden. The moon was riding high. She looked up at the sky and filled her lungs with the fresh air of the spring night, with all that it promised and threatened. My father, she said to herself, my real father, whose name I shall renounce tomorrow, I am now Anna Makó, born in Bolita. Father, my real father, I said of that wonderful man that he was cowardly and stupid. I even dared to write that in an essay, the one the Bishop read out. My dear father, so far away, I have been rude and hurtful to him at every possible opportunity. How can I ever make up for the fact that I never realised Mr Kőnig was Abigail all along?

MAGDA SZABÓ was born in Debrecen, eastern Hungary, in 1917. From 1949 her work was banned by the Communist Party after two volumes of verse had won her the prestigious Kossuth Prize. *Katalin Street* was published in 1969, and *Abigail* in 1970, and she was awarded the country's three major literary prizes. In 1987, publication of *The Door* brought her international recognition. She died in 2007.

LEN RIX was shortlisted for the *Independent* Foreign Fiction Prize in 2006 and won the Oxford-Weidenfeld Translation Prize in the same year for Magda Szabó's *The Door*. In 2015 *The Door* was chosen as one of the ten Best Books of the Year by the *New York Times*. In 2018 he was awarded the PEN America Prize for his translation of Magda Szabó's *Katalin Street*.

A New Library from MacLehose Press

This book is part of a new international library for literature in translation. MacLehose Press has become known for its wide-ranging list of best-selling European crime writers, eclectic non-fiction and winners of the Nobel and Independent Foreign Fiction prizes, and for the many awards given to our translators. In their own countries, our writers are celebrated as the very best.

Join us on our journey to **READ THE WORLD**.

www.maclehosepress.com

Magda Szabo's *Abigail* is the most widely read of all her novels
The item ...ly. Now, fifty years after its original publica-
tion, it is published in English for the first time.

Gina, the only child of a widowed general, lives a cosseted
and carefree existence in Budapest, even in the shadow of
the Second World War. When the general sends her to girls'
boarding school in Debrecen, in the east of the country, she is
devastated. Her belongings are taken away on arrival, and she
is initiated into the peculiar rites of her peers. She soon finds
herself ostracized and, desperately unhappy, tries to escape.

When brought back to the school, all she can do is entrust
her fate to the legendary and mysterious Abigail, a statue of a
woman in the school grounds, to whom the pupils confide their
troubles in handwritten messages. But who is the mystifying
figure behind Abigail, who wishes her well? Eventually Gina
achieves hard-won solidarity in a restrictive environment, and
begins to discover her place in the world.

Rich in imagery, and with Gina's internal world beautifully
realised, *Abigail* is a tale of suspense and revelation in a shifting
world where things are often not quite as they first seem.

Also by Magda Szabó in English translation

The Door (2005)
Iza's Ballad (2015)
Katalin Street (2017)